DANGEROUS VISIONS

A delivery van had stopped beside the sidewalk, and a man in a brown parka was leaning against a lamppost, smoking. Catherine stopped beside him. He straightened up and stamped out the cigarette.

"Excuse me," she said. "I'm looking for the ruins. Are they far from here?"

The man frowned. "Ruins? There ain't no ruins around here, far as I know. Hey, Louis, know of any ruins in this neighborhood?"

Louis, a stocky, red-faced man, raised his eyebrows. "No, I don't." He turned to Catherine. "Someone told you there were ruins around here?"

"No. I saw them myself this very morning. I went . . ."

Suddenly the man's face cleared. "Hey, no problem. It's a vision. If I were you, I wouldn't talk about this to just anybody. They don't like it much, you know."

Catherine set off once more, trying not to walk too fast. She couldn't remember ever hearing of such a thing. She ought to have known, shouldn't she? And then that remark: "They don't like it much." Who were "they"? And why didn't they like it much?

RELUCTANT VOYAGERS
by Elisabeth Vonarburg
winner of the Philip K. Dick Special Award
and the Aurora Award

Don't miss any of these highly acclaimed titles from Bantam Spectra Books:

BY WILLIAM GIBSON
  Mona Lisa Overdrive
  Virtual Light
  The Difference Engine (with Bruce Sterling)

BY SHERI S. TEPPER
  The Gate to Women's Country
  Grass
  A Plague of Angels
  Raising the Stones
  Shadow's End
  Sideshow

BY CONNIE WILLIS
  Doomsday Book
  Impossible Things
  Lincoln's Remake Dreams
  Uncharted Territory

BY ROBERT CHARLES WILSON
  Mysterium

Reluctant Voyagers

Elisabeth Vonarburg

Translated from the French
by Jane Brierley

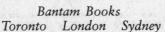

Bantam Books
New York   Toronto   London   Sydney   Auckland

The translator wishes to thank the Canada Council for generously awarding a grant-in-aid for preparing the English version of this work.

RELUCTANT VOYAGERS
A Bantam Spectra Book / March 1995

SPECTRA and the portrayal of a boxed "s" are trademarks of Bantam Books, a division of Bantam Doubleday Dell Publishing Group, Inc.
Reluctant Voyagers was first published in French as *Les Voyagers malgré eux* by Éditions Québec-Amérique Inc. (Montreal) in 1994.
All rights reserved.

ISBN 0-553-56242-8
Published simultaneously in the United States and Canada

Bantam Books are published by Bantam Books, a division of Bantam Doubleday Dell Publishing Group, Inc. Its trademark, consisting of the words "Bantam Books" and the portrayal of a rooster, is Registered in U.S. Patent and Trademark Office and in other countries. Marca Registrada. Bantam Books, 1540 Broadway, New York, New York 10036.

PRINTED IN THE UNITED STATES OF AMERICA
RAD   0 9 8 7 6 5 4 3 2 1

To Norbert Spehner, whose basement is so inspiring to dreamers—and without whom modern Québécois SF would be in a whole other universe.

Acknowledgements

This novel was written with the help of a grant from the Canada Council—an institution that is almost unique—which I thank for its generous support. With similar generosity, the Quebec Ministry of Culture provided funding assistance for the publication of the original French version.

I would also like to thank those who waded through the first version of this novel and offered their comments, especially, and in the following order: Denis, Joël Champetier, Yves Meynard, Jean-Claude Dunyach, Jean-Pierre Vidal, and Phyllis Gotlieb. Last, but not least, I wish to thank my translator, Jane Brierley.

My particular gratitude goes to Michel Lamontagne, who introduced me to Edmond Jabès just in time.

Somewhat different versions of certain events in this novel may be found in a short story written in 1977, "Le Pont du froid," published in the collection *L'Oeil de la nuit* (Montreal: Préambule, 1980), now out of print (subsequently translated by Jane Brierley and published as "Cold Bridge" in *Invisible Fictions*, ed. Geoff Hancock, Toronto: Anansi, 1987), and in the series of short stories written between 1977 and 1986, set in the same context, which I call "the Bridge Cycle": "The Knot" (translated by Aliocha Kondratiev, in *Amazing*, 1992), "La Machine lente du temps" in *Janus* (Paris: Denoël, 1984), and "Le Jeu des coquilles de Nautilus," in the anthology *Aurores Boréales II* (Montreal: Préambule, 1986), subsequently translated by Jane Brierley and published as "Chambered Nautilus" in *Amazing*, (December 1993). Resemblances and differences between the characters in the novel and those in the short stories are entirely intentional.

Like the title *The Book of Steps*, the citations on pages 239, 240 and 282 are derived with admiration and respect from the work of Edmond Jabès (cf. *Le Livre des marges*). But the poems of the fictitious author Pierre-Emmanuelle Manesch in the fictitious book *The Book of Steps* are truly the work of Pierre-Emmanuelle Manesch and no other.

E.V.

Part
One

Prologue

She is in an oblong capsule that follows the contours of her body exactly, without touching her. She's floating, although no tactile sensation indicates in what. She's naked, knows she has to be naked. She has been very cold but now she's all right. She also knows that if she leaves the capsule she'll be lost, and that if she stays she'll be lost. She chooses to leave because this is the choice she's always made. In response to her will, the lid of the capsule opens and disappears.

She is outside, but outside is nowhere. No perceptible dimensions, no texture, almost no color—something neutral, white perhaps, or slightly bluish-gray. No shading to indicate visual depth, a distance, a horizon. No smell, no taste. No sound, not even the gentle whisper of silence in her ears. She opens her mouth in a brief cry she cannot hear, cannot feel vibrating in her throat. She shakes an arm, and it's as though she had none—no skin to feel the air pressure, no muscles or tendons to contract. Yet she can see her arms, her hands. When she rests them on her belly, on her breasts, she can see them but cannot feel the contact. She sees, that's all. She sees, and supposes she is standing, but the sensation of vertical gravity has also

*been denied her. Has she left the capsule only to enter a
more hermetic prison?*

*She takes a step forward. Left leg, right leg. No sen-
sation. Is she advancing or staying in the same place? Impossible to tell. She is filled with an insidious sense of
anguish, an awareness somehow given her in response to
the incomprehensible silence of her other senses—for this
anguish has weight; it smells/tastes of burning, of vomit,
and it scrapes her flesh like sand, emitting a shrill, plaintive sound. It is directionless, coming from everywhere at
once, yet for that very reason it defines a space. A spherical space. That is shrinking.*

*She—she thinks. She thinks that if space is a sphere,
there must be a limit to this sphere, an outside to this
space. She must go beyond the wall of anguish. Suddenly
she's afraid of being unable to pass through—but fear
gives her the missing sense, the sense of a direction. She
holds out her arms, fists curled, and strikes. She doesn't
know whether she'll meet any resistance or whether the
anguish is a solid wall or a thin, viscous capsule. She
strikes. Fear has also given her a tool: anger. And now
there is space, space where she can run, where she is running, but space with only two dimensions, the dimensions
of fear—in front, forever receding, and behind, about to
catch up with her.*

*She runs without knowing whether she advances, turns
right, left, but it's always straight ahead. And fear, the good
clean fear, dwindles as anguish once more gnaws at her. If
in front is everywhere, if behind is everywhere, she's running nowhere. Is she trying to escape space itself? But you
don't flee from space, you flee from what's in it. For a moment, the idea of a monstrous shape chasing her is strangely
soothing, a new handle on the tool of fear. She starts running again, filled with anger, rancor, and hatred against the
unknown monster.*

*And with a suddenness that makes her stumble, she's
got her body back, the physical consciousness of her
body—lungs on fire, thigh muscles burning, acid sweat
streaming into her eyes, the constant shock of feet hitting
the ground. She revels in the pain wrested from the invisible Presence. It seems like a victory, and she tells herself*

with savage joy that she'll keep on running until she can't take another step, and then she'll fight.

She drops without warning. A brutal fall, winding her. Rigid with fear, she waits to be crushed, annihilated. Nothing happens. She simply isn't moving. Still that nonspace, grayish, bluish, but now she has the shield of her body, the armor of her pain, the sword of her anger. She gets up and swivels around belligerently, conjuring up all her childhood nightmares, defying the amorphous mass to condense into fangs and claws, into long, hairy paws or strangling tentacles.

Nothing appears. She should cry victory, but the longer she waits the sharper is her sense of time passing, becoming an exquisite torture, the agony of a thousand needles pricking. And once again uncertainty, doubt, and anguish seep in through all these pores. She regrets the absence of claws, of muzzles with drooling fangs. She could conquer such monsters, for she'd make them up herself. This invisible thing that refuses to take on their shape is far more terrifying. Has its own will. Is not some thing but some . . . one. Someone else.

She starts running again, but no longer with the simple, clean terror of mindless flesh. There's an indefinable panic, all the more terrible for its abstraction. Her body isn't in danger, it's her essence, the nucleus of her being, her soul. She runs but knows she's not moving in any direction. She flees but knows it's hopeless. The Presence doesn't need to catch her: it's everywhere. And it isn't the perverse but familiar space of her own brain that envelops her: it's an alien mind, immense, less a will than a violent, irrepressible desire to grab her, assimilate and decompose her into myriads of particles, only to spit her out, reconstituted but transformed, forever separated from herself.

$$1$$

Catherine wakes up. In her bed, in her room, in her house. She knows this from the sensory landscape that unfolds in her consciousness. The position of her body is familiar: right hand under the sheet, spread flat on her diaphragm, left hand outside, right leg a little bent to one side, left leg slightly raised. And almost in the same fraction of a second, another continuum of sensations explodes in her head, in (or out of) her body, a tidal wave, no, a whirlwind with herself in the middle, in the eye of the storm, a supernatural calm where each of the unknown sensations assailing her is identified, perceived in a completely expected, familiar, *normal* way.

This dream (because surely it is a dream) reaches her through the medium of senses she doesn't possess, providing comprehensible but apparently useless data. A voice (her own voice, since it is her own dream) is enumerating facts with nonchalant curiosity, as though this were a routine operation: *Atmosphere terrestrial in type, traces of pollutants indicating a developed society*—an observation that seems to fill the commentator with satisfaction. *Gravity slightly lower than normal, but atmospheric pressure terrestrial in type also, assuming this is sea level*—about which the commentator is uncertain.

Catherine feels her fingers brush her sheet and night-gown. *Cotton and synthetics.* A muffled, sustained throb rises from somewhere in the depths of the house, and the commentary continues *Ah, oil-fired forced-air heating ...* as a fairly precise image of the room takes shape—no, not an image, for her eyes are not open to see it, but she knows it's her bedroom, nevertheless.

In the dream she opens her eyes, curious about what she will see. For a fraction of a second, nothing, yet too much: light, a deluge of vibrating light that blots out everything at first, then divulges silvery networks, a little greenish, perhaps bluish. But almost immediately everything sharpens into focus with the same amazing familiarity. *Infrareds, not many ultraviolets, numerous radio waves, weak electromagnetic signals from a nearby gadget*—the tone is ironic—*definitely civilization.*

Then, as Catherine looks round the metamorphosed room: *Morning. Winter. Furniture of western type. Possibly Americanoid.* Well yes, it's morning, winter, North America, more precisely Eastern Canada, even more precisely the francophone Enclave of Montreal. So what? It's absurd—she might as well wake up for real!

Without transition, without any sense of opening her eyes, with the convulsive breath of a swimmer too long underwater, Catherine threw off the covers and deliberately offered her body up to the coolness of the room. Straightaway she forced herself to sit on the edge of the bed, to stretch, not knowing for whom she performed this show of waking up. Troubled by the persistent feeling of uneasiness, she groped with a foot for her bedroom slippers and found them as she switched on the night-table lamp and fumbled myopically for her glasses. A flash of sharp distress—for an instant she had the impression of seeing things with crystal clarity. Heavens, am I still dreaming? But the anxiety quickly subsided. She put on her glasses and let them slip down to the tip of her nose as she stared over the frames at the green, blue, and white pattern of the wallpaper across the room (blurred, the way it should be), then pushed the glasses higher (artificially clear, now), and shrugged with a grudging half-smile. Now *there* was something she wished would pass from dream to reality!

In the bathroom, she let herself be caught up in the routine of waking. Familiar. Strangely so. Why? Decidedly, this dream was going on too long. Nothing surprising about the face reflected in the big mirror above the sink. The smell of complexion soap, toning lotion, daytime face cream, the colors glimpsed out of the corner of her eye as her fingers worked—all normal. Objects, contours, dimensions, toothbrush, toothpaste, bath towels, pale green wall tiles—all familiar, yet with this upsetting, nagging impression, like a pebble in a shoe, of seeing them for the first time. A persistent dream, all right; she'd enter it in the notebook. Must find a name for it.

Catherine had her share of the usual dreams—dreams of falling, of chases, staircases, pointless arguments with people she loved. But real nightmares. . . . There was the Little Spoon Dream that had occurred just once. In it, she was sitting up in bed in the morning gloom of her student room in France, in Dijon, eating a scoop of vanilla ice cream out of a small, short-stemmed metal cup, like those used in restaurants. She felt faintly surprised, although apparently not disturbed. Did people eat vanilla ice cream in bed, so early in the morning? The sensations were totally clear and very real, however: the damp warmth of the bed, the smooth, cold metal in her left hand, the straight, hard spoon in her right, the unmistakable tactile sensation of ice cream on the tongue. She took another little spoonful, testing, checking the reality of all these ordinary sensations just to be sure, and the ice cream was indeed real, very cold, very creamy, very vanilla. . . . Still disconcerted, she bit the spoon gently—it was good and hard—tapped it against the cup, metal against metal—tin-n-ng! And a bright streak of anguish suddenly wakened her, sweating, every muscle knotted, in the damp bed in her small student bedroom, in France, in Dijon, at daybreak, but with no ice cream.

Now *that* was a nightmare, a genuine one: no longer knowing which was reality. The dream she'd just had belonged to the same category, possessed the same characteristics of perfect clarity, the absolute certainty of being awake—the logic of total absurdity. The dream before that hadn't been the same kind of nightmare. No need to describe that one in detail, just call it the Dream of Presence and record it in the notebook without further comment. A variation on escape dreams, only interesting for its sudden appearance and recurrence since ... since when, in fact? She'd have to check the notebook.

Catherine gave a start as the toaster oven beeped. The bagel slices were done. She removed them, burning the tips of her fingers as she did so, sat down at the dining-room table beside the steaming teapot, and consulted the small alarm clock placed where it could be easily seen. Just six-thirty! She could indulge in the luxury of dawdling a little. The news? No. Damn. Music. Still holding her teacup, she went into her study, fished randomly for a tape in the basket where she kept her favorites, and slipped it into the tape deck without looking. And the winner is ... Pergolese's *Stabat Mater*, the fine, full canonical version, with Mirella Freni and Teresa Berganza, *Stabat Mater Dolorosa*, not a particularly cheerful winner, even in Latin. The soprano and alto began to develop the motif in ascending waves, serenely tragic: "The Mother stood between the crosses, full of pain, of pain." *Dolorosa, dolorosa.* ...

Catherine stared through the frost ferns on the study window, looking at the small courtyard garden beginning to take shape in the faint dawn light. François and she had decided to buy here mainly for the garden. They would have preferred something on the Île Sainte-Hélène or the Île des Soeurs, something in the middle of the river, but those neighborhoods were reserved for the Enclave elite and were hopelessly expensive. In the end they'd had the good luck to find this house. A bit far from the college and the business district in Old-Montreal, of course, too small, badly planned, and rather stifling with its low ceilings and dark woodwork. But built around the garden. They'd bought the house in summer. The garden, ablaze with color, came as a surprise, a dream amid the concrete. In winter, and in this morning's uncertain light, you could barely see anything. The snow sketched the branches of the dwarf maple and outlined the little white pine, otherwise unrecognizable. There hadn't been time to shake its branches free for Christmas lights. She ought to do it soon. The colors looked so pretty at night, a childlike frivolity against the black and white of winter.

Catherine went back to the dining room. The two
divas continued their duet, alternately supporting each
other like the two Marys going up to Calvary. *Dolorosa,
dolorosa.* ... A faded, framed photograph across the
room, standing in the middle of the mantelpiece above the
fake fireplace. A blurred background, a garden or park
(walls and grillwork, in any case), two shapes: the unknown grandfather in his white colonial suit, European to
the hilt, holding a hat and walking stick, his bald head
shining in the sun, large, fat, with the assured joviality of
the powerful. Her mother beside him, fourteen or fifteen
(she'd said how old, but Catherine couldn't remember),
tiny, slim, brown as a berry, more like a Hindu than an
Annamese in her long, narrow skirt and short-sleeved
white blouse. The girl balanced shyly on one leg, arms behind her back, even the arm her father was holding, head
tilted as though to hide her eyes, revealing only her large,
timid, dutiful smile. *Dolorosa,* yes, always the same smile
in all the photos where she smiled, the one on her student
card, and the pretty, overly retouched one taken at
twenty-five, when she no longer wore the heavy braids
coiled around her head, the photo she'd always said didn't
look like her.

No recent photos on the mantelpiece. Never. François
had been surprised by this. When people in his family got
married, they were given "their" photo album—from the
baby posed on red velvet to the young groom on the
church steps, with snapshots of brothers and sisters, parents and relatives. No question of escaping time among
the Rhymers. When she and François had separated, he'd
taken the photo album with him. It was the first thing
she'd handed him when he'd begun to pack.

Catherine had always kept her family's picture history
jumbled in a box. Except for this montage of three youth-
ful photographs of her mother who would now have
been—seventy-five? With a sigh, Catherine buttered her
last slice of bagel. She never could remember the exact
year of her mother's birth. Anyway, in another century—
well, another universe. Let's see ... 1913, yes, and in
Cambodia, once Indochina. How's that for another universe? And now me, in yet another universe, across the
Atlantic. I was always separated from her, not just by

space, but by time—by generations, by cultures; that's what happens when you're the child of old people. Except that she never was old for me, of course, apart from the times I went to see her in France, and I forgot, oh so quickly, each time I came back to the Enclave.

She felt herself cringing in expectation of the familiar heartache, but nothing came. Suddenly "France," "dead," "mother" were just words. The memories remained, but pale, shallow. Flat, that was it, as if she had read the history of someone else in a dream. In a dream. . . . What was wrong with her this morning, anyway? Talk about wallowing in the past! What had possessed her to fish out the *Stabat Mater*? With a class to teach, this really wasn't the moment for melancholy musing. She'd do better to get herself in the mood.

Catherine went back to her study, cut short the second movement aria in full flight, substituted some good, grinding, heavy rock, and gathered up her books and course notes. Nelligan and modern poetry today, children. Yes, I mean modern, as proven by the fact that the rock group October put several of his poems to music at the end of the sixties. Wait—she should bring the tape to class just in case they didn't believe her. Most of them were born around 1970; it would give them a healthy shock to find that their favorite group had been going well before then and that this was the second glorious time around for October. For once she found the tape where it should have been, in the drawer with the blue-lettered label: "Say Gran—what didya listen to when you were little?" *October Sings Eugène Nelligan.*

She stood motionless for an instant, holding the tape. That was the face, all right. She recognized the paste-up on the cover, Nelligan's fine, fiery head surrounded by members of the group in flowered jackets, with the Gerry Boulet of that era sporting his caveman beard (they didn't go to much trouble with record covers in those days). But why this weird feeling? There was no other term for what had made her stop so suddenly. Weird. *October Sings Eugène.* . . . She shook herself, feeling annoyed. This morning's dream just can't stop pushing through. I'm too impressionable. She slipped the tape into her bag, remembered to switch on the answering machine, and turned on the radio as an illusory protection against burglars. As she put on her coat, she checked the garden again through the kitchen window, trying to gauge the temperature. It was a reflex action, the habit of a European raised in the countryside in the old way, without television. She'd never been able to shed the habit, even after twelve years in Montreal. It didn't look very cold, minus twenty-five centigrade, perhaps, and no wind. Since she had the time, she could walk part way to the college along the banks of the Dorchester Canal.

She went down the steep wooden staircase and opened the inside door. The inner handle of the outside door was covered with frost. Oh-oh. It might be colder than she'd thought. A gust of icy air hit her as she opened the door, making her hunch her shoulders for protection. She'd forgotten that the garden was sheltered from the wind. So much for European-style weather predictions, my girl; you'll be taking the bus. She looked at her watch, reluctant to go back upstairs. The 24 would be coming along Sainte-Catherine in ten minutes. It went the long way round, but she had plenty of time, and she'd have a chance to look over her course notes. She closed the outside door carefully and hurried along the sidewalk, sidestepping the iron-colored patches of ice where the wind had cleared the snow.

The Rue Montcalm lay cold and desolate beneath the yellow glare of the street lamps. Here and there, Christmas decorations blinked from behind double windows. Toward the west, beyond the Enclave, the illuminated skyscrapers of Montreal-City stood out against the brightening sky, a decoration of another kind. The distant rumble of the city had not yet reached its height at this early hour. The Enclave was awake, but only the heavy black-and-green buses lurched through the streets. There were almost no passengers; the night workers had already gone home, day workers who breakfasted at home hadn't left yet, and the rest were huddled in small, smoky restaurants along the Boulevard de Maisonneuve. As she emerged from the Rue Montcalm into Sainte-Catherine, she tapped the pole bearing the street sign—her patron saint—but this habit of hers seemed curiously childish all of a sudden. She crossed the street to walk along the canal bank. Another habit, but what a lot of habits she had! Why did it seem so noticeable today? What was special about today anyway, apart from that stupid dream?

A fine dusting of snow had fallen during the night, just enough to restore the virgin white of the sidewalk. It wasn't quite so cold, now that she was out of the Rue Montcalm where the wind whistled straight up from the Saint Lawrence River. But here she was protected by the buildings and warehouses along the south bank of the canal. Catherine slowed her steps. She loved this part of her morning walk, especially when it wasn't too cold to saunter along, loved the long, straight opening of the pale canal, its sharp horizontal and vertical perspectives simplified by the snow, the bridges edged with evenly-spaced splashes of light from the street lamps. During the early winter months, hundreds of grownups went to work on skates or cross-country skis. Catherine had done it for years. Less often now. The winters were getting colder and colder; they came earlier and stayed longer. *A minor ice age? Curious, considering the quantity of carbon monoxide in the atmosphere. . . .*

Catherine skidded on a treacherous ice patch hidden by the snow, but managed to catch hold of the parapet, heart pounding. What had she been musing about? The winters. Yes, colder and colder winters. Or else she was lazier than she used to be—that, more likely. A sudden, incomprehensible irritation pricked her and she grimaced a little: Well, old girl, forty-three and feeling decrepit? She'd take her skates to be sharpened tomorrow—no kidding.

There was a shelter at the bus stop on the corner of Grand-Condé, its walls lined with unintentional Op-Art collages of old, torn posters. Catherine closed the door behind her. Only a half-dozen people, their sex indeterminate beneath the thick coats and tuques pulled down past the eyebrows. Not enough of them to warm the shelter. Too soon for her regulars, people she'd exchanged smiles and ritual conversations with over the years. She went and stood in a corner, gloved hands jammed into her pockets, hunching her shoulders slightly like everyone else and staring into space, or rather, staring at the bit of parapet visible through the thick, dirty glass. Old graffiti, half obliterated, whitish phantoms on the gray stone. One was clearer than the others. BORN FREE or BOOKS FREE? Someone had tried to recycle one into the other. "Born free" must have come first: it was the most popular slogan of the moment. Appropriated by some booklover, no doubt, furious after reading the new Index list published last week. A sobering thought. Catherine shuffled from one foot to the other to get warm. She'd better hurry up with her class on Nelligan before *he* turned up on the Index as well. Surely they wouldn't dare? There'd been riots in the Enclave over less. Perhaps they'd just forbid the revolutionary poems—but no, even they wouldn't indulge in that kind of bureaucratic bumbling.

A new form entered the shelter and stamped its feet. A heavy old man with white eyebrows beetling between his fur hat and woolen scarf. One of Catherine's regulars, M. Labrecque, a former mailman. Their eyes met, and she smiled, waiting for the ritual, "Not warm today"—"No, not warm." Instead, he walked over to her with a mumbled greeting and took a newspaper from one of the pockets of his voluminous jacket. "You've seen it?" Without waiting for an answer, he unfolded the paper and read the headline. " 'Bomb Blast Hits Office of Secretary of State for Minority Language Groups.' A stink bomb, can you believe it? Old man Smeller'll be a skunk's uncle!" The old man gave a laugh that threatened to turn into a coughing fit. "How I'd like to have seen that ratfink's face!"

"In any case," a man said, "it'll mean more patrols in Montreal-City and tighter controls at the checkpoints. If they find out who did it, we'll have our passes revoked again. It's another student prank; if you want my opinion, those snot-nosed kids really go too far."

"Put yourself in their shoes," retorted Labrecque benignly.

The speaker, a man wearing a stiff denim jacket lined with fake sheepskin, turned toward Labrecque. "In their shoes! If I were in their shoes and able to go to college, I'd be very grateful and shut my trap! We got them a community college, didn't we? Went on strike for them—I lost six months' pay for those snivelling bastards, and they start throwing shit around!"

"I was on the picket line, too," said Labrecque amiably, "and I think they're right. If we'd done all we should have at the time, we wouldn't be in this fix. When the young people take to the streets, it means the grownups haven't done their work. This lady is a teacher at the college; I'm sure she'd agree with me."

The clanking arrival of the bus saved Catherine from having to reply. She mumbled something affirmative, then climbed onto the bus and sat down on the right-hand side where she could see the canal. Labrecque sat down beside her. Was he going to continue the conversation? But he merely winked and shook his head knowingly as he undid his coat and opened up his newspaper.

Catherine couldn't resist the printed word, not even an Enclave tabloid. She glanced over her neighbor's shoulder. The inner pages had smaller but usually more significant headlines: "Talks between Canada and the American Union Suspended." Again? It looked as though Canada's demands for a corridor through American territory to its Western Province were on the back burner. What went wrong this time? Did the Canadian representatives insult the Amerindian Federation delegates again? The old man rattled the paper noisily as he turned the page. General news, now. A few fuzzy photos, no doubt bloody, and one headline amid many: "He Loved Her Too Much, She Killed Him." Catherine couldn't help smiling: that summed it up so nicely! A possible subject for her third-year class in creative writing—but no, that might be tempting the devil, perhaps the subject was too daring. Being allowed a trial writing workshop with final-year students was already a big concession.

Catherine closed her eyes. The buses were always too hot in winter, and she felt an overpowering desire to sleep. There was still some way to go before her stop— five stops to Berri, seven more to Notre-Dame, and two to Gosford. A roundabout route, but the bus would drop her almost at the college door. And this was the scenic route, at least in summer when it ran beside tree-lined canals, passing the occasional multicolored calèche along the Berri Canal promenade. The more austere winter beauty of this early hour wasn't unpleasing, either. Nevertheless, Catherine forced herself to open her bag and take out her course notes. Nelligan, here we go! Beginning with the juvenile poems, of course, the ones he'd had published right after his father's sudden death. *It was a vessel of gold. . . .* She ought to go to the audio-visual room as soon as she reached the college, requisition a tape deck, and play the tape in class first thing, without saying a word. A real, revived Nelligan, not the Great Poet of Francophone America, the icon fossilized by a century of official adulation. To think there was a Nelligan University in New Orleans! Louisiana, that's where she'd first thought of going with François. But there'd been no job openings there at the time and they'd both wanted to leave, no matter what the conditions. After the Events of May '76 in France they'd no longer wanted to stay in that wicked stepmotherland, old and hypocritical, with its sleek rich and its smug politicos. Anything, then, the first offer that had come along, this double posting to the new French college in the Enclave. Oddly enough, up to that point the only thing they'd known about Canadian francophones had been the Enclave strike of '75–'76, aimed at winning the right to open just such a post-secondary college recognized by the two Canadian provinces. The Enclave's victory had happened at the same time as the Events in France, and Catherine, like all the other contesting teachers, had signed the congratulatory card sent by their union.

"The Events." She was annoyed to find herself using this expression, so favored by reporters still looking for an acceptable handle twelve years after the fact. But how else could you describe it? May '76 hadn't been a revolution, not even a real revolt, despite the deaths. It had been a way for members of the younger generation to cry out to the old that, twenty-three years after the official end of the war, Reconstruction was really over in Europe and they were fed up with restraints. No one had been able to find new words to describe the general and disorganized desire for change, and the old words had won out in the end. So "the Events," and why not?

The very vagueness of the term was appropriate, after all, even if it evoked very clear images in Catherine's memory—burning barricades in the Latin Quarter, wounded students brutally pushed into police vans. . . . May '76. She'd been thirty-one with a brand new posting at the University of Dijon, and she had thrown it all up to take the students' side. The occupation of the Radio-France relay station, the sleeping bag timidly offered by a long-haired François whom she'd taken for a student. François was in Louisiana now, and happy to be there. He'd never liked the Quebec climate—oops, the *Eastern Canadian* climate, as the English Language Bureau would have them say. In fact, he'd have gone to British Columbia, the other Canadian province, had it been possible in the beginning, but his English wasn't up to it. In any case, being a francophone from France was enough: they'd refused his application.

The bus lurched with unusual violence, jerking Catherine back to her open textbook and the last verse of the poem: *He foundered in the dream abyss.* Well, he isn't the only one. What's happening to me today, for instance? If this keeps up I'll start woolgathering in the middle of class. But those two dreams would tug at her consciousness until she'd sat down to record and comment on them in her diary. She pondered for a moment—what should she call the weird new dream? The Dream of Hyperceptions? Really: atmospheric components—with statistics, yet! She'd already forgotten the details, which was perfectly normal since she'd never known them anyhow. *Azote 78%, oxygen 21%.* It didn't matter, *argon 0.09%* she still had a good general idea of the dream *atmospheric pressure about 2.63 kg per cm^2* and of the almost supernatural perceptions. There wasn't really any connection with the Little Spoon Dream, except for the sense of anguish, perhaps. . . .

The bus shuddered and screeched as gears crashed. Catherine raised her eyes to check her whereabouts. Saint-Denis already? And not far from Saint-Antoine. Get on with it, girl: more than four stops left. Let's have a little Nelligan.

The next-to-last stop. The bus doors slapped shut with an exhausted wheeze of compressed air—hardly an encouraging start to a work day. Catherine checked her watch. Still much too early! The audiovisual people wouldn't even be there yet. The prospect of the deserted staff room, as cheerful as a clinic, made her reach for the bell cord with one hand while collecting her books and briefcase with the other. She strode toward the rear of the bus, pushed back the flap that triggered the doors, and found herself on the Notre-Dame sidewalk. She crossed in front of the bus against the traffic light, smiling apologetically at the stolid driver as he grumbled inaudibly behind his windshield.

The light grew stronger. It would be a fine, cold day, with one of those sharp azure skies that Catherine loved. Come on, girl, an invigorating ten-minute walk won't kill you. Luckily the wind seemed to have dropped. She'd be all right if she breathed through her scarf, although it made her glasses foggy. She started walking briskly. Rows of historic houses overlooked the canal on both sides, a little rickety, but meticulously maintained. Not much traffic on the ice yet—some delivery sleighs, a few snowmobiles, two or three intrepid cross-country skiers, their breath rising in plumes behind them. "Montreal, Venice of North America." So said the tourist folders sent by the French Ministry of National Education with their joint hiring notice from the Enclave college. It was strange, all the same, a network of canals in a city that lay under ice and snow half the year. But the weather hadn't been so cold when the first settlers arrived. The general cooling hadn't begun until ... when, exactly? How stupid: she couldn't remember. What a sieve I am today: one more memory lapse and I'll begin to get worried! At least two hundred years ago? After colonization. An odd idea, in any case, building canals here. There weren't that many settlers, after all, and they surely must have had better things to do than dig ditches. *And who did the digging? The natives? Not enough of them. Slaves? But that would require enormous numbers, presupposing widespread slavery in this particular New France, and before 1600 as well, which is doubtful. You'd have to know when settlement really started.*

Catherine stopped suddenly and reached for the parapet to keep from falling. She stood still for a moment, eyes closed, trying to overcome her sudden rush of distress. Vertigo, now? Or hadn't she eaten properly this morning? Flu, maybe? She took several deep breaths through her scarf, welcoming the searing cold in her lungs, then opened her eyes. Her mind was a blank. How long had the vertigo lasted? A few seconds? A minute? She couldn't even remember what she'd been thinking about. Something to do with . . . the canal? She looked automatically downward to jog her memory.

This wasn't the Notre-Dame Canal. The sidewalk ran for about fifty yards in three wide steps descending to disjointed segments of tall, rusty grillwork. Beyond, running gently downhill, lay a vacant lot covered with bare bushes and saplings. The occasional clump of yellow grass poked through the patches of snow. It wasn't really a vacant lot. There was no rubbish lying around, and you could make out little paths of white gravel. A movement caught her eye: a marmalade cat, almost perfectly camouflaged until now beneath a tuft of dried grass. It had just risen to cross a stretch of snow. As though in response to a signal, other furtive shapes began to move about the landscape. More cats, dozens of cats of every kind.

For an instant, Catherine couldn't move or think. Then, as her heart pumped frantically, explanations crowded in. She must have been daydreaming, must have gone past Vauquelin and turned into the wrong street. Or else her mind had simply gone blank as she automatically continued walking; her brain had subconsciously registered the error and had stopped her, with the accompanying sensation of vertigo. Whatever it was, she'd never been here before.

She went down the stairs toward the cats. They ignored her and continued padding about, dozing, or grooming themselves as before. They didn't seem to be starving—must be some old ladies in the neighborhood playing nursemaid. Curious how the snow had melted here. Probably heat vents from underground construction; Montreal was riddled with them. A sort of microclimate had been created, and naturally the cats were quick to take advantage of it. She looked at the half-exposed mounds in the snow between the bushes, suddenly realizing that they weren't rock piles, as she had thought, but the remnants of dressed stone walls. She recognized the outlines of arches and columns, eroded bas-reliefs, and stairways burrowing into the darkness beneath the mounds. Like the cats, so intimately blended with the landscape, these details only emerged if you looked closely. An old archeological dig left uncovered, perhaps? She walked a little way along the steps, looking for a plaque that might give the name of this place, and came upon a space between two segments of fence with the beginnings of another path, wider than the others. A questioning miaow made her turn her head to see a white shape half a dozen yards away, standing in the dark mouth of an opening partially hidden by the bushes. Catherine hesitated. The mewing began again, imperative this time. "I warn you," remonstrated Catherine with a slightly rueful smile, "I've nothing to eat."

It was a big cat, so luxuriantly white and velvety that Catherine couldn't resist its appeal. She crouched on her heels, took off a glove, and held out a hand to the pink muzzle to be sniffed. When the golden eyes had blinked lazy approval, she laid her hand on the immaculate fur. "Hello, my beauty, do you spend all day licking yourself clean?" The fur was incredibly soft and warm, the pleasure of touching it almost electric. Catherine gave a spontaneous, jubilant little laugh. The cat purred, eyes closed. After a moment, as Catherine suddenly woke up to reality and was about to look at her watch, the cat rose and arched its back in a classic, quivering, feline stretch, with tendons, bones, and muscles pushed to the uttermost limit. Then it backed a little way into the dark opening and scratched the ground with a soft, cooing sound. Catherine noticed a thick bed of moss. She lifted it slightly, aided by the cat's deft paw, and found a sort of nest dug in the soil and lined with grass and leaves. In it lay a wriggling mass of white blobs that uncurled to reveal six round-eared kittens, their eyes still shut, mewing almost imperceptibly, tiny pink mouths open to reveal tongues already furled to welcome their mother's teat. Delicately, the white cat settled into the middle of her litter and rolled on one side to offer the swollen, rose-pearl nipples to her young. Catherine lifted out a kitten caught under the others, placed it on the cat's abdomen, and watched it nuzzle between two siblings. Slowly but surely it reached its goal, attaching itself to the teat with the rhythmic clicking sound that is the purring of very young kittens.

Catherine stood up, laughing. "My warmest congratulations to the happy mother, but I'm afraid I have to go."

Once back on the sidewalk she looked at her watch with a sigh. She must be terribly late. . . . No? Only twenty-five minutes to nine! Maybe she could get to class on time, after all. Forget about the October tape; she'd play it next time. She looked around to get her bearings and saw the familiar parapet of a canal across the street. She'd obviously kept going on Notre-Dame instead of turning into Vauquelin, that was all. She walked back, looking carefully at the street signs and keeping an eye out for the black-and-green of a taxibus or a roving taxi. But it wouldn't be necessary after all: she'd reached the Saint-Laurent intersection with its hideously flamboyant Second Empire lanterns; then the parade of saint streets—Saint-Jean-Baptiste, Sainte-Gabrielle, Saint-Vincent, and here was Vauquelin, six minutes to go, and home free!

The corridors were practically deserted, except for late-comers hurrying to class. The teachers stood at their doors, watching. Catherine's students never waited for her before entering the classroom. They had soon become used to her down-to-the-wire arrivals. And yet someone *was* waiting by the door—a young girl leaning against the wall. Tucked under her arm was a mauve felt parka decorated with brightly-colored geometric designs. Not a girl, really, but a young woman of at least thirty, slim and poised in a shirt of fine white wool and one of those newly fashionable retro skirts from the fifties, long and narrow with a slit to the knee. Thick, brown hair coiled around the head; high, prominent cheekbones; slightly slanted black eyes, liquid and sparkling; full, curved lips, but a slender nose and palish skin: an Amerindian Métis. Who stared at Catherine with brief, disconcerting intensity.

"Mrs. Rhymer? I see you're in a hurry. Is there a moment when we can talk?"

Catherine automatically shook the cool, hard hand, almost surprised at not feeling a small electric shock, so vivid was the sensation of familiarity. "Have we met?"

The young woman smiled slightly. "Not yet. Joanne Nasiwi. I would like to audit your creative writing workshop next semester."

The hum of the waiting class penetrated Catherine's consciousness. Out of the corner of her eye she could see her colleague, Professor Marchand, standing on the threshold opposite. "Well, my office number is E-416. I see students Wednesdays and Thursdays from two o'clock on—"

"I saw the notice on your door. But I really can't get away. They're very strict at work. In fact, I had to tell them I was sick in order to come here this morning. I work at the Botanical Gardens, and I thought that maybe, if it's not too much bother, you could meet me there and—"

Catherine lifted a hand to stop her. "No problem. I haven't been there for ages, and it would make a nice outing. I've no classes tomorrow. Would the morning be all right?"

A big, bright smile. "Eleven o'clock in the main pavilion?"

"I'll be there."

The young woman put on her parka, bowed slightly, and hurried off, padding silently in her thick, fleece-lined leather boots. Like her parka, they were decorated with geometric figures.

"Curious." Marchand's insinuating voice taunted Catherine's back. She tried to ignore it, but as she was about to enter the classroom, he added, "Your workshop certainly attracts . . . curious people."

She couldn't let it pass. With a wide, friendly smile, she turned and said, "Well, yes, curious people. Curiosity is an excellent character trait. That's what makes good students, don't you find?"

"That isn't what I meant."

Oh, really?

"You don't think that accepting auditors will affect the, uh, uniformity of your seminar groups?"

Female auditors and halfbreeds, you mean, and possibly—horrors!—all kinds of black, yellow, and brown skins? Catherine managed to keep smiling. "It didn't occur to me, actually. Very few ask to audit." Not surprising, with the entrance requirements you've imposed on the department, you old hypocrite! "Could we discuss it at the next faculty meeting? I'm in a rush now. Excuse me."

She gave him no chance to reply before she plunged into her class. "Good morning, everyone." She threw her bag on the desk and took off her coat as grinning students chorused a greeting. They were well aware of her tilts with ex-Father Marchand, S.J., an incompetent teacher but one of the college founders, and therefore impossible to dislodge. Catherine looked at all the familiar young faces for a moment. They seemed to get younger every year, even though third-year students always ranged between eighteen and twenty in age. Henri Lapointe and Jacques Lévesque still absent? Since Monday, too—a real spree. What with their parents looking for them and a memo from the college principal to all the profs. . . . The shit was certainly going to hit the fan when those two resurfaced! Did Jacques imagine he could get away with this kind of escapade, let alone lead his classmates down the primrose path, simply because his father was vice-governor of the Enclave? Hmmm; Annie Leboeuf had switched her seat again. Off with the old love, as usual. But with only three girls in the class, what could you expect? So many boys, so little time! Female students had been behaving pretty predictably since first being admitted to the college three years ago: either they were indulging in orgies or keeping strictly to themselves. It would probably be that way as long as there weren't more of them, particularly while high school still wasn't co-ed.

Catherine smiled at them with a wistful inner irony

aimed at the young, fire-and-brimstone feminist that had been herself, twenty years ago in France, in another universe. "Since we're late, let's be really late. Juliette, would you get a tape deck from the audiovisual room? And while we're waiting, the rest of you can show me where you are with your end-of-term assignments."

2

The Montreal French College (that was the name carved in Roman letters above the main door, minus the "Enclave") stood at one end of the Rue Vauquelin, a severely angular building raised to the greater glory of functionalism—a style popular in France during the Reconstruction period as well as being the received architectural wisdom of the Enclave until the end of the seventies. The Enclave always lagged ten years behind what some of its older inhabitants still referred to as "the mother country." Why, at the time, hadn't the Vauquelin mansion just across the street been renovated and adapted? It was the handsome but decaying residence of the Marquis de Vauquelin's descendants, who had moved to the Île Sainte-Hélène. But no, the college had to be a modern building, and everyone, students, professors, and office staff, had to work in this antiseptic concrete box with its glaring white light and endless corridors. When Catherine walked along the hall to her classroom, she sometimes felt there was hardly any difference between the college architecture and an industrial henhouse— probably because the general view of education had something in common with the fate of the unfortunate fowl. It was certainly true that when the end-of-class bell rang, the students charged into the halls like a flock of cackling chickens freed from a fate worse than death.

She might often have done the same herself, but she knew all too well just how far you could go with the administration, to say nothing of the students. Irritating, of course, considering her past history ("My dear young people, I was in France in May '76"), to find herself in a classroom playing the thickheaded adult foil to some young man or, less frequently, some young female rebel who'd suddenly decided to take a stand. But Catherine was used to it now. Avoid pretending to be a fellow traveller, shut up, be tactful, and, when they actually want to tell you something, make them feel they can talk to you. And keep on repeating your mantra as you smile inwardly: "They'll grow up—I did." From one year to the next she held her own pretty well, once the inevitable jokes about her European French accent had run their course. "Hey, you're not from here, are you?" recurred with tiresome regularity as each new student generation moved up—a question that usually masked an almost instinctive respect for the French-from-France on the part of some Québécois (as the Enclave people insisted on calling themselves). It had maddened her to begin with. More than that, it upset her to think what lay behind it: their difficulty admitting that being different didn't mean being inferior, and the secret, painful scorn of so many Canadian francophones for their own mode of speech, their accent, their *patois* as some of them put it.

At the foot of the main staircase, Catherine hesitated. Should she go to the cafeteria? If Marchand nabbed her. . . . And that big, noisy room. After three hours of Wednesday morning classes she longed for a bit of peace and quiet. She walked out of the college. There were lots of little restaurants along Notre-Dame West, between Vauquelin and Saint-Jeanne, and she'd be sure to find an empty table in one of them, even if it was past noon.

The Lapin Blanc was full, however, as were Chez Sophie and Le Troquet. There were Le Domino and La Traverse, but they were cafeterias, and although the food was better she might just as well have gone to the one in the college.

The sun was at its height and the wind off the river had softened to a light breeze, making the cold bearable. Why not go a bit farther? She wasn't all that hungry, anyway. One of the girls had brought Christmas fudge (oh, the biological female urge to nurture!). Everyone had eaten some at the break, including herself. Why not try to find the ruins and the cats? It was in this direction, beyond Saint-Laurent. Not very far beyond, surely, perhaps one or two blocks. Before Notre-Dame Church? After? She didn't remember passing the church, but she hadn't paid attention, that was all. Saint-François-Xavier, Sainte-Jeanne. . . . So far? She halted, disconcerted, and looked at her watch. Quarter to one! It couldn't be much further. It hadn't seemed such a long walk this morning.

A delivery van was parked beside the sidewalk, and a man in a brown parka was leaning against a lamp-post, smoking. Catherine stopped beside him. He straightened up and stamped out his cigarette.

"Excuse me," she said. "I'm looking for the ruins. Are they far from here?"

The man frowned. "Ruins? There ain't no ruins around here, far as I know."

"Or an archeological dig? A vacant lot with bits of wrought-iron fence?" She hesitated to add "and cats." The man was already giving her a rather puzzled look. He shook his head doggedly as he fumbled in his jacket for a pack of cigarettes.

"Nope, ain't never seen nothing like that."

Was he having her on, taking her for a tourist? But his surprise seemed genuine. The delivery men were coming out of the building, and he called out to one. "Hey, Louis, know of any ruins in this neighborhood?"

Louis, a stocky, red-faced man, raised his eyebrows. "No I don't." He turned to Catherine. "Someone told you there were ruins around here?"

"No. I saw them myself this very morning. I went. . . ."

Suddenly the man's face cleared. "Hey, no problem. It's a vision." But his expression became serious again, and he seemed a little taken aback. "Ruins, you say?"

Catherine was still digesting "vision." It was the driver who replied.

"She said ruins or an archeological dig, a vacant lot with iron fencing."

"That's a vision, for sure," opined Louis. He sniffed

and wiped his nose on his sleeve. "But I never heard tell of one like that until today."

They were having fun at her expense! Well, she wouldn't get angry; that would be too stupid. Anyway, they were putting on such a good act that she might as well play along; they'd end up giving her the information she wanted. She smiled knowingly. "A vision, eh? So what's the usual type of vision you guys have around here?"

"You ain't from around here," said Louis. Oh, no, not that! But it was a statement, not the veiled challenge she would have expected.

"I teach at the college, but I live on Montcalm."

I teach at the college. The magic words had the desired effect, and Catherine felt the three men's attitude change. Good: maybe now they'd tell her what she wanted to know.

"So, about those ruins?"

"Ain't never heard about no ruins," repeated Louis, truly sincere. "Don't know much about how these visions work. Never had any myself. But it seems most of the time there's a kind of promenade with huge trees. Usually on the Quai Saint-Paul. And then farther up, around Notre-Dame Church, there's a kind of park full of statues. That's the sort of visions they have around here, mostly. But ruins, no. Ain't never heard about them."

Catherine listened, spellbound. A vision. Of course: she'd had a vision! How could she have forgotten? She'd actually thought the men were playing a joke on her, as though she'd never heard of visions. Decidedly, you're going off the rails, my girl. Better get your head screwed on straight.

The third man stood by, a stocky individual with a cap, hugging his hands in his armpits for warmth. Now he joined in the conversation. "A vision? What was it like?"

Catherine tried to describe the vacant lot, the ruins that were . . . medieval, that was it, or even vaguely Roman, the underground openings, the cats, and particularly the white cat, so unbelievably real. . . . She stopped, a little uncomfortable at noticing the three men listening to her with embarrassed expressions.

"Don't know much about how these visions work," repeated Louis, looking away from her. "If you don't live around here, perhaps it's normal, and then, you being a Frenchwoman—you're from France, eh?"

She nodded, once more at sea. What did he mean by "normal"? All visions were normal, weren't they? They must have noticed her puzzlement, because the driver took his cigarette out of his mouth and leaned toward her to say, in a fatherly way, "If I were you, I wouldn't talk about this to just anybody. They don't like it much, you know."

"Hey, Louis!" yelled a female voice from the depths of the building, "are you going to be all day?"

Louis gave a final sniff, muttered something, either "Sorry," or "So long," and bellowed an earsplitting "Just leaving!" The stocky man touched his cap with a forefinger—"G'bye, Ma'am"—and jumped into the truck after Louis.

Catherine set off once more, trying not to flee. Were some visions normal and others not? Did visions vary according to neighborhood? She couldn't remember ever hearing of such a thing. She had actually forgotten that it was completely normal to see things that didn't exist—or existed only briefly (she could still feel the white cat's fur beneath her fingers). Were there two kinds of vision? And then that remark: "They don't like it much." Who were *they*? And why didn't *they* like it much?

Brakes screeched, making Catherine jump. She found herself in the middle of the street with the traffic light against her. An incensed taxibus driver glared at her. Miming her apologies, she hurried to the sidewalk, then made herself stop. She was panting. What's happening to me? That time lapse this morning, and now these memory gaps. . . . Perhaps there was a link between this morning's incident and the vision, but she never remembered hearing that visions might be accompanied by vertigo.

Except that her memory wasn't exactly reliable today.

She moved on again, walking purposefully. At the first telephone booth, on the corner of Saint-Laurent, she stopped and phoned the clinic for an appointment. Next Monday, twelve-fifteen? Fine, perfect, she'd be there.

She headed for the college, vaguely amused. Even at

a distance, the ritual contact with Medicine had fulfilled
its reassuring role. Perhaps there was nothing really serious the matter. She must be tired, just tired. Her body was
trying to tell her so. She hadn't taken any time off since
classes started in September. What with her teaching, setting up the new third-year program, and the endless
wrangles with Marchand and all his gang of defrocked
old farts. . . . Physical and mental fatigue. Lucky thing the
Christmas holiday was approaching. Let's see what Sarah
says on Monday. Tomorrow there'd be time to relax, at
any rate. The Botanical Gardens in the morning, and
whatever she liked in the afternoon—shopping, a movie.
How about a whole day outside the Enclave? Good idea.
Outside. In the other Montreal.

3

Catherine arrived late at the Botanical Gardens. Getting there by the usual means was complicated, and she'd thought she had lots of time when she left home at nine o'clock. But she hadn't counted on the recent stink-bomb attack on the Secretary for Minority Language Groups and its consequences. As usual, the government was treating the whole thing with ridiculous solemnity. Nearly all the bridges leading out of the Enclave were closed. The only open checkpoints were the ones on Sainte-Catherine West, Berri, and Maisonneuve East. Catherine had to wait for half an hour in the Maisonneuve checkpoint lineup. "French from France, eh?" muttered the guard when she presented her pass. He disappeared to verify heaven knew what mysterious fact with his superior. Catherine reached the 235 stop on Du Havre only to see the back of the bus retreating. Of course, bus drivers on this side of the checkpoint never stopped when they saw someone running behind them, waving like mad—on the contrary. At least the red double-decker buses in Montreal-City were more frequent than those in the Enclave, and she didn't have too long to wait in the freezing shelter. There was another lineup at the Montgomery Metro, and a security check on the train at Hochelaga, then at Saint-Patrick. Really, for a stink bomb, it was ridiculous! When she finally got out of the taxibus (hailed, resignedly, at the exit to the Harness metro), it was after eleven-thirty.

The Nelson Park entrance was lit up and decorated with the kitsch of a Santa Claus cruise ship. She paid for her ticket and passed into the first geodesic bubble of the Multidome complex. Above her hung the giant noticeboard with messages in letters eight inches high, announcing the weekend sports attractions—the eternal hockey game, the semifinals of the Molson tennis tournament. Smaller characters (it figured!) announced the Impressionist exhibit and the Arts and Crafts Show. Mmmm . . . Botanical Gardens, Botanical Gardens . . . yes, there it was, half hidden beneath a huge wreath of plastic holly. On the moving sidewalk in the tunnel leading to the gardens, she pushed her way as best she could through the clusters of chattering retirees and shrill schoolchildren who paid no attention to her plea of "Excuse me . . . sorry . . . I'm late," and emerged at last into the big hall above the garden domes—an airlock to accommodate the transition from one atmosphere to another. A quick look at the map of the gardens: all paths led to the central pavilion. She hurried toward the revolving door.

The warm, moist air hit her like a soft wall as she entered the greenhouse complex. As she walked, she struggled out of her coat. She should have checked it in the cloakroom, but she was in too much of a hurry, couldn't even take the time to look at the riot of greenery and color in the beds. She'd find Joanne Nasiwi first, then admire the decor. There was a cafeteria housed in a kiosk, a sort of enlarged bandstand with tables around the edge—all full, naturally! She forced herself to slow down, trying not to scrutinize the customers too obviously, yet embarrassed and at the same time disgusted with herself for being so. She didn't know which was worse: to be seated and secretly fretting, or wandering about looking like a lost dog. An arm rose, hope leapt up. For her? Yes! Joanne Nasiwi, wearing shorts and a tight, sleeveless, red top, the employees' uniform, coming toward her with a tray and deftly tossing it into a waste bin, almost without stopping. She interrupted Catherine's apologies with a smile. "I know: the checkpoints. I got to work late myself this morning. Shall we go somewhere quiet?"

The young woman led the way, and Catherine followed, first into a wide alley running across the main greenhouse, then into a small alley. Amazing: just a few steps, and the hum of the crowd vanished, as did the odor of frying food, to be replaced by the earthy green smell rising from the beds. She heaved a contented sigh, although her head was spinning a little from the contrast between her race through the outdoor cold and the peaceful warmth of the gardens.

"How lucky you are, working in all this greenery! What do you do?"

"I work in the nurseries. One does what one can."

Catherine nodded. Outside the Enclave—and even inside—only low-level jobs were open to people of color and the rare Métis. "And you want to register in third year at the college."

"Let's wait until we're somewhere quieter," protested the young woman with a little laugh. "Don't worry, I've plenty of time. I skipped the ten o'clock break, so I have until twelve-thirty."

Things seemed quiet enough for a talk right here, as far as Catherine could see, except for the buzz of flying insects and the chatter of invisible birds among the branches. These geodesic bubbles were miniature ecosystems. This first one featured temperate zones and was bathed in the trembling, luminous warmth of a late summer afternoon beside a river. Suddenly Joanne knelt down and groped in the grass. She gave a little grunt as she lifted a square of lawn to reveal a steep and narrow metal staircase. She looked at Catherine. "Come on!" she said, with a wink and a wave.

Catherine climbed down after her, clutching the handrails. It's like a submarine companionway, she thought with amusement. It did feel almost like a submarine in the innards of the bubble. The walls were lined with various colored ducts of plastic and metal, nourishing viscera bearing cryptic inscriptions. "A shortcut," said Joanne over her shoulder, walking briskly. Catherine wanted to believe it, although she had been totally lost after the third turn—but then her sense of direction was hopeless.

At last they surfaced again, climbing a staircase as steep as the first, but without a trap door. They emerged at the foot of a species of weeping willow with twisted branches, on a tiny island linked to *terra firma* by the narrow arch of a red-lacquered bridge. Watery-lily leaves covered the pond, with the occasional pink star of a blossom opening to the light. Catherine had no names for the reeds and water plants that crowded the banks, nor for the contorted trees trailing bright green leaves in the water. It was hotter and more humid here, and the light had a breathless quality. Sharp cries pierced the air. Catherine looked up. The sky was closer than she would have expected—a luminous, white sky, millions of fiberglass filaments transmitting solar light to the re-created environments, bathed by almost imperceptible waves of air wafting through the ventilation system.

"This is the new addition to the tropical environment," said Joanne, hands on hips. "It's almost finished. It should be hooked up to the bubble next month. You're getting a sneak preview."

Catherine didn't like the moist heat, although she wasn't about to say it to this young woman who seemed so bent on pleasing her. She wiped her brow as she followed Joanne over the bridge. Off came the woolen pullover, and she unbuttoned her cuffs and rolled up her shirtsleeves. As they sat down on a bench, sharp cries still echoed through the air—so close that they made her start. Monkeys? No, smiled Joanne, a tape. Birds and insects were allowed in the greenhouses, but not mammals. Catherine looked discreetly at her watch. Only five past twelve? Extraordinary, the way the gardens were arranged in the available space; it seemed as though they'd walked for much longer. Well, better get down to business. "So you want to register at the college."

Joanne smiled with some embarrassment. "Mainly for your third-year workshop. But I'd have to register in the program. I've already taken two years of college-level courses at Victoria College."

A perfectly bilingual anglophone? Interesting. Catherine could almost have understood Marchand's remark about this "curious" young woman, except that he had no way of knowing that particular fact. He just wanted to make trouble because she was an adult, a woman, and a Métis.

"Was that very long ago? Pardon me for asking, but how old are you?"

"About twelve years ago. I'm twenty-nine. Victoria had the old system, but I have the required equivalents."

"Did you submit your file to the college?"

There was a small silence, a muscle suddenly quivering in the smooth cheek. "Not yet. I wanted . . . to meet you first."

Get your agreement, your support, Catherine translated. Anglophone, adult, woman, and Métis. Yes, she'd probably need it.

"Were you born in Montreal-City?"

A brief hesitation. "Kingston."

A Métis from the Amerindian Federation? "And you want to complete your college education in the Enclave?"

The black eyes stared at her intently, then looked away. Catherine remarked the elegant arch of the eyebrows and the length of the eyelashes. "I'd like to attend *your* writing workshop."

Catherine refrained from laughing. Should she be flattered? But the young woman seemed completely serious, even grave. "Why?"

"Henri Lapointe spoke to me about it."

"You know Henri?"

Joanne made a face. Was she embarrassed? "A little. A workshop led by a woman—I thought it might be different."

Oh dear, what have we here? "You write?"

"I'd like to."

Now for the usual little warning. "These workshops aren't designed to produce writers, you know. The idea is mainly to approach literature from the practical angle, rather than the theoretical."

"I know. One wonders why the college administration made such a fuss."

Catherine shrugged. "It upset college routine."

"Not only the routine . . . and not only the college."

And just what did she mean by that?

"Well, the top brass don't like people to use their imaginations."

"Typical of people at the top," remarked Catherine noncommittally. "They're prone to dizziness."

A silence. Joanne sat with her head bowed, resting her elbows on her knees, scuffing the white gravel of the path with the toe of her sandal. "Did you know that there isn't a single writing workshop left anywhere else?" she said finally. "Not at Victoria, nor any of the other colleges, nor McGill University? Profs who've tried to organize one recently have had their knuckles rapped."

"Well then, the Enclave is more liberal," said Catherine with a smile, hiding her surprise.

The young woman chuckled to herself. "No, they're all the same: they want to preserve the status quo." She straightened up and looked into the distance, her expression suddenly hard. "Enclave, Montreal-City, Quebec-City, or . . . beyond. All they want is to stay in power. The older they are, the tighter they hang on."

Catherine couldn't help agreeing. The incumbent gerontocracy in the Enclave, and particularly in the college, had made her gnash her teeth more than once. So, Joanne Nasiwi, you're a protester? Fine. Let's just hope it's not too evident in your file.

"Apart from the fact that this workshop is run by a woman and is the only one in the area, have you other reasons for wanting to join?"

Another hesitation, and then Joanne said with slow determination as she looked Catherine straight in the eye, like a poker player laying down an uncertain card, "To tell the truth, those are my main reasons. That and the fact that no one expects somebody like me to register."

Catherine nodded sympathetically. The Métis appeared deep in thought for a moment, then said: "In fact, what with the Index on one hand, and the difficulty of finding published works of original fiction. . . . And have you noticed that there isn't a single book about visions? It makes sense, somehow, that they've practically forbidden writing workshops. Fiction, visions, fantasy—the powers that be clearly find them unsettling. They all agree on that point, whether they're from the Enclave or somewhere else. So, your workshop. . . . Well, I just had to register, didn't I?"

Now that Joanne had jogged her memory, Catherine remembered that it was true: the Index didn't originate in the Enclave but in Quebec-City, the seat of the Canadian government. Here lists were made, books authorized. Very little new fiction, and yes, no books on visions. Neither normal visions nor the others—for there must surely be other kinds. Catherine couldn't be the only one to experience them, could she? She felt a sudden urge to talk about them to her companion, but felt awkward about broaching the subject.

"To get back to the subject of your workshop," continued Joanne, "could I send you my file first? And what I've written?"

"I see that writing isn't entirely a secondary motive," smiled Catherine, feeling reassured. "You really do write."

Her companion dropped her head and almost blushed. "Not really. I'd like to do better. The legends, the myths of . . . my people. I'd like to be able to do them justice."

"Your people?"

"I'm a Montagnais by birth."

Born in Kingston? But the young woman had answered rather abruptly, and Catherine didn't pursue the point. A painful family history, perhaps? She could always learn more later. Meanwhile she smiled at Joanne. "All right, send me the whole file and if we hurry you'll be able to register in January."

The two stood up spontaneously. Catherine gathered her things.

"Have you visited the Japanese dome yet?"

"No."

"Well, follow the guide!" said the young woman, beginning to walk along a path, and again Catherine admired the play of muscles on the straight back molded by the red top. "There've been some interesting additions to the bonsai collection. Would you like to see them?"

Miniature trees in their miniature environment had always fascinated Catherine. She liked to imagine them with doll-sized towns and tiny people. What if there really had been several kinds of humanity on Earth—giants, for instance, and dwarves? She had in mind a picture, probably something from a childhood book, showing part of a huge face bending benevolently toward a giant hand and the small creature standing on it.

Joanne suddenly slowed down, her expression odd, puzzled, vaguely . . . afraid? But it was only a child, a girl of about ten, blonde hair hanging freely to the shoulders. She wore a sleeveless royal-blue dress with white lace applique. There was something curiously familiar about the dress, despite its outmoded look. They came level with the girl, then passed by.

Joanne made as though to turn around, visibly checked herself and walked a few steps farther, then stopped abruptly with a little cry. "Oh, I'm so sorry—I've got to get back to the lab. There's something I forgot to do." She smiled apologetically, adding just a little too eagerly, "The bonsai are just over there, to the west. I'll send you the file and the writing samples. Thanks for coming. I'm sorry to rush off like this. Have a good day!"

She turned on her heel and disappeared into a narrow path at right angles to the alley. Catherine, totally taken aback, started walking again. Something blue at the edge of her field of vision made her look up. The little blonde girl again. Had she turned back? How had she managed to get there? Their glances met, and she looked into a pair of blue-green eyes, wide with curiosity, or so she supposed. Then the child skipped off along a flowered border. Catherine gave a disconcerted laugh and went in search of the bonsai.

Predictably, she was lost within five minutes. "Just over there to the west," indeed! Which way was west, anyhow? She'd left the wide alleys and was now walking along a series of small, tiled paths. Turning back, she did her best to retrace her steps, cursing herself for failing to note landmarks. Let's see—had she passed by this bush of starlike mums before? Weren't there any signs in this damned greenhouse? If she didn't meet someone soon, she'd wander about this maze until closing time and be stuck here all night!

A splash of blue at a turn in a path. The little girl? Catherine hurried toward it. She wanted to call out, but what? "Hey, you?" Not very dignified. "Little one?" If it isn't the child, I'll look like an idiot. The blue splash reappeared a little farther to the right, and Catherine abandoned the path, walking straight through the bed just in time to see something blue turning into a path at the corner of a small grove. Good—a path, at least! At the next intersection she found a sign. It seemed to positively jeer as it announced the presence of the bonsai fifty yards ahead. No blue dress anywhere, though, just a couple of doddery old ladies going into genteel raptures over the azaleas.

Naturally, now that she'd finally found the bonsai she didn't much want to look at them. She lingered by the sign for a moment, unsure. But no: she'd definitely had an overdose of color and greenery. This lush, mercilessly invasive profusion was suffocating. It made you feel like becoming a mindless vegetable yourself. She longed for the cold (how perverse could you get?), longed to be out in the honest black and white of winter, in the stripped-down landscape that reduced her to basics, to a core of hard, warm life, threatened but thoroughly stubborn.

All right: if the bonsai were "over there to the west," then this way was east, right? And the main entrance was. . . . She gave up, turning instead to a passerby, an elderly man with a pipe. She humbly asked the way, repeated the directions, and set off to the north. That film she was so desperate to see, what was it called? The last Peter Brooks, anyway. Where was it playing? Cineplex, McGill Metro station. Do a little shopping, dine at the Mandarin—well, why not, since she was missing the bonsai? By yourself? Yes, by myself. You don't need a man to go to the movies or a restaurant. *She* didn't, anyway, or so she'd learned over the past six years. "Six years!" She could still hear the slightly la-di-da voice of Lucie Saint-Onge, the other female literature prof, as well as the look on Marianne Sutaud's face as the two exchanged glances. Marianne was a Latin teacher and Lucie's sidekick in the gossip department. Once they had asked her why she hadn't gone back to her maiden name. "I didn't choose my father, but I chose my husband," Catherine had retorted, eliciting raised eyebrows, puzzled looks. She'd made the rare mistake of getting trapped in the staff room. She could tell what they were thinking. "Do you think she hasn't made love for that long?" Well, ladies, you may also be surprised to learn that you can service yourself very handily! It's really rather pleasant to be in control of your own life—fearlessly to face the prospect of building a bookcase, fixing a jammed drawer, repairing a light switch, or unplugging a sink on your own. Or to come home at three in the morning and put on a rock or opera tape, whichever you want. And have the whole bed to yourself. She hadn't said any of it, of course—her oddball reputation was already too well established in the college.

4

—

Friday, December 17, 1988

I dreamed of Mama last night. In the house at Sergines. She's on the big bed, legs curled under her rather like Hans Christian Andersen's Little Mermaid on her Copenhagen rock. I'm sitting beside her. There's a big wooden box by the bed, as high as we are, like a large desk. I open it. It smells of cedar. Inside is a board, and underneath it some little animals are sleeping. Curious and captivated, I lift up the board gently so that I can see without disturbing them. Not mice or cats, but white-and-black things, raccoons, even skunks, but I'm not afraid, I tell myself their scent glands have been removed, that they're tame. The board is hard to put back, and I'm scared of crushing the tiny things because they've begun to shrink.

It's very dark, very humid. I turn to Mama. We talk. About what, I can't remember. I'm worried she might be tired. Her head hardly reaches my chin, and I feel very moved because she's so little, so fragile with her black, liquid eyes. I think she even has her little-girl braids wound around her head. I don't realize it at first, but while we're talking, I see that she really *is* small, smaller and smaller, and all of a sudden I'm looking for her in the folds of the sheet. She's minuscule, I can't see her and I hardly dare move for fear of crushing her. Then all at once, maybe because of the thought of being crushed, the dream almost turns into the Dream of the Presence—not for long, just like . . . a shadow, with me being the one about to be crushed.

Of course I woke up crying, every muscle tensed. How I hate waking up with that kind of dream in my head, having to spend the whole day mulling it over! Especially a work day, when I can't stop to think, just scribble down some notes before going out. It almost makes sense, I almost understand what the little animals mean. Crush and be crushed. Are they meant to be me? But what's the connection with Mama? And with the Presence, especially afterward. Poor Mama never stifled me. Brought me up to be independent, rather. Although I've always felt guilty about leaving. Even now, when she can no longer reproach me for it. Or when I can no longer imagine her reproaching me.

Warm, moist—the Botanical Gardens. And the little animals—are they the kittens in the vision? Is there an interplay—if dreams determine visions, then are some visions determined by our dreams?

At the college, Catherine hadn't even time to grab her ritual hot drink from the coffee machine. Just in time again
for her ten o'clock class. She disappeared into the empty
elevator and got off at the third floor. All the doors were
closed by now, but the noise filtering through them meant
classes hadn't started yet. Catherine walked into her classroom and put her things on the desk. Her students were
talking at the back of the room and didn't even notice her
arrival. She caught snatches of conversation that sounded
astonished, frightened, shocked.

"All right, kids, what's up?"

Dead silence as the group turned to face her. Annie
Leboeuf had a purple bruise on her left cheek, Daniel
Lemire an arm in a plaster cast. Several had visible traces
of contusions, some sported patches of adhesive tape, and
she could see a white bandage here and there. She felt the
blood rush from her face. "What happened?" she asked,
her voice husky.

"You don't know about yesterday's demonstration?"
asked Juliette Miville incredulously.

"In Longueuil at five o'clock?" added Daniel Lemire.

Catherine shook her head, dumbfounded. She had
gone from the Metro into the underground downtown
mall, and then straight from the movie to the restaurant,
then back to another movie, all in the Cineplex. She'd got

through the checkpoint just in time for the Enclave cur-
few, eleven o'clock, but she'd missed the late-night news
at home. Had people been reading their papers in the bus?
She'd been in a hurry, too busy going over her notes to
pay attention.

A demonstration. Of Enclave students outside the Enclave. That went awry. But a demonstration for what? Or
against what? Why in Longueuil? Catherine had the painful certainty that she ought to know about it. Her students were looking at her with a mixture of disbelief and
mistrust. They obviously thought she must be aware of
what had happened. She leaned against the nearest desk,
feeling her knees go weak.

There was a knock, and the door opened brusquely.
Two men walked in without waiting for an answer, each
dragging a half-collapsed figure by the arm. Crew cuts,
heavy khaki parkas lined with sheepskin, dark-green trousers, and high, laced boots. Enclave Security. The policemen shoved their charges toward the front row of empty
desks and sat them down.

The students crowded around, but the police intervened. The older of the two cast a belligerent eye over the
group. "Where's your teacher?"

Catherine, incapable of speech, stepped forward from
the group. The officer looked at her skeptically. "We're
bringing you back *this*," he said, jerking a thumb at the
two desks and their occupants. "You can turn them over
to their parents." He sniffed, ran an angry eye over the silent group, and added, "Students are supposed to study.
And you profs should do a better job. They ought to be
in class, not in the streets."

With military precision, the two men turned simultaneously and walked out, slamming the door.

Catherine looked at the form slumped in the first
chair. She recognized Henri Lapointe, head swathed in
bandages, arm in a sling, face covered with cuts and
bruises. One of this week's two absentees. The star scorer
on the college hockey team, a dark-haired boy of twenty,
muscular, well-built, proud of his strength and agility. He
didn't move as she walked over to him. He seemed completely oblivious to his surroundings. Instinctively, she
kneeled down so that they would be on the same level.

His left eye was shut and the left side of his face was swollen and blotched. His hands hung listlessly on his lap. Catherine reached out to take one, then started back with a horrified shudder. The knuckles were covered with dried blood, some of the fingertips, too. It looked as though the nails had been torn off or crushed.

"My God, Henri . . ." she whispered. Still crouching she turned to the other desk. Jacques Lévesque, the other absentee. All she could see were bruises and a swollen, cut lip. But his usually plump and rosy face was haggard. Catherine stood up and looked at the others. No one moved. She turned back to Henri and Jacques. "Tell me what happened," she said hoarsely.

"The CNP arrested us last Saturday," croaked Jacques, his voice trembling with rage. "Because of my father, they let me off lightly."

"The National Police? Is this connected . . . with the stink bomb in Quebec?" stammered Catherine.

The young man shrugged, then grimaced with pain. "Obviously!"

"The CNP arrested you in the Enclave?"

"No. We were in a meeting with . . . we were near the Botanical Gardens."

"And they let you go? With Henri in that condition?"

"They escorted us to a checkpoint. A warning, they told us."

A warning. For the Enclave. Of course. To the parents via the children, who were shouting out loud what so many adults thought in silence. To the Expansionists, who demanded more land for the Enclave in the territories across the river, the Longueuil/Saint-Lambert county with its fields.

Catherine took a deep breath: her heart was beating too fast, as though she'd been running. "An unfortunate mistake," no doubt. But it was bound to happen. The unrest had been going on for months. With the hundredth anniversary of the Enclave's independence coming up next year, it could only get worse. The CNP wanted to make a show of force. And the Enclave Security had brought the boys to the college, not to their homes? Classes had gone on as though nothing had happened, and the college hadn't reacted in any way?

"Henri, you've got to get to a hospital. You should call your parents."

"They've been told. They're coming to get us," said Jacques. He no longer seemed fired by the same rage, perhaps because he'd begun to imagine how his father would take the news. A sobering thought—the Enclave vice-governor having to collect his son from the college. Not at a police station, no, the insult had been carefully calculated to have a more immediate public impact. The warning. The lesson.

But Henri—he hadn't just been maltreated, he'd been tortured. This couldn't be allowed to go unnoticed!

Beneath Catherine's incredulous shock and anger lay some uncertainty, however. She had no idea where it came from, and decided to ignore it. She stood up and contemplated the young, bruised faces surrounding her, taking in the surprise and hope that her reaction had aroused. "No class today, not with me, at least. I'm going to see the principal. Wait here."

Once out in the corridor, heart thumping with rage, Catherine hesitated. Those old croaks must have some limits to their legalistic posturing! A student *tortured* by the CNP, even if he were "guilty" of helping organize an unauthorized demonstration. . . . And he'd been detained for several days, too, instead of being brought back immediately to the Enclave, as stipulated by law!

She hurried up the stairs and arrived somewhat out of breath. "Good morning, Marielle," she said to the principal's too pink-and-blond secretary. "May I see Mr. Touchard? It's urgent."

The woman barely raised her eyes from her screen. "He's waiting for you."

Speechless, Catherine moved toward the principal's office and knocked on the door.

"Come in, come in!"

Roger Touchard, principal and chairman of the college board, was a tall thin man between forty and fifty. Somehow, with his crown of iron-gray hair thinning on the top, he still seemed to be wearing his cassock, transmuted into the phony casualness of dark, close-fitting turtleneck sweaters and impeccably pressed black trousers. He invited her to sit, then remained standing beside her after she'd taken a seat. He said nothing, merely resting his hands benevolently crossed over his belly—fine, white hands, the middle finger of the left hand sporting a ring with a purple stone worthy of a cardinal. He looked down at her, the expression thoughtful on his long, closely-shaven, slightly waxen face.

"You were waiting for me," Catherine found herself forced to say.

He smiled. "They brought Jacques and Henri to me first. I hope it will be a salutary lesson for your students."

"Henri Lapointe has been tortured, Mr. Touchard!"

"That isn't the version given me by the CNP chief, Mr. Gallagher, when I phoned him just now. Henri Lapointe and Jacques Lévesque were indulging in clandestine, illegal activities when they were arrested. They resisted, and young Lapointe later tried to escape from the police station by jumping from the first floor. That's how he was injured—a slight concussion, broken arm. . . . And that's why they kept him under observation at the Royal Hospital before bringing him back here."

"The parents weren't told?"

"The authorities weren't obliged to tell them: an inquiry was under way."

Catherine rose to her feet, unable to remain seated. "And you believed them!"

"Catherine, Catherine, you're so impulsive!" Touchard smiled, aiming somewhere between the paternal and the friendly. She could see it coming: he was going to grab her by the shoulders and sit her down. She moved away, folding her arms in an effort to contain her anger.

"Even though we sympathize with some of these young people's demands, Catherine, you should be fairminded enough to agree that we can't endorse their methods. Rush-hour traffic was blocked on the Jacques Cartier Bridge for three hours. There was inexcusable vandalism in the Longueuil Metro station, and five policemen were injured, three of them with a baseball bat."

"And how many students? Have you seen the state they're in?" said Catherine through clenched teeth.

"There isn't one in my class that doesn't bear marks. I'm sure it was meant to be a peaceful demonstration!"

"My dear Catherine, you seem to entertain certain illusions about your students, illusions—how shall I put it?—from another age?" Touchard had hooked a thigh over his desk, and now leaned back, hands still folded, shaking his head with gentle reprobation. "We aren't in France, you know, and this isn't '76 anymore. . . ."

"A lucky thing, too. Some people died in France, in '76! And it could happen here if someone doesn't put a stop to it."

"But that's exactly what we're doing, because all these young people are far more resolute than those you knew in France. Times have changed, you realize. Our students aren't all imbued with pacifist idealism, as you seem to think. A policeman was wounded by a bullet." He raised a hand to cut off Catherine's argument. "And it wasn't a caliber used by the CNP."

Catherine shrugged. "Some hothead. . . ."

"Several heads, and not all hot, my dear Catherine. It wasn't young Lapointe or Lévesque that the CNP planned to arrest in Nelson Park. Your 'peaceful demonstration,' like all the troubles we've been experiencing recently, wasn't only the work of a few contentious students from the Enclave. They're being manipulated from the outside; they're too young and inexperienced to realize it, but you of all people ought to understand, my dear Catherine. They're being used to achieve aims that have nothing to do with their demands—which, by the way, are fairly legitimate. It's our duty as educators and parents to stop them sliding down that dangerous slope and to forestall any further, more serious incidents. That's why the college board has issued a directive. In future, all students participating in this kind of activity will be suspended for the semester. And if they're suspended twice, they'll be expelled. As for young Lapointe, since he will appear in court he is *de facto* expelled from the college and won't be allowed to re-register. If you'd found time to visit the staff common room this morning, you'd have seen the directive. You were supposed to read it aloud to your students."

"What!" Catherine gasped, ignoring the implied reprimand.

Touchard leaned over and placed an insistent hand on her arm. "My dear Catherine, surely you understand that we have to make an example?"

"With one of the college's best students?" she asked, shrugging him off. She was about to add, "And why not Lévesque? He was arrested, too!" But she bit her tongue, knowing what Touchard would say. Something like, "But he didn't try to escape." That wasn't the reason, of course. The Montreal French College wasn't going to punish the son of the Enclave's vice-governor with irrevocable expulsion. Henri Lapointe's father, on the other hand, drove a taxibus. . . .

Thoroughly disgusted, she made one last effort. "If you expel Lapointe, and if, as you say, the student movement has more radical elements, you'll push him into their arms. I know him: he won't calm down."

Touchard raised his eyebrows and sighed. "You don't seem to understand, my dear Catherine. Henri Lapointe has long been on the side of the 'more radical' elements, as you put it. There were Northern agents at the Nelson Park meeting, despite the fact that they all managed to escape—deserting their young and naïve accomplices."

And they'd brought the boys back to the Enclave? She had barely time to be astonished before another and more distressing emotion filled her mind. "Northern agents." Touchard's tone implied that she knew what he was talking about. The connotations were easy enough to grasp in the context, but they didn't correspond to anything in her experience or memory. Once again she was overwhelmed by a feeling of total ignorance, an unmistakable sense of strangeness. Touchard's innuendos, his "my dear Catherine," and his furtive hands, she *knew* she'd been trying to avoid them ever since she'd begun working at the college, but she couldn't *remember* it. She remembered nothing, no definite incident. And "Northern agents" triggered no response at all. A blank. No resonance.

Catherine stumbled into the chair, her head whirling. An alarmed Touchard bent over her. "My dear Catherine. . . ." She almost slapped his face. He must have recognized the impulse, because his hands stopped in midair. "Good lord, you're taking this too much to heart!" He rushed to the cooler and came back with a glass of water. Catherine stifled a hysterical gulp of laughter at the obscene burp of the water cooler, but accepted the proffered glass. She drank too fast and began to cough. *If he pats me on the back, I'll scream!* But Touchard remained at a respectful distance. *All this swooning and coughing must be a bit too physical for him.*

When she lifted her head, eyes swimming with tears, he was again half sitting on the desk, arms folded while one hand thoughtfully plucked at his fleshy lips.

"You seem truly upset, my dear. I can well understand. Perhaps you'd better forget about teaching this morning. The ten o'clock class is half over, in any case. Get some fresh air instead, or perhaps lie down in the infirmary. We could lunch together outside the college between noon and two o'clock to discuss all this. . . ."

The old goat doesn't miss a trick, thought Catherine, stifling the hysterical laugh that threatened to burst out again. She managed to say in a suitably anemic tone, "No thank you, I don't think I'm hungry," as she rose and walked out without further ceremony. Touchard would put it down to her upset state. She ignored the secretary's inquisitive stare and went into the deserted hallway. Ten to eleven. It wouldn't be empty for long. She tried to think of simple, practical things. Coat. Hat, gloves, bag. In the classroom. She'd have to go back.

Vice-governor Lévesque passed her in the hall, a bear swathed in fur from head to toe. He held his son by the arm and glared fiercely at Catherine as they went by, daring her to so much as speak. She said nothing, but tried to catch Jacques' eye. The young man shuffled along, eyes lowered.

In the classroom, Henri Lapointe was still slumped in his desk chair. The other students crowded around Catherine, but she shook her head, suddenly exhausted. "There'll be no eleven o'clock class. We'll meet next week. Why is Henri still here?"

"His father works the morning shift today," volunteered Annie. "They didn't give him permission to come for Henri."

"Take him to the infirmary and get him to lie down."

"I'll stay with him," said Annie.

Catherine nodded but said nothing, although vaguely amused. Someone had found her hero. She studied the young man's swollen face. He seemed a little less dazed and had raised his head to follow the conversation. Suddenly, a question rose unbidden to her lips. "Henri, how long have you known Joanne Nasiwi?"

There was no mistaking the flash of alarm in Henri's one open eye. "Who?"

"Joanne Nasiwi, a Métis woman. She wants to register in the writing workshop in January. I met her yesterday. She told me you'd spoken to her about it."

Henri's face relaxed as she talked. She added in a careless tone, "Where's she from in the North, anyway?"

"Chicoutimi," said Henri mechanically. Then, as though suddenly aware of the implications, he added, "But she left ages ago."

When the eleven o'clock bell rang, Catherine followed the flow of students down the staircase. They moved in clusters, and she noted the occasional Band-aid and strip of surgical tape, as well as various cuts and bruises. Once in the main hall, she walked idly toward the staff room with the vague idea of reading the directive. It was still early, and the Friday between-class crush of teachers hadn't begun. There must be some heavy discussion going on at the end of class. Catherine found the directive prominently displayed on the notice board. The same old administrative claptrap, virtuous circumlocutions disguising the fact that the college was prepared to sacrifice the futures of dozens of students on the pretext of protecting them. The feeling of déjà-vu was almost unbearable. May '76 all over again. Protect them from what? If they didn't learn to take risks for their beliefs and to accept the consequences, what sort of citizens would they become, what sort of human beings? Protect them! Muzzle them, that was all. And as for the hackneyed argument that they were being manipulated from outside—it was the same old scare tactic trotted out by aging paternalistic governments, unable to face the fact that the children had grown up and could think for themselves, even if it meant making their own mistakes!

She turned away impatiently from the bulletin board and saw that someone had come in and was standing behind her. Robert Ducharme. One of her earliest students, now a Spanish teacher at the college. The young man winked in at attempt at irony, but his discouragement was obvious.

"Immortal prose, isn't it?"

"Very lethal in its way," answered Catherine, clenching her teeth. "They're expelling Henri Lapointe. With no appeal. Two Security men brought me Henri and Jacques Lévesque. Afterward, I went to Touchard. . . ."

Ducharme raised his eyebrows, and Catherine made a silent face, admitting her naïveté.

"You must have known long ago that there's not much to expect in that quarter," Ducharme said. "He's a Concentrationist: the Expansion can only take place on Montreal Island, nowhere else. Completely unrealistic, of course, but he won't budge. Neither will those old Natalist reactionaries. They'd actually like us to withdraw from the three satellite islands—Notre-Dame, Sainte-Hélène, and the Île des Soeurs. You can imagine what heresy it is to ask for south shore settlement! And once the revenge of the cradles has driven all the English into the river, what'll those old bastards do? Build a wall around the island, I suppose? They're stuck in 1758 with a last-stand mentality."

Catherine fought against mounting anxiety. She felt dizzy. Concentrationists. Natalists. As before, she could catch the context, yet the words aroused no memory. But there must be at least two hundred years of history behind them. They surely couldn't be recent labels!

Suddenly, as though her distress had reached a threshold beyond which it ceased to exist, a curious calm invaded Catherine. Very deliberately, she repeated Touchard's words. "They say Lapointe and the others are being manipulated by Northern agents."

Ducharme pulled an incredulous face. "For street demonstrations? Do they take us for imbeciles? The Believers—" He glanced around the room, but it was empty; now he spoke more softly, but with the same con-

viction as before. "The Believers don't go in for that kind
of thing, and you know it. Politics, our Southern-style
confrontations.... Well, they'd be more likely to try to
dissuade us. They'd consider it useless agitation, a fatal
distraction. They're totally against violence."

"Who are totally against violence?" said a voice by
the door.

"The Northerners, according to Robert," said Catherine smoothly, turning to face the squat form of Georges
Chiasson, one of the two geography professors. She still
felt the curious calm, now mingled with an amused curiosity that was equally strange.

"The Sags?" Chiasson shook off his heavy coat, his
face already darkening with the forthcoming diatribe.
"They'd *like* us to believe they're pacifists, all right! As
though the wolf could become a lamb! They're all a
bunch of communists, and we know what that lot wants
for dinner! Their idea is to overthrow the Canadian government and swallow us whole."

"Since when are you defending the Canadian government?" retorted Ducharme.

"Don't give me that argument, my young friend. I
fought the Fascists in Spain in '39, and there were En-
glishmen in my brigade. I fought by their side in '51 as
well, during the Normandy Landing and after. They saved
our skins several times, and my men and I did the same
for them. We have our differences here, that's for sure, but
when it's a question of defending democracy, we know
what side we're on. Make no mistake. The Sags are just
like Hitler or Mevdeiev. Whether they're bleating freedom, equality, and brotherhood, or government of the
people, by the people, for the people, I'm not fooled. I've
already heard that come-on."

"The Believers aren't into politics!" protested Ducharme.

"Hah! You kids are unbelievably naïve. No wonder
those poor students are being infiltrated so easily."
Chiasson turned to Catherine, but she was merely keeping
score, completely divorced from the actual conversation.
"The people in Quebec-City are right. We've got to stop
this now, strike quickly. A surgical procedure instead of
letting things drag out for weeks and bemoaning the fate

of poor innocents. We'd do better to look to our own, the ones who haven't yet done something stupid but might be tempted. Strike quickly, strike hard. Then they'll stay quiet."

Ducharme was choking with rage. "A surgical procedure! Can you hear yourself talk? What kind of surgical procedure, pray tell? Air raids over the North, blowing up the whole place? Why not the final solution while you're at it? Gas, viruses, the lot!"

The squat geography professor drew himself up indignantly to his full but modest height. "I never said any such thing! Don't put words in my mouth. I fought in Europe, Ducharme, cleaned out the Nazi labor camps when you weren't even born!"

"It doesn't appear to have taught you anything."

"Listen, you shit-faced little toad—"

Catherine closed her ears to the sharp voices, drifted to the door. Oh, she'd understood the words, but the references still escaped her. The Spanish Civil War in '39? The Normandy Landing in '51? Something to do with World War II, obviously, but the dates seemed odd. "Hitler or Mevdeiev." Hitler, yes, of course, but Mevdeiev? Again a blank, a gap, something forgotten.

Alzheimer's. Might as well face up to it. But wasn't that a slowly developing disease? She couldn't remember any such episodes before—let's see—Wednesday, the day of the vision. And since then, an avalanche.

She couldn't *remember*; that was the trouble.

Or else, equally odd, she couldn't remember and suddenly it would all come back.

Standing still in the bustle of the hallway, Catherine recognized the feeling rising within her, her response to everything that frightened or hurt her, almost always inadequate, but compelling. Anger. She preferred it to the thoroughly disconcerting calm that had overtaken her in the staff room. And she certainly preferred it to panic. Anger was a source of energy, of action. Like the time when she was little and had suddenly been angry with her fear of the dark. She'd made up her mind to leave the flashlight at home on winter evenings when she had to go down the hill to the grocery store, past those terrifying black chasms at each farm gate along the road.

Well, those were memories. She had memories after all—she hadn't forgotten everything!

Absurdly reassured, almost glad to be angry, Catherine headed for the library. So she lacked facts? She'd go after them, find out what came back on its own, and what didn't come back at all.

When she and François had been taken around the college on their arrival, twelve years earlier, she had entered the library with trepidation. The rest of the college—both the architecture and the interior arrangement—had been very like the barracks-style schools of her youth, but here she had been pleasantly surprised. Northern Louisiana had given the college a fully-equipped library: all the basic materials, shelves, books, a librarian, and the latest computer hardware and software, with a promise to update the technology. The library still bore the name of the then president of the Louisiana Federation, Georges d'Iberville.

The library was a bright, airy space occupying the entire west second floor of the college. Catherine relaxed as she walked in. The studious silence of libraries and all the soft noises that accompanied it always evoked cheerful memories, from the little library of her provincial secondary school to the huge factory-library in the university at Dijon, where nobody had the right to penetrate the sacred stacks except the employees.

She hesitated in front of the main desk, a little semicircular island at the entrance. She felt completely lost, perhaps because she'd been thinking of the Dijon library with its huge main hall and long, straight counters. She consulted the main cataloguing system, found the call number for a fairly recent reference work on Canadian history—dated 1982—and attacked the shelves in the section indicated.

Settling herself at one of the large tables nearby, she noticed a redheaded student sitting opposite, surrounded by an impressive array of books and periodicals as well as scattered sheets of squared paper on which he was writing feverishly. "End of term!" he said, lifting his head and smiling at Catherine. She returned the smile, feeling a pang of anxiety. Was she supposed to know him? To avoid conversation, she quickly opened the book taken from the stacks and looked at the table of contents. *Colonization: first arrivals . . . colonizing peoples . . . the British . . . Amerindian tribes. . . .* No, that wasn't it. *The Conquest.* Perhaps. *Emigration to Louisiana . . . The Twenty Years' War . . . Treaty of York . . . New Canada . . . Eastern Province . . . Western Province. . . .* Nothing on the North. But was the North part of Canada? Chiasson talked about it as though it were a separate state. Back to the Treaty of York. Catherine's eye skimmed the page: *1870 . . . natural expansion of American settlement toward the northwest of the continent . . . English blockade . . . Franco-Canadian unrest in the East . . . partisan units . . . involvement of Louisiana,* yes, she remembered everything so far; at this point, all the Canadian francophones had been rounded up and resettled in Montreal-Enclave in order to neutralize their activity and influence.

Still nothing on the North. Ah—a colored map showing the American Union with the three major federations: a splash of blue for French-speaking Louisiana, running the length of the Mississippi, spreading eastward down to the tip of Florida and westward between the Missouri River in the north and the Platte and Arkansas rivers in the south; the Amerindian Federation in green from the Missouri up to Hudson Bay; and to the right of it, the red splash of Eastern Canada—the map said "Québec," as the book had been published in France. The yellow splash indicated the Hispanic Federation along the Mexican frontier, including the western half of the Red River, the northern end of the Rio Grande, and then up the length of the Colorado as far as San Francisco. (Who chose these colors, anyway? Were they simply picked out of a hat?) The Eastern American Federation was pale pink, a sprinkling of little states along the east coast, linked to the mountainous territories of the Western Federation by the corridor between Louisiana and the Amerindian Federation. Pink arrows penetrating from Missouri into what had been Saskatchewan showed where the American armies had marched in. It was still called Saskatchewan, but the red had turned to pink after the Treaty of York in 1888.

And still nothing on the North. No wave of abrupt memories. Wasn't there normally a kind of logic in the memory gaps of Alzheimer's? Why would she remember all this, and not the rest? She could even close the book and recite the chain of events by heart. The Canadian-American War, 1868–1888, each side incapable of carrying the day, the compromise peace, the loss of the central Canadian plains to the American Union, and more particularly to the Amerindian Federation. And the transformation of the Enclave from a forced resettlement camp into an independent francophone "state," a concession by the Union negotiators to Louisiana to compensate for the fact that Lower Canada hadn't been recovered.

But when had the "North" been created, then? The other maps in the book didn't show it, and there'd been no more boundary changes in Eastern Canada, anyway. The two world wars had brought alterations in the Enclave's status and its relations with the rest of the province, culminating in the 1955 agreements: a common currency, the right to circulate freely in the two provinces with only a passport and in Montreal-City with a pass, joint management of immigration with Quebec-City, settlement of most litigation surrounding the Enclave free port and traffic on the Saint Lawrence (the major bone of contention since 1888). The wholesale slaughter of World War I and especially World War II had at least opened the lines of communication between the two communities, Chiasson was right about that. But it was over thirty years ago. Everything had settled back into the status quo since then, the old sociopolitical forces had re-established their sway, and now, under the most conservative government in Canadian history, Enclave students got themselves clubbed by the CNP, as in the good old days.

Catherine closed the book, discouraged and struggling to retain a spark of the anger that had propelled her as far as the library. She went back to the main desk and found Gérard Duplain, the head librarian, who flashed his white dentures at her in his habitual smile. "I'm looking for something on the North," she said. He looked blank. "The North of the Sags—or the Believers. That North."

Duplain's change of expression caught her interest. Was it embarrassment? He coughed. "There are no books on that subject. You'll find something in the green bank, but that's all."

Catherine's expression must have surprised Duplain in turn. "Only professors with an access card can use it," he said. "You've got yours, haven't you? The green card?"

Card. Green. She felt a relief that was difficult to hide as she fished in her wallet. Bank card ... there, green card. She put it on the counter in front of Duplain, who again smiled hesitantly.

"You run it through the slot in the green room door."

Catherine took her card back, feeling herself blush. "My head's not screwed on right today. It's time term ended." She hurried away from the desk, managing just in time to find the sign saying "Green Room" with an arrow pointing left.

So: in a separate data bank. Not on the Index, but almost. Catherine couldn't figure out which was weirdest—forgetting these details (although in a perverse way she was beginning to get used to it), the fact that the history book seemed to have left the North out entirely, or the library's precautions surrounding information on the North. The small, pale green room was empty except for a single terminal in front of a large screen. Catherine slid her card into the slot beside the huge keyboard. The screen lit up. Surname, given name, work code—it was on her regular library card; address, telephone, social security number. ... What was the point of all these data? You couldn't use this terminal anonymously, it seemed. A good way of supervising unorthodox interests?

She shrugged with a surprised little laugh. What a silly idea? As though the Enclave were a police state!

Not the Enclave, perhaps, but the rest. Montreal-City, the Canadian government?

Her fingers stopped on the keyboard. Paranoid fantasies, now? Things were getting more unpleasant by the minute. She couldn't wait for Monday and her appointment with Sarah at the clinic.

She typed the required keystrokes and a summary appeared on the screen: *At the time of the Conquest, there were two main francophone immigration movements between 1758 and 1765. The largest was to Louisiana, the other to the Saguenay region and territories to the north, where a fairly large native population lived (Montagnais, Cree, Inuit). The isolated situation of this territory, the difficulty of access, and what had been considered its limited resources had, until then, caused various colonizers to ignore the region. . . .*

Catherine closed her eyes and clutched the arms of her chair. The rush of memory was like an electric shock. She knew, she remembered everything perfectly! Helped by the natives to survive under difficult conditions, the francophones intermarried with them to form a society isolated by geography—by Laurentide Park in the southern portion (a hundred and twenty square miles of wild, mountainous terrain), by the steep cliffs on either side of the Saguenay fjord (the river that flowed into the Saint Lawrence), and above all by the terrible climate, the winters that lasted almost nine months. When the Enclave was set up there were fresh immigration movements to Louisiana and the North. The authorities made no move to stop them, judging that dispersion would effectively neutralize francophones. Early in World War I, however, things began to change. The authorities turned to the North during conscription. The population melted away before the recruiting sergeants—those who had succeeded in getting there, despite the traps laid for them on the way.

Catherine stared at the screen, breathless, heart pumping. There'd been none of this in the table of contents of the book she'd consulted earlier. But there should have been, shouldn't there? Along with the sequel between the two wars—the establishment of a revolutionary government vaguely modeled on the soviets that were then sprouting in Russia.

She frowned, distracted by a detail despite her astonishment. Pseudo-soviets? In a region mainly occupied by seminomadic hunters and fishers, and no doubt totally lacking in industry? Ridiculous. But not more so, or not less so, all things considered, than the name chosen by the secessionists: the Independent Realm of the North. That was about as much as anyone knew, however, since the Northerners had completely sealed off the area. All Canadian attempts at military penetration had failed, vanquished by the terrain and the climate. The attempts were no doubt half-hearted—after all, there was nothing up there but spruce trees and then tundra.

Catherine hesitated briefly, then quit the summary and typed SAGS.

In recent years, the North has been sending secret agents to the South, especially to Montreal and Quebec. Their apparent aim is to use violence to foment public disorder that will first paralyze, then overthrow the Canadian government. Popularly known as "Sags," an abbreviation of "Saguenites" (although they come from the entire territory, not just the Saguenay region), they are particularly active in the francophone Enclave, where they believe there is fertile ground for their communist propaganda, designed to aggravate political, economic, and cultural antagonisms that. . . .

Exactly what Chiasson had said in the staff room. Catherine returned to the menu and typed BELIEVERS. The screen blinked NOT FOUND.

She stared at the words for a moment, trying to assess her reaction. There was still the question of her sudden recovery of memory—but at least this had occurred with almost no help from the data bank, apart from minimal prompting. It still bothered her, though; she felt worried, puzzled, and angry, but with a strange kind of anger, more like dissatisfaction, frustration—yes, intellectual frustration, such as she might feel when faced with a logical pattern that had some elements missing, and where some of the elements present didn't quite seem to fit together.

So now what? She looked at her watch: half past twelve. Had she really anything more to learn from the green bank? No. And she was getting hungry. Leaving the green room, she thought of the book left on the table in the history section. Could there really be nothing in it about "the Independent Realm of the North"? Perhaps she had read too fast. Or was it in a chapter where she hadn't thought of looking?

She felt rather stupid as she walked to the history section. The redheaded student had disappeared, leaving his things on the table. Gone to eat, probably. She sat down and opened the book at the table of contents. *The Conquest.* Subheadings: *Emigration to Louisiana . . . Emigration to the Saguenay.*

Her heart seemed to skip a beat. She closed her eyes, opened them again. "Emigration to the Saguenay." There it was, in black and white. She could have sworn. . . . How could she have missed it? *Part of the francophone population, especially from Québec and the surrounding area, opted for internal exile by taking refuge in the Saguenay region. This was still wilderness territory. The emigrants founded the towns of La Baie and Chicoutimi, the latter subsequently becoming the capital of the Independent Realm of. . . .*

Catherine's hands trembled as she flipped through the book looking for the chapter on the Treaty of York. There was a section on the northward migration of francophone populations.

An index at the back of the book. Had there been an index earlier?

She went back to the index and looked for "Believers." *Recently, a marginal, apparently religious movement has begun to spread through Eastern Canada. There is no written material on this sect, which appears to carry out its teaching on an exclusively oral basis. However, most "Believers" appear to be Métis and/or francophones. The sect's sacred place is somewhere in the North, and followers are obliged to make a pilgrimage to this place. The movement may possibly be another attempt by the IRN to further muddy the political waters.*

As she read, Catherine waited for the flash of illumination, the sudden, dizzying flood of facts in her brain. Nothing. If she'd ever known anything about the Believers, she had no memory of it.

She went back to the table of contents and stared at the subtitle that she'd missed the first time around. Words she should have seen, simply couldn't have failed to see. Was there a rational explanation? A selective blindness? Possibly, but why would it strike precisely the information she was looking for? And why hadn't it lasted?

She closed the book. A rather wild idea crossed her mind: if she went back to the green room now, would she find "Believers" listed in the data bank? Good heavens, I must be losing my marbles—but wait, there *is* something. Something like . . . a vision? Only the reverse. Instead of seeing what wasn't there, she didn't see what *was* there.

And now she did see it. A sort of twisted logic. She should ask whether there were—should she call them "anti-visions"? But so intermittent? So . . . specialized?

Joanne Nasiwi's remark came to mind: no books about visions. And in the green bank? No, she was too hungry to go back at once. She'd eat first, then see how she felt.

But when she came back, she found that the green room was closed in the afternoon. That left her with nothing to do at the college before next Tuesday.

Back home in her kitchen she fumbled to find a place for her frost-covered glasses on top of the fridge and gazed at the impressionist picture postcard that was her snowbound garden. It was going to be a long weekend. Two full days before her visit to the clinic and Sarah, before knowing what was the matter with her.

She made herself eat and go to bed early, where she watched the television news. The previous day's "student troubles" were covered with brief banter and not even the courtesy of a film clip. She switched off the set, feeling exasperated, and picked up a book, hardly aware of what she was reading. Finally she gave in to the temptation of a sleeping pill, something she hadn't done since the painful days following her separation with François.

That night, despite the sleeping pill, she dreamed of the Presence.

6

Sunday, December 19, 1988

I've spent the whole weekend grappling with the concrete reality of this world—my usual remedy for inner confusion. I waded into the snowy garden and put the Christmas lights on the little white pine, cleaned and tidied the house from top to bottom, filed old papers, course notes, letters, and various documents, and reorganized my whole filing system. I don't fool myself with this frantic ordering of externals, but after all there's a sort of sympathetic magic between mind and matter that guarantees cross-pollination, so to speak. Restore calm and order to surrounding matter, and some of it will always rub off on your state of mind. All this unaccustomed physical exertion has left me with creaking joints but dreamless nights, or at least no memory of dreams. The Presence made a brief visit on Friday night, but hasn't been back since.

I'm being a bit too cheery, all the same. I've used humor too often and for too long. Can a sense of humor wear out? Or am I more out of sorts than I thought? Humor doesn't work too well, anyway. Neither does physical activity. I was glad to have got all those old letters filed, but I have to admit that my main feeling now is one of melancholy. Liar! It's sadness, even good old depression if I don't get a grip on myself. Why should I get a grip on myself, though? But what good would it do to let myself go? Adolescent maundering—and at your age. Aren't you ashamed?

Let's look at the bright side. I undertook this visit to my past in alphabetical order as a sort of exorcism, or perhaps a challenge: are there blanks, gaps in my memory, names that mean nothing or to which I can't put a face? Well, no. Rereading a few of the letters written to François before our marriage, I remembered the things mentioned perfectly clearly—people, places, smells, music: "While My Guitar Gently Weeps" thirty times in a row on the university cafeteria jukebox, even now I smile when I hear it. . . . *Oh darling, they're playing our song. . . .*

Does he smile when he hears it, does he even remember? All those memories, all that time together, and I don't even know if he remembers. Sometimes I have the feeling that he forgot everything the moment he walked out the door.

I don't know which is worse: that he should forget or that he might remember things differently. But there's no way I can ever know whether, somewhere in his head, there exists another image of us. . . . And another history of myself, a part of myself that I've lost forever. I kept the letters I wrote him; he didn't ask for them when he left. Forgetfulness/indifference, plain forgetfulness, or a conscious decision? And if the latter, was it a silent commentary on me, on us? He had so few things to pack, there was so little of himself in this house where we lived together for six years. He left, and it's as though he'd never been here.

Tears—just a few. Let them come; crying is comforting if it doesn't get out of hand, but my old strategies certainly aren't working and I haven't another house to put in order. I'll have to think of something else.

After all, why am I so upset by the thought that I'm perhaps the only one who remembers? Because when I die everything will disappear? No children . . . but you don't create children just to pass on a bunch of memories.

In any case, my personal memories are coming through loud and clear—too clear, but that's really no cause for regret. No lapses, no strange twists. "Who am I, where do I come from, where am I going?" Well, as that long-dead French comic used to say, I'm myself, I come from home, and I'm going back. In a manner of speaking, that is. I can't go home because I'm already there.

7

Sarah Mayer's clinic was in Old-Montreal on the Quai Saint-Paul, in a former mansion that had been renovated a few years earlier. Only taxibuses and taxis were allowed in the narrow streets of the Old Town, but there was no taxi waiting at the 24 bus terminus on the corner of Gosford and Notre-Dame, and the two taxibuses that went by were going in another direction. It was eleven o'clock. There wasn't much wind off the river, and the pale gray sky took the edge off the sharp cold. Another chance for a little walk. Catherine set off briskly, walking west along Notre-Dame and every once in a while looking in the shop windows with their swarm of Christmas decorations. Fake frost, fake snow, fake spruce laden with fake presents, red-and-white cardboard Santas with over-flowing sacks, all of which were secondary to the word SPECIAL in big letters beside a percentage sign accompanied by suitably large exclamation marks. The end-of-year consumer orgy was in full swing. Catherine knew that her sense of disgust around this time of year came from comparing her childhood Christmases with the bogus frenzy of the modern celebration, which threatened the simple, true magic of her memories. Nowadays she merely adopted an attitude of indifference for several weeks. She wasn't going to join in the festivities just because it was expected of her, as if it were an obligation.

She stopped in front of one window, however, entranced by a miniature village with its stable and crèche a little to one side. It was beautifully made, with figurines and little houses of handcarved wood painted in vivid yet harmonious colors. Instead of clumsy wads of cotton wool for the white snow, the decorator had used some powdery substance that caught the soft glitter of freshly fallen snow. The tiny electric bulbs were concealed, so that the mother-of-pearl light seemed to emanate from the actual scene—the snow, the houses with their lovingly reproduced detail, and the crèche with its two Children, Jesus dressed in red, Lilith in blue. Several people had stopped. A mother was telling the two-thousand-year-old story to her small daughter, having loosened the child's blue scarf so she could see properly. Catherine listened for a moment, at once amused and touched, then started walking again, feeling somewhat reconciled to Christmas in the Enclave. After all, Christmas was mostly in your mind. Perhaps that small girl in blue would also have magical memories, one day.

And several of the stores really did have pretty things. She lost track of time staring in the windows, then remembered her appointment and looked around to find how far she'd gone along Notre-Dame.

A muffled shape in a red parka stopped abruptly a few yards away and crossed to the other side of the street.

The same parka had got on the bus at Grand-Condé, stepped off at Gosford, and stopped in front of the window with the miniature village as she had. But how did she know this? She could swear she hadn't noticed anything!

She immediately started walking again as if nothing had happened. At the Jacques Cartier intersection she turned left and walked quickly down toward the port, crossing over and turning into a narrow side street. She followed it to the end, turned into another street . . . and knew exactly where she was without once looking at a sign: on Saint-Thérèse, headed west after Vauquelin, with the college over there to the north-east, and the clinic on this side.

The red parka had stopped in front of a shop window across the street, a little behind her. Catherine knew that it would start walking again as soon as she did, and that she was being followed.

Left onto Sainte-Gabrielle, into the warm humidity of Le Restaurant Laverdure, stuff her foggy glasses in her pocket, ask for the telephone, clamber downstairs without a backward glance, telephone here, washrooms there, kitchen door in the middle, push open the door, steam, cooking smells, shapes in white aprons, faces looking up, somewhat surprised, smile and keep walking confidently, too fast to give them time to speak, head for the back door giving onto the delivery lane between Saint-Jean-Baptiste and Sainte-Gabrielle, it must be open at this time of day, yes, climb the area stairs, look right, look left, nothing, back along the Quai Saint-Paul, past Saint-Laurent, up Saint-Dizier, no more red parka, make for the taxibus lot on Le Royer with an exit on the Quai Saint-Paul, dodge between delivery vans, still no red parka, past Saint-Sulpice, through the clinic door, lucky thing the elevator's waiting, first floor, look out the window at the sidewalk, along the quay, still no red parka, tail lost.

In a daze, Catherine found herself staring at her reflection in the window as it steamed over. She was out of breath, not shaking, but numbed by the shock, by this distance between herself and herself. From far away she felt herself take off hat, scarf, and gloves, undo the coat, return to street level, and walk through the corridor leading to the clinic. Calm—split in two, dazed, but calm. She smiled at the receptionist, "Hello, Julie," heard Julie say, "Mrs. Mayer is expecting you," crossed the empty waiting room to Sarah's office, entered, took off her coat, and felt the shape of her glasses in the pocket, glasses she hadn't put on since the restaurant, took them out, propped them on her nose, saw clearly again. Really? Again?

Sarah had risen on seeing Catherine come in. She walked quickly around her desk and took Catherine's hands in hers. "What's the matter? You're as white as a sheet!"

"I don't know."

And even as the seconds ticked by, the memory of what had just happened began to blur, as though her brain refused to retain a sequence of events so at odds with its usual experience. The certainty of having been followed—and yet she had been so calm, so detached, so incredibly . . . routine about it—now crumbled and fell away in fragments. And that mad, circuitous detour, that total mastery of space and body that had suddenly taken over: like a dream—yes, a dream.

"I'm having visions, Sarah. That's normal, I know. But mine. . . . Are there abnormal visions, Sarah? I don't remember things. Lots of things. And they suddenly come back to me."

Sarah straightened up, the professional once more. "One thing at a time. You're having visions and you don't know if they're normal, and you have memory lapses, is that it? And you had a vision just before coming here?"

"I don't know what it was."

She tried to explain, her sentences jerky, knowing how paranoid the whole thing sounded. ". . . and I didn't even have my glasses—"

Sarah raised a hand to stop her. "You know, it isn't that extraordinary. Emergencies sometimes bring out quite unexpected capacities. Part of your brain knows Old-Montreal very well, and it took over because you believed yourself threatened, or followed, at least."

"Not necessarily threatened. Wanting to lose him was like . . . a reflex."

"It was a man?"

Catherine realized that she had no idea. She'd never seen a face. Just a sexless red parka. But she had said, "Lose *him*." An automatic assumption, that was all; it was generally men who followed women, wasn't it?

"An admirer, maybe," Sarah said, echoing her thought. She went back behind her desk. "What really worries me are those memory lapses." She opened Catherine's file, added a fresh sheet of paper, and took up a pen: "Tell me."

"Well, I forgot how things were done in the college, in the library. And I forget things everyone knows. Someone speaks to me about something that's common knowledge, and all of a sudden I realize I haven't a clue. Then it comes back to me. It was the same with the vision: I suddenly remembered that having visions was normal, yet I still found it . . . weird that it should be normal."

She fell silent, astonished at the accuracy of what she had just said. Since the subliminal uneasiness had taken hold of her almost a week ago, she had never expressed its effect this way. *Normal, but weird that it should be normal.* Like the house when she woke up after the Dream of Hyperceptions. Completely familiar but at the same time . . . strange. Alien.

Sarah noted this, nodding slightly as she wrote. "How are things physically? How about eating and sleeping?"

"Fine—well, still a few pounds overweight. I've let my exercising slide and I get tired more easily, but apart from that. . . . My appetite has fallen off, but my digestion and bowels are normal, thank you. My periods, too." Catherine couldn't quite prevent the small sarcasm in her smile.

Sarah repeated smoothly, "And sleeping?"

"No problems. Most of the time, anyway." Then reluctantly, because the next question was so predictable, "I have some rather odd dreams now and then, but—"

Sarah smiled, waving a careless hand. "We all have strange dreams from time to time. It doesn't mean much." She stood up and went into the small examining room. "Come along, let's check you out."

Catherine followed her, amazed to find Sarah brushing off the basic material of her profession—she was a *psycho*medic, wasn't she? It was almost vexing: Catherine had thought the dreams important enough to note in her diary.

"Everything seems completely normal," Sarah said as she finished up and went back to her office. "Your blood pressure is a little high, though."

Catherine talked at the open door as she dressed. "It's just fatigue, I think. This semester has been rather strenuous, what with the workshop and all. And the students being beaten up has upset me a lot. What can you expect? I can't change the way I'm made." She went into the office and sat down. "So, Doctor, what's the verdict?" Her laugh sounded hollow in her ears. "I wondered whether it was Alzheimer's."

Sarah made a small face. "There wouldn't be such

pronounced effects so soon if it were. I think you're tired, though. Tell me a bit about your visions."

Unlike her experience on the way to the clinic, Catherine remembered the vision with the ruins and the cats perfectly. She described it, amazed. "I could almost draw it!"

Sarah opened a drawer, took out a large sketch pad and a lead pencil, and handed them over.

Catherine hesitated, then took them, surprised to find herself feeling disconcerted yet again. Apparently it was normal to draw your visions if you could, judging by Sarah's completely routine response. She almost made a comment, then bit her lips and set to work. She had a way with a pencil and a natural talent that she periodically regretted never having developed, although she knew it wasn't her real vocation. Words, they were her vocation— except that she didn't believe in the term "vocation." A "call," etymologically speaking. No one had called her, except possibly that inner voice, that insistent urge to tell the story of her life, or of life in general, if only to herself. Yet she'd been content with teaching others' words and writing in her journal. François had never really understood. Often he was sarcastic. Jealous, maybe? Perhaps that was why he'd left behind the letters she'd written him. Because he somehow felt they weren't only addressed to him, that she could have done without a correspondent if necessary, because she was talking to herself first and foremost. But it wasn't true. She'd really wanted him to understand, share everything, even the most exacting candor, the most profound doubts about herself, about him, about them. A mistake, probably. Was love a shared misunderstanding? For them, for the couple they had been, yes it was.

There, the drawing was finished and really captured the effect, as always happened when she thought about something else while she worked. She handed the sketch pad to Sarah, who examined it with interest. With really a lot of interest, frowning. Finally Sarah got up. "I've seen this somewhere—wait." She walked out briskly, carrying the pad.

A few minutes later she came back with a large volume in a cardboard sleeve. The shiny cover had "Paris" printed on it in vaguely Gothic lettering. Sarah opened it at a full-page photograph. Black, heavily ornate iron grill-work, grassy slopes slightly below, and white-and-gray stone ruins that seemed familiar, but much smaller, more compact, as though the vision had been compressed. In the corner of the picture two seated cats were licking one another.

Sarah read the caption. "The entry to the cata-combs."

Catherine looked up in response to her puzzled tone. "I know, it's not what you usually see in that corner of Old-Montreal," she said, feeling nettled. "What *do* you normally see there, anyway?"

The young woman appeared to hesitate, then went over to a cupboard—a locked cupboard, Catherine sud-denly noticed. She took out a large book with a thick gray cover, marked simply "Volume II." After leafing through it for a moment, she laid it on top of the first book. "This and the following pages."

Framed by tall, tropically lush trees was a perspective of a huge, open promenade on the edge of a sparkling blue sea. Catherine realized she was holding her breath and let it out as she slowly turned the page. The prome-nade again, this time from another angle, apparently from the sea. Next, a big park with white statues everywhere, even in the trees if you looked carefully. Catherine turned back to the first of these inexplicably familiar images—she was so very sure she'd never seen them before, could have sworn to it. She examined the details, the benches with their carved armrests, the lacy balustrade over-looking the sea, also decorated with complex geometric figures.

"Can you photograph visions?" murmured Catherine in amazement.

"Heavens, no! It's a picture based on several draw-ings, but we try to make it as precise as a photograph where possible."

Catherine suddenly noticed something and turned the pages to check. "Are there never any people?"

"No, no live people, no live animals. Have you for-gotten that, too?"

"It's coming back now." Me and my cats. Goodness,

am I a special case? She began to understand Sarah's interest better. But the insidious feeling of anguish was still there. She continued leafing through the book to preserve an air of calm, noting Sarah's brief but immediately controled impulse to stop her.

After several pages of forests with curiously close-growing trees along the edge of an oily river littered with sand bars, she stopped again with the same painful sense of familiarity. A castle—no, a snow-covered palace or a fortified temple, vaguely Tibetan with its tall ramparts, its many levels, its turrets and pinnacles silhouetted ocher and red against the deep blue of a high-altitude sky. A halo of light mist hung like a transparent cupola above the buildings. *A force field.*

Force field? Why a "force field"? Where did she get that idea?

"And where do you see that?" she said, trying to sound indifferent.

"On Mount Royal—in place of Mount Royal, that is."

A mountain superimposed on a hill. . . . There was a certain logic in "normal" visions.

The next page brought her up short, but only because it was so genuinely surprising. An enormous purple moon hung in a night sky, surrounded by several small moons, one amber-colored, one pearly white, and the third almost silver.

She tried to joke: "And that, in place of the Planetarium?"

"No, it's scattered pretty well all over the east coast at the spring equinox."

Catherine stared at the book with an abrupt yet strangely detached curiosity, possibly calculating. So, not only the "normal" visions of the Enclave were to be found in that book, but also those of Montreal-City and the rest of the province? Were they collecting them? But not for public consumption, only for the psychomedics—

Sarah leaned over, removed the book out of Catherine's hands, put it back in the cupboard, and turned the key in the lock.

"To make a long story short, my vision isn't really abnormal at all," said Catherine, watching the young woman closely, all the while dismayed and grieved to feel that she was in fact *scrutinizing* Sarah. What was wrong with her? Sarah had been her physician for five years and was practically a friend!

Sarah went back to her desk, sat down, and leafed through the Paris book thoughtfully. "It's unusual. Insofar as it's recognizable. In most cases we can't link the visions to any known localities. They reflect . . . other worlds."

Catherine repeated Sarah's words without inflexion. "Other worlds. Imaginary worlds."

"Well, that's hard to check, isn't it? But yours are clearly the Paris catacombs. That's never happened before, as far as I know."

Hard to check! Catherine was amazed at Sarah's nonchalant treatment of such a fundamental point. But the young woman was flashing her a big, reassuring smile: "But don't worry, it's not important as far as your health is concerned." She became serious once more. "No, I think you're mostly tired and that you've been that way ever since last spring. Not only physically, but mentally. You kept on going afterward as though nothing had happened, but. . . ."

Afterward? After what? Catherine exploded with exasperation. "What happened last spring?"

Sarah's eyes widened. "Have you forgotten your father's death?"

So this is what it was like to be petrified? Afraid of moving, because if you moved, even by so much as a hair's breadth, you'd crumble? After an eternity, Catherine began to breathe again. No, she wouldn't disintegrate. But her chest ached and there was a pain under her ribs, as though she'd been hit. Did memories come from the chest? Because that's what was lodged beneath her heart, suffocating her—this explosion of memories, images, sorrow. She repeated, almost inaudibly, "My father's death."

Sarah got up, left the room, and came back with a glass of water. Catherine drank, feeling a crazy urge to laugh as she thought of Touchard: water, the universal panacea. Thank you, Doctor. Yes, folks, I'm really feeling very unwell, very unwell indeed. Forgotten my father's death, only seven months since it happened, but

I've forgotten it. Wanted to forget, at least. That's obvious; and the rest, all those memory lapses: they may just have spilled over from it. To block out such a memory so completely, you'd have to get the energy from somewhere. Are there communicating vessels of this kind in the brain?

Sarah was looking at her with affectionate concern. "I wonder—"

What? What now?

"You passed through Paris when you came back from the south of France last spring, didn't you? I've never heard of a case of this kind, but perhaps your vision has something to do with all that. From the purely material point of view, you went to Paris, you may have passed by the catacombs, and ... well, they are the catacombs, a subterranean ossuary. Death. Don't you think it might be connected with your father's death? In a—how shall I say—symbolic way?"

Catherine stared incredulously at her for a moment. "Now you believe in psychoanalysis?" she said, unable to contain her sarcasm. Sarah's reaction was completely unexpected. At first the young woman's face was a picture of surprised incomprehension. Then her eyes grew round and her lips widened in a smile. Appreciative.

"Psychoanalysis! Now there's an appropriate term for you! Had you already wondered whether the visions might have some connection with ... psychological problems? Psychoanalysis. Hmmm." She savored the word approvingly, staring into the distance. "Yes, that's it exactly; if one were to prove that visions. ... It would be the term to use. 'Analysis'—'of the psyche.' Excellent. Did you think it up? May I borrow it?

So excited, like a child with a new toy! Catherine nodded, completely taken aback, yet hearing herself answer in an almost normal tone, "Oh, it's a term used by someone named Freud in the last century." She was *watching* Sarah again.

Sarah merely raised an eyebrow: "Really? Never heard of him." She scribbled a few notes on the page beside Catherine's drawing, then looked up, once more the cool professional.

"All right, make an appointment right away for the

tests; they're always heavily booked at Saint-Luc's." She took out a form from her desk, ticked off the required tests and pushed the papers toward Catherine, who folded them mechanically and put them in her bag.

"You know," said Sarah suddenly, a little hesitant, "you ought to get away, go somewhere different, take advantage of the Christmas holidays."

Catherine stood up, feeling a little dizzy. Sarah was partly right, of course, despite her baffling ignorance and her equally odd remarks. Perhaps the strange idiosyncrasies of the past hour were not even Sarah's fault. Perhaps it was more Catherine's doing—like the index in the Canadian history book in the college library. If she'd been able to forget her father's death. . . . Yes, she certainly was in bad shape. It was almost, well, psychotic, a memory lapse of that dimension! But if she could actually think of herself as parapsychotic, *was* she? Ask Sarah—but Sarah mightn't know the word "psychotic," either. Well, enough of these surprises. Let's concentrate on the concrete, the positive. Get a change of scene, yes. Perhaps all she needed was a little action. Some easy skiing, for instance, just to get back in shape.

Sarah came around from behind her desk to shake Catherine's hand. "Call me if you need anything—anything, all right?" She held Catherine at arm's length and looked at her affectionately with genuine concern. "You're so independent, Catherine, so used to going it alone, that you forget one can't always do it. There's nothing wrong with needing someone now and then, you know."

Catherine gently disengaged herself and looked at Sarah for an instant, uncertain what to do or say. No, she'd simply have to think about all this in peace and quiet, by herself. Find the right questions. Why the "right" questions? Well, there must be some right questions. She was also convinced (but why, she couldn't say) that whatever questions she might ask herself, Sarah's answers would be of no use.

She found herself leaning on the parapet overlooking the Quai Saint-Paul, although she didn't remember crossing the street. The frozen surface of the Saint Lawrence lay below, a medley of shades from steel gray to greenish-white. Smooth white drifts had accumulated between two sheltering heaps of broken ice. A little further to the west, opposite the Franciscan convent, was a skating rink where bright spots of color bobbed back and forth with small, distant cries. Her eyes were streaming—must be the wind—and her glasses were fogging up. She removed them, and the line between the sky and the southern shoreline became more blurred than ever, as though the river had leaped its banks and was flooding upward.

Well, now what? Normally, I ought to seek help from someone. But who? A psychomedic who'd never heard of Freud & Co.? That needn't affect professional competence, though; after all, psychology existed before Freud. Anyway, I'm still functioning. I forget things, but then I remember. That's all it is, really, a delayed reaction to trauma. I should be able to manage, now that I know what's involved. Luckily we're almost at the end of term. I can hold out until Wednesday, at least! Then I'll get out of the Enclave. Skiing is a good idea—yes, Quebec-City. See what Christine and Dominique are doing for Christmas. Maybe nothing special. We could spend Christmas together. Annette must be ... thirteen, now? And Bertrand ten. Still good for a real old family Christmas. I haven't been to Quebec for ages.

She stuffed her hands in her pockets and turned away from the river, satisfied at having made a decision. She looked around somewhat defiantly for a red parka. Nothing. Too bad. She felt in the mood to walk right up to whoever it was and ask him what he wanted. But probably no one had been following her; it was just that her mind was unhinged by the effort to forget, to avoid thinking—the mind was a strange thing ... there she was, sliding away from it again. She forced herself to stem the feverish flow of images/ideas flitting into her mind like small fish, to formulate clearly what they were trying to dodge: *my father's death*.

She began walking quickly eastward toward the bus terminus. It wasn't just her father's death. It was everything connected with it. So sudden, the telephone call at

that Paris conference, the journey south, too slow in spite
of the turbotrain, with a knot in her chest and her stomach a bundle of nerves, as her mother used to say. Finding
him in bed, thin as a rail, waxen, one leg propped up on
a pillow, the foot all purple, in a rather fetid-smelling
room.

The admitting desk in the little Cavaillon hospital
was in the new wing, where the illusion of modernity was
maintained. But after that you went on to the other wing,
the geriatric wing, and yes, there was a room, a single,
you are in luck, Madame. It was like a hospice, not even
something dating from the forties—more the thirties or
the twenties. The noise was unbelievable for a hospital:
dishes clattering somewhere, the screeching of stretcher
wheels, the voices of nurses trying to calm an old man
moaning invisibly in another room. At last her father was
in bed, tended, washed, one end of the oxygen tube
plugged into his nostrils, eyes closed. She took his left
hand in hers. It was dry, scaly, and warm with fever. He'd
said nothing when she walked into his room at home,
nothing in the ambulance during the journey to the hospital. Now that they were here, he opened his eyes, the
vaguely reptilian eyelids of the very old lifting halfway to
reveal wet, pale blue eyes. "You shouldn't have come," he
croaked.

She protested, but it was useless. He didn't hear, and
anyway he'd closed his eyes.

After that she simply held his hand in hers, and soon
the rapid breathing slowed down and became a noisy
snore, a snore so well remembered from all the childhood
nights she'd kept awake, frightened she might not hear it,
sure that he was dead.

She spent three frenzied weeks trying to clear up all
the problems at once. Find him a place in an old people's
home that accepted bedridden patients, visit, make sure
everything was the way he liked it. There was no possibility of bringing him to Canada, of course, not right away
in any case. He had to get back on his feet again. Clear
out the house, that horrible house they'd rented after their
retirement, much too big, her mother worn out with trying to keep it clean and tidy. Clear out forty, fifty years of
accumulated life, of possessions, for they'd brought every-

thing with them when they'd left the house at Sergines. Half of it had never even been unpacked, and on top of it they'd stored twenty years of papers, empty bottles, plastic containers, magazines, broken household appliances— because of course one never threw anything out, it might come in handy. How quickly, how fiercely she had sorted everything, filling countless garbage bags, amazed at not feeling more sad, but no, it meant nothing to put aside articles for charitable organizations out of the useless and unused heap of clothing, dishes, and all those *things* with which they'd cluttered up their entire lives.

She hadn't cried, she'd been in a fury the whole time, swept along by a maniacal energy, lugging heavy cases of books, piles and piles of her mother's sugary romances of later years, detective novels, spy thrillers. Not even when she happened on familiar objects did she give in to nostalgia. Not even for forgotten things, such as her little-girl hair preserved in tissue paper by her mother, cut off when she went to high school—a heavy auburn rope, thick and crackling with static, still braided. . . . Into the trash, into the trash, and no regrets!

It had been the same when it came to selling the furniture and other valuables. She had watched, almost without a qualm, as things were taken away, objects that had illustrated and nurtured her childhood with dreams. The big, baroque, iron-bound seaman's chest, in which she'd gained the right to store her childish treasures as soon as she was strong enough to lift the cover herself. ("If you pinch your fingers, don't come and complain." "No, Papa," and she'd never pinched her fingers.) The series of handpainted Russian boxes that had come from the Tsar's court, according to family legend: soaring horses and troikas on a dull black background, and the lingering gingerbread fragrance of mild cigars. Odd pieces of the silverware set that wasn't all silver, like the pieces of period furniture that weren't really antique, but merely Second Empire copies, all those relics of a slowly decaying family of *grands bourgeois,* oh, how she loved them, hated them, all those things that held on to her so fiercely, things as familiar as her skin, her nails, but also things she'd fled from by leaving for the New World, she now realized. It hadn't really been France she'd left, but her heritage, the past, the invisible but rising drift of duties, obligations, absurd codes of behavior transmitted from generation to generation—the past, that abusive survival that she had dragged in garbage bags as far as the court-yard gate, the heritage that she had watched disappear at last in the antique dealers' vans.

The parents she'd left behind. All the guilt in the world hadn't been able to hold her or make her come back for more than a few weeks, the shortest possible stay each time. Her mother, that old mother, killed by her ob-stinate devotion to a capricious, tyrannical, and possessive old husband. And he himself, now lying in hospital. "You know, I get the feeling he doesn't really want to fight," the exhausted young doctor had said to Catherine. Tell me something I don't know, Doctor. It had been ten, fifteen years since he'd not wanted to fight, since he'd become deaf, then increasingly helpless, what with his game leg from the war and the heart aches and pains of a long life catching up with him, fossilized into a single stone that beat like a heart, with ever increasing difficulty.

Catherine went to visit him at the Cavaillon hospital at the end of each day—a day spent tidying, sorting, throwing things out, cleaning, and haggling since seven or eight o'clock in the morning. She took the little local train from the village station. It was spring in the south of France, hot, scented, luminous, and young girls in low-cut dressed occupied the plastic benches of the autorail. The track ran through apple orchards in blossom, cherry or-chards, fields of strawberries and melons protected from the mistral by tall hedges of cypress or bamboo. The sky was bright blue, and it was six o'clock on a May after-noon. The days were long now. She entered the room and remained there for an hour, sometimes an hour and a half, until it was time for visitors to leave. She kissed him, took his hand, talked to him a little about what she'd been doing all day just for the sake of saying something. She had to shout in his left ear, but even so he didn't hear her, didn't want to hear her, really. He soon withdrew his hand, as though the contact of another flesh, another life, had become unbearable.

Toward the middle of the second week he regained some of his strength, and they made him sit up in an arm-

chair so that he would move about a bit. He had protested violently—so the nurses told Catherine when she
came that day. Whether because of the effort of sitting up
or the vexation of being forced to do so, he had had a minor stroke. Now the right side of his face was paralyzed,
and an arm and leg lay twisted on the sheet, naked and
often uncovered during the day because of the heat. The
line of his thin-lipped mouth, sucked inward because his
dentures were no longer there, drooped toward the right
and gave his emaciated face a vaguely contemptuous expression. He no longer spoke. And yet, toward the end of
the second week as she was kissing him upon arrival, he
whispered with what was clearly a great effort, "Go
away."

Her father's last words to her: "Go away." She
straightened up, convulsed with distress and anger. She
stayed as usual, left as usual, took the autorail home. It
was empty at this time of night, past eight o'clock. The
sun was sinking in an aureole of orange and honey-gold.
Its slanting light filtered through the long line of gnarled
old plane trees on the road to the house, the rays almost
horizontal, picking out each blade of grass in a quivering,
electric green. She walked, trying not to think, unable not
to think about her father's words; he hadn't meant it, he'd
meant to tell her to live her own life and leave him there
to die. That was also what he'd wanted to say at the beginning, probably: "You shouldn't have come." It hurt his
pride to have her see him in this condition. . . . The temperature was just pleasant now, after the grueling heat of
the day, and there was even a slight coolness in the air.
The swifts were whistling, black dots skimming through
the pristine sky. It was beginning to take on that luminous
tint, neither green nor blue, that as a child she'd always
despaired of capturing with her colored pencils and later
with her paints. She felt a smile coming in response to the
innocent, senseless beauty of evening, and suddenly, in the
middle of the empty road, she stopped and began to cry,
she *had* cried—once, just once.

But not when the telephone rang to say he was
dead—she'd been preparing for this news for ten years.
And not when she saw him laid out in his coffin, already
tiny, at peace, his skin slightly yellowed. She had seen him

asleep so often, had told herself so often that he would look like this when he was dead.

After the burial, where she shed no tears, she went back to Paris, to the airport, to being torn from the soil of a motherland now and forever rendered harmless, promising herself not to return for a long, long time.

8

_

Tuesday, December 21, 1988

Last night I dreamed of the Tannerre house where
we'd taken shelter, my parents and I, in 1951 as the allied
troops advanced on Paris between April and July. I was
nearly six. As soon as the Landing was announced, Papa
packed Mama and me into the car with the minimum
amount of baggage, and we left. It was a day laborer's
house, really, very modest. But for me, a child of the city,
it was my first home in the country. That's where I first
thought he was going to die. I'd been wakened by cries
and groans in my parents' room. It was Papa's voice. I ran
to see what was happening. Papa was twisting in pain on
the bed. My father, the hero with the gentle smile, the
quiet strength, or the large hand that slapped me, the
voice that told me stories, all that, twisting in pain on a
bed. I fled in terror back to my small room, climbed
under the eiderdown, and began to pray. It must be my
fault, I hadn't been a good little girl, but I'd never do it
again—I'd begun to masturbate at that period—never
again, never, but please don't make my Papa die! Then
Mama came to find me, and we went for the doctor in the
village on foot, two and a half miles away. And after we'd
disturbed the doctor at his Sunday dinner, what happened? Our gray Peugeot drove up and out stepped Papa,
laughing hilariously and feeling better. The doctor diag-

nosed a sharp attack of sciatica—in fact, it was his Indochina wound acting up. We went back to the house. And I felt . . . cheated. Still terrified, though—it was after this that I began to listen to him breathing at night. I was scared stiff he'd die, but felt cheated that he didn't. And he held it over me for ten or fifteen years. "When you come back next year I may not be here, you know." "Come on, Papa, don't talk nonsense."

Of course I was furious. Of course I was relieved. Of course I still feel guilty.

Just before waking up, I dreamed of another house— normal, I suppose, after yesterday's flood of memories. The house in Sergines, this time, the true childhood home—we lived there for ten years before they sold it to go and live in the south of France. In the dream I'm in the garage. It's totally dark in there. I'm moving toward the back, but without fear, or only a brief uneasiness that I quickly suppress. It's not in any way a nightmare. There's a wire hanging within arm's reach. I pull, the lamp lights up. It's a globe hanging from the central beam, but the light is very weak and flickering.

I move forward, still without fear. At this point the garden door opens, and I turn toward the rectangle of light. For a moment I'm blinded by a sort of afterimage, but I've had time to see a black cat slip into the garage. I go over to close the garden door, because, as I rationalize to myself, my eyes must remain accustomed to the darkness so that I can see.

Everything goes black. A velvety, breathing, downy black, almost maternal, and yet there is a muffled anxiety: I would like to see. But I have no desire to be anywhere else. The silence moves slightly, like a great bird perched in the darkness, a bird with soft gray wings, perhaps a barn owl, but not a contorted monster, no cruel beak or talons, just a mute, attentive presence. But in my dream I'm not sure I haven't invented it, this tutelary spirit in the darkness, in order to reassure myself.

Darkness, almost tangible, and a vague smell of mushrooms. I want to touch the walls to get my bearings. I walk straight forward, hands outstretched, trying to re-create the floor plan in my head. I touch something. Warm earth, a little damp. Why am I not horrified? I never think of sticky little animals squirming in surprise beneath my fingers. Just this earth, blacker than black, the welcoming feel, almost sensual. All right, so it's the back of the garage, but there's earth, an earthen wall—why not? If I turn forty-five degrees to the right, I'll touch a wall, a real wall. . . .

But there, too, I find earth. I move laterally to get nearer the invisible wall on the right. Earth again. I turn, stretch out my arms again, move forward . . . and touch earth again, but it's not possible, I think of running and suddenly the space closes, an earthen fist; I revolve, arms outstretched, and all around me at the tips of my fingers is earth, damp, warm, malleable, crumbling a little, and I'm in a hole in the earth, I am buried.

Alive. Buried alive. Living death, invisible but black, breathing in the darkness.

And yet, despite the horrified flash of total terror that shoots through me, this earth is so warm, would embrace me so completely . . . it's clean, healthy, alive—innocent. But I can't stay, I don't *want* to stay.

And then, in waking, I seemed to stop on the frontier of sleep for a fraction of a second, and in this instant of equilibrium a whole series of thoughts raced through my mind, half spoken, half experienced, ideas about how to *end*—perhaps tame?—the dream. I could dig steps. But not upward, the earth would crumble too much. Steps going downward, that was it. I'd smooth them flat with my hand, feel the pleasure of the earth against my palms and under my nails, moist and warm. I would dig, surrounded by the fertile smell. There'd be no worms. Yet the farther I'd go the more inhabited the earth would become, with tunnels opening up. Tiny? Gigantic? I couldn't even tell my own size, would have nothing to measure myself against, but I could crawl . . . no, walk, upright. What should I do: explore the tunnels or keep on digging? Maybe all the tunnels ran into each other, or into the rest of the hole. No, I'd have to go to the bottom, keep on digging steps, get there on my own, not make use of the tunnels. And so I'd keep on digging steps in a downward spiral, keeping to the wall of the hole, perhaps going on all fours, head first. And I know there'd be (want there to be?) a light at the bottom.

Then I really woke up. Feeling a kind of excitement, my heart pounding, as though I'd won a victory.

I don't know why, but this impression of liberation has spread throughout the rest of the day. I still feel it. It's probably because yesterday, after seeing Sarah, I finally consented to remember. A liberation, yes, but not a final liberation. There seems to be something else to do, another step beyond that. It's absurd, I suppose, but all the incidents of these last days take on another perspective in this light (this light *to come*, from the bottom of the well?). I'm certain that somewhere inside me is a key to these incidents, some explanation. So what if Sarah hasn't ever heard of "psychoanalysis"? I know why, now, it's come back to me: it's on the Index. I only know about Freud & Co. because of my European education. When I came here, I had to sign a statement along with my contract, agreeing never to mention works in class written by authors on the local Index, as long as I remained in the college—authors whose books I could have read in France. François and I fought for a whole evening about whether to sign, and I finally gave in; I signed. I admit that I'm amazed, even staggered at how effectively the Index works, even outside the college!

Well, no matter, I feel positively bursting with confidence and ready to take any dream in my stride, any weird memory lapse thrown my way. I'm not afraid. My arms are wide open. Whatever little beast emerges from the tunnels will be welcomed by me, without animosity, and I'll examine it carefully. I feel that nothing will happen to me that I haven't somehow brought upon myself. If I have something to tell myself, I'm ready to listen.

After her last class at six o'clock, Catherine went gift shopping along Notre-Dame. Christine and Dominique had been delighted to learn she was coming for Christmas, and had decided to invite two of their mutual friends for Boxing Day. As Catherine listened on the phone to names and anecdotes about them, she'd had the now-familiar, fleeting sense of never having heard of them, but her newfound equanimity had helped her take it in stride. Then, almost immediately, she'd been able to put faces to the names, dates to the anecdotes. Charles-Henri, Antoine: also former students who'd decided to live in Quebec-City where there was still a franco-phone community—legally assimilated, but very much alive.

And while she wandered from one little shop to another looking for something that would catch her fancy—*that* for Charles-Henri, *this* for Annette—Catherine became aware of being followed.

As with the first time, she couldn't tell what had alerted her. But unlike the first time, she couldn't pinpoint whoever it was. Puzzled, she noted the difference as something to think about later and continued walking. From time to time she switched sidewalks to look at other shops, occasionally going in and out, noticing no one in particular. A wind had sprung up again, and the fine snow that had been falling all day rose in powdery swirls that stung her exposed skin. She saw a taxibus that still had a light blinking on its roof. It was headed for the Misericordia Hospital on Dorchester. Good: there was a bus stop in front of the hospital, and she could take the number 12 right to Montcalm. She dove into the little van, paid her share of the fare, and clambered to the back to sit in the last free seat, storing her packages underneath it. So long, whoever you are!

If there *had* been someone following her. After all, this could very likely be another secondary symptom of her mental fatigue. An annoying relapse, though, when she was feeling so much better. Well, my girl, which would you prefer: a small but explicable setback, or to be followed by someone for reasons you couldn't begin to imagine? To tell the truth, she *could* imagine—again supposing she lived in a police state, which was patently not the case.

Her small, sarcastic smile froze. Not the case? The Index, the green room, Sarah's collection of normal visions, all of it applied to the whole province, not just the Enclave. What were these visions, anyway? How did they work? Where did they come from?

She'd have to see if there was something on the subject in the library, or more likely in the green room. But why would visions be classified data, or restricted? "Legal" visions at least, since the government "didn't like" the others. And why didn't it? What did it do to people who had abnormal visions? But she was being paranoid again. Sarah's reaction had been neither worried nor threatening. Surprised, that was it, and interested. Normal visions. The very notion implied that most people had the same visions. In the same places, too, since they seemed to be fairly localized. Shared hallucinations, then? No, if the accepted term was "visions," it meant what it said, something *seen*, real (and yet that huge moon with its little satellites . . .), not a hallucination, not something imagined, phantasmagoric, a mental projection. Nonexistent. That was the accepted meaning, at least. If you thought about it, what exactly was a hallucination, anyway? A special functioning of the brain that allowed you to perceive things that weren't there, or to *create* for yourself things that weren't there for others.

But no one else had ever seen her particular vision, according to Sarah. Which would make it a hallucination. And when did a hallucination become a vision? How many occurrences did it take, seen by how many people? Did all so-called normal visions start with just one person and become generalized later on?

And why didn't I ask myself these questions before, and why don't I know the answers?

But she'd merely "forgotten." A little trip to the library would give her memory a nudge. After a psychological trauma, the brain must require a period of adjustment before beginning to function properly once more. All the same, these hiccups in her mental system were very irritating. Her memory lapses seemed so arbitrary! Logically, according to Indexed psychoanalytical theory, at any rate, there should be some hidden connection between the main repressed element and the rest. Everything relating to authority, for instance, everything even vaguely representing the father-figure: the college, Mevdeiev (her father had lived for a few years in Russia with his adoptive father), Spain, the Normandy Landing, the North, and the Sags ... well, they could represent images of war, confrontation—her father had been a career soldier. By extension, the policies and politics of the Enclave? And Roger Touchard: the old female Oedipus complex reversed into a desire to be seduced by the father-figure, and a former priest to boot—it had to be!

And the visions? But of course! The vision of the ruins could be linked to the father-figure indirectly, as Sarah had suggested. Wouldn't it be funny if Sarah reinvented psychoanalysis all by herself? "Never heard of it." Was the Index really so effective? How about foreign symposia—how did the psychomedics manage to ignore such subjects? After all, they must read some of the current literature and keep up with what was happening elsewhere, in Europe or the American Union.

Or else I'm the one who *invented*—"hallucinated"— this part of our conversation, like the index in the Canadian history book that I didn't "see." That would fit, somehow. Freud whisked away, another authority figure down the drain. Except that I'm not the one who forgot him; I only imagined that Sarah didn't know about him. But Sarah could be an authority figure, couldn't she?

Catherine stirred uneasily in her chair. All this felt like rationalization, a smoke screen. She was playing with all the possible permutations, not taking them seriously. To protect herself?

The taxibus came to a halt and the passengers got off, hurrying toward the revolving doors of the Misericordia Hospital. Catherine slipped between the cars in the hospital parking lot. She could see her bus coming toward the shelter, and she arrived just in time to climb thankfully aboard, relishing the warmth and light inside. The December warm spell, with its relatively mild temperatures and abundant snowfalls, was coming to an end. Soon it would be far too cold to walk. No more promenades, my girl. If you want exercise, you'll have to go back to the gym: no more excuses!

She got off at the Rue Malloret and walked toward Montcalm. At least, coming from this direction, she didn't have to walk practically the whole length of her street.

Someone was following her.

She forced herself to keep walking. Unbelievable. Surely not since Notre-Dame! She was just imagining things. But as she walked, passing a few hurried, bundled-up shapes like herself, the impression grew stronger.

Suddenly overcome by exasperation, Catherine stopped in front of her door and put down her packages. She turned and walked back briskly toward the figure that had stopped a dozen yards back, just outside the cone of light falling from the nearest street lamp. The figure stayed there, making no attempt to get away. It wore a white parka, not red, and wasn't tall or heavy . . . it wasn't a man beneath the flimsy blue cap, but a delicate-featured boy in his teens! Catherine slowed her step and halted beside the figure. "Who are you? What do you want?" she asked, but not in the aggressive tone she'd planned on using. The other said nothing, but stared at her, his large eyes darkened by the surrounding dusk. Catherine took a closer look. The features were too delicate, even for an adolescent. He didn't move.

To make sure, Catherine snatched off the blue cap. Thick blonde hair fell in waves over the parka. A girl, yes, fifteen, perhaps less and . . . oh, no, she seemed familiar!

"Who are you?" she asked, more gently this time. "Why are you following me?" The girl would no doubt say she wasn't following her, and it would end there.

But the adolescent was still looking at her with that expression of . . . curiosity? Or was it puzzlement? "You're not the same," said the girl at last. Her voice was light, clear, and conclusive. A gust of wind blew hair across her face. Catherine handed the cap back, feeling a little embarrassed, but the girl didn't take it. She kept staring at Catherine, who stared back, this time with distressed compassion. Now she could see that the parka hung loosely on the spindly form. A homeless urchin, perhaps, a bit simple in the head, or else starving and delirious? Or perhaps stoned to the eyeballs. Catherine tried a smile. "Let's not stand in the cold. I live here. Would you like to come in for a moment?"

The urchin shook her head after a moment's hesitation. "I'm not cold. Why are you different?"

"Different from what? Or whom?"

As the child said nothing, Catherine tried once more, taking her gently by the arm—a small, skinny arm, as she could feel through the parka. "How about talking it over at my place?"

"There's someone up there."

Catherine turned toward her house. The lights were on. She turned back to the girl, laughing kindly. "I always leave the lights on. Don't you want to come?"

The child appeared to reflect for a moment, then nodded. Relieved, Catherine turned to walk to the house, then stopped as she realized the girl hadn't moved. She came back. "You want to come in with me, don't you?"

The girl shook her had. "No. Go with you."

"With me, then. Are you coming?"

"No. With you. Beyond. We've got to go beyond."

Catherine stamped on the ground to warm her feet and give herself time to think. She felt appalled and annoyed. "I'm cold. I'm willing to go beyond, but first I want to go home."

"Beyond," said the girl, her voice crystal clear. Then she ran toward the main thoroughfare.

It took Catherine a few seconds to react. She raced after the girl, idiotically waving the blue cap. "Wait. Don't run off like that!"

The girl disappeared onto Dorchester. Catherine reached the intersection a few seconds later and stopped abruptly, almost skidding on an ice patch. She grabbed the traffic light pole, out of breath and mystified: no girl running, no white parka, just a few obviously adult shapes hurrying along, bent against the wind. No nearby shops where the girl could have gone.

A gust of icy wind hit Catherine in the face, bringing her to her senses. She walked back down Montcalm, at first pausing occasionally, then hurrying, cap in hand. Another vision? No living creatures in normal visions, all right Sarah, but obviously I don't have normal visions! A girl, a blonde urchin in a white parka. A vision. That talks. And leaves a blue cap behind as a pledge. Is that the sort of thing that happens? And what's the connection, anyway? Still more puzzled than upset, she reached her door and climbed the steep stairs. Entered the kitchen, holding her fogged glasses in her hand, put down the parcels, took the key out of the lock, closed the door, removed her coat, hat, and scarf, and hung them up. And turned to see Joanne Nasiwi sitting at the dining room table, the contents of Catherine's photograph box spread out before her.

A thought flashed through Catherine's mind: *the door hasn't been forced.* And another: *she's taken off her coat.* And a sense of calm. Catherine walked slowly over to the table, incredulous but calm. Joanne Nasiwi was calm, too, but . . . watchful. Her two hands were clearly visible on the table. Why remark this, though? Catherine stopped beside the table, so close that she only had to reach out to grab the edges and tip it onto . . . but what an idea!

"Did you find anything interesting?"

A slight shrug, no answer, but the young woman

had been caught short. She was wearing a tight pullover of dark red mohair; no weapon could possibly be hidden there. *Weapons?* The thought astounded Catherine. She pulled a chair out from the wall and sat down, balancing on the two back legs. (*Far enough from the table to be able to kick it over while leaning against the wall and . . . not again!*) "I haven't received your file or your writing samples," she heard herself say evenly, smiling a little.

Her visitor relaxed in her chair. "I mailed them today."

"You should have brought them, in that case. I'm leaving for Quebec-City tomorrow."

The other was suddenly still. Then she leaned forward, her hands folded on the table, her eyes still fixed on Catherine. "Quebec-City?"

"I'm going skiing, visiting friends. Spending Christmas there."

A nod, then, with seeming regret, "That's not very wise."

"Why?"

Silence, eyes lowered, a slightly obstinate expression that remained as the young woman lifted her eyes and said, "You've been followed ever since you went to see Sarah Mayer."

"Since before I saw Sarah," Catherine heard herself say. Not, "How did you know?" or even "So what?" No: "Since before I saw Sarah." And hardly any surprise at the response:

"No, that was me."

"That red parka isn't very good camouflage."

"I didn't necessarily want good camouflage."

"To what do I owe the honor?" asked Catherine, suddenly clenching her teeth. Her ridiculous calm was beginning to crumble. Should that worry her, or ought she to be relieved?

"Routine procedure." A cold little smile, and always that watchful stare. "You got rid of me pretty neatly."

Catherine forced herself to keep looking at Joanne. Say nothing, force her to show her hand.

"Have you had other visions?" Joanna said at last, with unconvincing nonchalance.

This time Catherine couldn't help reacting. But why shouldn't she? What was the good of this idiotic, calculating calm? This woman had entered her house while she was absent and had rummaged through her things. A Northern agent, who had drawn poor Henri Lapointe and Jacques Lévesque into her machinations! And who was now coming after her, Catherine—God knows why!

The young woman suddenly leaned forward and stretched her hands across the table. "You don't seem to realize that you're in danger," she said, her voice low and urgent. "And that it may be even worse in Quebec-City."

Catherine had instinctively recoiled in the chair as Joanne leaned forward. Her heard was pounding, her mind a blank. "In danger?" she muttered, "But that's ridiculous! Why?"

"They don't like new visions. I told you, everything that threatens the status quo. . . . From the moment you talked to Mayer, you were under suspicion."

"Sarah?" stammered Catherine, totally lost.

"The psychomedics are under constant surveillance. Their offices are bugged. She has no idea, of course. 'The government takes charge of the subjects,' they're told, and that's enough for them!"

The young woman made an obvious effort to regain her calm. "Listen, go to Quebec-City if you like, but be very, very careful. Don't stay by yourself; surround yourself with people as much as you can. And if something happens. . . ." She pulled a small ballpoint out of her pants pocket, picked up a photo without looking at it, wrote two lines on the back, and shoved it at Catherine. "Just in case you need help."

Catherine didn't look at the address. Her heart had stopped pounding, and she felt relatively calm once more. Nothing like the sense of total control she'd had at first, but enough to say, "You're a Northern agent."

The other shrugged and stood up. "Yes, if you like. Don't lose that address; it might come in handy." She took her parka from the other chair—the mauve parka of their first meeting—and slipped it on.

Catherine stood up, too, suddenly panicking at the

idea that the young woman would leave without answering the questions buzzing in her head. "For heaven's sake, explain what this is all about! What's wrong with my visions? Why. . . ."

Joanne shook her head and drew on her gloves. "I can't. I've already stayed too long."

And before Catherine could stop her, she had clattered down the stairs and disappeared into the night.

It's a narrow traverse, curving between two ridges of blue-gray rock. Under the powder is the hard surface of compacted, high altitude snow that never melts. Above, the sky is an intense blue, emphasized by a few frayed white clouds. Catherine climbs slowly, methodically, breathing with shallow regularity in the thin air and placing each foot so as to obtain maximum traction with her crampons. Her knapsack's padded straps and aluminum frame are pushing into her back. Here between the two ridges she is sheltered from the wind but not from the dry cold, as tangible as the wind on the few uncovered surfaces of her skin, despite the protective grease. She climbs. She isn't far from the summit and has come a long way. She's in a hurry to reach her goal, knows the route—this isn't the first time. Several minor storms have forced her to stop now and then, but there's been nothing really dangerous. The autumn hurricanes won't hit before two weeks at the earliest, leaving plenty of time for her to get there. A steeper bit after the traverse, and then she'll see the ocher walls silhouetted against the sky, with the pennants snapping in the wind above each pinnacle, red and yellow, the colors of welcome.

When she reaches the end of the traverse there is no summit, no distant, grand panorama of the other ranges striding over the violet horizon. The mountain softens into long white slopes with occasional rocky stretches and, less distinct, the shadows of some frail little spruce trees covered by snow. Below lies a sea of fluffy white clouds rimmed by a vast circle of mountains as far as the eye can see. The sea of clouds resembles a huge ring, really, because from where Catherine stands she can see that somewhere in the center of the sea is an almost circular space.

Her surprise is momentary. She adjusts her sack and sets off again. Her round snowshoes sink a little into the crisp surface of the snow. She won't, can't look at the person walking with her. She must keep on descending. She is walking in the sea of clouds, now, walking in the fog, unable to see more than two steps ahead, but she knows exactly where north is, and she strides between the small spruce trees that grow higher and more luxuriant as she descends toward the edge of the fog. It's a real forest, now, with huge trees, oaks—she pushes a low branch aside and is again slightly surprised to see the deep indentations on the green leaves, but the surprise quickly fades. The fog is a mere mist floating half way up the tree trunks in large, frayed patches, then a damp, heavy atmosphere, bright green mosses that feel soft beneath her feet, silver trickles between the high grasses, glittering filigree threads linking the rocks where huge ferns grow, their lacy network dripping with dew. It's warm, getting to be almost hot. Her old hiking boots are dirty and wet. She stops a moment to wipe her face, her neck, her bare arms and thighs in the sleeveless T-shirt and shorts, although resisting the temptation to take off the sodden socks. She switches her bag from one shoulder to another and sets off again.

The forest echoes like the interior of a cathedral, the air shot through with luminous rays of sunlight and the twittering of birds. It is immense, perhaps infinite. In the distance is a different, golden light that grows brighter, shining between the thinning tree trunks. The edge of the forest is near. Catherine hurries forward, not bothering to check whether anyone is following her or not. The damp, interlacing green vaults above her are beginning to be oppressive. At last she comes out into the sunshine. She is in a wide meadow running gently downhill toward a valley and a lake.

Catherine contemplates the lake of the North, amazed at first, then at peace. She has difficulty judging distances: everything is too distinct, the clarity of the atmosphere deprives it of light and shadow. But whatever its actual size, the lake is triangular, bright orange, with a fairly round island in the center. It is covered with dense, almost blue vegetation. North is exactly there, on that island. That's where she must go to plant the blue and white flag in her hand.

She's standing at the water's edge. There is no boat, not even a floating tree trunk. For some reason, she hesitates to dive in. The water must surely be unpleasantly warm and sticky. The color is so strange—probably the effect of minute animal life held in suspension—and the idea of swallowing it is repugnant.

Behind her, a commanding voice says, "You must go beyond."

Two hands against her back, pushing. She falls into the lake.

And she is in her bed, in her room, in her house, but not awake, toppled without transition into the Dream of Hyperceptions. But this time she knows, she understands the distorted images that come to her: this is her room seen in infrared, then ultraviolet, those quivering networks are electromagnetic waves, and that's the alarm clock providing a picture of the room in the entire audio spectrum, from ultrasound to infrasound.

Now she wakes up, just as the alarm clock stops ringing. She jumps out of bed and rushes through the familiar routine of the morning. Yes, absolutely familiar, nothing strange about it; that's her face in the mirror, a face where the wrinkles look pretty deep this morning. Fatigue, nothing serious. Last day of classes, she's off to Quebec for the holidays. *Toward the north.* More exactly, the northeast, but of course dreams don't bother too much about accurate compass points—in fact this is typical of her dream, a surrealist mixture of her forthcoming journey and her meeting with that poor urchin yesterday in the street, with echoes of her visit to the Botanical Gardens and the images seen in Sarah's book. One of those "blender" dreams, as she calls them, with everything thrown in, obviously due to more or less random activity in the brain as it runs through and sorts the engrams stored during the day—dreams not really worth noting in detail in her journal, because they're superficial rather than deep.

The Dream of Hyperceptions has come back, however, and that should be noted. Definitely a power fantasy: supplementary senses, no less! Catherine smiles at the mirror, a smile foaming with toothpaste. So, old girl, you're becoming a megalomaniac in your dotage? Superior senses, of course, the opposite of aging.

10

At the end of the last class, Catherine exchanged Merry-Christmas-and-Happy-New-Year greetings with her students. They gave her a group present that took her by surprise and touched her deeply—a small china box in the shape of a heart, with a bronze-colored metallic finish. "I wish I could have done more," she murmured once she'd unwrapped the box and hugged Annie Leboeuf, who had offered it on behalf of the others. "So do we," said Jacques Lévesque. She looked at him. The bruises on his face were beginning to turn yellow, and she felt they were both talking about the same thing.

Toward noon she reached home feeling rather sad, a sadness tinged with anger. She probably wouldn't see these students again. Most were graduating, and some would begin working while others left for universities in France or Louisiana. Some weren't finished, but they wouldn't be in her courses next semester. As they sat in the cafeteria during the ten o'clock break talking of their plans for the future, Catherine knew that, like her, they were all thinking of Henri Lapointe. He had hardly any future to speak of, certainly not the one he'd hoped for and deserved. When classes started again, she must take the younger teachers aside and find out discreetly whether there wasn't some way of counteracting the phalanx of elderly reactionaries.

A white envelope was sticking out of her mailbox. Her name was written in a large, firm hand that she didn't recognize. No stamp or address. It had been delivered in person. *We absolutely must meet before you leave. Crêperie Bretonne, corner of Saint-Denis and Sainte-Catherine, three o'clock.* It was signed "J."

Catherine tossed the sheet of paper on the kitchen table. She felt annoyed and worried. What now? She'd been planning to take the first afternoon bus for Quebec, at one o'clock! Nevertheless, she picked up the phone and called to say she would be arriving in Quebec-City later than planned. When? "I don't quite know. . . . Listen, I'll call you from the bus station when I get there. All right?"

"I hope at least it's a romantic tryst," said Dominique.

"Heavens, no!" protested Catherine. "It's—well it's a little too complicated to explain, but—"

"Fine; tell us about it this evening! See you soon."

Dominique and she had kept up a running joke about mythical lovers ever since she began living alone, but after six years it was beginning to wear a little thin. Catherine hung up, slightly annoyed. Her eye fell on the box where she had dumped the photos after Joanne's impromptu visit. She hesitated for a moment, then emptied the box onto the table. There was no hurry, in any case.

For the hundredth time, she told herself she ought to arrange them in albums once and for all, although pinning all those memories to paper smacked of the butterfly collector. At least she'd be able to find a photo more quickly, like the one where Joanne Nasiwi had written the address just in case—just in case what? It was grotesque! But if it really was grotesque, would she be going to this meeting? No, she informed herself with a shrug: she only wanted to hear what Joanne would have to say, out of simple curiosity, that was all.

She stopped rummaging and held a photo in her hand as she slowly sat down. She'd been six—it was marked on the back, but she didn't need to look. She remembered it well. Her birthday. At the door of the beautiful, big country kitchen in the Tannerre house. Her mother was seated on the bench in the background, in the shade, with a smiling, exhausted expression: she'd worked all morning to get the meal ready. The small Catherine stood on the doorstep, her braids wound round her head in a crown above her face. She was holding the white puppy-present awkwardly against her cheek, smiling and squinting because of the sun, and she had dimples everywhere. Her straight-cut dress was made of royal blue velvet, sleeveless, with appliqués of white lace at the collar and armholes.

The same robe worn by the girl at the Botanical Gardens.

And suddenly a second shock: the blonde girl, yesterday! She looked like the girl at the Botanical Gardens; that's why I thought I recognized her!

In a state of bewilderment, Catherine laid the photograph on top of the pile she'd already gone through and went on rummaging, all the while trying to picture the girl of the previous evening, trying to check the resemblance. Somehow she couldn't keep their faces apart, they kept fading into one another. . . . She wasn't even sure of their relative ages. Let's see, the girl in the gardens was no more than ten. And the one yesterday, well, she was taller, but so thin, perhaps not even fifteen. It can't possibly be the same girl, of course, but it's curious, all the same. . . . Ah, here's the address!

Catherine slipped the photo with the address into her bag without a second glance, took another quick look around the house, and called a taxi. She'd check her baggage at the Berri Terminus and have lunch at the Crêperie Bretonne, not far away. She could eat and read a little, and then it would be time for the meeting.

The Berri-de-Montigny Terminus on the corner of Berri and Ontario covered a whole block. It was one of the three main checkpoints for the Enclave, and had been built in 1955 during the brief honeymoon between the two communities of "founding peoples" after the Second World War was officially over. It served both the Enclave and Montreal-City as a terminus for all bus links with the rest of the province. Green-and-black uniformed police patroled the Enclave sector of the building. There were more of them than usual. When she took her bags to the checkroom counter on the City side, Catherine was asked to give the names and addresses of the people she was staying with in Quebec. She felt her hackles suddenly rise, and out of pure devilment gave the coordinates of Marcel Éthier-Domville, a former student whom she hadn't seen for ages. When she wanted to go back into the Enclave zone after checking her suitcases, a policeman in a Canadian uniform accompanied her into the baggage room and made her identity her bags for a regulation search. She swallowed her irritation—after all, these men were only doing their job, and the policemen looked a little embarrassed. "Orders, Ma'am."

She wasn't as surprised as she had been the previous week when patrols had checked the metro. After all, there really were Northern infiltrators working in the South. She quelled a bubble of slightly nervous laughter. Here she was, actually on the way to meet one of these Northern agents. That part of it hardly seemed believable, though. "An agent, if you like," Joanne had said, which probably meant a sympathizer at the very most. And as for Joanne "manipulating" poor Henri Lapointe . . . well, Henri hadn't said so. He might have met her at the Botanical Gardens for reasons that had nothing to do with conspiracy. Anyway, if they'd met for such a purpose, why would he have spoken about the writing workshop? I'm the one who's been extrapolating wildly on the basis of mere coincidence!

It was nearly two o'clock when she entered the restaurant. She sat down at the only free table from where she could see the door. The Crêperie Bretonne tried to live up to its name with a rustic decor, a heavy, hobnailed door and windows with small, dark green panes. Not very good for seeing anyone coming—but not bad if you wanted to avoid being seen from the outside. Catherine's smile at this ludicrous idea earned her a rather surprised grin from the waitress who had come to take her order. Let's be original: a crêpe bretonne with mushrooms, ham, and cheese, and she'd see about dessert later. She always left herself time to think about it—usually a pointless ritual, and today was no exception: she kept the menu to look at the list of sweet crêpes.

After the crêpe bretonne and the dessert, she left her

half-consumed tea to cool as she read, keeping an eye on the door. It was a quarter to three; Joanne shouldn't be much longer. Ten to, five to ... not an early bird, evidently. Five past. Not punctual, either. But perhaps Northern agents ("if you like") had reasons for being late. She decided to wait until half past three, not a moment longer, and called the waitress over to settle her bill. If there was a chance of making the four o'clock bus, she didn't want to miss it: Quebec-City was three hours away, but if you arrived around seven you could still enjoy a good portion of the day afterward.

Three-fifteen. She fidgeted in her seat. Just because I was late for our first meeting, does she think she can be late for this one? Three-twenty. Twenty-five. She began to gather up her things, really annoyed now. Two hours lost for nothing! If Joanne couldn't come, she could at least have phoned. Three-thirty. I'm leaving.

Her hand was on the handle of the restaurant door when she became aware of a strange noise rising above the drone of the piped-in music, a distant rumble punctuated by muffled explosions. It was getting nearer. The other customers also heard it and murmured questions to neighboring tables. She opened the door and stepped out.

People were running on the sidewalks and between the cars on Saint-Denis. Young people. Coming from Sainte-Catherine. The rumble was a roar now: thousands of voices shouting. Another demonstration? The door was still open; someone shoved past Catherine and disappeared into the restaurant. Pressing against the wall to avoid the fleeing crowd, she went around the corner of the Crêperie to take a look at Sainte-Catherine. Not a vehicle in sight. The street was full of people, most of them running. Some turned into Saint-Denis, but the rest kept going along Sainte-Catherine. They were brandishing small fleur-de-lys flags. Two boys running at the same pace were having trouble holding up a large banner displaying the words NO TO POLICE BRUTALITY. The banner had no vertical slits and billowed like a sail, slowing them down. The muffled explosions increased from the west, and clouds of smoke—no, it must be tear gas—floated toward the Rue Sanguinet. Catherine, paralyzed with shock, watched the crowd flee. Were her students among them? They'd said nothing. Perhaps they'd thought she knew about it. Was Joanne Nasiwi late because she'd been caught up in the mob?

Suddenly, as if time and space had telescoped, the contact line between students and anti-riot squad reached her. A gray avalanche sped by, a blur of outsize heads and bodies in anti-gas helmets and padded uniforms, shields held out, clubs raised, vaguely monstrous shapes charging forward, heavy but inexorable.

Her brain begins to tick, 15:38, 15:39.... Head for the Sainte-Catherine entrance to the underground malls, about fifty yards to the west—if the entry tunnels haven't been closed off. Pick up some snow, rub it on the scarf to moisten it, keep going against the flow, hugging the walls and shop windows, scarf over the face—there's a wind, good, it'll blow away the fumes. Slowly but surely she moves forward as terrified bodies hurtle against her. 15:41: just as she reaches the Sainte-Catherine entrance, the reinforced windows of the glass shelter around the entry shatter under the pressure of demonstrators trying to get through. They swarm over the breach, and with them come gray, club-wielding forms, some stopping at the entrance, others moving onto the stairs and escalators, shoving and toppling the people already there. Shouts of surprise, anger, and pain rise from the crowd as clubs flail indiscriminately at every moving thing. Catherine takes off, half climbing, half pushing to get past the crush of bodies around the doorway. She does the same inside and gets to the bottom of a staircase in the main underground mall where shoppers have been swept aside, first by fleeing demonstrators, and now by the police in hot pursuit. If anybody sets off a tear-gas grenade in here.... But the police are more occupied in trying to corner the demonstrators. Someone with a torn black parka passes in front of Catherine, pursued by two gray shapes. A club descends on the figure, and it topples against the wall beside her. She jumps back just in time as the two policemen attack the parka. A dark-skinned waif, his face already bloody; he crouches, trying to offer as little of himself as possible to the blows, then suddenly goes limp. The policemen keep on beating the inert form.

A rush, two feet in the back of the first policeman.

He twists and tumbles head first against the wall, falling
on the victim. The other policeman stops beating and has
just time to turn toward Catherine before she kicks him in
the neck, sending him sprawling. As he struggles to his
feet she grabs the first policeman's club and whacks the
second, who lies groggily on the ground. She bends over
the dark-skinned form, feels for the pulse at the base of
his neck, finds it, straightens up—15:44, no time—and
starts running northward through the tunnel, at one moment almost neck and neck with a gray form too intent
on its own race to care about her. She lets the form get
slightly ahead, sticks out a leg, and then jumps out of the
way as the other trips and falls—15:45—now she's ahead
of the fleeing crowd and someone else is running beside
her, out of the corner of her eye she sees a white parka,
streaming blond hair, no it can't be, but she keeps on
running—15:46—dodges into a secondary tunnel leading
to the terminus—15:47—clambers up the escalator past
people half-turned at the sound of pounding feet, pushes
her way to Gate 12, QUEBEC, the white parka still beside
her, takes her passport and ticket out of her bag (she still
has her bag!)—15:48—the Enclave policeman is studying
her, must have noticed her panting, her eyes streaming,
must know. . . . From behind her comes the sound of
shouts; the man raises his eyes, frowns, looks back at
Catherine—15:49—but he stamps the passport and mutters "Hurry up." She walks unhurriedly through the metal
detectors and gets a brusque nod from the guard on the
City side—15:50—heads for the platform where the large
double-decker bus marked QUEBEC-CITY EXPRESS is
waiting, and joins the line of last-minute passengers now
boarding.

The timer in her head stops as she boards, her ticket
held out for inspection. She immediately climbs to the second level, not bothering to check for empty seats below,
and collapses into a seat with a right-hand window. She's
out of breath, her chest squeezed in a painful vice, her
eyes stinging, but she's made it, she's leaving Montreal-
City, going to Quebec, safe. She has no idea from what,
but she is safe.

The white parka appears from nowhere and sits
down beside her. The face beneath the thick, tawny hair is

oval, the forehead rounded, the skin smooth, with a small, slender nose, large eyes, neither green nor blue, staring at Catherine, and full lips trembling on the edge of a smile as a clear timid voice says, "Beyond?"

Catherine searches for the lever with the tips of her fingers, finds it, and lowers the seat to a reclining position. She'll try to comprehend it all in a minute, but not right now. Even so, she answers, eyes closed, not knowing quite what she's responding to. "That's right. Beyond."

She opened her eyes a few seconds later, feeling horribly hot. The excess energy from her headlong rush had caught up with her. She took off her coat. The bus was cruising along Sherbrooke East, a lighted boulevard stretching away beneath a sky that was still blue, despite the early winter dusk. As she sat down again, still out of breath, she couldn't help smiling: through the fading sunlight glimmered the wreaths and neon-lighted shop windows, the overhead lights running the length of the avenue, the traffic lights, all twinkling like electric jewels. Everything stood out with exquisite precision from the blue vault, itself slowly paling with a fragile luminescence. At this moment of the day, Catherine could almost forgive the city its brutal shapes, its heights and distances so incompatible with the human scale. And of course everything looked different when seen from the top level of a bus, behind high, hermetic windows, this world on wheels that rode through the cold and the ambient roar of the city, so self-contained in its warmth and whirring silence. Perhaps she was also influenced by the knowledge that soon the city would be behind her. Once past the big expressway that ringed the Enclave then soared over it to the Jacques Cartier Bridge, once over the bridge with its metal lace suspended between sky and water (how vast the sky suddenly seemed!), the bus would be rolling across untrammeled spaces, through snow-covered fields with the horizon stretching almost infinitely in the direction of the barely undulating plains of the Bois-Francs and the Beauce.

The first time she'd gone to Quebec-City, the journey had seemed endless until she suddenly realized that this really *was* a new world with different dimensions from the one in which she'd grown up, a world where neither space nor time had the same meaning. It had been summer, everything green and gold beneath a blue sky—nothing you wouldn't see anywhere else, but grass and trees hadn't seemed to carry the weight of history the way they had back in France. As she remembered it, everything there was old, almost immemorial, from the hawthorn hedges in Tannerre to the Roman road on the hill behind the Sergines house. The least plot of land had been dug and redug by generations of human beings, and the stones of the houses in villages and towns seemed still to bear the mark of all those other buildings for which they'd been used before being disassembled and reassembled. Here it was different. Here, she had thought exultantly, memory was less cluttered.

With time, she had come to understand that it was less the collective memory of the inhabitants and the country, which after all was at least three hundred years old, than her own, a clean slate, bare of any personal memory of the New World. But it was different, all the same. Here there was space, you could move. Even living in the Enclave hadn't obliterated Catherine's first revelation of a land where heritages were built rather than handed down. The Enclave people's constant determination to remain francophone, to be different, didn't arise from a link with a transatlantic mother country (which they often accused of having deserted them, even now), or with a Louisiana to which others had "fled" three centuries earlier. The Enclavers demanded their right to the place where their ancestors had put down roots in the huge expanse of the New World. The irony of their situation, their confinement within the Enclave, made no difference to this specific view nor did it alter the special relationship between the inner eye and the physical horizon—a dynamic in space and time very different from that of the Old World.

"They filched their New World from the Indians," François never missed a chance to say. She had to admit that it was true, a tragedy; but, she hastened to add, at least in the American Union this tragedy had been somewhat compensated for by the creation of the Amerindian Federation. François asked her why they were both still in Canada, in that case, after which the discussion always descended into wrangling. Catherine couldn't help feeling uneasy when faced with the undeniable contradiction of her position. She only knew that she had no desire to go to Louisiana, and that if she went back to live in France it would be with a profound sense of failure. For her, there must be some vital reason for living here and not somewhere else, something more than just wanting to get away from an oppressive motherland. . . . A hidden link between herself, the Enclave, the general condition of francophones in Eastern Canada, and what else? Perhaps her almost automatic sympathy for oppressed minorities? She had been so ready to help Joanna Nasiwi, an Amerindian, a Métis, a woman. And was that also why she felt so furious at having been . . . betrayed? Whatever designs the Métis woman had on her, it certainly didn't include establishing friendly relations!

What designs, in fact? Of what use could I possibly be to her? Why take any interest in me? Because of a supposedly *anormal* vision? Paris ruins and cats . . . ridiculous! Joanne has simply invented it all to frighten me. Perhaps she's a mythomaniac, makes up cloak and dagger scenarios to give herself importance and traps people in them, including poor boys like Henri Lapointe, who want to believe her stories.

Catherine felt annoyed and looked out the window again, trying to lose herself in the landscape sliding by the other side of the glass. Forget all this. If Nasiwi starts bothering me again next semester, I'll deal with it then. Now I'm going to Quebec, it's holiday time, this will blow over. Admire the sunset, instead—the polluted air makes the colors look so pretty. To the west, picture-postcard clouds were rimmed with incandescent violet. One resembled a tiger *rampant* . . . now a crocodile with gaping jaws, now more like a dinosaur in the process of being chewed away by invisible teeth. The huge bank of cloud on the horizon looked like a landscape in itself, with roofs and a church spire rising beside the estuary of a great orange river. . . .

Catherine stopped breathing for a moment: the clouds had broken and formed anew, the imaginary town had disappeared, and in its place was a triangle of molten lava with a round bit of blue-green sky in the center. The lake in the dream!

"The lake," said the girl's clear voice.

Catherine started, turned; the child smiled innocently, pointing her finger at the window. "You see the lake?"

Catherine responded with a vague nod. The girl had taken off her parka and was holding it on her knees. She had nothing but a dress on underneath—the blue, sleeveless dress of the Botanical Gardens, of the photograph. Almost frightened, Catherine touched the blue velvet, the white skin. "Aren't you cold, dressed like that?" she asked. And added rather idiotically, "I haven't got your cap."

The girl shook her head, as she had done last night in the street, and said, "I'm not cold," in a tone that implied, *I'm never cold.*

Hard to tell how old she was, really, with such a slender body and those porcelain features. One of those perfect faces that grow old very slowly, that look fifteen at thirty, and ten at fifteen. It could well be the "little girl" of the Botanical Gardens. But she certainly wasn't thirty, or even twenty! Last night's theory, then: a half-witted girl without a home?

Who had an up-to-date passport, nevertheless, and enough money to buy a ticket to Quebec-City. "Would you mind showing me your passport?"

The blue-green eyes widened. "Passport?"

"Your papers. The little book you showed the man in uniform at the checkpoint." She was talking to this girl as though she were a mere child! But she *was* a child: the surprised expression showed no comprehension at all, merely an interest full of good will. "A little book like this?" said Catherine desperately, taking out her own passport.

The girl leafed through it and put a triumphant finger on Catherine's photograph. "That's you!" Then she frowned. "You're not the same."

Catherine stopped herself from repeating last night's question, certain she'd get the same answer. She nodded approvingly, "Yes, that's me. My name is Catherine. What's yours?"

Again that slightly vacant expression, tinged with curiosity at first, then thoughtful. At last the girl said something that Catherine thought must be an attempt at her own name. But she said it again, louder and with more apparent conviction. "Atana." Or was it "Athana"? There was a slight sense of the fricative. An anglophone? Curious: their brief conversations had been in French, and there'd been no trace of an English accent until now.

"Would you rather speak English?" Catherine suggested, switching languages.

The girl shook her head. No.

"But you *do* speak English? You understand it?"

A slight frown. "You want me to?"

Good, at least that was settled. "No," Catherine smiled. "How old are you, Athana?"

"I don't know."

Not a complete surprise. "Is your home in the Enclave?"

Again that flash of interested surprise.

"The Enclave. That's where we met yesterday evening. Do you live there?" Perhaps "home" wasn't exactly the expression to use with a stray child.

"No."

"Where do you live? Where do you stay, usually?"

"Everywhere."

As though it were a matter of course. Not in the Enclave, not in Montreal-City, and therefore in both. To be quite sure, Catherine took out her Montreal-City pass. "Have you a card like this?"

No, again. A little outlaw, then, who found ways of getting by checkpoints without a pass. Or who avoided the checkpoints altogether. It could be done. It took acrobatic talents most of the time; apart from the bridges, the wall surrounding the Enclave was a good eight meters high, even though the barbed wire had gone. Catherine considered the slender shoulders and the delicate wrists. Underground passages, more likely. And she'd never been caught.

But how had she got through the terminus checkpoint?

Still, Catherine hadn't actually seen her go through the checkpoint, had she? That racket at the last moment must have been some of the crowd reaching the top of the escalator, no doubt with the police on their heels. Perhaps the girl had taken advantage of the guard's inattention—and once she'd crossed into Canadian territory there were no further checks.

What about the bus ticket? She must have had a bus ticket; they wouldn't let her board, otherwise. Stole one, probably. In any case, here she was, ticket or no ticket.

"Going to Quebec, are you? Have you friends there?"

Still that innocent look, ignorant but confident. "You are going to Quebec."

"Yes, but you. . . ." Catherine was taken aback. "You mean you're going because I'm going?"

The girl nodded with a delighted smile. "To Quebec."

Catherine stared at her. This conversation would have been almost laughable if it hadn't been so pathetic. The child must certainly be retarded. It wouldn't be easy to get any useful information out of her. Might as well forget about things like surname or place of birth. Did she have parents or friends? A smile and another "No," without distress or reticence, as though "parents" or "friends" weren't very different from a passport or an article of clothing. Catherine settled into her seat once more. She'd have to see what she could do for this waif when they got to Quebec. Alert the social services . . . but maybe that wasn't such a good idea. There must be private organizations that would take charge of her, act as a buffer between the child and the bureaucratic efficiency of government services. Catherine turned to the girl, who looked at her expectantly. "Would you like to stay with me for a bit in Quebec, Athana?"

Enthusiastic nod.

"I'm visiting some very kind friends in Old-Quebec. You could live with us for a little while. Would you like that?"

"Yes."

Total trust. The child may not have even heard "a little while," and thought it was forever. Catherine suddenly felt embarrassed. "But you can't stay with them all the time. I'm not staying with them for long. I'm going back to Montreal, afterward. They'll find other friends for you to stay with in Quebec."

A little frown, now, but no lack of comprehension—more a sort of reproach: "No. With you. Beyond."

Catherine didn't insist. "We'll see in Quebec," she murmured, feeling discouraged. All at once she remembered taking a mint as she left the restaurant. She found it in her pants pocket and handed it to the girl, who fingered it curiously. Hadn't she ever seen a candy? Catherine unwrapped it and handed it back. It was a bit sticky. "That's a candy. You eat it." She had to act it out, but the girl finally caught on and put the candy on her tongue, closed her mouth, and began to suck, astonished at first, then delighted.

Catherine turned toward the window. It was unbelievable, depressing. Where did this waif come from? How could this girl be out on the street with no shelter, no one to care! To think this was the end of the twentieth century in one of the richest continents on the planet! Human universes were forever existing side by side without touching.

Night had almost fallen, and only the reflected light of the vanished sun lit up the western clouds. Ahead of the bus lay the night sky, a dark blue of immeasurable depth in which the first stars would soon be twinkling. Waterman blue, Catherine always thought, the color of the ink she used to put in her fountain pen in days gone by. She no longer wrote with a fountain pen. Advanced technology, now: ballpoints, felt-tips. Or, as in the last five years, computers and word-processing software. Even her diary had become electronic. The only time she wrote by hand, nowadays, was when she corrected her students' homework. "A Waterman-blue sky." A bit of imagery that would be meaningless to her students, who'd never written with a fountain pen. Meaningless to an increasing number of people, a survival from an almost vanished world. That was part of growing old, too: fewer and fewer things to share with others—expressions, comparisons, metaphors, slang, colloquialisms. And she, for good measure, had been transplanted into a society that spoke a different kind of French! But it was better, in a way: the feeling of growing old was less acute because she remained the-one-from-somewhere-else, a curiosity, always a little exotic whatever her age.

"Transplanted." Odd how she still used this term after twelve years; and yet she had put down solid roots in her adopted land. But she'd never lost her not-from-here accent and all the other things that showed she wasn't from here. She was no longer French-from-France, although she'd probably never be what was meant by "Québécois." Somewhere in between, that was it, not so much transplanted as in a state of unstable equilibrium on a thread; with her double vision, she could look at the New World in a different way from those who'd lived here for generations, and also see the Old World differently from those who'd always lived there. She was a sort of third world in herself: by partly belonging to two worlds she belonged to none. Anyway, to belong totally, to lose herself—she couldn't do it. Virtue or sin—she'd rather not say.

It wasn't egoism, strictly speaking, it was just . . . the fact of being alive, a deeply-rooted sense of selfhood that set off compelling defense mechanisms whenever she felt her integrity threatened. Her father had not been wrong; after all, there was a "well-understood egoism," the kind that kept you strong, that left enough of yourself intact to allow you to exist, gave you a chance to live with others and for others, if need be. "Well, *I'm* certainly not an egoist," said her mother when they discussed the subject. And each time Catherine would bite her tongue to keep from saying, "Too bad." She almost did say it, one day, toward the end. It was in the south of France, in the room that was always too hot; her mother was tiny—yes, shrunken—almost disappearing in the folds of the sheet. They were probably talking about what would have to be done for her father "afterward," about all the difficulties he'd be sure to cause, his irascible stubbornness . . . she lost her temper and her mother said, in a little-girl voice, "Don't shout, Catherine!" Instead of the usual, "I'm not shouting," Catherine suddenly said, "Perhaps I have to shout, Mama, for all the times you didn't." She said it gently, without anger. And her mother had not protested, merely nodded with a sudden sad wisdom and said, "But I couldn't, my little one."

Catherine blinked as she felt a tear roll down her cheek, and she turned her face more toward the window to stare at the darkened landscape and starry sky. They were deep in the countryside, now. Distant farm lights twinkled here and there, and headlights loomed up from the opposite side of the highway. The snow gave everything a faint luminescence. She loved traveling in winter during the day, loved the vast, stripped black-and-white horizons beneath the wide sky, but night journeys were perhaps even more enchanting, with the darkness hiding the winter vastness, leaving only a phantom without dimensions, as though all the life and color of the universe had taken refuge inside the bus—a tiny spaceship plunging through the interstellar void, the glimmering farm lights now galaxies, the headlights comets, and the pale shoulders of the highway infinitely distant nebulae. . . .

The sky is enormous and black. Above, below, all around Catherine, there is sky. She is under a transparent dome, on a transparent floor, in front of a transparent wall. It's not the first time she's been here, she's had time to get used to it, but even now she would experience vertigo if she weren't careful. She contents herself with touching the curved wall with her fingertips to feel the reassuring contact, smooth and cool, and the comforting thickness as it vibrates when she taps lightly. She knows her hosts don't consider this a weakness. In any case, she's not the only one in need of reassurance. Out of the corner of her eye she can see other hands touching the wall from time to time. Long hands with brown skin, rather rubbery-looking hands with four spindly fingers that flatten into spatulas where there should be nails, fingers that end, she knows, with a depression—a vestigial suction pad.

She looks at the sky, at space: a majestic vision with nothing to obscure the view, since the observation bubble is located at the end of the link conduit, quite far from the mother-ship. This space is not really black. Once her eyes become used to the darkness after leaving the tunnel, they notice small points of light to the right of the bubble, registering the fact that the bubble is moving. The mother-ship is in geostationary orbit, caught up in the same slow course that is leading the planet far below toward the extreme edge of its small solar system, itself at the extreme edge of its galaxy. The points of light slip slowly to the left and disappear one after another from her field of vision. And it's not over: no longer distracted by the vanished lights, the eye now distinguishes others of much weaker intensity, an almost subliminal blinking in the depths.

But the bubble, the vessel, and the planet keep on turning, and a collective sigh rises, to which she adds her own. Now the outside is truly black; now the planet, the vessel, and the bubble are hanging over the immense gulf that separates them from other nebulae, other galaxies, other suns. The Rift: a tear in the fabric of the cosmos hundreds of thousands of light years wide, so vast that if there are waves crossing it they haven't yet reached this small planet on the edge of its galaxy. The Shingèn are on the lookout, listening carefully each time the Great Year rolls around, bringing the planet into this quadrant of its orbit; but they've never seen anything, never picked up any signals. Two hundred years ago, as soon as they were capable of it, they themselves sent signals, and they send new ones each time their technology improves. They don't really hope for an answer. It's more an act of faith. Below, far below on their planet, on the southern hemisphere continent, it is spring in the Great Year, the time of renewal of life. For them, it's associated with this unrelenting black sky. They call it "the sky of a thousand colors." And since she hasn't understood what it means, even after reading their modern poems and ancient myths, they've asked her to wait and see.

Both hands on the glass, she contemplates the immense blackness surrounding her—but no, you can't contemplate it. You have to let the blackness seep in. Her reason tells her that this void isn't really empty, that there is plenty of interstellar dust floating about, especially in the vicinity of the planet's invisible magnet. But the darkness overrides her reason. After her hosts' warnings, she'd thought she might be overwhelmed by terror. But her reason isn't crumbling. The surrounding blackness strikes her like a thunderbolt, but she emerges reborn, becoming gradually exalted, transmuted, enlarged to unsuspected dimensions. She sees the colors—perhaps not a thousand, but hundreds of delicate tints and bright hues, no doubt a hallucination constructed by a brain deprived of visual stimuli, but at the same time she knows these colors are real; better still, they are true. And she now understands why the Shingèn have more than thirty words to describe black, which for them is the most mysterious, the richest of colors.

She doesn't know how long she has stayed like this, arms stretched toward the blackness. An intense, bluish light begins to grow in her righthand field of vision: the bubble and the ship are coming around to the sunlit side of the planet. A hand falls on her shoulder, a slightly whistling voice says her name, reducing it to two syllables. "Katrin." Regretfully, she lifts her hands off the glass, which feels as warm as a skin to her now, and turns toward the girl who has fallen asleep to the regular rocking of the bus. As the bus follows a curve, the girl is gently thrust against Catherine, head lolling on her shoulder.

For a long moment Catherine doesn't move, breathing softly and listening to the last drops of blackness patter away inside her. Then she stirs cautiously in order to get herself more comfortably ensconced without disturbing the sleeping girl. She turns to the dark window and the sky. Without thinking; she doesn't want to think, just take a look. Then she removes her glasses, the gesture with which she has always insulated herself from the rest of the world by limiting herself to the blurred periphery of her vision. The window and the sky become hazy, as the memory of a dream ought to be. After a few minutes of gazing into the distance, Catherine closes her eyes and lets herself slip once more (once more?) into sleep.

Part
Two

It was snowing when she woke up again. The bus was just pulling out from the boarding platform in St. Foy, the first stop before the downtown terminus. The seat on her right was empty. Alarmed, Catherine leaned over and spoke to her neighbor across the aisle. "Excuse me. The young girl sitting beside me hasn't got off the bus, has she? The blonde one in a white parka?"

The man looked at her with polite surprise. "Sitting beside you? I didn't notice her."

Catherine sat back in her seat. The child had probably gone downstairs to use the washroom at the back of the bus.

It must have been snowing for some time, because the sidewalks were completely white. A fairly thick layer of snow covered the cars parked in front of the big shopping centers bordering the avenue on one side for a nearly a mile. There was no wind, and the snow had a resolute look about it as it fell straight down. Seven-fifty-eight according to the huge Greenburg Plaza signboard. The bus went by the gate to the Lowell Campus and turned into McDougall Avenue. The girl hadn't come back. Just to make sure, Catherine climbed down the narrow staircase and glanced at the back of the aisle. The washroom light showed the toilets were empty.

She climbed back up and sat down, feeling despondent. Perhaps the child had thought St. Foy was the end of the line and had watched in puzzlement as the bus pulled out. No papers, no passport, probably no money—she'd certainly be picked up at the first checkpoint. Did they always process passengers from the Montreal bus? Judging by the security checks at the Berri terminus, they must have set up a similar procedure in Quebec City. The child must have been caught right away. Contact the police at the downtown terminus, invent a plausible story. . . . Difficult, though, without papers to explain the child's existence. Or she could notify them that the girl had gotten off the bus at St. Foy by mistake, she's a little, uh, simple, you see, *Sir*, and when they found her she'd have a fit because the child had "lost her papers."

Feeling gloomier than ever, Catherine watched the fine and forbidding Victorian mansions along McDougall Avenue slip by, then the painfully modern government buildings that jutted up here and there in this part of the Upper Town. There'd be no way of retrieving the child if she got caught up in the wheels of the social services, unless false papers could somehow be obtained. But where did she get such a harebrained idea? How did you get false papers, anyway? You could hardly put an ad in the newspapers, could you?

There might be worse things than being taken up by the social services; at least the child would be fed and housed. It was stupid to take it so much to heart. After all, she didn't know the child, had barely exchanged a few sentences with her. But she couldn't convince herself that it didn't matter. To have brushed against this half-guessed world of solitude and incoherent need was already too much. The child even had a name—funny name, Athana, but still a name! Catherine couldn't help thinking of the blonde head resting on her shoulder and the trusting smile, the slender shoulders in the blue velvet dress . . . and to her surprise she felt tears welling up.

The terminus loomed into view. Catherine retrieved her things from the luggage bay. When she was finally off the bus, and as a last sop to her conscience, she went to the driver. "You must have seen a fair-haired young girl get off at St. Foy? About fifteen years old, long hair, wearing a white parka?"

The man gave her a puzzled look. "No."

"Maybe you didn't notice her," murmured Catherine, discouraged, ready to turn away.

"I know exactly who gets on and off my bus, lady! I'd know if I'd seen this young girl," growled the driver.

"She got on at Montreal, just behind me."

"I remember you perfectly well. You were out of breath and you were the last. There was no one behind you."

Catherine stared at the driver. There wasn't even a trace of mockery: he seemed completely sincere. They looked at one another in silence, until Catherine lowered her eyes in embarrassment. The man coughed and muttered, "I'm sorry," as he walked off to help the baggage-handlers unload.

Catherine hurried through the snow to the terminus building. Sorry? Why sorry? Because he thinks I'm a nut case? Then it hit her. She almost stopped in the middle of the revolving door: he thinks I've had a vision.

A weird vision, not "normal." No ghosts in blue dresses on my bus, lady! She checked the baggage carrousel, saw that nothing was coming down yet, then headed for the phones. She fumbled in her wallet for a fifty-cent piece. A vision. The idea had already occurred to her the previous evening. But it was impossible, wasn't it? No living beings in visions, no conversations, no blue caps, no blonde head resting on a shoulder. And an itinerant vision, what's more: in the Botanical Gardens, in the Rue Montcalm, in the Berri tunnel, in the bus. No, the only likely theory was that the driver, despite his protests, simply hadn't seen the girl get on and off the bus, not because she didn't exist, but because he hadn't paid attention.

She could hear the phone ringing at the other end of the line. Someone picked it up, "It's me," said Catherine, smiling in spite of herself on hearing Christine's warm voice.

"I'm on my way!" said Christine. "Give me a good half hour with this snow."

Catherine waited for forty-five minutes, but this time it didn't bother her: everyone waits in a bus station. She saw Christine come in and registered all the small changes as her friend approached, yet she couldn't remember the

last time they'd met—a thought she resolutely put aside.
She'd remember sooner or later. It was Christine, that was
enough. Still the same fair hair streaked with a lighter
blonde swinging about her ears, same scent of oranges. As
they kissed each other, their glasses clashed. They laughed
and removed them in unison, then kissed again.

Christine Chantaraine lived in the old section of the Upper Town, like many Quebec-City francophones. They
had left the Enclave at the end of the Twenty Years' War
to return to their original homes, even if it meant living
officially in English. Within a century they had produced
enough surviving children to create a French quarter in
the old city once more. In fact, everyone called it the
French Quarter, even the anglophones—although they re-
garded the phenomenon with a jaundiced eye and had
never agreed to the name becoming official.

The traffic was light. Beneath the old part of the city
lay an intricate network of tunnels, making it possible for
the inhabitants to leave their cars at home in winter much
of the time. Summer traffic formed the subject of an on-
going, covert battle between francophones and the munic-
ipality. By establishing a network of one-way streets, for
example, the city could make life very disagreeable for the
residents of the French Quarter.

This struggle didn't extend to business concerns, for
the most part. Money spoke its own language, whether it
came from local francophones or the thousands of tourists
from Louisiana and Europe that congregated in the city
each summer. The small francophone community of
Quebec-City had played its cards well by preserving and
developing solid contacts with several of the big business
and industrial families of Louisiana. North-South mar-
riages took place at least once every two generations, and
the young people went to New Orleans for a French education.

Catherine felt an absurd satisfaction at remembering
this information as Christine's small car dodged through
the labyrinth of streets leading to the old section of town.
The Chantaraine house wasn't far from the Château Pitt,
a green-roofed, red-brick monstrosity that had loomed

over the old city since the end of the nineteenth century.
The huge fake-French-Renaissance hotel was a wildly incoherent pile worthy of a moviemaker with more money
than architectural or historical knowledge. The old
sixteenth-century houses on St. Michael Square were built
of sober gray stone with a minimum of carving and
looked quite solemn by contrast, especially in winter
when the fiercely-pruned linden trees on the square were
merely pale, snow-hooded trunks. But it was all exactly as
Catherine remembered it: the benches, the large basin of
the fountain where pigeons and turtledoves congregated
in summer, the small baroque church filling the east side
of the sloping square, and the gray stone Chantaraine
house with its tall windows and roof of yellow-and-green
varnished tiles. The roof cost an arm and a leg to repair
each year, but it was something of a family duty to maintain the genuine French style. The original tiles had come
from Burgundy, brought over in the same boat as the first
Chantaraine, and the carefully-matched replacements
were always purchased at great cost from the same region.

Christine Chantaraine had been thirty, almost the
same age as Catherine, when she came to the Enclave to
pursue her undergraduate studies at the newly opened college. She hadn't been the only mature student; others had
also waited for the chance to complete their studies in
French. Dominique Patelin, for instance, had come from
Vancouver. Afterward she and her daughter Annette had
gone to Quebec-City to live with Christine in the handsome house on St. Michael Square. Christine had brought
a child of her own from Montreal, a brownskinned baby
of two, Bertrand, whose father was known only to her.
The flock of aunts and great-aunts had almost choked with
indignation, but had finally bowed to the inevitable—after
discreet inquiries as to whether anything in the disposition
of the will under which Christine inherited the house
would enable them to overturn it on the grounds of mor-
ally reprehensible (although legally permissible) conduct.
Since Christine and Dominique each had a child, they were
allowed by law to marry one another.

Charles-Henri and Antoine also lived together, but
weren't married—they couldn't have married legally even

if they'd each had a child. They didn't, and had no intention of doing so in the so-called natural way. For years they'd fought for the right to adopt children, but without success. As Christine parked her car deftly in a narrow space in the underground garage beneath the square, she finished recounting the latest episodes in this legal battle.

"This double standard is really becoming intolerable," she concluded. "Dominique tried to involve the diocesan authorities, but they're infinitely cautious, as usual."

Catherine responded with a simple nod, saddened to note another memory lapse. Diocesan? What had Dominique to do with the church? The Roman Catholic church, that is. Did it have a progressive hierarchy prepared to fight for gay rights? Rather odd. But "infinitely cautious"—yes, very likely!

The two women took the elevator up to the square. It wasn't snowing so hard, now. The Christmas decorations and the triple-globed street lamps were lit—a real picture postcard. They hurried to the graceful wrought-iron gate, which opened with a click as they approached. Someone had been watching for them. Catherine glimpsed Dominique waving at them from a first-floor window. The front door at the top of the stone staircase was open, letting out a warm, yellow light. Annette and Bertrand rushed out and began arguing over who would carry Catherine's luggage, then they dragged her into the combined living-and-dining room to show her the Christmas tree. The room was warm, and mouthwatering smells floated in from the kitchen. Catherine looked at her two friends and the bright-faced children, astonished and embarrassed by her sudden emotion. You must be worse off than you thought, old girl, if the mere idea of "family" makes you want to cry! Christine must have noticed, for she said, "You must be tired. Come on, we'll get you settled."

Catherine followed her gratefully up the stone stairs curving upward from the ground floor, then up the spiral staircase of creaking but elegant dark wood to the gabled room on the third floor. As she entered, it seemed as though she'd never seen it before, but she resisted the temptation to lose heart and forced herself to appreciate what must, after all, be considered the unexpected pleasure of experiencing this pretty little room for the first time. She took in the exposed rafters, the fragrance of cedar and wax, the puffy, floral eiderdown on the antique bed—one of those narrow, girlhood beds that only needed a china doll with pink cheeks and a lace dress to make it perfect.

Catherine started unpacking while Christine sat on the bed.

"You really needed a holiday," Christine said after a moment.

Catherine looked up and met her friend's green gaze. Once again the tears rose. What was the matter with her, anyway?

She found herself sitting on the bed, sobbing in Christine's arms as her friend rocked her gently and stroked her back. Between sobs, Catherine tried to tell her everything at once, but Christine shook her head and murmured, "Later, love, later. Weep first."

Catherine wept.

2

It's warm, salty, and red, filling her mouth, her nose, her eyes, she's drowning, flails her arms and legs in the pinkish dusk, her feet touch bottom, and a viscous cloud looms up, enveloping her—but she floats up again and breaks through the skin of the waters. Her throat is full of salty phlegm as she glimpses a beach, and then the wave unfurls to toss her flat on the sand. Half unconscious, she crawls forward. The hot sand scrapes her skin raw. A monstrous pile of rocks eats into the sky. It's cold in their shade. She hugs her knees, pressing her heels against her thighs and tucking in her chin, smelling the bitter odor of water and sand already hardening into a crust.

The shade has disappeared, the sky is a burning mirror. At the end of the beach she can see colors. The furnace-hot sand forces her stinging feet to move faster, to run, and the colors get nearer, bringing with them the smell of cool undergrowth.

Hunger, a merciless void that fills her and must itself be filled. Grasses tall as trees, bushes tall as mountains, a placid lake surrounded by giant reeds. She falls forward into the coolness. Drinks. Grabs a blade of grass taller than herself and sinks her teeth into it, but the rubbery vegetable flesh won't give way. Tears run into her open mouth, and she reels at the water's edge.

The smell of honey fills her nostrils. She follows the

promise of food to its source, an immense flower with no stalk, its corolla spread open. A pink light filters through the pulsing petals with their network of red veins. Farther inside the warm, fleshy folds of this cavern lies the source of honey, a bouquet of gold-rimmed pistils. They caress her mouth, melt on her tongue. The flower closes over her. Warmth. Silence. Peace. The muffled music of the wind gently rocks the flower. Peace. Silence. Warmth.

The damp, warm dusk splits with a crackle. The pistils disappear. She bounces between the elastic walls and each bounce brings her closer to the rip. The flower shakes itself, shakes her, throws her out, and snaps shut. She screams, beating against the petals, bending her nails backward in her efforts to claw the flower, mad with rage and despairing hatred.

It is dark. She pulls back the curtain of hair from her eyes. So long? And her fingernails are long, too. Some are torn off, and there is coagulated blood on the ends of her fingers. She isn't cold, but she hugs herself, shivering. And opens her arms instantly, patting her body in the shadow, horrified. Flab, everywhere! Hair and nails keep growing on cadavers, but the dead don't get fat, a reassuring thought. She looks around her. Night is falling. The points of light in the sky form unfamiliar patterns. She falls to her knees, her head thrown back, mouth gaping. Somehow she knows, is sure she's somewhere else, sure of being through, of having come through . . . but her memory stalls, can't complete the thought, and after a moment she rises and walks a few steps, her mind a blank.

The uncomfortable bouncing of her breasts stops her. And also the pit in her stomach. Eat. The flower? It's closed. Fish in the lake? It's already too dark. Plants, then. Everything around her is huge. Has she shrunk? Are there animals proportionately as big as the plants? She can hear noises all around her, rustling, clicking, quivering, snapping—is it the wind, or is there something alive out there? Yellowish clusters of fruit hang from a shadowy bush. She tears one off, sniffs it, touches it with the tip of her tongue. Sweet. Are there sweet poisons? She can't be sure of anything on the other side . . . the other side of what? Here. It's up to her to choose: life or death. She eats one fruit, then another, then the whole cluster. *Qui vivra verra*.

As she walks along the water's edge, she finds a shard of rock, long and sharp. She winds grass around the wider end. Feels less naked, tries to forget the quivering flesh of her belly. And the hunger, for the yellow fruit wasn't enough. She pushes her way underneath the bush, through moss as high as grass, makes herself a hole, and curls up in it. Tomorrow she'll make herself some clothing and explore. And devise a way of marking time.

Is it another day? She swims in the lake: she must get her muscles back in shape and forget about being hungry. The fish elude her and the fruit is hard to find. But she hasn't ventured farther afield. Seated beside the water, she watches the flower in the distance.

The flower that is moving. Opening.

She gets up, runs toward the flower, eyes wet with grateful tears, but a small, long-bodied animal, half otter, half lizard, slips into the warm, pink cavern before she can get there. The flower closes over it. She rushes forward, hears noises, dull thuds, as though the small animal were struggling. She tries to force the petals apart, wants to see what's happening, but it's no use. She steps back, trembling with rage and disgust. The obscene corolla is already opening, the odor of honey has gone, and the small animal crawls out, exhausted, its coat dusted with gold.

She goes in hesitantly. The flower seems dead. She looks at the savaged pistils, lifts the weapon in her hand, and adds another slash to the wounds in the pink flesh. A whitish liquid begins to ooze out. Horrified, she runs out.

Shift. Another part of the forest. Here the plants have normal proportions. It is the kingdom of the trees. The trunks rise straight and smooth in the glimmering shadows. A living, murmurous silence bathes the wooden pillars; it is their breath that makes the forest quiver like the sea—a tranquil sea of soaring depths where it is impossible to drown.

And here is the king of the forest, a tree so high, so broad, so luxuriant that perhaps she has been unconsciously responding to its call. She must lie flat on the ground to see all of it. Hundreds of birds sing in its mighty fronds. A hut built in its branches would be a good shelter. But the branches begin too high up. The trunk is too smooth, too wide. She tries to jump, to climb, but her fingers slip.

No, she can climb it after all: she's holding a braided vine rope weighted with a stone, manages to swing it over a branch and tie it to the trunk. She reaches the first limb amid a green, leafy tangle; invisible birds take wing like a gust of wind. A menacing snarl rises very close to her. The leaves move, part. A flat-faced head, short white fur, round bronze eyes with vertical pupils. . . .

She slides the length of the cord, palms on fire, grabs her knife, presses her back against the trunk, heart beating, certain she's going to die . . . but the beast has vanished among the leaves.

She thinks resentfully of the shelter she could find in the arms of the tree. She takes cover and watches for the beast. It comes down at last, clinging awkwardly to the trunk. This isn't a feline, in spite of the long, sinuous body—more like a giant frog: the front legs are articulated like arms, the long back legs are drawn up but splayed on either side of the haunches. It goes off at a jolting gait, half running, half jumping. It's not slim, it's scrawny; sick, perhaps? It won't be difficult to catch.

There, the beast is hanging from a branch, half strangled in the snare. She undoes the rope and the beast falls to the ground. It seems inoffensive lying there on its side, knocked unconscious by the fall. Tie it up and build a cage, that will be enough.

Shift. From the hut built in the fork of the large branch, she is watching the exiled beast in its cage. Sometimes it stands and grips the bars, shaking them as it snarls, but wearily. Soon it lies down again, its large, dull eyes fixed on the tree. Then she goes in search of fruit, the plum, red, oblong fruit of the tree, far more nourishing than the yellow berries by the lake. She hugs the round branches like a lizard, shinning up to the highest branches, close to the clouds. Later she'll feed the beast and tease it.

Shift. A lowering sky, turning the forest to stone beneath a gray, glutinous light. All is silent. The clouds become heavier, gathering noiselessly across the sky as though self-propelled; not a breath of wind moves in the forest, and the leaves hang listlessly. She hears the first distant rumbling, and a pale light bathes the forest as the last bit of open sky is engulfed by the clouds. A murmur of wind lifts the foliage briefly, and an instant later howling demons are unleashed upon the forest. The branch supporting the hut pitches like a ship, and water streams over her as the wind penetrates the fragile walls and tears them away. The whole sky is bright as lightning flashes and peals of unending thunder roll over the forest. She clings to the glistening trunk, blinded by the rain. Below, the beast screams and shakes the bars, maddened by the storm. It will injure itself—she must go down and free it. The rope swings, threatening to smash her against the trunk. She is just about to jump to the ground when a tremendous crash rips through the air, an unbearable light closes her eyes and every muscle contracts in an electrical spasm. She falls into the grass far from the tree, body hair standing on end, skin tingling, heart pounding.

The tree burns, split in two.

The beast has been wounded. Its left foreleg is broken, its left eye destroyed by fire. Black leopard-like scorchmarks dot its fur. It's lying on its face, forelegs folded on its chest, rolling its head from left to right in a curiously human movement. With sudden pity, she gives the beast something to eat. It stretches its long, articulated fingers to grasp the food and carry it to its mouth.

Shift. The beast has recovered. With help, it can stand and walk.

Shift. She braids vines into rope for lashing together the branches to reinforce her future shelter. The beast slowly ties a knot in the vines.

Shift. She's lying in front of the fire, very weary, light-headed, body wracked with pain, curled up to concentrate the heat on her taut belly. The muscles relax little by little. Cheek resting on her hand, she watches the blood-red shimmer of firelight on the skin of her thighs and on her pubis. She's been on the other side a long time and hasn't menstruated once. Has she become sterile? Does it matter? She's somewhere else, now, probably the only one of her kind. Alone. Forever. And suddenly she rolls onto her stomach, arms between her thighs, panting, head thrown back, mouth distended, hands kneading, clawing, wanting to tear her flesh, and the spasms come but bring no relief, only pleasureless cries.

Another skin on her skin. The beast. Placing a ... hand on her shoulder, warm and dry. The claws are sheathed, the tips of the ... fingers caress her arm. She scrutinizes the feline mask, the single eye, the thin lips strangely curled back, looking for a human expression that isn't there, has never been there, and she shudders violently. The claws on her shoulder instinctively emerge halfway from their sheath. She cries out. The beast recoils, drops to the ground, and crawls to its litter. The flickering firelight gleams in its single eye.

Shift. She's in the forest with the beast in its winter-thickened fur. It has been raining. There are fresh tracks in the mud. Boot marks; no animals would leave tracks like those. The beast growls, refuses to move. She tells it to come, walking on without waiting. In three bounds the beast is in front of her, snarling and blocking the trail, all four paws planted in the mud. She threatens it with the spear—for a moment she thinks the beast will attack, but it goes off, head lowered, and disappears into the undergrowth, limping a little and deaf to her calls.

The trail takes her to the edge of the forest, where trees grow in abundance, smaller brothers to the one destroyed in the storm. Autumn has quenched the colors, and empty fruit husks cover the ground occasionally crunching beneath her calloused feet. On the harder soil, the trail fades.

A slithering sound in the branches, she looks up, too late. She is pinned to the ground by a cold dry mass winding itself around her shoulders. A gaping mouth hangs near her face. She struggles vainly as the giant snake tightens its coils, and a red veil dims her eyes.

A roar, a jolt; the vise slackens and she rolls dizzily away. The mesh of claws and coils suddenly untangles itself and the snake slithers off through the bushes. The beast pursues it for a while, flailing viciously, then comes back. She sees its inscrutable mask bending over her, but her vision is fuzzy, breathing hurts, something in her chest is broken. She hears no noise, but the beast turns its head to listen to something and disappears from her field of vision. She tries to lift herself to see what's coming, but curiosity and fear are locked in her brain, unable to reach her muscles. Her eyelids close, she hears distant footfalls, then from a greater distance feels the touch of a hand. With a gigantic effort, she lifts her eyelids: a triangular face, bronze eyes, a large mouth, a round shock of curly hair behind pointed ears. She knows she should speak, say her name, but she hasn't thought of her name once since coming from the other side, doesn't know her name, and feels an immense, stifling terror.

She wakes, and in waking remembers and shouts at the darkened room, but it is only a murmur. "Catherine."

3

Christine still had some shopping to do the day before Christmas, and dragged Catherine into the big St. Foy shopping centers. The main mall of the Greenburg Plaza was filled with music and twinkling lights—a consumer temple in the throes of its major celebration. People had congregated around the central hall where a succession of Nativity scenes was being acted out rather stiffly by animated figurines: the arrival at the inn, Mary's dream, the great light of Creation shining down on the village (a highly successful effect, resembling an almost tangible wave of light), the villagers walking behind Mary and Joseph to the abandoned stable, the discovery of the Miracle in the manger. Only Jesus appeared in this Unicist version, since this was Quebec-City, a Protestant stronghold.

Catherine stopped to look at the figurines, conscious of an inexplicable irritation. Was it this apotheosis of the male Child that rankled? The Unicists weren't the only culprits, though: Roman Catholic iconography often displayed the Infant Jesus as larger than the Infant Lilith. Jesus, created first for the Catholics, the first to be crucified, the first to rise again. To think that generations had fought long and bloody wars over this issue, but that, even now, the members of the international men's movement secretly agreed on the supremacy of the male!

Christine had walked on ahead, and Catherine followed her, feeling uneasy. It wasn't really irritation she felt, more like . . . surprise. The idea of the two Infants in the crèche seemed totally *improbable,* all of a sudden. She hadn't felt that way in the Enclave in front of the Rue Saint-Jacques crèche. Such different doctrines, two Infants or one: how could Catholics and Unicists have ever made peace? And not only with each other, but with the two other religions of the Book that accepted neither the two Infants nor a solitary Messiah. She tried vainly to remember the history of the great wars of religion, the Catholic Crusades, the Unicist Reformation. Her memory was being selective again, offering her all the details of various doctrines with perfect clarity, but nothing more. And she didn't remember how she'd learned this information, either. Since when was she so very learned on the question of religions? Was she *that* interested in them? Or was it simply a side issue in her feminist concerns?

A sentence suddenly took shape in her mind, at once mocking and incredulous: *With a male and a female Messiah, there should be no need for feminism among Catholics.* She felt obliged to reply that biology and the international men's movement were stronger than religion, even revealed religion. Why did this seem like such a weak argument, all of a sudden? Hadn't she had this conversation a hundred times? But she couldn't remember a single one of these conversations. . . .

It was too weird, exploring her memory like a tooth with a possible cavity—cautiously, for fear of stirring up a sudden pain. Catherine rejoined Christine, who was standing in front of a jewelry shop. The gems were spread around an imitation seabed, with dozens of exotic shells for decoration. Shells that fixed Catherine's attention with the same disagreeable impression of some mental hiccup. Why? What was weird about the shells? Why did some of them seem out of place? Shells from the south seas, warm countries that weren't so warm now, what with global cooling—but surely these shells could have survived even farther south, couldn't they? Or else the collection dated from before the advent of global cooling.

And when had the cooling begun, anyway? Her memory provided no answer. Catherine turned in exasperation to her friend. "How long has it been since the cold set in, Christine? I mean the cooling?"

Christine replied without hesitation, "Sixteenth century. Why?"

"The shells," said Catherine, pointing vaguely to the shop window. She started walking again, puzzled. Sixteenth century. And there were *lindens* growing in Quebec-City, in a region where temperatures of minus thirty degrees centigrade were usual in winter? Linden trees simply wouldn't survive in such temperatures. Perhaps it was a genetically-altered species? Was there a highly developed genetic science here?

Christine was watching her rather worriedly.

"Perhaps we should stop for a drink," Catherine said, feeling desperate.

Christine agreed without comment, and they headed for the restaurant section.

"Which would you like?" asked Christine. Catherine looked at the names on the signs. McGerald's, A&A, Rodger's, Kameka, Milo's, all the usual fast-food chains . . . she knew this, but with a sense of some break in continuity, some imbalance, an error somewhere. She turned away, muttering, "It's all the same to me," and sat down without caring where she was.

Christine sat down opposite her. "Something's really wrong, isn't it?" she said gently after a while.

"Yes." Catherine had never been able to hide anything from Christine, and didn't even try. But how to explain, where to begin? She felt lost. "I forgot about Papa's death. Really forgot. Total denial." She kept her eyes on her hands, not wanting to see Christine's expression. "And lots of other things as well, history, politics. Then suddenly it all comes back. Or doesn't, and I have to check it out in books and data banks, and then it does." She almost stopped there—but no, this was Christine, she must tell all. "And I have visions . . . weird visions."

"What kind of visions?" said Christine gently.

Just as Catherine was trying to reply, a figure suddenly dropped out of the crowd streaming by the tables. It sat down beside her. A young man in black leather, medium height, slender and lithe, with glossy brown curls falling to his shoulders. The round face of an adolescent, big black eyes, intense and ... anxious? The mouth was smiling, but not the eyes.

"Don't look surprised," he said in French, bending over to kiss Catherine's cheek. Dumbfounded, she returned the kiss mechanically. His cool skin smelled of eau-de-cologne. "You shouldn't be here. Haven't you seen the signs?"

"What signs?" she heard herself ask with amazing calm.

"The white letters. On the advertising, all over the place." He looked around the restaurants. "And here, too."

She followed his eyes, and saw nothing but multicolored letters spelling the names of restaurants. The white letters? Yes, there were white letters, a C, an H over there, an O, a G ... WAY. ...

"So what?"

"CATHERINE GO AWAY," said the boy, as though it were obvious.

"How do you know my given name?"

The boy smiled, a real smile, this time, conspiratorial, a little mischievous. "The words tell all when one knows how to read them. You know that."

"Who are you? What do you want?" Why didn't she simply tell him to get lost? But she felt drawn into the conversation in spite of herself.

The boy now turned to Christine. "Explain to her," he said. "She's in danger here."

He rose and said softly, "Happy reading," then walked jauntily off into the ever-increasing crowd.

"An Adept," said Christine, following him with her eyes. Her voice was a mixture of puzzlement and incipient laughter. She turned back to Catherine, looking attentively at her friend. "A Book Adept. In capitals. Don't you remember that, either?"

"Yes," said Catherine, annoyed but wondering, for as she spoke the mere juxtaposition of the words "book" and "adept" had seemed like a signal, jarring a whole segment of memories into place, not memories, really, but data, detached from space and time, unconnected to their context. Book Adepts, sort of the same thing as Believers, a marginal sect. "This world is a great Book, where all is written for those who know how to read." People obsessed with anagrams, who saw revelations in graffiti and slashed posters. . . . "CATHERINE GO AWAY" indeed! You could find plenty of other messages in those letters. With an incredulous little laugh, she exclaimed, "Don't tell me you're one?"

A little late, she realized that the way she'd phrased the question and especially the tone might hurt Christine's feelings.

Her friend didn't seem offended, however. "No, but I know them," said Christine mildly. She seemed rather pensive. Even worried. The boy *had* said "in danger here."

"A whacko," said Catherine. "You're not taking this seriously?"

"Your name *is* Catherine," remarked Christine equably.

"Do these Adepts have some connection with the North?"

It was the only rational explanation. Joanne Nasiwi knew she'd come to Quebec. Could describe her. Maybe someone had followed her. But what was all this ridiculous cloak-and-dagger stuff about, anyway?

"Yes, with the Believers."

And the Believers had contacts with the "revolutionary" branch—all clear and accounted for, then.

"They're Ultimists," Christine added, still pensive. Her tone implied Catherine would understand the significance of this remark.

Catherine gave up and asked, "They're what?"

"They believe in the advent of the Ultimate Infant." Christine watched Catherine attentively. "According to them, the fusion of both complementary Infants into a single, Ultimate Infant will determine the fate of the world."

Catherine shook her head in discouragement: no inner echo. She'd better set Christine straight, though. In blunt sentences, she described her meeting with Joanne Nasiwi, the student demonstration, Henri Lapointe. . . . "It's very simple," she heard herself say. Very simple! Well, yes, in a way; it explained the silly Adept episode perfectly. But Christine seemed more puzzled than enlightened, and still worried. "Let's go home," she said, rising and putting on her coat.

"You haven't finished your shopping!"

"It wasn't anything important, just a couple of things for the meal. We can easily do without them."

"But this is ridiculous! Anyway, Joanne told me to stick with lots of people. You could hardly get more people than there are here." Catherine was joking, but Christine seemed to take it seriously, looking around carefully. She made a small face and muttered: "That's true—but let's get a move on."

What had happened to Christine? Since when did she believe in this claptrap? Catherine followed her friend, dumbfounded at her reaction and extremely upset. Would Christine be like a stranger because of Catherine's intermittent memory?

They finished the last of the shopping and took the main elevator down to the central plaza. In front of the escalators leading to the underground parking lots, there was a big advertising poster that Catherine glanced at mechanically as she passed.

She stopped in her tracks and walked back.

A bit of forest on the edge of a lake. In the background, bushes with clusters of yellow fruit among glossy, blackish-green leaves. In the left foreground stood a form dressed in a short, brown tunic decorated with blue geometric patterns, a braided belt at the waist. A male form, it seemed, judging from the shoulders, the proportions of the body, the arm and calf muscles ... covered with golden fur, more a fuzz, really, but less pronounced on the face, which was triangular in shape, leonine, with a somber mouth and large, browny-gold eyes. A curly mane formed a halo around the head, and behind it two small, rounded ears protruded from the top of the skull.

On the right-hand side of the picture was a flower, almost as high as the humanoid figure, its fleshy petals slightly open, reddish, with a network of paler veins. No stalk or leaves, just the huge corolla that seemed to grow right out of the ground.

Catherine felt a hand on her arm. Without moving, still staring at the sign, she said, "Christine, what do you see on that billboard?"

"*Death and Rebirth in the Land of the Marrus*," replied Christine, reading the English title inscribed in gold letters on the forest foliage at the top of the poster. "*Royal Museum, Canadian Center for the Arts, December 20th–January 15th*. It's an exhibition."

Catherine felt her legs buckle. "You see it—you see it!" she exclaimed, leaning on a worried Christine.

"Of course I see it. It's an advertisement. Cat, what's happening?"

Catherine had managed to get a slight grip on herself. "Nothing. I see it, too. I thought . . . it was another vision."

"A vision?" Christine turned and touched the poster. "Well it's possible, but I don't think so, you know. I've seen these posters around town before." She looked guardedly worried again.

"When?"

"I'm not sure. The day before yesterday, I think."

"You think."

"Well . . . yes. Cat, what's going on?"

Catherine thought a moment, then settled for the most rudimentary explanation. "I dreamed it."

"The poster?"

"No, the world of the Marrus. I was in it."

Christine stood utterly still for a moment. Finally, she said, "How about visiting the exhibition? It's open between noon and two o'clock."

Catherine ignored the exhibit at the entrance—a three-dimensional solar system showing the planet of the Marrus and a flat projection, although in relief, of its three continents. She walked over to the first tableau. Electric light combined with the noonday sun to produce an almost painfully bright illumination. It showed a pile of enormous rocks and a sandy beach running down to a large, irregularly-shaped basin filled with a reddish, syrupy liquid. At the foot of a rock lay a black, gleaming form, round and tapering like a seal, but with four limbs and articulated fingers, rather like an otter. Catherine moved on quickly. The other tableau was that shown on the poster, although here the lake was just a mirror-like stretch of water surrounded by grass. Catherine studied the humanoid figure. It was a little taller than herself. The tinted glass eyes held no expression, but it was the face in her dream.

She bent over the little stand displaying a description of the scene. "A young Marru male from the western continent. . . . On his tunic are ritual symbols designed to protect him from the spirits of the forest. The second most important spirit is embodied in the carnivorous flower shown here." Carnivorous?

Catherine followed the arrow showing the route of the exposition. On the threshold of the next room, she stopped in amazement. Although the walls were lined with tableaux and display cases like the first, the center was entirely given over to a reproduction of the dream tree. Half-hidden in the branches was a motionless figure, white, long, and sinuous.

Catherine spun around and stumbled into Christine, who grabbed her firmly by the shoulders before she could fall.

"Is it your dream?"

Catherine nodded, eyes closed.

"Look at me, Cat. You mustn't be afraid. It happens. Even if you don't remember. Not often, but it can happen. Come and sit down."

Catherine sank into one of the benches placed around the walls of the first room. Her heart wasn't pounding quite so hard, and the burst of perspiration had faded. She wiped her forehead, swallowed hard; she wasn't going to be sick in the middle of the oh-so-grand Royal Museum! She looked at the shapes of the Marru and the flower, then at the model of the solar system floating in front of the main door. A faint curiosity stirred once again: no obvious wires or threads, how did they keep the spheres in the air? And keep them turning, as well? An animated hologram—but did they have such advanced holograms here? That "here" again! Here in relation to where? As in the dream, that's it—"passing through to the other side," but to the other side of what, in relation to what frontier?

"You say it's normal?" she said at last. "You dream of something, and then it really happens?"

Christine was still looking at her, full of solicitude. "It's not . . . usual. But there have been cases. I don't know what you dreamed, but yes: parts of dreams occur in real life. They aren't dreams, but an anticipated memory."

"An anticipated memory." What a useful label. And what did it mean, exactly? "An anticipated vision?"

"No, visions are different. They don't exist in the same way. You can touch some, but not others. Some visions can be seen by several people at once, others can't."

Out of the corner of her eye, Catherine saw a white spot enter her field of vision. She stiffened. Then something gave way inside her once again, and almost relieved, almost thankful, she let the welcome sense of calm wash over her. Amused and curious, she turned to look at the girl, at Athana, who had stopped in front of her. Tall and slender, her parka open over the blue dress. Had she been that tall before? But the blonde hair and blue-green eyes were exactly the same—and the trusting smile.

"Christine, I'd like you to meet Athana. Athana, this is one of the friends I told you about. Christine Chantaraine."

The girl held out a hand rather timidly. Christine shook it, looking puzzled.

Catherine's jaw dropped. "You can see her!"

Christine hesitated, keeping the girl's hand in hers. "I see her, I'm touching her," she said with studied calm. "Why? Is she one of your visions?"

"I don't know," murmured Catherine, astounded. "She has no passport and managed to get through the checkpoint. The bus driver couldn't remember seeing her, and I thought. . . ." Should she have been relieved at this confirmation of Athana's material existence? She wasn't sure.

The youngster—this wasn't a youngster, though, but a rather gangly adolescent—sat down beside her and took her arm. "Are we going beyond?" she asked with smiling approval.

Catherine couldn't help a brief burst of dazed laughter. "Well, you're certainly persistent!" She stood up. "That's right. Let's visit the rest of my . . . anticipated memory."

They all went into the second room and stood underneath the tree. The branches cast chimerical shadows on the wall. Athana pointed to the white figure. "She stopped."

The placard enlarged upon this comment. *Among young Marrus, reversion to the animal state does not always occur in the same manner. This seems to depend not only on complex endocrinal processes, but also on the place where their pilgrimage ends. Ideally, it leads them from the Red Sea to the coastal villages. Those who stay on the shores rather than going back to the villages take on an ancient aquatic form of their race. Some stay in the wilderness area known for its carnivorous flowers. It is not known what form these young assume, since not one has ever been found. Others stay in the forest and are closest to the modern Marru form. These are without doubt the most pathetic victims of the peculiar biological development of their race, since some of them show unmistakable signs of sapience. Attempts to force them into the villages have always failed, however, even with the sophisticated biological science of the modern Marrus. The metamorphosis linked to adolescent endocrinal phenomena is apparently a threshold that the young Marrus can only cross in one direction.*

Catherine remembered the feline mask of the white beast, its single eye glimmering moistly in the night on the other side of the fire. "Yes," she murmured, "she stopped." Why should she feel so sad? It was a dream, wasn't it? No, an anticipated memory. But what did that really mean? She turned to Christine, who was studying the tree with awe, her head tilted back.

"Will my dream come true, Chris?"

Christine came back from wherever she was, and looked at Catherine. "What did you dream?"

"That I was on the seashore, and inside the flower, and in the forest with a white beast."

"Well, it's come true, hasn't it?" replied Christine, with a little wave that took in the whole exhibition.

"But it was a . . . a story," persisted Catherine, not sure why she protested "With a plot. It was . . . complex. Very . . . personal."

She had almost said "very symbolic." It was an interesting concept. Maybe her mind had simply combined her own fantasies with the so-called anticipated memory of this exhibition? But "simply" wasn't the right word; it didn't explain how anticipated memory worked, although it might account for the construction of the dream, in part at least, and the intense, almost hallucinatory quality of its emotions and sensations.

Her stomach began to rumble, and she smiled almost gratefully at this reassuring organic manifestation. "Chris, why don't we grab a bite? All these discoveries are making me hungry."

Christine nodded, also smiling, and they retraced their footsteps. As they passed by the model of the solar system, Catherine slowed down. She glanced around to make sure no one was watching, then tried to touch the small blue and green planet of the Marrus. Her finger passed right through it. They certainly did have sophisticated holograms "here." And an imagination run wild. Were these exoethnographic displays a new art form? Based on visions, perhaps; the idea of "other worlds" had set artists off on new trains of thought. She couldn't ever remember hearing anyone talk about such a thing—but the fact that she couldn't remember was less and less of an argument.

They were walking down the stairs giving onto Wolfe Square and the St. John Gate when Catherine realized Athana was no longer with them. She looked back at the museum entrance. Nobody. Christine had stopped, too, and was looking at her with concern. "Did you see her go?" asked Catherine, feeling exasperated and crushed.

"Who?" Christine said.

Catherine forced herself to breathe deeply, once, twice. "The young blonde girl whom we met in the museum. Athana. In the white parka. You shook her hand."

"Oh yes!" But Christine still looked somewhat perplexed. "No, I haven't seen her since then. Maybe she stayed inside."

She was already walking back up the stairs. Catherine almost stopped her, then followed, suddenly sure they wouldn't find the girl. No one in the first room, nor the second, nor the third, where a film had been shown on the daily life in the Pilgrimage villages. The lights were on between showings. There was no other exit, either. For reasons best known to the municipal authorities, although the Royal Museum was partially underground it wasn't connected to the maze of tunnels underneath the old town.

They emerged once more into the bitter cold. The wind coming from the river swept the snow from the roofs in smoking swirls. Catherine pulled her cap down over her ears and hurried after Christine, head bowed against the wind. "That kid sure has breezy manners," she said, gritting her teeth to stop them from chattering. The intended humor was more for herself than her friend.

"Who?" queried Christine.

4

December 24, evening

And it's the same each time. If I remind her, if I describe Athana and our meeting, she remembers. Otherwise she forgets. But only Athana; she remembers everything else. It's something to do with this girl, obviously. If a vision can be touched and shared, does that prove it *is* a vision? What if visions could walk and talk—but according to Christine that never happens, at least as far as she knows. I wonder if Athana's blue cap is still in my house?

An itinerant vision, one that follows me around—not a "normal" way for visions to behave. Who triggers it, Athana or myself? Chris couldn't answer this question, like many others. But that isn't what makes me so uneasy or intrigues and distresses me. She's fully aware that all this is very important to me, she's worried about me, but she's quite out of her depth. It's as though she'd never wondered about visions, apart from what she knows already, which is precious little when you come right down to it. And when I asked her how she knew, whether she'd had visions of her own, she looked vaguely embarrassed and said no, but everyone knew. Did she *learn* about them? This question made no sense, apparently. She has *always* known. There have *always* been visions. Since colonial days? Since *always*. Since the Middle Ages? Roman times? I saw a flash of anguish in her eyes . . . and stopped questioning her. Maybe the anguish was for me, though, at seeing my memory so bad.

But if I don't ask questions, what can I do? Submit. Passive, powerless, uncomprehending, like . . . an animal. No! And full of fear, too. No again! I'd rather ask questions, even if there are no answers. Asking questions helps. After a while, I forget *I'm* the one with the problem; it becomes more general, a case to be solved. My emotions subside, I calm down. Schizoid? Why not? It's not a bad thing to be two, from time to time.

December 25, 8 a.m.

I had a dream. A new one. I'm in the middle of a very violent demonstration, or at least one that is being very brutally repressed. Smoke, buildings and cars burning, bursts of tear gas, but I have a mask, many of the demonstrators have masks—very well organized, the demonstrators. And they're all women. Did it start out as a peaceful demonstration? I don't know. I'm in the middle of it, and we're being chased by anti-riot squads. I'm running, I'm afraid. The soldiers are armed and will surely end up shooting. I run. Not the way I often do in dreams, light, agile, graceful. No, this is very realistic, my lungs hurt, my thigh muscles are burning, but terror carries me forward and I run. Definitely a nightmare (a recall of the Montreal demonstration?). I fall and roll myself into a ball, someone walks on me, someone else hits me. Suddenly I'm in a dark room, strapped to a seat with a light shining in my face. Someone is interrogating me. I'm a member of a feminist organization. Feminist organizations are forbidden by law? *Women* are outlaws? Anyway, whoever it is slaps my face, burns me with cigarette ends. I tell myself this is a bad spy movie and I should wake up, but the pain is excruciating and keeps on and on. I know that I possess vital information—but not what it is—and that I'll die rather than talk. And I'm filled with hate, a fierce, unbelievable hatred.

Now I'm in a long, narrow room, small, more a slice of a room, really, with high walls of an indescribably repugnant color, the ceiling almost invisible behind the blinding light streaming from it. I'm naked. Curled up in a corner. No sign of injury, nothing. I'm seeing myself from somewhere up high: I tell myself that I'm dead and having an out-of-body experience. At once I'm back in my body. It's cold. A voice comes from the walls around me. I can't hear the exact words, but I know someone is trying to brainwash me, and I sing nursery rhymes to block it, chant multiplication tables, Latin declensions.

Shift again—curious, this latest tendency of my dreams to present themselves like film clips. I'm being rolled into an operating room. I've been injected with anaesthetic but am still conscious. Totally powerless, totally horrified, I know what is going to happen. They're going to mutilate me, change me, slip implants into my brain to make me a puppet. And send me far, far away, never to return. I feel my consciousness waver, collapse, darken, and the flash of despair is so strong that I wake up shouting, every muscle rigid. It took me at least half an hour to relax.

In other words, a charming nightmare, unlike any other I've ever had. Never have I had so many new dreams in such a short period. If indeed they are all dreams. Let's not get confused: the Marru episode is supposed to be an anticipated memory. And what about my dream of the Shingèn, in the bus coming to Quebec? I haven't dared mention it to Christine, haven't dared to really talk to her at all. Would I have the nerve? If I can't feel free to talk to her, I'm done for.

No tears on the keyboard, if you please.

On the other hand, I've also had the good old Dream of the Presence. With tiny variations: the Presence isn't so determined to hound me, doesn't dog my heels so closely. Perhaps it's getting fed up, too, tired of always having the same dream with me?

Change in continuity. My subconscious must be a progressive conservative—like the government!

All right, Rhymer, enough of that. You're beginning to babble. Go and get ready for Christmas.

5

Catherine had felt vaguely fearful as she waited for Charles-Henri and Antoine. Would she recognize them? Or only half remember them? But Charles-Henri's bear hug and joyous guffaw were thoroughly familiar, like his aroma of cinnamon and mint. Her memory even obligingly came up with their first meeting in Montreal. He had written from Quebec-City to ask about the literature syllabus of the newly opened college. She'd been interested enough by the tone of his letter to answer it personally instead of passing it on to the department administrators. After that they'd corresponded for several months and occasionally spoken on the telephone. He was intelligent, impulsive, had a great sense of humor, and was forever coming up with something new. The thought of having a student of his caliber in her class had delighted her. When he'd arranged to meet her in one of the small Enclave cafés along the Sainte-Catherine canal, however, she'd wondered how they would recognize each other.

It was the kind of waiting she hated, alone in a café filled with couples and chattering groups, staring at each person who came in and who seemed to be peering through the fog of smoke. And then he came in, walked by her table as though looking for someone, and she didn't even consider him—until he returned to her table

and said, "Catherine Rhymer? I'm Charles-Henri Neveu."
She recognized the voice at once and was embarrassed at
her astonishment.

His skin was a rich, gleaming brown, his thick, frizzy
hair was cut in the current geometric fashion, and his
smile shone like a lighthouse in his round, dark face. A
black. She'd never thought of the possibility for an instant.

Ashamed at what this revealed about her *a priori* as-
sumptions, she invited him to sit down, and they took up
where they'd left off in their letters and phone calls, skip-
ping the customary smiling commonplaces. Suddenly he
asked her, "Well, am I what you expected?" She thought
of putting him off with, "Am I?" But it would have been
a cop-out. She looked him straight in the eye: "I wasn't
expecting you to be black." Their friendship dated from
that moment. She called him "my demolisher of preju-
dices." Later, she had experienced a sense of satisfaction
at her lack of negative reaction as she watched the developing love between Antoine and Charles-Henri. She had
grown up at the war's end and during Reconstruction,
and like all those in her generation she knew what horrors
any kind of discrimination could lead to. She'd seen the
movies, read the books. But her consciousness had been
entirely intellectual. She'd never actually encountered
those other worlds—people of color, homosexuals. She
had viewed them with an abstract tolerance. It was encouraging and comforting to discover that, once she was
confronted with the daily reality, she'd found nothing to
"tolerate."

Reassured by the flood of reminiscences about
Charles-Henri and Antoine, Catherine began to relax. The
new arrivals put their presents under the tree, and everyone settled in for the cocktail hour, chatting, joking, and
exchanging news all at once. Catherine said little at first,
her real news being difficult to share. But the conversation
suddenly turned to something she could talk about. The
demonstrations in Montreal-City had caused repercus-
sions in the capital. Three days earlier, about a hundred
young Quebec-City francophones had staged a surprise
protest in front of the parliament buildings, demonstrating against the brutal repression of the previous week in

Montreal. The anti-riot squad had moved in swiftly, attacking the demonstrators, injuring many and arresting several. Antoine had witnessed the whole thing and could testify to the needless police brutality, even toward people on their way home from work. His car had been enthusiastically bludgeoned. The windshield and windows had been smashed in, and he'd been lucky to emerge without a scratch.

"We hadn't given them any provocation—just hooted our horns a little because there was a traffic jam and we didn't know why!"

"The news didn't mention it at all," said Catherine, not remembering to hide her surprise.

"Have you forgotten it's the state network, Catherine?" exclaimed Antoine sarcastically, too focused on his returning anger to notice her sudden stiffening.

"Why so much violence?" murmured Dominique. "These demonstrators are just kids, not armed combatants."

"A policeman was shot and wounded in Montreal," remarked Catherine hesitantly.

"A policeman is *supposed* to have been shot and wounded in Montreal," corrected Antoine, frowning. "No reporters saw him afterward, and I wouldn't have believed it even if they *had* shown him publicly. Not even if they'd produced the sniper with a confession. They can make anyone say anything."

"You're exaggerating," Dominique said. "They couldn't even prove that Martel was a Northern agent."

"Martel?" murmured Catherine, lost again.

Christine leaned toward her. "The one who tried to blow up the parliament buildings in '83."

"It was before the implants, that's all," said Antoine to Dominique, as Christine was speaking. "Today, with implants, Martel would confess."

Catherine shuddered. Implants? Her dream . . . another anticipated memory?

"Martel was handed over to the Enclave immediately and judged there," said Dominique. "There are limits to—"

"What do you mean, limits?" Antoine glared at her indignantly. "There are no limits. Don't tell me you're be-

ginning to believe their propaganda! They control the Enclave, too."

"That's a pretty strong statement," protested Dominique.

"The Enclave isn't any more sympathetic than the
provincial government, as far as the North is concerned.
They work together against it. Even you have to admit
that!"

Catherine listened to this exchange, hardly daring
to breathe, miserable at the realization that her memory was again hopelessly inadequate, or that since she'd
last seen them (when was that?) her friends had developed differences of opinion she didn't know anything
about. At the same time, another part of her mind was
recording the facts with curiosity, and she heard herself say smoothly, "It was only Expansionists who
were demonstrating in Montreal, not Northern partisans."

Antoine turned on her. "But the official position in
Quebec-City and the Enclave is that the *North* is using
brain implants among other control techniques, and
therefore Enclave demonstrators are obviously manipulated by the North!"

"Are they?"

Antoine stared at her with disbelief.

"Some of them are in touch with Northern agents,"
broke in Charles-Henri, unusually circumspect. "But the
. . . official policy of the North doesn't include fomenting
unrest."

"What does it include?"

"Changing hearts and minds."

"One doesn't exclude the other."

Charles-Henri hesitated, visibly perplexed. "You
know very well that they don't advocate violence!"

Catherine gave him an artificial smile. "Let's pretend
I don't know. Give me a detailed explanation." She
couldn't stop her voice from grating harshly, and Charles-
Henri stared, completely at a loss for words.

Christine laid a firm hand on Catherine's arm "Catherine has a problem," she said decisively. "Recently she's
been having memory lapses. It's better to say it right out,
Cat, so there'll be no misunderstanding."

Catherine, head lowered and muscles tensed, nodded her agreement.

"You mean to say you don't remember. . . ."

"Maybe I once knew something about Northern political ideology, but I don't now. Not a thing." She clenched her teeth. "I had to find out what the North was from the college data bank."

"The data bank?" There was a note of alarm in Charles-Henri's voice.

"Yes. Why? Is it also under surveillance?"

Charles-Henri didn't react to her aggressive tone, merely nodding and keeping his eye on her.

"An Adept spoke to us in the shopping center yesterday," said Christine suddenly. "He told Catherine she was in danger."

Charles-Henri and Antoine exchanged rapid glances. "Tell us," Charles-Henri said.

Catherine stared at her friends, one after the other. It was unbelievable—everyone totally serious, the children all ears, the Christmas tree twinkling in the background . . . and they all looked as if they understood . . . God knows what! The whole thing was absurd, crazy, grotesque!

The whole thing was a huge chunk of missing memory.

She threw herself back in the sofa and folded her arms, desperately trying to control her trembling body. She closed her eyes and began to tell them everything in a monotone, everything, from the beginning.

When she had finished, there was a long silence. She opened her eyes. There would be no answers here either, she realized, flinching at the thought. In a confused way she'd hoped they could help her. But no, their faces all registered the same puzzlement. A chilling sense of calm permeated her. She was alone. She'd have to get out of this predicament all by herself.

Antoine spoke first. "But they don't know about all this," he said thoughtfully. "Only what her psychomedic knows. And the data bank, that's not so serious. Perhaps she's fairly safe. A lot depends on earlier incidents. And she certainly has no previous record. The writing workshop is hardly a subversive incident, is it?"

"Isn't the fact of knowing *you* subversive enough?" remarked Catherine, testing the ground and pleased to note that her voice didn't shake.

Charles-Henri pulled an amused face. "We're discreet."

"We?"

"The Believers," said Christine.

"Are you part of this 'we'?"

"No, she isn't," said Charles-Henri, smiling affectionately at Christine. "But she has an open mind. To tell the truth, Antoine and I aren't really Believers, either. Sympathizers at most. I think their doctrine makes a lot of sense."

"Which doctrine?" asked Dominique, slightly defiant.

Charles-Henri burst out laughing—his special laugh, the delighted chuckle of a child who is surprised and likes it. He leaned toward Catherine and winked. "There are several. Too many for Dominique."

"She already has enough problems with her own church," remarked Annette, seated at her mother's feet.

"You should thank your lucky stars she's not a Unicist," retorted Bertrand. "She'd be in over her head!"

Antoine chortled. "You're right: Is Jesus an androgyne or a hermaphrodite? Tune in to our next gripping episode!"

Catherine listened to them, feeling a little at sea. The atmosphere had suddenly changed: this was a familiar topic, one you didn't fight about, good for friendly teasing.

"Since Dominique's ordination, they won't let her alone," Christine said. Then, a little embarrassed by Catherine's blank look, she added, "Dominique was ordained as a priest last year."

"Priestess," noted Antoine, raising a finger.

"But they say priest," chorused the children.

Dominique shook her head with a smile. "It's not labels that matter," she added in a singsong voice.

"It's the sacred calling!" chanted the children in response.

The general laughter was hushed by the expression

on Catherine's face. "Please don't mind me," she said.
"Tell me all about it."

They were all content to let Dominique explain the
difficulties within the Catholic hierarchy. The progressive
wing was insisting that the strictly egalitarian interpretation of the Infants be re-adopted, and was fighting to have
the term "priestess" accepted as the official designation
for ordained women.

How strange it all sounded! "It is usual for priests to
be women?" Catherine asked diffidently.

"It's usual for women to be priests," Dominique
stated.

Catherine noted the correction, aware of its
implication—I don't think women should be priests, was
that it? And yet I seemed to be so very knowledgable
about religions, yesterday. . . .

"What about the Unicist religion?"

Antoine burst out laughing. "Don't hold your breath!
Unless they decide Jesus was a hermaphrodite, in which
case they might consider female pastors."

"They have their own progressive wing," explained
Bertrand solemnly.

"The presbyteries are hotbeds of intrigue!" Annette
chimed in, giggling.

Dominique was mildly reproachful. "A religion that
doesn't question itself is a dead religion."

"And the Northern religion? Or religions?" asked
Catherine, astonished to find herself feeling almost
amused once more. Was it just a nervous reflex? All right,
then; it was more convivial, in any case.

Christine must have sensed her change of humor, because she stood up with a smile. "Well, people, could we
continue the discussion while we eat?"

They moved to the table amid cheerful confusion.
Soon the conversation fell into other channels, as though
they wanted to give themselves or Catherine a breathing
space. She was grateful. The awful feeling of solitude that
she'd experienced earlier in the evening was nearly gone.
These were her friends, after all, even if they didn't comprehend her situation very well. They'd try to help her,
she was sure. They would all try to understand or at least
explain what the trouble could be.

As the meal progressed, however, she felt a growing impatience to pick up the earlier conversation. Nevertheless, she forced herself to wait until the dessert was served. It came—a splendid Christmas log-cake made of three different kinds of chocolate. By then it was almost midnight, and the children were clamoring to open their presents now instead of waiting until morning. She let herself be drawn into the general excitement, deliberately at first, then with growing enthusiasm. It was with genuine delight that she received everyone's gifts—each an unexpected pleasure, as thoughtfully chosen as hers to them. Afterward Annette insisted on trying out her new synthesizer, and Antoine, being a musician by trade, felt he had to show her "Silent Night." Dominique began singing in her high, clear voice, joined by Christine's full contralto and Charles-Henri's smooth bass. They moved on to other Christmas songs. Catherine sang along with the others, her memory keeping up fairly well, but when there was a pause she said firmly, "Now, what about those Northern religions?"

They turned toward her as though they didn't understand what she was talking about. Shaken, she repeated, "The Northern religions. We were talking about them earlier, don't you remember? You were supposed to jog my memory."

Recollection dawned in Charles-Henri's black eyes first, and then the faces of the others lit up, although there was a lingering puzzlement on some. Catherine tried to catch Christine's eye, but her friend was looking elsewhere. Perhaps Christine didn't remember their discussion yesterday about the so-easily-forgotten Athana. Struggling to master her distressed disbelief and the anger that threatened to replace it, Catherine settled more deeply into her chair and forced herself to smile. "All right, who's first?"

December 26

Nearly three o'clock in the morning, a pounding headache and almost equally painful hyperlucidity. Only a few sheets of paper in my bag, and I can't use Dominique's computer at this hour to update my electronic dairy. So let's summarize. Extraordinary difficulty keeping the conversation on track. Everyone always running off on tangents, with me continually herding them back to the subject. Felt like a collie with a bunch of sheep. At first, hurt: can't they pay attention? Then suspicious: are they trying to hide something? At last I understood. It was like Christine with Athana. Not a deliberate evasion, simply a symptom of rather subliminal uneasiness. Sometimes they seemed surprised, not so much by the kind of questions as by the mere fact of my asking. At other times it seemed as though they'd suddenly discovered a blind spot within themselves—I began to have some hope—but no, they'd go off onto another tangent. By the end of the evening I gave up pushing them where they were plainly incapable of going.

Charles-Henri, Antoine, Dominique—and Christine! My best, my only friends, and no way to talk with them! Not because I didn't want to, but because they *couldn't*!

No handwringing, haven't enough paper. At least make a note of the information gained, although it's little enough. The North, politics and religions. Main impression: great confusion, possibly more the messengers than the message. Nothing new. Pacifism, nonaggression, concern for the ecology. Anything else is "Canadian propaganda." Almost succeeded in getting them to admit to the existence of a more radical movement willing to use violence, but they started discussing the deeper Northern philosophy among themselves. It's linked to Northern religion. Or religions. They have different views on this (Dominique holds one, the rest another). *Grosso modo:* Northern religions are a bastard version of Catholicism (for which Dominique criticizes them), with elements borrowed from poorly-digested Asiatic religions. Nothing to do with a continuation of the Old Testament, in any case. In the beginning there is a Sleeping Deity (?) who created the world and the Infants while sleeping (or maybe it was the Infants who created the world). A hundred different interpretations as to the nature of the Infants, but everyone agrees on one thing: there is a male Infant and a female Infant, and both are still walking around on this earth in one form or another.

On the Infants' role, hundred of opinions and as many sects! For example, the Book Adepts belong to the Ultimist sect—a crackpot fringe, according to Antoine (Christine and Charles-Henri don't agree). Their creed: the Infants will fuse into the Ultimate Infant, whose coming will be heralded by various portents. All the sects seem to agree on one thing, though: the Sleeping Deity must be wakened. Then it will *confirm* the reality of this world, which as far as I can understand is an illusion at present. A fairly bizarre variation on the Vishnu myth: there, the world disappears when the sleeper awakes, whereas in the Northern religion it's the opposite. Logical, though, for a culture that is supposedly pacifist: why interfere with the affairs of this world if it's just an illusion? No, no, they all protested, pacifist doesn't mean passive. What the Believers want to do is convert the blind Southerners to another kind of action, the Quest for Liberation. (Politics in the South have something to do with the magical *maya* of the Vedas, then?) Many different versions of this quest, but in general it has something to do with discovering within yourself characteristics of both Infants. The goal is their fusion (or perhaps the characteristics of one win out over the other—not clear, either). This is meant to speed up—I suppose through sympathetic magic—the Infants' own Quest (or the victory of one over the other) and the completion of their task: i.e., the awakening of the Deity and the confirmation of the world's existence, or some such thing. Or else it's a question of "opening up to the future reality" of the world, and thus helping this reality to come about.

Other elements borrowed from Hinduism: the Infants have supernatural powers—reincarnation, immortality. Telepathy, too—we're into theosophism, now! Tried to get Charles-Henri to admit that it was a bit redundant—reincarnation *and* immortality—but according to him they're not the same thing at all. Why not? He quickly changed the subject. These Infants are clearly a bastardized version of Jesus and Lilith—odd, in a religion that wants to get away from the Bible! Not entirely kosher, their Lilith, if I may say so. More likely a heresy from the early Christian era, in which the Infant Lilith of the New Testament is the reincarnation of a first Lilith that God created before Adam, but Adam found her too independent for his liking, so God replaced her with the more accommodating Eve. . . . And yet the Northern religion considers the Infants as equals. Or at least the dominant sect does, the Believers. In others, Jesus is Good, Lilith Evil; and in still others it's the opposite. More remnants of medieval heresies eliminated by the Catholic church. They must be having a fine old time of it in the North with all these sects, I said. Not at all, retorted Charles-Henri. Everyone is free to find his or her own way toward Liberation. I'm skeptical.

Most of all I wonder how this religion got going. The North is supposed to have been settled by Catholic francophones who intermarried with Amerindians. As far as I know, the Amerindian religion of this region hasn't much in common with Hinduism. Was there some prophet, some individual who saw the light and who concocted and disseminated this doctrine through the North at one point? They don't know. How long has this religion been extant? They don't know.

The only interesting digression came from Christine on the subject of visions. She is right: the Northern religion takes very kindly to visions, the idea being that if the present world isn't the right one, and if the Infants are fighting over who'll determine the reality of the world to come, it's only natural to find the empirical framework heaving a little and visions slipping in through the cracks!

But when I tried to push the question of visions, I hit a wall. It was beyond them to envisage a rational, scientific explanation of visions. Even Sarah's "symbolic" hypothesis, the so-called softest kind, got almost no reaction. Antoine launched into a diatribe against psychomedics being Establishment watchdogs, and Christine went on about anticipated memories and their being among the signs collected by the Adepts, who apparently also spy on the psychomedics to keep abreast of visions, dreams, and other "indications of the reality to come." But why would the Southern government think this threatened law and order, since it doesn't believe in the reality to come? Well, said Antoine, everything that doesn't agree with the dominant materialist ideology and breaks down people's mental stability is considered a threat, that's all. And off he went into another tirade about the implants that the Canadian government accuses the North of using, this being an out-and-out lie, since it was the South, not the North, that reportedly undertook research into this technology five years ago. This fact was leaked somehow, after which the government pretended it had initiated research in order to understand and combat this "new Northern weapon," and that was the last anyone heard of it. According to Antoine, this is clearly part of a vast government conspiracy to manipulate and control society.

And that's why Joanne Nasiwi wants to recruit me, because my "unusual visions" make me an antisocial element? Well, I have no love for the present Canadian version of law and order, but the idea's ridiculous, all the same!

They all seemed genuinely worried about me, though, even Dominique, who appears to be the most moderate in the group. That's what really gets to me: they all seemed so sincere. My question, my doubts, my sarcastic remarks when I couldn't take it anymore, nothing registered for long in their minds. A hesitation, a slight pause, that rather clouded expression in their eyes, a little lost, and then they'd go back to their original position. I even said straight out that they could be seen as brainwashed by Northern propaganda. Charles-Henri smiled indulgently and said it couldn't be very effective since it wasn't consistent enough. I was speechless, although it *is* an argument, I suppose. Charles-Henri and Antoine are of the same mind—more "politicized," if such a term still has any meaning here—but Charles-Henri is more of a pacifist than Antoine, Christine is more mystical than Charles-Henri, and Dominique tries with difficulty to reconcile her Catholic faith and her Northern sympathies. They certainly aren't unanimous! But it could also be said that since the aim of the North is to destabilize the South, all means are acceptable and confusion is as effective a tool as any.

Highly effective in my case, anyway!

It's a good thing writing puts things in perspective for me! Feelings, anyway, if not ideas. Here I am, almost calm, and even my headache has virtually disappeared. Four-thirty. Time to go to sleep.

6

___

She woke early, around ten o'clock, feeling rested and in pretty good shape considering the previous night. She seemed filled with a purposeful energy, perhaps the result of knowing for certain she'd be alone in trying to discover what was really happening to her. She whistled as she entered the tiny bathroom under the eaves, took off her nightgown, ran the shower, then stepped under it. She soaped herself and shampooed her hair, smiling all the while. There was nothing like running water to put her in a good mood. Or water, period. She really must start going to the Y pool again when she got back to Montreal. She began scrubbing her head vigorously, eyes closed beneath the steaming jet of water.

Her fingers encountered a bump, above and a little behind each ear. And two others at the front of her skull.

She explored them, dumbfounded. Each tiny bump had the same circular shape.

She rinsed herself off quickly, toweled herself with equal haste, and wiped the steam off the sink mirror. The bumps on top of her skull were too far back for her to see by parting her hair. She fumbled in her toilet bag for her make-up mirror and held it up to examine her skull once more. Yes, two small, round whitish scars. And above the ears . . . the same thing.

Her hand trembled as she put the mirror down on a

shelf, trying not to drop it. She leaned against the sink. They couldn't be implants! And why would she only notice them now?

The index in the history book—it had been there all the time, but she hadn't realized it at first, either. And the dream about the demonstration . . . but that was a *dream*! And even if it had been a memory of the past instead of the future, when would these implants have been inserted? Defective implants, too, since even in a dream she had remembered the operation. And who had inserted them? The Canadian government? Why? Because she was an antisocial element, as Antoine had said last night, and the government wanted to brainwash her?

And nobody had the slightest inkling of this—either at the college or here, among her most intimate friends? Maybe everyone had been given implants to make them forget . . . but that was perfectly silly. And if she *had* been given government implants, they weren't much good— they may have interfered with her memory, but they hadn't inhibited her insubordinate tendencies! Or were the implants just beginning to be defective and that was why she'd noticed them?

Maybe I made them come on my own, dreamed about an operation (they talked about implants yesterday evening) and developed the scars. Like the stigmata of victims of hysteria or people who undergo hypnosis. A touch on the hand, the suggestion that it's a white-hot rod, and blisters form. I'm going mad. Totally bonkers and hysterical to boot—certifiably hysterical.

But why do the scars seem so old? Because I *made* them seem old?

She turned on the cold tap and splashed her face with water. KEEP CALM. There must be a reasonable explanation. An accident, she'd had to have an operation but didn't remember it. Christine and Dominique would surely know. Ask them first whether they could actually see the scars. Too bad if I wake them up. Confirm the fact. One thing at a time. Proceed in an orderly, scientific manner.

She slipped into her dressing gown and clambered down the small staircase. Everything was deathly quiet on the first floor. Undeterred, she walked up to Christine and Dominique's door and lifted a bent index finger to knock.

The front doorbell rang. Surprised, Catherine glanced through the curtains of the window overlooking the square. Two black cars were parked in front of the house. Beside the first stood two men in bulky khaki parkas.

Catherine started back from the window. The doorbell rang a second time as she ran across the upstairs hall and up to her room. Get dressed—glasses, thick pullover, socks, slacks, boots, ski jacket, gloves, fur cap. Toss the diary pages and diskette into her bag. Money, papers, all there. Wait until Christine started down the front stairs grumbling, "Coming, coming," as the bell pealed steadily. Tiptoe down behind her, nip across the front hall into the back passage and through the small door leading to the basement. Hear the front door open, a male voice say, "Police," close the door, pull the string for the light, and start down the uneven stone steps. Once in the basement, head straight for the murky back cellar, move the empty cardboard boxes piled against the wall. See the outline of the door beneath the dust and spiderwebs. Locked. No door handle. Go back to the workbench along one wall and calmly choose the right tool as heavy boots hammer on the ceiling. Work the tool into the lock until it clicks, pull open the door, slip into the slightly damp, earthy-smelling darkness—the disused seventeenth-century passage—stick an arm through to replace a few boxes, and close the door.

Black. Not really. An almost subliminal, greenish-blue glow illuminates the walls of a narrow space. There are sources of infrared radiations almost everywhere—vents, pipes, electric wires that give off energy as well: the underside of the house. Half-crouching, Catherine runs unerringly through the little passage. Her body knows exactly where east is, as well as west, south, and north, knows exactly where it is and where it's going, and she lets it lead her, bewildered and terrified by all these certainties that she doesn't understand, by the icy calm that has filled her from the moment she saw the cars and men in the square. In her head, like a blueprint overlaying the semidarkness, she sees a map with a network of red lines and knows they represent the tunnels under the Upper Town, those of the French Quarter *there*, the tunnel under St. Michael Square *here*, crossing the disused passage *here* (she kicks open the grating over the opening, drops down into the main tunnel), and *this* right turn will get her to the series of underground stairs going diagonally through the cliff down to the port. And in the port is the Argonauts' Tavern, the address given her by Joanne Naiswi.

7

It wasn't far from the Ramsay Bridge, at the point where the St. Charles estuary had been dredged and widened to build the main north shore port installation. On this Christmas morning all was silent beneath the snow. Traffic lights blinked on and off imperturbably for the absent traffic. Lewis Avenue was deserted, and not a hydroglider was to be seen on the ice road that had been cleared along the river. Puffs of creamy smoke mounted slowly from the buildings toward the white sky, only to curve softly onto a horizontal plane as they hit the atmospheric inversion layer. The weather was bitterly cold despite the lack of wind, and Catherine hurried along, huddling into her parka.

The ugly buildings of the waterfront section huddled together, flat façades with blind windows, mysterious shops squeezed between warehouses and sleazy boarding houses where sailors with a night or two of shore leave amused themselves. The tavern shone out in the midst of this dinginess like a peacock in the middle of an ostrich herd—a one-story building tucked between two tall, cube-shaped warehouses. It sported a thirty-yard mural, an orgy of color featuring an improbably blue sea on which some kind of trireme sped proudly along, sails billowing in the wind, with "Argonauts" inscribed in pseudo-Greek lettering on the side of the

boat. Jason and his intrepid mariners could be seen
leaning on the gunwales, dressed in striped jerseys like
seventeenth-century buccaneers, complete with three-
cornered hats and eyepatches.

Catherine had no illusions, but she tried the door
anyway. Locked. No doorbell, of course. Someone should
be there, though, unless Joanne Nasiwi was really a
phony conspirator and the address useless. Better go
around the block first, past the warehouse—yes, a delivery lane, snow piled high on either side with two deep
ruts in the middle, frozen hard as steel. Unlike the flamboyant front of the tavern, the back was adorned only by
sheets of tin. She saw a pair of low double doors and a
doorbell. The button on the bell wouldn't move. Frozen?
She kicked the door several times. It must be thick, judging by the dull thuds.

"*What is it?*" queried an English voice from the wall.
Catherine gave a start, then noticed the small intercom
grille that had looked to her like just another spot of
grime. "Joanne Nasiwi," she said, with a momentary hesitation.

Silence. The sound of bolts being drawn, the door
opening, a slice of darkness releasing a gust of warm air.
Catherine held out the photo, address side up, and a
large, male hand grabbed it. The door opened wider.
"Come in quick, I'm freezing my balls off!" growled the
voice, this time in French, although with a strong English
accent.

Light suddenly flooded the room into which Catherine stepped. It was the tavern storeroom, containing racks
filled with large jars of pickles, sacks of noodles and rice,
various bottles, cases of beer, and soft drinks. It was
warmer than the outside, but that wasn't saying much.
She took off her foggy glasses and was able to make out
a man standing on the other side of the shelves, a hand on
the light switch. He was a hairy six-footer with a black
beard, a little paunchy, in slippers and black pajamas,
with an orange parka thrown over his shoulders. His
other hand held a door open. "Through here."

The passage smelled of stale cooking oil and cheap
wine. Wiping her glasses as she walked, Catherine followed her guide through a kitchen with big, shiny stoves

and caught a glimpse of the actual tavern, a dim cavernous space that seemed immense. They entered a tiny office with walls almost entirely covered with flyblown notes, bundles of paper, posters for old shows, and beer advertisements.

Catherine sat down and unzipped her parka, calmly removing her gloves and cap and placing them on the floor beside her. She folded her arms, a picture of self-confidence that was entirely lost on the bearded man, who had subsided into another armchair behind a cluttered desk and was yawning as he rubbed his face. He still had the photo, and now examined the other side before handing it back to Catherine. "Who's that?"

His tone was strangely neutral. Catherine took the photo and gave a start. It was one of those photographs from the beginning of the century, brown and ocher on thick cardboard. He's young, seventeen. Seated in an armchair, half facing the camera, on a balcony looking out on the rooftops. Despite the suit, he isn't at all stiff—legs crossed, one hand resting carelessly on the arm of his chair while the other is held under the chin but not touching it. Slightly affected, all the same: he's posing for the photographer. Even so, a lock of blond hair has fallen on his forehead, and the seemingly insolent half smile is really just timid. His clear gaze is fixed on a distant point—on the blue line of the Vosges mountains, but he doesn't know that yet; he's a student at the École des Hautes Etudes Commerciales, with all his life before him. Paris, 1913. The following year his brutal adoptive father will enlist him in the French Army without so much as a by-your-leave, to fight in the War to End All Wars.

Catherine put the photograph back on the desk. "It's my father."

"Your father."

Didn't he believe her? Catherine stared at the bearded man. "Joanne wrote your address on the first thing that came to hand," she snapped. "She told me I could come here in an emergency. This is an emergency. The police are after me."

"In uniform or not?"

"Not."

The bearded man was chewing pensively on his mustache. "May one ask why?"

"Will you throw me out if you don't like my answer?"

"No, but it'll tell me who to contact."

Catherine hesitated. The sense of calm that had kept her going this far was beginning to crumble. Couldn't these personality shifts last just a bit longer? "To tell the truth, I really don't know. I've been having . . . weird visions."

The bearded man nodded as though this last piece of information solved his problem. "I see." He yawned again, then scratched a hairy stomach as he stood up. "You can stay here while I get in touch with the right person."

He led Catherine into a sort of cubbyhole—an arched gable, really, fairly high. There was a mattress on the floor, a table and a chair. An upside-down case of Pepsoda served as a night table.

"Here you are," he said, as though he'd just opened the door to the royal suite in the Château Pitt. "Are you hungry? Since I'm up anyway, I may as well make breakfast. It'll be served in the tavern. My name is Max, by the way."

"Catherine," she said to the massive back as he walked away.

She put her parka and other things on the bed, sat down at the table, and ran her fingers through her hair. It was still damp. If I escape without catching pneumonia, I'll be lucky. She suddenly felt empty—the reaction to pumping all that adrenaline. She dropped her head onto her folded arms and tried to think about what she was going to do. Was there anything she *could* still do? No doubt about it: she'd put herself in the hands of people who'd act for her, do things. Do what? Get her out of Quebec, send her to the North? She straightened up with an inarticulate cry of protest. Never! It was absurd, this couldn't be happening to her—why on earth had she run off like that? She didn't even know what those plainclothes men wanted. They weren't after her—the police thought she was staying at the Éthier-Domville house, not at Christine's! Maybe they were coming to . . . check out a name Athana had given them, that was it, Christine's name!

With two cars and a paddy wagon? At almost the same moment a sudden fear chilled her heart. Christine. Dominique. The children. Had she unwittingly exposed them to danger? Telephone—no, of course not, or not right away. But why would they be in danger?

As if imbued with a will of their own, her fingers touched the small lump of a scar on top of her skull. Because they'd harbored a brainwashed criminal or a Northern agent about to self-destruct?

A Northern agent was the most likely, all things considered. This sudden ability to get her bearings, first in Montreal, then here. The old underground passage— Christine might have told her about that. But the underground map ... she hadn't been seeing things, nor had she made it up. It was a good map, she hadn't got lost. Where did it come from? In any case, it has appeared when needed, presto! like magic, like her sudden talent for commando combat during the demonstration, to say nothing of her ability to shed someone shadowing her on the Rue Notre-Dame. Weren't those the sort of talents spies had? But who was she spying for? North or South? If Joanne Nasiwi wanted to help her, they must be on the same side. Perhaps the government wanted to catch her because she possessed some information. A waste of time, in that case! Unless her memory unexpectedly returned. Or maybe she was supposed to infiltrate the Northern spy network. But if so, how long had she been spying for the South? And—

"Grub's on!" shouted Bearded Max from afar.

Catherine got up with a sigh and went out into the corridor, rubbing the small of her back. She ached all over. The smell of eggs and toast made her stomach twist in knots, and she glanced at her watch. Past noon. She followed the smells into the tavern. All the lights were on, and she stopped at the door, transfixed. The tavern was a gigantic, circular well descending in tiers to a central stage, a good fifteen yards lower down. The seven circular tiers were divided into private booths trimmed with red leather, each with a table. The tiers were linked by staircases with banisters of dark, gleaming wood, carved to represent mermaids, dolphins, and seahorses. On the round stage at the bottom of the well, a girl was dancing silently, her graceful naked body and her long black hair undulating in streaming banners. The projectors caught the mother-of-pearl tints of her gray-pink flesh.

Fascinated by the incongruity of the spectacle, Catherine walked down the stairs. When she reached the foot of the slightly raised stage, the dancer stopped in front of her. Their eyes met and the girl smiled. Her eyes were an impossible purple—contact lenses, probably, and her skin was covered with tiny scales. Glued on? Unlikely—too time-consuming and difficult. A body-suit? It must be made of gossamer, then—a virtual second skin. Catherine was tempted to touch it, but stopped herself in time. She opened her mouth to ask a question, but the girl had moved off and begun dancing again to the soundless music heard by her alone.

"Hey!" shouted Max. "Breakfast is up here!"

She went up the stairs and found Max in a booth on the first tier, seated in front of a plate overflowing with fried potatoes, sausages and eggs. A carafe of orange juice stood in the center of the table, along with a small basket of toast and a plate of butter. "I made you the same. Is that okay?"

"Fine," said Catherine, laughing. There was no third plate; a little surprised, she slipped into the semicircular red padded bench. "What about the young mermaid down there? Has she had breakfast?"

"What young mermaid?" Max said, puzzled and about to stand up to see what Catherine was pointing at.

"The dancer, that young girl down there!"

"He doesn't see her," said a clear, familiar voice behind her.

She turned around. Athana was leaning on the back of the partition, mischievous green eyes, blue dress, white parka and all. Catherine stared at the girl, speechless, then heard herself ask, "And does he see you?"

"How did she get in here?" asked Max, astounded.

"Now he does," Athana said. She took off her parka and sat down on the bench, sliding over close to Catherine. Her breasts seemed to have curves that weren't there the last time Catherine had seen her. But the smile was the same—somewhat timid, but trusting.

"How did you get in?" asked Catherine in turn.

"The back was open," said the young girl.

Max pushed his plate in front of her and stood up, scratching his chest. "I'll go make some more," he growled, sounding vaguely surprised. He took a few steps, then came back. "What did I want to . . . ? Ah, yes!" And he headed for the kitchen.

The dancer had disappeared from the stage.

Catherine watched as Athana explored the plate with a fork, curious at first, then enthusiastic. Her own stomach clamored for attention. She buttered a piece of toast and slipped it into the egg yolks. After several mouthfuls, she gave in to her curiosity. "Did you see the dancer, Athana?"

"Yes. She was beautiful."

"She was a vision, wasn't she?"

"Real. Somewhere else," answered the young girl through a forkful of potatoes.

"But Max couldn't see her."

"Just you and me." A big smile smeared with egg yolk.

"And Max didn't see you, and then he did."

"Just a little."

"Do you mean he's forgotten you already?"

The girl nodded, her lips forming a sad, small *moue*. "Just a little." The smile returned. "When he comes back."

"He'll remember?"

"Yes."

Catherine reached out and touched the girl's cool skin. The girl dropped her fork and held out her hands questioningly. "No, it's all right," said Catherine. "Eat." The girl obeyed. She was real enough—talked, ate. . . .

"How did you find me, Athana?"

The fork stopped in midair, and the smooth, pretty face took on a somewhat puzzled expression. "I don't know."

She's homing in on me? My implants are transmitters?

She has implants?

Max came back carrying a steaming plate. He paused a moment, looked curiously at Athana, sat down, and began to eat.

Catherine passed a hand over the girl's head, feeling for the round scars of implants. Nothing. Athana stroked Catherine's hair in return, smiling at her. Catherine felt a little embarrassed and turned her attention to the contents of her plate.

"Weird visions, eh?" said Max suddenly. "There was a dancer down there?" He studied Catherine, squinting a little.

"Yes, with scales on her skin," said Catherine, continuing to cut her sausage.

"Weird visions," he said by way of confirmation. "And who's this?"

"Athana. She's been following me since I left Montreal. Athana, meet Max."

"Hello Max," the girl said in her clear voice.

He smiled back mechanically. "What kind of a name is Athana?"

"It's my name," replied the girl.

"She doesn't seem to have any other," said Catherine.

"Are the police after her, too?"

"I don't know." Catherine looked at the girl. "Athana, you remember Christine Chantaraine, the young woman who was at the exhibition with me?"

"Your friend. She saw me all by herself," said the girl approvingly.

"Did you give her name to the police?"

Athana shook her head, her mouth being full of sausage. Catherine turned back to Max. "I don't think the police are after her."

"And she's been following you since you left Montreal?"

"I don't know how she finds me, but she's certainly following me." It gave Catherine a perverse kind of pleasure to emphasize the ridiculous nature of the situation by adding, between mouthfuls, "And she keeps growing."

"She keeps growing," murmured Max. Catherine looked up. Max's bearded face wore a curious expression, hesitant disbelief bordering on respect.

"I have particularly twisted visions," she said, disconcerted.

Max shook his head, still staring at Athana who was wiping her plate clean. "She's no vision."

"Really? What is she, then?"

Max stood up and picked up his empty plate and Athana's. "I don't know, but she's no vision."

8

Max went out after their brunch, telling them to stay put. He was probably going to consult the "contact."

"Will you be long?" Catherine asked.

"Dunno," he replied. He was bundled up like someone setting off for the North Pole, which was more or less the case judging by the blasts of wind rocking the building. He turned toward her as he pulled on his gloves. "You can cook something for yourselves if you're hungry. Everything's in the kitchen." Did that mean he wasn't coming back until tonight? "Maybe."

The thought of a whole day of doing nothing rather depressed Catherine. Was there anything to read, she asked? It would be better than passing hours worrying about how things might be developing. "In my bedroom," Max said, waving vaguely at nowhere in particular. As she watched the orange parka disappear, Catherine wondered what she'd do if Max didn't come back. We'll cross that bridge when we come to it, she told herself firmly, heading off on a determined search for the bedroom and the promised books.

To her surprise, the room was lined with shelves. That would teach her to typecast! This huge bearded man of few words was a great reader. Or else he thought books were as good a form of wall insulation as any. Whatever the motive, he possessed all the great French and English classics. Catherine closed her eyes and picked a book at random. Lewis Carroll, *Through the Looking Glass.* Well, why not? The luck of the draw.

Back in her own room, she read the two first chapters. Athana watched her with interest. After a while Catherine's eyes began to prickle, and she handed the book to Athana. "Look at the pictures if you like. I'm going to sleep for a bit."

But the girl snuggled up to her with complete abandon, and Catherine made no objection. Athana would keep her warm, since the blanket was none too thick.

Catherine is dreaming. She knows it's the Dream of the Presence. The beginning skips a lot, as if she's reading a synopsis of previous chapters: she fled, she fell, she tried to impose her own form on the formless thing, realized she couldn't, that she was confronted by another will, by desires unlike her own . . . by fears other than her own? The idea is born gradually, hesitatingly. Can this invisible presence surrounding her know fear? If it's pursuing, enveloping, squeezing, stifling . . . is this to make its fear disappear?

But why would the Presence be afraid? It is immense, all-powerful, it is all things, everywhere.

It is not all things everywhere, though; it isn't me. I don't belong to it, I'm not *of* it. I'm like a thorn in its nonexistent flesh—or possibly it does have flesh, the bluish nonspace surrounding me? I'm an irritant, making it itch, making it angry. Perhaps I'm hurting it. The Presence wants to get rid of me. But it has only to let me go! I can leave. I *want* to leave.

The Presence doesn't want me to leave. It cannot let me leave? The Presence is afraid to let me leave. Catherine can feel it, a terror as immense as the Presence itself: every single atom is terrified, millions and billions of private terrors weeping in unison. And that whirling desire to seize and assimilate, to transform, a desire so intense that it is pain. . . . A sudden compassion mingled with incomprehension flashes through Catherine. She looks into the bluish nonspace, trying to find eyes, hands, a body to which she can say the "you" that spontaneously rises to her lips; but the Presence tightens its hold as though to take advantage of this sudden weakness, shooting out thin, invisible tendrils at Catherine to bind, then penetrate her, dispossess her of herself! Catherine stiffens.

The tendrils shrink back. The Presence is not all-powerful. Surprised and triumphant, Catherine concentrates on this thought. When I fell, it didn't finish me off. When I defied it, it didn't crush me. It wants to seize and transform me, but it doesn't do it. It can't! Because I don't want it to. Its strength and mine are equal: its desire, my rejection. Are we going to stay like this, locked in confrontation?

With every ounce of strength, Catherine wills this question into the nonspace surrounding her. The Presence doesn't respond. And yet there is a subsidence in the incessant movement of its desire, as though the idea of a possible lull has formed, a suspension. And in this relative calm, something diffuses across the nonspace. Catherine isn't sure; it seems like a sharp, penetrating perfume, an acid taste on the tongue, the sudden constriction of taste buds followed by an explosion of saliva. . . . If curiosity has a flavor, a smell, thinks Catherine a little crazily, it's like the taste and smell of lemon. And she suddenly begins to laugh. Curious, that's it: the Presence is curious! The Presence has suspended its appetite and its fear for an instant, and it's curious!

And the nonspace seems to undulate timidly, like a shy smile.

When she awoke in the wan light falling from the dormer, Catherine was surprised to find Athana still sleeping beside her. Before drifting off herself, Catherine had thought the girl would be gone by the time she awoke. She studied her thoughtfully. Has she really grown, as I told Max? She seems so young—seemed so young every time that. . . . But each of Athana's appearances had wiped out the memory of the previous one. The girl slept like a dreaming cat, eyelids quivering, a leg jerking, convulsive movements of the hands folded under the chin. She eats, she dreams, she must be real—an unorthodox definition of existence. Catherine crawled gingerly off the

bed, her spine cracking as she straightened and stood up.
What an idea, putting a bed on the floor! She glanced automatically out the window. It was covered with frost,
but she could tell it was dark outside. She looked at her
watch. Four o'clock in the afternoon. She was feeling
much better. It seemed as though she'd slept longer than
that.

The girl was sleeping with totally admirable conviction! Catherine smiled as she pulled the blanket up over
the bare arms and the slender legs in their white socks.
They'd have to find her something other than this dress.
Catherine went and looked in Max's cupboard, amazed at
how little compunction she felt about snooping among
other people's things. A thick pair of leotards and a mohair pullover of non-Maxian dimensions, two short-
sleeved body-stockings, and a titillating negligee of frothy
black lace. Dancers' leavings. She ignored the negligee and
took the rest back to the room, along with a thick pair of
socks. That would do it.

Athana was still sleeping. Feeling at loose ends, Catherine wandered through the darkened building, switching
lights on and off as she went. The silence was oppressive.
There was a radio as well as a television set and loud-
speakers in the tavern, but she didn't want to wake
Athana. She went back to Max's room, leafed through
two or three books, and finally sat down on the bed with
a sigh, discouraged by the abundance of choice. So this
was the exciting life of a secret agent: being bored stiff for
hours on end while others acted in your place? But I'm
not necessarily a secret agent, Joanne. Maybe just a common criminal. She stood up in disgust, determined not to
embark on useless speculation.

Her eye fell on a small portable radio covered with
dust. She turned it on, not hoping for much. A metallic
whine, Christmas music—oh, *please*! She turned the dial,
crackle, crackle, Christmas music, radio-wave whistles, a
commercial for a local snowmobile outlet, crackle. . . .
There ought to be news somewhere at this hour. She recognized the tag end of the CBC news intro and turned up
the volume. Weather bulletin, blizzard warning for Quebec, Christmas truce all over the world respected more or
less by distant countries where Occidentals were at-

tempting to sort things out, bumbling as usual, trying to settle the aftermath of the war and Reconstruction. The two newscasters, a man and a woman, seemed in a good mood. There must be a party going on in the studio.

The tone became abruptly more serious as the newscaster moved on to the national news. The tranquility of Christmas had been disrupted in Quebec-City, where the empty car of the Undersecretary of State for Immigration had been blown up. The police had several suspects and were arresting people throughout the province, especially in Quebec-City among known Northern sympathizers. In Montreal the Enclave had started a full-scale cleanup operation. According to a well-informed source, a dangerous agent had gone to Quebec-City to carry out the assassination. His capture would no doubt be a severe blow to the Northern terrorist network.

Catherine turned off the radio, hardly knowing whether to be amazed, offended, or amused. "Terrorist network," "dangerous agent"—stink bombs and blown-up cars! And they were using these pretexts to harass citizens, especially francophones, of course. Her heart sank as she thought of Christine and the others. Maybe the police really *had* been coming to arrest them—nothing to do with her at all.

She started as she heard a noise in the back of the building, a door opening, closing, footsteps, two people. Then Max's voice calling in English, "I'm back!" and the almost painful sensation of her taut muscles going limp with relief.

She went out into the passage. Two figures, Max's and a smaller, more delicate one. She guessed just as the light went on: Joanne Nasiwi, wearing the mauve parka and the boots trimmed with colored beads.

"Are you the dangerous secret agent they're talking about on the radio?" asked Catherine rather acidly. She felt annoyed yet relieved at seeing her.

The Métis shrugged. "Not really." She looked along the corridor, then back at Catherine. "You're not alone."

"No. Athana's here." *The little girl who scared you off in the Botanical Gardens the other day?* No. She wasn't sure it was the same girl, after all. "A girl who's been following me."

"Why didn't you tell me, Max?" snapped Joanne, taking off her gloves with impatient haste. "Where is she?"

"I'd ... forgotten," said Max rather sheepishly.

Max hadn't told her? How did she know of Athana's presence, then? Her "You're not alone" hadn't been a question.

"She's sleeping," said Catherine, backing instinctively toward the bedroom.

Joanne pushed her aside and stared briefly at the sleeping girl. She swung around. "Where did you find her?"

"Nowhere," said Catherine drily. "She finds me."

"She finds her ... all the time," said Max from the passage. The words came slowly as his memory returned.

Joanne scrutinized Catherine. "Where did you first see her?"

"With you in the Botanical Gardens."

Joanne nodded. Had she expected this answer? "And after that?"

"In front of my house. Then in the demonstration, when you'd made a date to meet me. We took the bus together but—"

"She had a ticket? A passport?" Why was Joanne suddenly relieved?

"I don't know about a ticket. But no passport."

Joanne's face clouded once more. "And then?"

"She got off at St. Foy, but she found me again at the Royal Museum in the Marru exhibition."

"In the exhibition," muttered Joanne. She had stuffed her hands deep in the pockets of her parka.

"And people seem to have trouble remembering her once she is out of sight," Catherine added, just to see what effect it would have.

A muscle quivered in the brown jaw, but Joanne merely said, "I see."

"I'd like to see, too!" exclaimed Catherine, tired of playing cat and mouse.

Joanne suddenly looked weary as well. "I told you not to come to Quebec." She glanced over her shoulder, then remarked evenly, "She's awake."

Athana, sitting up on the bed in the growing darkness, with her blonde hair streaming over her shoulders, stared at them with friendly curiosity.

"We must get them out of the city," said Max.

"Impossible. It's too risky at the moment."

Catherine felt like saying, "It's all a misunderstanding, I'm going back to Montreal." She said nothing, however; the scars on her skull were a sure sign that the misunderstanding was too serious and too absolute for that.

Joanne stood, hands behind her back and eyes on the floor, apparently meditating a solution. "Keep them here until things have calmed down," she said finally, turning to Max. "We'll get them out afterward."

"But there's a transfer tonight!" protested Max.

"No, cancel it. Too risky. With these two hanging around, the police will double and triple the surveillance. Call the others and tell them to stay where they are and wait until they're contacted."

The huge man shambled off, leaving the two women face to face. Catherine, with a sudden, incongruous calm, examined Joanne's impassive features. "You won't tell me anything, will you?"

"The less you know, the better for everybody," muttered Joanne, turning her eyes away.

"Has it ever occurred to you that you don't know everything about me?"

"Several times," replied Joanne, with a shrug and a small embittered laugh.

Catherine grabbed one of Joanne's hands and placed it on her head, searching until her fingers found one of the round scars beneath the hair. "What's that, in your opinion?" *What am I doing?*

It was the only way to make Joanne talk: take her by surprise.

The cool, hard fingers lifted up the short hair and felt the scars. The Métis suddenly let go of Catherine and stepped back, perplexed. "What is it?"

Surprise tactics, eh? A resounding flop. Or a revelatory one, maybe? She stared hard at Joanne for a moment, but the young woman was genuinely surprised—or else a better actress than Catherine would ever be. She resigned herself to being truthful. "I hoped you'd tell me."

Joanne's eyes widened: "You thought they were implants? Implants don't leave that kind of mark—they're much less conspicuous." A compassionate expression crossed her face and she said more slowly: "You thought they were implants. . . ." Quite unexpectedly, she touched Catherine's arm. "Forgive me if I sounded disagreeable. The circumstances aren't exactly . . . ideal." A brief smile, almost timid. "Don't hold it against me."

"You did tell me not to come to Quebec," Catherine admitted as a peace offering.

Behind them, Athana's clear voice rose, eager and full of hope. "Are we going beyond?"

Catherine couldn't help smiling. "She's always saying that. She seems to like traveling."

Joanne turned round and contemplated the girl, who was still sitting on the bed. Slowly, as though forcing herself, the Métis walked over and crouched down on her heels—the easy hunkering of small children that Catherine had always envied. Joanne turned the bedside light on and silently examined Athana. After a while she stood up, her face inscrutable. "Yes, you are going on a voyage."

Catherine had supposed Joanne would leave after having decreed their fate, but she decided to stay to supper. "Max is a fine cook when he has the time," she remarked. He had enrolled them both as cook's helpers and given them vegetables to chop for the Chinese dish he was preparing. She and Joanne were sitting opposite each other at a table on the top tier of the tavern. The empty, brightly-lit hall echoed as they worked, surrounded by the sweet smell of carrots pared with gusto. This domestic interlude was as strange as anything that had happened these past few days. All it needed was for a scaly-skinned dancer or some other exotic creature to pop up beside them, elbows on the table. But only Athana appeared, sitting down beside them to watch, apparently fascinated, and unaware of the slight stiffening in Joanne.

The atmosphere was one of such friendly conviviality, surely the Métis would open up a little? She was wondering how to make her feel more relaxed when Joanne suddenly spoke with the abrupt tone of someone who has taken a hazardous decision. "What do you know about the North?"

"That its inhabitants are supposed to be pacifists, and that you come from Chicoutimi."

Joanne seemed taken aback by Catherine's terse summary. She smiled thinly. "It's a long time since I left," she murmured, echoing the words of Henri Lapointe.

Catherine was about to ask, "Why did you?" But the time for being polite was past, she decided. "Because you were less of a pacifist?"

Joanne finished paring her carrot with exaggerated care. "Because I'm an atheist."

It was Catherine's turn to be surprised. She tried humor. "Do you mean to say not one of their 258,000 sects suits you—or is it 259?"

Joanne's reaction was a disappointment. She glanced at Athana, began paring another carrot, and finally, in a curiously obstinate tone, replied, "No." Keeping her eyes lowered, she asked, "Do you know about the Quest?"

"Just the bare facts. The Sleeping Deity has to be wakened, right?"

Joanne shrugged a little and frowned. "Yes."

"And you think it would be better to let sleeping deities lie."

"There's no Deity, sleeping or otherwise!" snapped Joanne.

A sensitive point? "And Northerners frown on atheists?"

Joanne made a face. "No," she said in a calmer voice, "but it's annoying. For everyone."

"Annoying enough to want to move to Montreal?"

"I could be useful there without being annoyed. Or annoying."

Catherine attacked the celery. "And what does a 'not really' Northern agent do?"

Joanne laughed heartily, genuinely amused this time. "You still don't believe me?"

"Everything seems too much of a coincidence, that's all."

"Do you think I've got time to waste blowing up cars?" said Joanne disdainfully.

"And what about not turning up for our meeting in the restaurant?"

"They had me under surveillance. Those young rebels are pretty paranoid. Not that they haven't cause, mind you."

Catherine laid several stalks of celery side by side and began chopping them with a large knife. "And what did you have to tell me that was so important?"

"That you really were in danger. You're convinced, now."

Catherine thought about this for a moment. "Not really."

"What more do you want?"

"Well, I'd like to understand *why* I'm in danger, for example."

The two women eyed each other momentarily over the vegetables.

"Understand," said Athana thoughtfully.

They both gave a start and turned to look at her in surprise, but Athana had dreamily taken up the pieces of Joanne's last carrot and was trying to put them together again. Catherine went on with her work, although she saw that Joanne was staring at the girl in a daze, or so it seemed. To hell with the niceties. "Athana seems to upset you a lot," she blurted out.

Joanne set to work on another carrot with exaggerated concentration. "It will be difficult enough to get you to Louisiana. Two people double the risk."

"She practically made you run away in the Botanical Gardens."

"Of course not!" Joanne retorted with a shrug. "I had to take some cultures out of the incubator. That sort of thing can't wait."

She wasn't going to let herself be pushed into admitting anything. Perhaps another tactic might work.

"But you remember her. Everyone who sees her forgets her almost as soon as they've turned their backs."

"Some people have that effect," Joanne said. "Do you remember our first meeting? You felt you already knew me, didn't you?"

Catherine stopped chopping, astonished. "Yes."

"Me too. With Athana, it must be the opposite."

"But why?"

"It's just like that."

"An awful lot of things are 'just like that,' in my opinion!" remarked Catherine. "Athana, visions, anticipated memories. . . ."

"You've had anticipated memories?" said Joanne with a start.

"Technically speaking, only one, as far as I'm aware," said Catherine. The implant dream couldn't count, could it? "You know the Royal Museum's exhibition on the Marrus?" Better say it as simply as possible: "I dreamed about it."

"About the exhibition?"

"About the world of the Marrus. Why? Does it make a difference?"

Joanne nodded, eyes thoughtful as they rested on Catherine. Or perhaps calculating? "It's never exactly what you've seen before. Or dreamed," she added as an afterthought.

"Do you mean visions come true, as well as dreams?" That wasn't what Christine had said.

"Yes. Sometimes."

"Government manipulation?"

"There have always been visions."

"What proof is there?"

Joanne looked at Catherine with renewed interest. "Well, documentary evidence is difficult to find, especially in the South, what with the Index; but I've seen documents going back at least to the sixteenth century."

"The government is keeping track of visions."

"And it's trying to control heterodox visions by eliminating those who have them, yes. I've thought about it, believe me. But if the government were the source of normal visions, the motivation and techniques would be very hard to establish. Implants are a fairly recent development, and they have nothing to do with visions."

"You've thought about it," said Catherine, intrigued and relieved, remembering her frustrating conversations with Christine and the others the previous night. "You've wondered about it, too? Not many people do, it seems."

"Some people are like that," said Joanne with a joyless little smile.

Catherine watched her attentively. "Annoying people."

The black eyes rested on hers, suddenly warmer. "Very annoying."

They really smiled, this time, and went on slicing vegetables in an almost conspiratorial silence that Catherine was unwilling to break right away. She wasn't the only one to ask herself questions: the knowledge was comforting. On the other hand, it would have been nice to have a few answers before being shipped off to Louisiana!

Her hand came to rest on the red pepper she'd been about to eviscerate. *Shipped off to Louisiana.* Until now, those words had been just words, but suddenly the realization hit her. She had come to Quebec-City for a ski trip and she was going to end up a fugitive in *Louisiana* because people she'd never met, engaged in clandestine struggles she knew nothing about, thought her visions were "weird"? She hadn't asked for any of it, the visions, the implants, her intermittent memory! Sudden pain pierced her rage: she'd gripped the knife too tightly and cut her thumb. She licked the small cut as Joanne stared curiously, and went back to work on the red pepper. A leaden certainty had replaced her sense of revolt: she wouldn't be able to go back home. Probably never again. Never? Was everything she loved lost—her mother's Thai silk tester above her bed, her books, her music, the box of photographs, and the notebooks and diskettes containing her journal? She had left too many homes already: Paris, Tannerre, Sergines!

And yet she'd stripped her parents' house in the south of France, jettisoning all those things so lovingly collected over several lifetimes, not only by her parents, but by their families. She had allowed them to be dispersed, revirginized, free to build a new history in other lives. She had kept nothing, aware of having to tear herself away from them, yet proud of her resolve. Start from zero, she'd said to herself. No heritage. A liberation, not a loss. No children to give them to, in any case; the line stops with me, and it's just as well. Arrive at zero.

And now she was heartbroken at the thought of her Montreal house that she'd never see again, as though she were abandoning it, betraying a trust? She blinked away the tears. Anger was inappropriate, tears useless. She forced herself to think of more practical considerations, her bank account, for example: was there the slightest chance of taking out all her cash before leaving, or after she'd reached her destination? She asked the question aloud, just to show herself she'd regained her self-control. Joanne looked doubtful. "Maybe once you're in Louisiana, if they forget to freeze your account. But they rarely forget."

They had finished the vegetables. Catherine continued to think about practical considerations as she went back to the kitchen. No money. She would have to appeal to François. Now *there* was one who'd be surprised. But he'd help her, she was sure—to start with, at least. Find somewhere to live, find work. . . . At the thought of this whole existence to be started anew in unknown surroundings, Catherine suddenly felt so disoriented that she was almost dizzy and had to lean against the kitchen doorframe for support.

It all happened very quickly. A loud crash from the direction of the storeroom, the sound of things falling and breaking, several figures looming out of the dark passage, revolvers in hand. "Police. Freeze!" Reflexes snapped on instantly. She threw the two bowls of vegetables in the face of the first man, and with lightning speed knocked his gun hand then punched his solar plexus, automatically exposed as he raised a hand to his face. She felt the blow sink softly into the unexpectedly thick down of his parka, backed into the kitchen to gain momentum, bumped into Max who was coming out, lost her balance, and opted for a sideways retreat. The second policeman had grabbed Athana, who was fighting like a wild beast, silently using her teeth and nails. A third must have gone straight for Joanne, because she was nowhere to be seen in the passage. A fourth entered the kitchen, followed by the first, whose parka was now decorated with celery and sweet peppers. Not in uniform. Only four? Not expecting resistance—ordered to take us alive. Too big and too well padded for me, in any case.

She backed left, away from the door, keeping the stoves behind her, grabbing anything she found on the counter and shelves lining the wall, hurling them at the policemen, and knowing the whole time where she was heading—the hatch into the main room of the tavern. Max had disarmed one of the policemen with a backhanded blow of his frying pan and was dancing in front of him, looking for an opening, but the other was closing in on Catherine, glowering furiously. She heaved electric gadgets at his feet, as well as a row of ketchup bottles that exploded on the floor with a wet thud. While he jumped to avoid them, she did a rolling somersault through the hatchway and landed on the floor of the tavern.

Joanne and a policeman were standing side by side, she with arms folded, looking toward the passage, he turned in the same direction, his weapon pointed away from her. The sound of Catherine's landing made them both jump, and Joanne, as though suddenly awakened, grabbed the man's gun arm. There was a brief explosion, and Catherine felt rather than saw the wood chips flying from the nearest table. She rushed to help Joanne, but the policeman was now on his knees, completely stunned, and Joanne looked as though she could manage quite well on her own. Catherine took a moment to assess the situation in the passage: Athana was still keeping her policeman busy. The two others must be in the kitchen with Max. She looked for the first man's weapon, caught sight of it through the feet of Athana's assailant. Getting by the struggling pair would be difficult, since they took up the full width of the passage. She moved forward, watching for her chance to get an effective stranglehold on the man.

She saw the impact of the bullet in the dark-green parka almost before hearing the shot. The man stiffened, made as though to turn while keeping a grip on Athana, then staggered, looking astonished as he leaned on the girl, hands grasping and slipping as his greater weight pulled her down with him. Athana was on her knees now, still hanging on to him and apparently as surprised as he had been. From the kitchen came a dull thud followed by the crash of cascading crockery. Another policeman burst through the door, saw the two crouching figures at the last moment, tried to jump over them, and fell forward with such momentum that his head crashed against the corridor wall. Catherine turned around to see Joanne with the gun in her hand, arm rigid, and the tripped policeman lying senseless at her feet.

Through the silence came the sound of more preserve bottles crashing, then the clink of metal and china being kicked out of the way. Max appeared in the doorway, covered with flour, his lip split. He glanced at Catherine and Joanne, examined the policeman with the bullet wound, then stood up, shaking his head. He looked overwhelmed. "We're out of here."

He stepped over the two bodies and headed for his room. Catherine sensed that the other Catherine, the combatant, was no longer there. Her heart was pounding, and she felt a sharp pain in her wrist and lower back. As she tried to catch her breath, she leaned over the dying policeman's body.

"Come, Athana," she said. The girl continued to stare at the man without moving. "Come, Athana, we're going beyond," Catherine coaxed. It had no effect. She grabbed Athana's shoulder and shook her, but the girl resisted with surprising force. Catherine realized she wasn't staring at the policeman with horror or pity, but with an intense and totally disproportionate curiosity.

A silent flash exploded at Catherine's feet.

She instinctively leaped backward, but there had been no rush of air, no shock, nothing but a sudden heat and a searing, bluish light. Through the dancing afterimage before her eyes, she saw the man's parka, flattened . . . no, empty!

Thunderstruck and vaguely conscious that Athana was now standing with her back to the passage wall, Catherine was about to kneel down to feel the collapsed parka. A firm hand prevented her, and Joanne's voice spoke from behind. "Go and get dressed."

She obeyed like an automaton, came back wearing her parka, her bag slung across her back, and carrying Athana's white parka and boots. The girl hadn't moved. She was still pressed against the wall, eyes closed, arms held against her chest. Max was back, also dressed for the outdoors, the strap of a big knapsack hitched over one shoulder. He busied himself snapping police handcuffs on the two men in the hall as they groaned and began to come round. Catherine slid along the wall, avoiding the empty garments of the vanished policeman, and grabbed Athana by the arm. At her touch, the girl opened her eyes. She wore a puzzled yet delighted expression. "Blue," she said.

Catherine had no idea what Athana was talking about, and didn't want to know, either. She slipped a parka sleeve over one of the girl's arms. Athana finished dressing herself and smiled at Catherine. "Now we can go beyond." It wasn't a question this time. Catherine merely nodded. Joanne was in the tavern tying up the remaining policeman. When she had finished, she walked over to the bar, took down a full bottle of brandy, and slipped it into her bag. Her eyes met Catherine's. "We'll need it." Her face was stony.

It was dark. Blowing snow swirled in the icy blasts, cutting visibility almost as effectively as fog. The police van stood in the yard—a gray Nordica eight-seater with no particular distinguishing marks and plenty of clearance under the chassis. The interior was still slightly warm. Max took the wheel, turning the starter with a key found on one of the policemen. Catherine had expected to hear a burst of CB crackle, but there was nothing, just an ordinary radio tuned to a rock station. Joanne switched it off as she slid in beside Max. Catherine pushed Athana onto the middle bench. The van started down the alley, bouncing crazily in the ruts, and turned toward the port, going through the yellow light on Lewis Avenue as it headed for the Lower Town and McDonald Boulevard. There was hardly a vehicle in sight. The colored Christmas lights in the shop windows came and went between streamers of blowing snow, phantoms twinkling from either side of the boulevard beyond the long line of traffic lights that changed progressively from green to yellow as they climbed the steep hill to the Upper Town. The van turned right. Catherine made out the bus station and its platforms, with parked buses half hidden by the blowing snow. One, its red breaklights blinking, was either backing out or arriving. It must be the nine o'clock bus for Montreal just coming from the garage. She felt a ridiculous lump in her throat at this reminder of timetables and destinations, all those commonplace little details belonging to a normal life, a life that was now lost to her forever.

The van kept going southward along Brampton—*southeast, actually*. Well, well: was she suddenly able to use the homing-pigeon skills of her alter ego at will? With a small, inward start, she realized she'd used the words alter ego quite routinely, as though it were now a familiar idea. "Another me." She was certainly amassing a collection of psychopathological labels—paranoia, schizophrenia, hysteria, split personality, and what else? Were all these facets of mental disturbance compatible? A good thing having visions was completely normal! She folded her arms to contain the nervous laughter rising to her lips. It must have been a vision in the corridor, a lightning vision—another laugh threatened to burst out. Surely no one else had seen the flash. No one had reacted. Except Athana. Maybe. She glanced at the young girl, who was sitting on the edge of her seat, staring out at the night through the blowing snow. But this was hardly the moment to question an enigma about a mystery. Max had his hands full with driving. And Joanne. . . . What had happened in the tavern? Why had Joanne let herself be arrested without resisting, only to shoot a policeman later? Almost as though expecting the raid to finish without her.

As though she'd expected it to happen in the first place.

An idea to be filed under "paranoia"? But who knew of my whereabouts, apart from Joanne and Max . . . and Athana? Max and Athana fought their attackers, but not Joanne, not really. It doesn't necessarily mean anything; perhaps she'd been paralyzed, overwhelmed, thinking Max had denounced us? No, Joanne isn't the kind to be easily undone. Just an impression, I'm no judge of personality, particularly when it comes to secret agents, but still. . . . No, she was waiting. It would have been so easy to disarm the policeman while he was distracted. And why would his attention have wandered unless he'd known he was safe? And who was Joanne shooting at, anyway?

Catherine hunched into her seat, hugging herself—not so much to keep warm as to preserve her sanity. Talk about sticking one's head in the lion's mouth! And yet everything that had happened since her first meeting with Joanne seemed subtly inconsistent. Cracks, holes, discrepancies, yes, but none of it could really add up to Joanne being a double agent!

Lack of objective evidence. Let's try to get some. "Where are we going?"

"To find the two we're supposed to move tonight," said Max.

"I still think it's a mistake. There may be a general roundup," said Joanne through clenched teeth.

"We'll see when we get there."

So Max was the one in charge. His voice was calm. Did he suspect something, too?

"And then?"

"Toward the Saguenay."

"Beyond!" Athana said with satisfaction.

Joanne turned and gave the girl an exasperated glance. "This is utter madness. The checkpoints are going to be tighter than ever, and we don't have papers for the girl. We should have left *her* behind, at least!"

"No way," Catherine heard herself state without even thinking.

"Especially not the girl," said Max.

Joanne gave a disgusted grunt and turned her face to the window. "It's absolutely ridiculous. She's just a crazy kid."

"In which case we still can't leave her behind."

"If she isn't retarded, what is she?" murmured Catherine innocently.

Silence. Would Max let slip something revealing? Or Joanne? Max: "I don't know, really. But we can't leave her, that's all."

Not very revealing.

"Max loves to dream," sneered Joanne. The bearded man remained impassive. It was getting increasingly difficult to negotiate the streets. Despite studs on the tires, the van skidded and swerved on the snowdrifts. Impossible to see the street signs as they passed by a succession of intersections, small buildings, and the white spaces between where cars huddled like sheep in the whirling snow. Max turned off the headlights and began driving even more slowly. Oddly enough, it was almost easier to see with just the reflection of the street lights on the snow. There were no parked cars along the street. Max pulled up in front of a building that was indistinguishable from the others. "Seems okay to me," he said, pulling on his hat and stepping out. Wind and snow gusted briefly through the open door.

Joanne slid into the driver's seat and peered through the window. Catherine watched her, feeling exhausted. What do I do if she drives away without waiting for Max? Strangle her from behind? Jump out? I should have kept one of the revolvers.

Hysteria rising, Catherine?

But the Métis didn't move. After an eternity, shapes loomed out of the driving snow. Max and two smaller figures, one shorter than the other. Joanne stayed in the driver's seat and Max climbed into the middle seat, pushing Athana over beside Catherine. The taller of the two others took the passenger seat, while the second pushed the sliding door on the side of the van wide open. Catherine bent over to protect herself from the sudden rush of wind. The figure climbed aboard, lugging two large knapsacks. He tossed them into the baggage compartment at the back of the van, slammed the door shut, and sat down in the rear seat.

The van moved off. The passenger in the front seat struggled out of his parka. A familiar odor assailed Catherine's nostrils. Cinnamon and mint. The cut of the frizzy hair was also familiar. She leaned over and saw a round, dark face in the flow of a street lamp.

"Charles-Henri?"

He turned to face her, while from the back of the van came Antoine's voice. "Catherine?" they both said.

The storm swirled angrily, plastering snow against the side windows and the windshield. The wipers struggled to clear a triangle that disappeared as soon as it was formed. Almost an hour since they'd left Quebec by the 115, and they had barely got past Charlesburg where the four-lane highway ended. With the overhead lighting, they'd been able to switch off the headlights. The drifts weren't too high where the wind swept the flat surfaces clear. Then they had climbed the Charlesburg escarpment on the two-lane highway, running between rocky embankments that were now invisible. The guardrail on the right shoulder could just be glimpsed, and Joanne had to follow it as best she could: it was the only way of knowing where they were. Still, a snowstorm meant that no police car would be pelting down the highway after them. Anyone following them would be moving at the same snail's pace. "A white and stormy night," Antoine had quipped sardonically.

Christine and Dominique had been arrested. It wasn't the first time. They were among "known Northern sympathizers" whom the police routinely interrogated after each terrorist act. They'd soon be released. "But I was staying with them!" exclaimed Catherine. The police didn't necessarily know that, however, and since she'd taken her papers with her, her friends might get away with lying. She didn't press the point. Nor did she ask why Charles-Henri and Antoine were here with her: she simply assumed they were more than mere sympathizers. She huddled down in her corner of the seat, pressing her forehead against the padding on the van wall and staring blindly into the amorphous whiteness outside. Had she once known this and had she forgotten? Had she been ignorant of the fact and should she have suspected? She went over their conversation of the previous evening—but no, neither Charles-Henri nor Antoine had talked like militants. Sympathizers, yes. Protesting against the present government, nothing more, nothing to justify the need to flee like this toward the North through the storm.

Had Charles-Henri already been a militant when he'd written her for the first time, then when they'd met, and in the years that followed? She remembered nothing, not even one conversation about the North. She was terrified—she for whom the past continually helped define the present, its meaning, its direction. If she had really never known, if they had never told her anything . . . then she really would have preferred it to be the result of her failing memory, because if they'd hidden it from her, she'd have to re-evaluate everything—this special space in her life that was made up of Charles-Henri, Antoine, and Dominique (and Christine

... oh, no, not Christine, too?). If they weren't the people she'd imagined them to be, then she herself wasn't the person she'd imagined herself to be, and this entire part of her world would come crashing down, would have to be rebuilt—but how?

"What's the matter?" Charles-Henri asked.

She tried to shake off her sudden despondency, muttering elliptical sentences: "Saw the cops outside Christine's ... panicked ... Joanne warned me in Montreal, gave me Max's address. . . ."

"Yesterday we—well, this morning we alerted the network about you," Antoine said. "When you told us about your visions and all. . . ."

And the network alerted Joanne who, until then, had no idea where I was staying in Quebec. And who might well have been able to warn the police, therefore. But Catherine kept these thoughts to herself. Max had gone on about the police bursting into the tavern, the brawl, the death of the policeman. Without mentioning the bluish flash. It was a genuine hallucination, then, too brief to merit the name of vision—wasn't it? A hallucination. She tried to remember what kind of neurological breakdown could cause this kind of hallucination. Maybe she had a brain tumor, just for good measure! A white and stormy night indeed.

According to the original plan, they were supposed to take the St. Birgit turnoff, go through the village, and fork northwest along the Montmorency River. At the end of the road was a cache of snowmobiles, and from there they would continue along the Montmorency and then along the Snowy, according to Max (although the others called it the Rivière des Neiges), until they reached the barrier (they must mean the frontier), where someone was waiting.

"Someone will be waiting, all right, and well before the barrier," said Joanne sarcastically. "There'll be a roadblock at St. Birgit. We should keep going on the 115, since it's the quickest road to the frontier. We can stop just short of it and go over on foot. They surely aren't expecting us to do that."

"But there was no checkpoint in Quebec or at the city

limits," protested Antoine. "They must be counting on the storm, don't you think?"

"No, she's right," Charles-Henri said. "It would be better to keep straight on. Even if there is a roadblock at the frontier, they won't see us beyond fifty yards with this snow."

"Crossing the frontier on foot in this blizzard. . . ." Antoine's grimace could be heard in his voice. "And then how will the people on the other side find us? They were meant to meet us on the Montmorency."

"There's the frontier post just after the barrier," Max remarked. "We ought to be able to reach it without too much difficulty. Joanne is right."

"Is it a barrier or a frontier? Make up your minds!" snapped Catherine, aware she was using this small detail to focus her distress, but incapable of preventing herself. The silence that followed her remark lasted just a little too long. Then Charles-Henri said kindly, "Both. They are both, Cat."

The friendly nickname annoyed her even more. "What do you mean, both?"

"The frontier of the province, with guards and everything, and the barrier. The barrier is the frontier of the Realm."

"What's the difference?"

Another little silence. She could imagine Charles-Henri and Antoine making faces. Something else I ought to know and don't; go on, be charitable to the cripple, tell her!

"At the barrier, ammunition automatically explodes and motors stop functioning," said Antoine with the same gentleness as Charles-Henri, all the more exasperating because he was usually so biting. "And all the electrical gadgets. How do you think they could've resisted the South for so long without something of the kind? We say barrier because it isn't only at ground level: it goes straight up, like a fence. Nothing electrical works in the North."

Catherine turned to Antoine, stupefied. "A . . . force field? The North has that kind of technology? But if nothing electrical works in the North, how do they create their barrier? With magic? How long has it been there?"

"It's always been there," said Antoine. The hesitation

in his voice alerted Catherine. She'd heard this tone in Christine's speech. He didn't know.

Joanne chimed in, "That's simply the way it is. Right, Max?" Her voice dripped sarcasm. Then, more cuttingly, "Pipe down, you guys, I'm driving. It's hard enough to concentrate without your babble."

Catherine slumped against the back of the seat and folded her arms. Her mind was whirling as much as the blizzard. There'd been nothing about this in the data bank or the books, which was only to be expected. But her friends ought to have known. That Northern sympathizers or agents or *natives* (since Joanne was from Chicoutimi) could be ignorant of such details was stupefying. It was . . . alarming. On the other hand, didn't Joanne's tone indicate that she knew more? What were they really being taken to in the North?

She stared at the white walls of the blizzard. What could she do about it now? *Qui vivra verra.* After a moment she closed her eyes, wearied by the hypnotic, seemingly immobile spirals of snow. Fatigue began to make itself felt again. She didn't exactly have the physique for running around the countryside on wild adventures. Dear old stay-at-home Catherine, Secret Agent 000. It was grotesque. Or dear old Catherine, former criminal, former dissident recycled by the regime—would it be more believable? Like the serial murderers described by their neighbors, after the fact: "Such a nice man—used to mow his lawn so lovingly!" Pretty ridiculous. They couldn't have worked on her so effectively and so inefficiently at the same time, could they? Whoever "they" were. Anyway, did this really explain everything? Yes, if you put yourself in a strictly paranoid frame of mind: the Great Machination, not a single loophole, all neatly tied in a box with everyone inside. But in reality there are always a few grains of sand in the cogs. You can't manipulate everyone all the time, perfect control only exists in the minds of those who believe in it.

Perhaps this was the problem: too many minds with too many different opinions since all this began. The North, for instance. Chiasson or Touchard had their own idea: communists, God-haters. Ducharme had another, more or less shared by Christine, viewing the Northerners as pacifists who cared only about their religion. Charles-Henri and Antoine had their idea, too, more mystical and more political. . . . And Joanne and Max had yet another, mysterious for the moment, but surely different. Is any of them the real one? Or is the real one a combination of several visions? Perhaps the North is a badly-shared vision. Or the South, for that matter—all those machinations, all those factions: the mirror image of the Northern sects! Yes, a gigantic vision, and everyone revolving around it, like the blind men and the elephant. "It's a wall." "No, it's a tree." "No, it's a snake." Except that with this blizzard, they might walk right past the elephant and never know it was there.

Her thoughts were becoming increasingly incoherent. It was hot in the van, now, too hot, almost humid, with all this mingled breathing. . . . She gave up trying to think and abandoned herself to sleep.

There's a cat under a bush, looking at her. A long-haired cat, creamy-white speckled with brown, china-blue eyes in a round face, a Himalayan. The bush is in a garden, or rather—the perspective shifts backward—in a small park beneath a sky as blue as the cat's eyes. But not an open-air park. There is an almost imperceptible glimmer between the eye and the sky, a vibration, that of the dome protecting the Center from the atmosphere, which is too thin at this altitude. Invisible birds chirp and whistle in the foliage. It is hot and humid, too hot and humid for her, but they've sent her into the garden while they decide her fate, and she has to stay there. Anyway, she'd get lost if she tried to wander around the rest of the Center.

She ambles along a flagstone path and up to the large fountain, to the round basins arranged like flower petals. She sits down, all her muscles moving with precision beneath her skin—an agreeable sensation—and holds out a hand to the surface of the water, then pulls it back. In the bottom of the pool a furtive movement has caught her attention. She leans over, trying to see the enormous hundred-year-old carps they've told her about, but finds herself looking at her reflection silhouetted against the mirror-clear reflection of the sky.

She sees herself. Catherine sees herself. From afar, Catherine sees a young woman seated on the edge of the fountain, the young woman who saw her face in the water a second earlier. No, *she* saw her own face, she's dreaming that she sees herself in a garden protected by a dome, on what must be a Himalayan mountaintop. It's a dream, she knows that now, but there has been a kind of hiatus in this dream at the moment where she saw her face in the mirror-like surface of the water. Perhaps it's the fact of being surprised that has made her an observer in her own dream? The face is hers, but young, scarcely more than twenty, much harder and more angular than hers ever was. And she has never had a slender, muscular body like the one seated beside the fountain, dressed in a short, sleeveless red tunic fitted at the waist. But one way or another it's her in the dream, all right; she's in contact with this young Catherine, feels some of her emotions, guesses some of her thoughts, but intermittently, like puffs of smoke harried by gusts of some invisible and contrary wind, bent on sweeping them away.

Catherine-of-the-dream finishes inspecting herself. She straightens up, running her fingers through her hair to push back the brown strands that have fallen over her eyes. Involuntarily, her fingers touch the spots where the implant scars had been, but can no longer be found. The Catherine-who-dreams is dumbfounded, but the young Catherine seems used to the disappearance of the scars, and the dream wind scatters her thoughts on the subject. She stands up, satisfied: she has become herself again, the journey to the Center has restored her muscles and her strength. A brief picture of the Center flashes through her mind, just long enough to show Catherine-who-dreams a background of blue sky with a familiar cluster of ocher ramparts, towers, and turrets, with yellow-and-red pennants snapping in the wind. In any case, the breathless panorama of peaks and ranges in the distance is certainly the Himalayas, Roof of the World.

The young Catherine resumes her aimless walk along the alleys. At the sound of a rustle in a bush, she stops—just another cat, a miniature panther, a black, almost two-dimensional form with almond-shaped green eyes that look like cut-outs revealing the brilliant vegetation behind. The cats of the Center. The monitors asked her whether she was allergic to cats before sending her into the garden. It's one of the very few things they asked her. They don't say much in the Center. In the three days since her arrival, she's had time to realize that this is deliberate—"policy" she thinks. No matter: she has learned the basics from the Marrus, enough not to have to ask too many questions. The important thing is the machine, the "Bridge," as the Marrus said. That transfers people from one universe to another.

And something curious is happening, another kind of hiatus in the dream, but visual this time. Catherine-of-the-dream is standing near a tall cluster of bamboos, and the next instant she's a good ten meters farther on. Her thoughts have also jumped ahead. If her memory has shown her the famous machine, or the memory of the first time she saw it, Catherine-who-dreams has been deprived of such a memory. The ambience has also changed. Now there is a mood of grim satisfaction. How mistaken they were in her own world—those who used her as a guinea pig for their machine! This so-called Bridge can't be used for space travel, because it doesn't permit a Voyage *within* any one universe. In fact this machine isn't good for much. "Knowledge for its own sake," said the Marrus, because there's no communication among universes except through the Voyagers—a one-way street, so to speak, if and when they decide to divulge anything. Furthermore, the Voyagers aren't even able to decide where they'll go! She didn't really listen to the Marrus' explanations, except for the basic idea: the brain, or at least everything that isn't connected to autonomous systems, creates too much interference, even when conditioned, mutilated, even (and here the hand of the young Catherine automatically touches her scalp) with implants. With forced irony, she jams her chilled hands into her tunic pockets. She's been lucky in a way. The next guinea pigs will probably be the ones to be pitied, when the experimenters of her universe realize what's happening and transform them into brain-dead organic machines, just to see if that will improve the results! She's been lucky, in a way.

She sets off with quickened step, perhaps wanting to

leave the sudden, sharp pain behind. Her universe—it's very, very far away and she may never be able to go back. Well, she's not going to feel sorry for herself; it takes too much time, and what's she got to complain about, anyway? She's alive, in one piece, no more implants, no more conditioning! She's ready, she wants to leave, that ought to be enough—that's what the Marrus told her: the Voyagers are free to go or stay. But here, in this other universe to which the Marrus' machine transferred her, the Center people said, "Oh," and, "Hmmm," and finally sent her into the garden while they discussed her case! What case? She's not a case! She was sent against her will the first time, but she used the Marrus' Bridge of her own free will, which, according to the laws of the Center, qualifies her as a Voyager. And she's ready to set off again and again until she returns to her own universe. What's the problem?

Catherine-who-dreams sees a man entering the garden. Tallish and well-built, a man in his fifties wearing a long, dark blue tunic. He must have been blond, judging by his fading hair. An unruly lock falls over his high forehead. His eyes are a very pale blue, and there is the suggestion of an epicanthic fold, a strange thing in a man who is so obviously not an Asiatic. The face is square with an assertive jaw, a thin upper lip, and a strong, hooked nose. The overall effect would be solemn, not so say severe, if it weren't for the wrinkles fanning out from the corners of his eyes and the smile that lights them.

"Catherine?"

He pronounces the name as two syllables: "Ka-trin." His voice has a familiar ring for Catherine-who-dreams, but she hasn't time to think about it. Catherine-of-the-dream turns round. It's Egon Tiehart, the monitor who opened the door for her at the Center three days earlier, one of those who've been deliberating as to whether she'll be allowed to leave again. She relaxes—more or less. After being with the Marrus, she feels awkward with these human males who remind her too much of the men of her own universe.

"Well?"

He doesn't answer immediately. On the verge of losing her temper once more, she goes on. "I want to leave. I've told you. You have to let me go. It's your law!"

Egon sits on a bench half-hidden by the foliage. "Won't you sit down?"

Reluctantly, she accepts his offer. He stays quiet and pensive, hands folded in his lap. She's about to explode when he says, "The rules don't apply in all cases. We adapt them to the situation, according to the Voyagers who visit us. We've never had a case like yours, and that's why we have a problem."

"I want to leave. That's simple enough, isn't it?"

"It's the first time we've had someone like you, a Voyager who hasn't crossed with the Bridge of her own free will the first time, and who has never been prepared for the Voyage." Before she can open her mouth, he adds, "Not . . . adequately prepared, in any case. We know that this sometimes happens, but until now all our visitors had passed through universes similar to our own before coming here. They had the training and the surgery."

Catherine-of-the-dream and Catherine-who-dreams both shrink back. "What training?" the young Catherine asks, and more urgently, "What surgery?"

A sudden gust of dream wind carries off Egon's answer as well as a slice of time. The monitor has changed his position and is now bending over to stroke the black cat or its twin that has suddenly appeared at his feet. ". . . when the Voyage carries the Voyagers beyond the cold to near absolute zero. Only their body, their naked body. No clothes, no weapons, no tools. The transfer cures the body of what interferes with its normal functioning: diseases, injuries, and inorganic grafts, too— you've got rid of your implants, for example. However, if the body has undergone structural changes, and even certain types of nonorganic grafts, as with our surgery, and if the mind has fully accepted these changes, as with our training, then these remain. Apparently they're interpreted as being normal."

Catherine-of-the-dream gives a little snort. "If I've been a hunchback all my life and I travel by the Bridge, then I remain a hunchback?"

"If your psyche has become hunchbacked as well, yes."

She shrugs. "Cheap psychosomatic babble! The implants disappeared, but if what you say were true, I'd still be conditioned. They demolished and reconstructed my mind for months on end."

This young Catherine is very quick to spurn Egon's explanations. She'd be better advised to listen to this monitor who seems to know what he's talking about. And doesn't get annoyed by her obstinacy. On the contrary, he smiles. "But for your first Voyage, you arrived on Khorai, the planet of the Marrus."

The young Catherine shrugs again. What's that got to do with it?

"You're not the first. Khorai seems to be a knot, a junction of universes. You should have a look in the archives; there are at least three Voyagers' accounts of the Marru initiation. Each man—and woman—goes through a very . . . peculiar experience on this planet."

"There were hallucinogens and psychotropic substances in the pollen of the flower and in the forest fruits, that's all. And in my case, I was still being affected by the implants and the conditioning."

We had forgotten our name, Catherine-who-dreams reminds her—but it seems the communication is only one way.

"That's what I was just saying," says Egon, smiling again. He has her where he wants her. "The transfer puts your body right, but as far as the mind is concerned, it depends on how deeply the psyche is affected. Your conditioning was not yet very deep, you were lucky. Khorai . . . erased most of it."

But the invisible flurry blows away the rest of their conversation, and the black cat, and even the bench on which they were sitting. When Catherine-who-dreams finds them again, they have started walking through the alleys toward the fountain.

"It's a question of maximizing the Voyagers' chances of survival," the monitor is saying, "for example their total recall, a capacity to remember everything—or to forget, if necessary. We also train them in various forms of combat and survival techniques for several types of environment, as well as giving them the most varied possible scientific and technical education. It's very useful to have a good grounding in linguistics, for example. On the other hand, the world they reach doesn't necessarily have a ready-made Bridge. Sometimes it's just a prototype, other times only a theory. The Voyagers have to be able to make the Bridge *happen*! Besides, the time spent in training and surgery gives aspiring Voyagers the time to prepare themselves: the important thing is to be ready to leave."

During the patch of conversation that Catherine-who-dreams has missed, the young Catherine has become more impatient, more aggressive, more obstinate. She snorts again. "Ready?"

"Not only through physical or intellectual preparation. But emotionally. And spiritually."

Again the bitter laugh. (This young Catherine is certainly irritating! Can't she simply ask questions to learn about what she doesn't know, instead of automatically heaping scorn on it?) "Let's be serious: it transfers people randomly from one universe to another, so why the need to be 'spiritually ready'?"

"Not randomly," says Egon calmly. "And the Bridge is a means, but it doesn't effect the actual transfer. It makes it possible, but the true agent of transfer is the Voyager. The Voyager's . . . mind. You can use several other terms—the unconscious, the matrix, the soul. To tell the truth, we don't really know what happens. The machine cools the body until it's in the region of absolute zero, and there, when the molecules have almost stopped moving . . . something takes over, setting us in motion again and projecting us somewhere else. But not just anywhere else. Think about your stay with the Marrus, the flower, the beast—"

"Oh, no," the young Catherine cuts in, "not that psychomystic claptrap again! I want to leave by the Bridge, period. I'll get home in the end—all the more reason if the Voyager's mind is the essential element of the Voyage!"

Egon makes a visible effort to say nothing, but she doesn't see it. She's staring angrily straight ahead, elbows on her knees, hands curled in fists that she knocks together. The monitor merely murmurs, "The mind isn't necessarily just will." Then, louder, "And in that case, why not maximize your chances of surviving many Voyages if they turn out to be necessary?"

He has found the right argument: she's thinking now, frowning and pursing her lips without even being aware of it. Finally, grudgingly, she asks, "How long does the training take, and the surgery?"

"It depends on the aspirants. At least three years."

"Three years! Nothing shorter?"

"Three years is the strict minimum for physical preparation and the other learning processes. The results of the surgery depend mostly on the aspirants, on their relative ability to master their new perceptions quickly."

Catherine-who-dreams feels the delicious little thrill that accompanies the solution of a difficult problem: "their new perceptions" . . . but at this point the invisible interference obliterates the rest of the monitor's explanations to the young Catherine. Has someone decided to prevent her from hearing the good bits? It's beginning to look a lot like censoring! It's a dream, and she's the one who's dreaming; she has no reason to censor what interests her, has she? On the other hand, if she's able to censor things, she should be able to censor what *doesn't* interest her, shouldn't she?

The monitor is now sitting on the rim of the fountain pool, while the young Catherine strides back and forth in front of him, full of confidence. ". . . it can't be all that complicated! Like being reborn as an adult, but with new senses."

Egon makes a face as he trails a hand in the water. "It's not easy to be reborn an adult," he murmurs.

And she, aggressive again, "What do you know about it?"

Catherine-who-dreams decides that she has had enough of young Catherine's kneejerk reactions, but she can't manage to censor the next bit of conversation. This dream is really not very obedient.

The monitor seems to hesitate before answering. "I underwent the operations," he says at last. "I was an aspiring Voyager when I came to the Center."

Catherine-of-the-dream is suddenly as curious as Catherine-who-dreams. Almost. The young one doesn't admit it, still hiding behind an aggressive irony. "Why didn't you leave, then? Did you fail the post-op tests?"

"No, on the contrary." Egon smiles.

Oh, no! Not another obliteration? Yes! Absolutely no control over her own dream! The monitor is now seated with his two feet on the rim of the pool, hugging his knees. The young Catherine, sitting cross-legged, is pretending not to look at him, but listens avidly to what he has to say.

". . . to leave without being ready, in defiance, and I found myself in a Bridge capsule. In a Center exactly like this one, with Thénadèn and everyone. I concluded that I hadn't left, or that if I had, I was now in a universe so similar to the one I'd left that it amounted to the same thing. My true course was to stay, and so I stayed."

"But why did you want to travel in the first place?"

Egon sighs and straightens his back. There is a smile on his face, a distant tenderness caused by a memory known only to him. "Because of a Voyager. She was called, is called, Talitha. I had followed her to the Center. I loved her. She left, promising me that she would come back. And for a long time I thought—"

Another space-time hiatus. The young Catherine has turned to the monitor, abandoning all pretense of indifference. She's very excited, unaware of his indulgent gaze, just saying, ". . . proves that one can really and truly come back!"

"Sometimes. Sooner or later." He says this with a slightly melancholy smile. "Or in a universe that is so imperceptibly different from ours that we'll never know. . . ."

But she doesn't listen to him anymore. It is possible to come back: that's all she wants to know. Even if the Bridge sends you to a random destination, you can come back. She can do it. Her will to return will be strong enough to bend the capricious Bridge to her desires. She gets up. "All right. When do the training sessions and operations begin?"

The monitor gets up in turn, always with that same, slightly tired indulgence that she doesn't notice. "The process has already begun, since you've asked."

The garden implodes in silence. The blue sky closes

like a hand, and it is no longer blue, but black with white, whirling streaks. Trees and fountain shrink with bewildering speed into disconnected specks that soon disappear, swept away in a soundless tempest. A violent collision, and Catherine is projected back into Catherine, whose head has just hit the padded frame of the van and who finds herself half kneeling against the back of the front seat, just before she is thrown against her own seat.

9

"What's happening?" she shouts, breathless as she tries to straighten her glasses on her nose, but the bucking of the van prevents her. Over the roar of the motor she can hear a siren screaming, while light flashes through the rear window, first red, then blue. Catherine turns around and glimpses a dark mass surmounted by a revolving searchlight. As she watches, a gust of snow once more hides the police car following them.

"We're not very far from the frontier," says Joanne's calm voice. "The van is made of reinforced steel; there's a chance we'll get through. Attach your seatbelts. We're going to try to rush the roadblock."

Catherine searches frantically for her seatbelt buckle, and dimly sees Athana clutching the front seat with both hands. She doesn't look at all frightened. Catherine buckles the girl up, then herself, all the while jolting crazily as the van careens along the snowy road. She grabs the frame of the sliding door for support, feeling queasy. Nothing is visible from the side of the van except a moving whiteness that could be the side of the road, or the middle, or anything. Behind them, the police car can be glimpsed now and then, gaining on them, flashing red and blue between two gusts of snow, then disappearing in the blizzard again. In front is the same deceptive whiteness as all around . . . no, red and blue flashes between gusts, a blinking orange light: the frontier, the roadblock.

"Get down; they're armed," says Joanne. Catherine bends double and makes Athana do the same, she isn't thinking, only perceiving—the sudden roar of the motor, the jump forward, a voice from in front, a rhythmic groan that is perhaps Joanne saying, "Go, go, go," to encourage her mount, the creature of steel and plastic in whose belly they are locked. A first dull *crump,* a little to the right. A second—a direct hit, shattered windshield, ice-cold wind knifing through, carrying snow and shards of glass inward, a distant crackle followed by little thuds somewhere on Max's side of the van, and the whole frame vibrates in response: bullets, they're shooting—of course they're shooting, what did you think they'd do? The motor revs furiously, the tires skate, the van swerves, bursts of gunfire now, submachine guns or machine guns, another window shatters—an incongruous smell of brandy pervades the van: Joanne's bottle has been hit—the motor races again, the van skids sideways and slithers in the snow, but still they move forward. Catherine has closed her eyes, her chest is a small, hard knot as she huddles on the seat, her arms crossed above her head, jammed against the back of the front seat, and she is the wheels, the motor, groaning with them, "Go, go!" They hit something in front, metal crunching . . . crunching, and then something smashes into them from behind with a flash of red and blue, and the impact sends the van leaping forward, zigzagging crazily but still moving. A fresh burst of gunfire, the back windows explode, a hurricane of cold and snow and bits of pulverized glass spews into the van, above her head Catherine hears the clunk of a bullet as it ricochets off the door, but she isn't afraid, she is suspended in the cold, in the crash of metal, in the painful contraction of all her muscles.

Suddenly, silence. The bursts of gunfire have stopped almost simultaneously. Silence—the roar of the storm through the shattered windows. The motor has cut as they passed the barrier, but the van continues on its own momentum, free, not straight forward, but slipping steadily to the left. A muffled hammering, Joanne's hands as she desperately struggles with the rigid wheel, locked without power steering. They hit something in front—a pole? The van rears up, begins a majestic somersault, pirouettes with incredible slowness as it follows its new trajectory, and plunges into the drifts, sending up silent sprays of snow. The van tumbles once, twice, creaking and clanking amid dull thuds, and then, during a brief but eternal instant, free fall, her heart in her mouth, barely time to feel afraid, they're going to crash . . . no, the van bounces, teeters, and Catherine's whole body crumples against the seat in front, up is down and down is up, over and over again—then her head hits something hard, blinding pain, a weight on her chest, heavier and heavier until she feels something break, she screams, and at that moment the van hurtles backward into the ravine . . . a crash more violent than the rest, a sound more distinct because it is the last.

But Catherine can still hear—creakings, tinklings, hissings—can smell brandy and gasoline, hot metal and burnt rubber. Fire, she thinks, get out. She's on her back, her legs folded against her chest. The back of her seat is now the floor. She moves her hands, she can feel them; pats her abdomen, her waist, looking for the seatbelt buckle. Finds it. Pulls at it, once, twice, click, straightens up as best she can with the back of the front seat as a skewed ceiling. She can hear the click of a seatbelt being undone, says, "Athana," and can barely hear herself.

"It's all right, Catherine, everything will be all right," comes the clear, calm voice. From the other side of the seat-ceiling she hears, "Catherine? Antoine? Are you okay?" It's Charles-Henri, his voice faint with fright, but that makes three of them alive. Something moves above her, dull thuds, the van's carcass wobbles a bit, and the muffled voice of Joanne mutters, ". . . get the door unstuck." Four. "I can get out through the window." Max: five. We're coming out of it pretty well. Catherine examines her side of the van. Something has jammed into the frame and the sliding door will surely be stuck. No use trying it. She turns, gives Athana a shove. "That way, Athana, follow Max." The girl obeys. Catherine crawls after her, noticing that her left leg refuses to obey her, but she feels nothing and keeps moving forward, dragging it.

Hands pull her out of the wreck and help her to stand in the deep, powdery snow rolling like water around her waist.

Max's bearded face, powdered with snowflakes. Another face, bloody, an undone braid whipped by the wind. Joanne. A massive black shape: Charles-Henri. Athana? She is there, her white parka blending with the snow, a face and a pair of hands floating weirdly in the half-light. Antoine. Antoine was in the back. Dragging her inert leg, Catherine turns to the wreck sticking straight up out of the snow in the middle of its impact crater. The rear has been completely crushed, even the window is invisible. Charles-Henri struggles through the waist-deep snow toward the van, and Joanne wades after, trying to stop him. Behind Catherine, Max's voice: "No way he could survive that—no way."

"Let's get out of here," says Joanne. She grabs Charles-Henri by the hood of his parka. He's still trying to struggle forward, but he hasn't the strength. Catherine fumbles around her in the pockmarked snow. Pine branches stick out crazily, torn off as their vehicle hurtled by. She grabs one. A bit short, but it'll do. She tears off the twigs quickly, lowers her improvised crutch into the snow, feels the solid ground, and hobbles over to Joanne, who has convinced Charles-Henri to follow her. Athana and Max are ahead, invisible legs striding through the snow toward the relative shelter of a wall of rock. Catherine drags her numb leg. The wind slashes at her like icy razor blades, and the needling snow stings her, but her leg doesn't hurt at all. Strange. It must be the shock. The pain will hit her soon. The longer it takes, the better. Might as well make as much headway as possible while I'm disconnected.

She reaches the shelter of the rock, doesn't even want to look at her leg. She examines Athana instead—not a scratch. Charles-Henri ... like Joanne, superficial cuts. Max.... At this moment, she realizes she's been able to see them from the beginning, shouldn't be able to see them, see the crushed mass of the van, but she does, bluish-green, luminescent, faces, hands, no precise details, the injuries are brighter, that's all. Infrared vision, says her brain, although she hasn't asked. Okay for infrared vision. Max, leaning against the rocky wall, also seems to have nothing but cuts, but there is a more definite source of infrared on his chest. Catherine hobbles over to him, places her hand on the luminous spot, and pulls it back, all sticky.

"Max. . . ."

She has no time to finish the sentence. He crumples slowly against the rock, then falls forward toward her. She automatically holds out an arm, gripping her crutch to sustain the shock. But Athana steps in, catches Max, and kneels beside him. She has laid her hand on his throat, underneath the parka. Her head is tilted a little to one side, as though she were listening. In her clear voice, perfectly audible despite the wind, she says, "He's going to leave."

Catherine leans over Max as best she can, balancing on her crutch. He's barely breathing, just a feeble, luminescent vapor blown away by the wind. She gauges the location of the wound, the amount of blood lost—the whole front of the parka is dark with it. *No way* for him, either. A verdict, without pain, but not callous: detached, objective. She straightens up, shouts at Joanne, "Joanne, where is the frontier post?" For a moment she thinks Joanne hasn't heard her, but the Métis shouts back to her through the wind, "Don't know! Lost my bearings!" A pause. "About a hundred yards to the west of the road!"

Catherine tries to reconstruct the van's trajectory. With every ounce of energy, she wills the strange certainties of Montreal or the tunnels beneath the old part of Quebec to break through to her conscious mind, north here, south there, west . . . but it's not working. What she feels is an indistinct pain spreading through her chest. The period of grace is almost over.

"He's gone," says Athana. Catherine turns to her with a grimace—aware once more of the existence of her left leg. She observes Max's bearded mouth for a moment. No sign now of the luminescent breath of life.

"He is dead, Athana. Come away."

"But he's going to come back," the girl says confidently.

The body chills quickly in the wind that tears away at

its residual warmth. The luminescence dims visibly, then goes out. Athana removes her hand from the collar of the parka, she watches the body as though waiting for something. Catherine, with a sensation of déjà-vu, wonders whether another blue flash will blind her. But no. Just this darker blot in the whirling dimness, and the snow already beginning to cover it.

"Let's get out of here," Joanne says again. She's still holding Charles-Henri by the sleeve. He says nothing, turned to stone. Catherine realizes from the atonal voice of the young woman that she, too, is in a state of shock. Where can they go? Follow the ravine? The frontier post may be just above them. If only they could climb back up. Impossible. Catherine senses her thoughts begin to unravel. And the pain courses up her leg, spreads through her chest, and grips her head in a vice. It seems as though a gigantic bell is clanging inside her skull. Through the fog of her mind, she is aware that Athana has stood up, a luminescent phantom, and is disappearing along the ravine. Catherine shouts weakly at her to come back, but she can't even hear herself. She can't even see Athana, now. All she sees are the moving curtains of the blizzard. From far, far away, she senses she is falling, still grasping her makeshift crutch, and while she falls, slowly, slowly, the veils of snow seem to merge, condense, then spread into two great, downy wings, a beast, a bird, a great white owl that lifts off, circles her once, and flies off, beating its huge wings silently in the darkness, taking the light with it.

When she opens her eyes, she is in the garden at Sergines. It's a fine day, the sky is blue, luminous, arching above the intact trees. In fact she's floating above the trees too—another small, internal shock, thrilled and incredulous: she's flying, it's so long since she has flown! But she mustn't think about it too much, or she'll come down. She mustn't even *want* to fly too much. And so she lets herself be carried along by the dream, by the fragrant air of this late summer afternoon, above the trees heavy with fruit. She is very high—she can see the whole garden, with its neatly-drawn paths and its segments clearly marked by trellises, the kitchen garden to the left, the cherries and plum trees in the middle of one lawn, the pear trees in the other, with the pretty-by-night and blackcurrant on the terrace behind the kitchen, and at the very back, against the blind wall of the next door barn, the honeysuckle and the grapevine sending their bees zooming back and forth, near the fennel tall as a tree.

She's very high, but at the same time very close. She can see the two people who walk slowly down the main path very clearly. Two men in long, dark blue tunics and sandals; they might be priests, except for the lack of tonsures. One is shorter and older than the other. She recognizes the young one, but he shouldn't be there. He should be . . . she no longer knows where, but somewhere else, far, far away from here. The older one is worried. The younger is determined. But she doesn't want to know what they're thinking or feeling! For once her garden is peaceful, and they have no business being there. She tries to shout at them to go away, but she feels herself losing altitude slightly and decides to keep quiet. In any case, she surely hasn't a voice.

The younger one is resolute. All the monitors are in agreement: technically, he's more than ready. He speaks urgently, brokenly, continually brushing away a lock of blond hair that keeps falling over his forehead.

"But are you really ready, Egon?" says the older one, who knows full well that he isn't, and who is afraid because he's not sure he can convince him to stay.

"If I don't leave, I may never find her."

"If you leave, you'll certainly never find her. One travels alone, Egon. We have no example of Voyagers intentionally meeting. The archives—"

Egon interrupts him impatiently, because he must blot out the inner voice echoing the words of the old man: "The archives are constantly changing: we don't know everything, in fact we know almost nothing. I know I'll find her. Since the Bridge conforms to our deep desires, I will find her."

"Are you sure you understand your deep desires?"

Egon laughs, the brusque laugh of a young man, slightly insulting. "You're too old, Thénadèn, it's too long since you've loved. Have you ever loved? No, if you had, you wouldn't be here. I'm here because I love her, because I want to follow her. A love like ours can bridge universes."

Can he hear himself? How old is this kid? Twenty, twenty-two at most? A love like ours can bridge universes! How does the old man keep from smiling? But he doesn't smile. He's more and more afraid of losing Egon, of having already lost him because of the fable the young man has spun around himself like a blinding cocoon. In this fable, which Catherine sees unfolding before her like an animated picture book, there is a woman Voyager who one day comes to his small, sleepy village to wake him from the sleep of unawareness. To make him a man. Obviously his first woman, Catherine thinks, indulgent but slightly irritated. The Voyager is a slender, dark woman, over thirty, with big, black, almond-shaped eyes that seem a little sad, despite her smile, and black braids on top of her head. Familiar. . . . Then the shock of recognition: it's Mama! She didn't tell me about all her voyages, then. Where did she meet this young man? In Tunisia, or was it in the East Indies? But it couldn't be: at that age she was in Indochina, where she met Papa. And anyway, amorous adventures were not her style, poor thing!

Indifferent to Catherine's thoughts, the story continues to unfold before her, meetings in small cafés, walks along the seashore, nights in the small rented room above the boathouse, long, spellbound conversations. More monologues than dialogues, actually: he told her about himself, and she listened. And she understood, of course, she always had the right word, didn't judge. She loved him in her way, for his youth and enthusiasm and all that he could become, but she knew she would leave. Another misunderstanding taken for love. He didn't know her, had only seen in her what he needed to see, and she, indulgent, just passing through, agreed to play his game because she thought it was what he needed—at least she could give him that.

He wants to find her again, but she—she has left.

The old man walks on, wordless, overcome with grief, knowing that this young Egon will leave in search of lies and that he cannot prevent him. Yes, he's getting old; he had hoped for more from this aspiring Voyager. Yet he knows that not everyone leaves when ready. He thinks of the long, frustrating journey that awaits this young Egon on the other side of the Bridge, he links arms with the young man, an illusory bond, and walks in silence, head bowed, along Catherine's garden paths in the setting sun. And Catherine is now walking beside him, feeling his hand on her arm. She knows the old man's sadness and would like to console him, tell him that in other universes Egon has never left, but her mouth remains mute.

The old man turns toward her and strokes her cheek, murmuring, "Catherine?"

He has the black, round face of Charles-Henri. It *is* Charles-Henri, leaning over her. She's lying on a bed in a small room filled with the good smell of a wood fire. The frontier post. They've got as far as that? She remembers nothing. A vise squeezes her head, another her chest, another her left leg. She identifies them. Bandages, a plaster cast for her leg. The pain is there, but subdued. Drugged to the eyeballs. Bad prognosis. She feels as light as air, and if the bandages weren't holding her she would surely be floating. She concentrates on Charles-Henri, seated on the edge of the bed, holding her hand. The pink and white of the adhesive tape and bandages look rather silly on his dark skin. He appears tired. Of course he's tired, Catherine, don't be stupid! She concentrates a little more on the lower part of her own face. There must be a mouth, lips, she moves them with difficulty: "The others?"

"Joanne has contusions, like me. They've brought in the bodies of Max and Antoine. They were ready for casualties because of the events in Quebec. There's a small medical unit here anyway, and they were able to take care of you."

"Athana?"

"Not a scratch."

As though the mere mention of her name could summon her, Athana appears beside Charles-Henri and kneels beside the bed, contemplating Catherine anxiously, imploringly. "You mustn't leave! You may not come back either!"

Catherine tries to smile. ". . . no intention of leaving."

"They should have, you know? Come back. Max and Antoine."

"When people die, they don't come back, Athana," Charles-Henri says, tired but kind. He's still on the far side of heartbreak, protected by shock. "They've gone forever."

"But they must come back. They do come back. Like the man in the tavern."

Unexpectedly, curiosity opens Catherine's eyes. "The blue flash?" she manages to say. Then, more firmly, "What was it?"

"What was what?" asks Charles-Henri.

She takes a breath, and explains in brief sentences. The dark face expresses total stupefaction. She registers this stupor, and finds a last shred of energy to conclude, "Athana, what was it?"

The girl is perplexed, as though she had just realized that they didn't know. "They leave," she says as though it were obvious. "And they come back. The man in the tavern came back. He's here."

"Where?" breathes Catherine.

"Everywhere!"

Catherine closes her eyes, exhausted, divided between a feeble desire to be angry and an equally weak desire to laugh. Won't understand today. Maybe never. Maybe I'm going. Dying, say it. *Dying.* Weird, dying like this. I ought to have been told.

"Leave her alone," says an unknown male voice, while a strange face leans over her and a hand rests on her forehead, takes her pulse. She senses a familiar presence then hears Joanne's voice asking, "How's she doing?"

"Not too badly," says the male voice.

"Can she be moved?"

"Yes, but with this blizzard. . . . Anyway, her condition is stable, she can wait."

The presence comes nearer. Catherine makes herself open her eyes and look at Joanne, at the brown, serious face, slanted, liquid eyes, black braids gleaming in the lamplight. It almost reminds her of something, but she hasn't the strength to remember, and closes her eyes again.

A sharp gust of cold and snow hits her in the face, in spite of her cocoon of blankets. She doesn't know how much time has elapsed. A motor hums nearby. A thought, very detached from the painful body that is being loaded into the van: how can the motor run without electricity? By steam or the grace of God? It's warmer inside, at any rate. Someone arranges her blankets. Joanne is coming? How kind. She tries to open her eyes and smile at the young woman, but it isn't Joanne, it's Athana, who takes her hand in her own warm grasp, gazes intently at her, says, "I won't let you leave." Catherine smiles at the child, but the effort of keeping her eyes open is too great, and she lets herself slip once more into the blackness.

Part
Three

They are fighting in the kitchen across the corridor, but the bedroom door is open. Catherine wants to huddle in her small bed, but her body seems to be tied down around the chest and her left leg is stiff. She hugs her teddy bear close and squeezes her eyes shut. In the cavernous room the shadows thrown by the nightlight refuse to take on their usual forms. The smells are similarly stubborn. Instead of Mama's eau-de-cologne and the faint odor of naphthalene coming from the clothes cupboard, the room smells of wood and wax and smoke, a warm, peaceful smell, but it's not the right smell for the room where she sleeps with her parents. The fighting voices are familiar, though, and they're arguing over her. Snatches of sentences reach her, they must be walking round and round the big kitchen—as though they were chasing each other, but they never seem to realize this. There are moments when the words are meaningless, just noise. Papa is angry: Catherine shouldn't be here; Mama is trying to coax him: it's not for very long. Papa stops walking, his voice becomes clear: "I don't want to hear about it anymore. It's over, and that's the end of it."

"End? End?" Mama has also stopped walking. Catherine imagines her angry stance, hands gripping the back of a chair, fingers white, all of her white, Mama transformed, terrifying. "You threw up your hands, you mean!

You took it lying down. Of course they've left you alone. They've bought you off. What's *that*?" The rattle of an object being picked up and dropped, a funny little ringing sound—a telephone? "Eh? What's that? 'Never,' you said. 'I'll never have that in my house,' you said!"

Another rattle and the cracked ting of a bell. "Leave it alone!" Papa growls, and Mama snorts, "Ha!" and their voices are close together now, they're going to hit each other, he's going to hurt her! Catherine begins shouting as though she were crying, very loud, so as to distract them, and all at once she really is crying because it hurts so much. But through it all she hears the approaching footsteps and begins to be a little afraid. Will they scold her because she wasn't asleep, will Papa beat her, like he does sometimes even when she's not the one who's made him angry? She sees shadows moving on the walls, and Papa's face appears above her in an abrupt light; he's frowning, and instinctively she lifts an arm to protect her face. Her chest is hurting so much that she can't help crying out.

The shadows on Papa's face reveal worry, not anger. He takes the arm gently and puts it back under the blanket, murmuring, "It's nothing. Just lie still. It'll be all right." The blanket is very furry—she thought it was her teddy bear, but she's just holding the blanket against her cheek. Papa rests a hand on her forehead. "She doesn't seem to have a fever."

"She was dreaming," says Mama's voice in the shadows, half worried, half annoyed.

Catherine clutches Papa's hand. "A bad dream, Papa. Tell me a story."

He tries to free his hand. He looks very strange. Catherine starts to cry again, stammering, "It's not my fault, don't fight, please don't fight!" Mama takes Papa's place. She sits on the edge of the bed and strokes Catherine's hair. She is young, so young that Catherine stops crying and stares, astonished and delighted. "You have braids like mine, Mama!" Except that she can't feel her own braids, can't feel the familiar pull of the roots, can't feel the thick rolls against her neck. And then she remembers: she threw them away, threw her braids away when she cleaned out the house after Papa's death. She begins to cry again, great sobs that hurt her chest. "He's dead,

Mama. Papa's dead!" Except that he isn't dead, he's there, she can see him behind Mama, exactly as she remembers him when she was little. And the young Mama leans over her, clasps her awkwardly in her arms, and murmurs, "You mustn't cry like that, you'll do yourself harm. Go to sleep. We won't fight anymore." And Catherine hurts so much all over, now, in her chest, her head, her leg, her back, that she hasn't even the strength to be surprised that Mama doesn't smell familiar.

Someone else appears to the right of the bed: a young girl with pale eyes and blonde hair, like a fairy in a story-book, and Catherine knows her name. The fairy is called Athana. The fairy has cool fingers and when she rests them on Catherine's forehead and cheeks, the pain goes away and the distress isn't so sharp, and Catherine snuggles under the blanket-teddy-bear, yawns, and goes back to sleep.

She is in the garden in Sergines, at night. But a light is rising: the moon. She should go inside to avoid being moonstruck, but in defiance (of whom?) she stays in the garden. It's very cold in the silvery light, everything seems covered with a layer of ice—flowers, leaves, fruit. Horrified, she tries to comfort herself: perhaps it's just a kind of varnish that will preserve them, and anyhow it's too beautiful, it can't be death. She walks between the cherry trees, admiring the moonlight refracted in rainbows by the transparent coating, but she's very fearful of touching a leaf because it would break and there'd be blood in the wound.

She suddenly thinks that she has a sure way of knowing that the trees aren't dead: if they're alive, they'll be warm, if they're warm, they'll give off infrared rays. The hyperception faculty snaps on obediently, revealing a magnificent phantom garden, luminous networks of sap, ruby-colored filigree in the leaves, the flowers, the grass, everywhere (although she knows they should be silvery, not red, but why is that?). It's splendid, and she sees herself also transformed into a walking phantom-jewel, with her network of veins and muscles, a bit like the skinless bodies in natural science books but not at all horrifying—marvelous, moving, life has such fragile delicacy! Tears well up in her eyes. The air is transformed, too, right up to the sky, to the moon. She's enraptured: the universe is warm, alive, pulsating. She rushes to the kitchen window to tell her mother all about it.

Then she thinks she's tumbled into another dream. The quivering hyperception networks are still there, but a principle of order begins to establish itself. No personality-split this time: she's the one who controls and interprets the dream. Who sees the unknown room where she finds herself, a large room with a curved roof, wooden walls, and all the wavelengths within and beyond the visible spectrum, infrared, ultraviolet. . . . On her right she registers the characteristic signal of an underground electric generator, but this signal seems to be sucked down and thus kept from reaching ground level by a kind of energy that she can't quite identify. Also on her right, but on her own level, in the next room and almost at the limit of her field of perception, there's a sort of bubbling nucleus of the same unknown energy. She tries to lift herself up and turn in order to see it better, but a sharp pain stops her and she remembers: the chase, the accident. . . . Is she still in the frontier post? Wasn't there another journey, afterward? But for the moment she's interested in this knot of energy, a kind of stable . . . swirl, like a self-perpetuating reaction. Very concentrated. Not an electric battery, that's certain. A radioactive capsule? No hard radiations. She'll have to resume normal vision to see what it is, but how does she cancel the hyperceptions?

As though the mere fact of asking were enough, the networks fade and disappear. Athana is sleeping in an armchair pulled close to the big bed, her face turned towards Catherine. She's still wearing the oversized clothes borrowed from the tavern and sleeps carelessly, hands open on her thighs, her thick, golden hair spilling over her face. Not a mark on her. She was lucky. Max and I shielded her. *Max.* Catherine closes her eyes in sharp distress.

He was in the wrong place at the wrong time, an unexpected voice comments—the other Catherine, the one in the ravine who noted with detachment that Max was dead even though he was still breathing. It could have been you, it's not your fault. It's up to me to decide that, retorts Catherine with drunken determination—she must be drugged, ideas are lumbering through her brain one at a time like great, awkward beasts. The other Catherine remarks that she hardly knew Max, that it isn't like Antoine, and Antoine's dead, too. Exactly. She'd known Antoine for twelve years, and Charles-Henri is still alive, so in a crazy way it isn't so crazy, because there's someone to share the memories with; but she hardly knew Max and so can't even grieve for him the way she should. The other Catherine shrugs: as far as you're concerned, he barely existed. He didn't need me to exist, protests Catherine; he cooked, read, we would've had lots to talk about! The other Catherine has no desire to continue the conversation. Angrily, Catherine goes back to sleep, wondering where Charles-Henri can be.

2

I've caught a cold. This is Catherine's first thought on waking, before opening her eyes. The pain above her eyebrows, beneath her eyes, the aches, the burning sensation in her chest at each breath. . . . Then memory returns, just as she moves to touch her forehead and a preventing hand is laid on her arm. Joanne Nasiwi, one braid half undone, cuts and bruises on her face. A disconcerting thought springs to mind: has he beaten her? Then memory surfaces—no, it was a dream—and at the same time there's the troubling impression—no, not really a dream. Catherine makes an effort to shake off the shreds of images that refuse to go away.

"Where are we?"

"With a friend."

A terse way of putting it, considering it's a friend. The memory persists, the memory of the dream, all those arguments. . . .

"Athana?"

A little jerk of the chin toward the other side of the bed where Athana is sleeping. "That's all she's done for two days: eat and sleep," Joanne says, vaguely irritated.

"Two days?" Catherine tries to sit up, but a firm hand stops her. "Where's Charles-Henri?"

The black eyes look away, and Joanne fusses unnecessarily with the covers. "In Chicoutimi. He was taken by other friends."

"And this isn't Chicoutimi."

"No. Later. When you're better."

"Is it a hospital?"

"No. But everything will be all right. Don't worry. We've got what's needed."

Catherine senses that Joanne won't answer a question beginning with "Why?" The fact that she can't take a deep breath with this bandage around her ribs makes her sharply anxious. But she persists. "Where are we, how did we get here?"

"It won't mean anything if I tell you. It's on the Rivière-à-la-Chute, about fifty miles from the frontier. I brought you here in a snowcar."

"A snowcar? I thought nothing electric functioned in the North."

A sarcastic little smile. "Nothing does."

A vaguely familiar male voice makes Catherine forget about her puzzlement. "Is she awake?"

A shape appears behind Joanne. Before even seeing the man, Catherine senses that she will recognize him. Fiftyish, square face, hooked nose, thin lips, a former blond with pale eyes, his lids curiously slanted. He is wearing a thick black turtleneck sweater. Now where has she seen him recently. . . . At the same time, superimposed almost sickeningly on these sensations is another set of images and sensations telling her it was a long time ago. But she did know him—has she forgotten?

Catherine's amazement reverberates off Joanne and the familiar but unknown man. "What?" he says, surprised and already irritated.

"You look like someone I know," says Catherine, as though apologizing.

The man shrugs, picks up the nearly empty water carafe from her bedside table, and stalks out.

"What's the matter with him?" asks Catherine, surprised at feeling hurt.

"I didn't tell him I was bringing you here. He doesn't like surprises." An inference that only Joanne understands. She tucks back a stray lock of hair that has fallen on Catherine's forehead and strokes her cheek. "Don't worry," she smiles. "It'll be all right."

"You too, I felt I knew you when we met," murmurs Catherine.

"I know," says Joanne, still stroking Catherine's cheek soothingly.

Catherine is about to ask "How?" or "Why?" but another hand touches her lips. Athana is awake and kneeling on the other side of the bed. Joanne stiffens. "Try to sleep," she says, walking out of the room.

Athana examines Catherine, her face serious. Then she smiles and in turn strokes Catherine's forehead with cool, remembered fingers. "Sleep," she breathes.

Catherine closes her eyes, doubly obedient.

She had indeed caught a cold, as she realized with each passing hour. Her nose was blocked, and the feeling of oppressive weight had moved from her ribs to her lungs. At last an irrepressible, painful sneeze shook her. Joanne came into the room and did the usual things, hand on the forehead, little green pills to be swallowed. . . . The other Catherine was apparently continuing to register these facts with interest—the Northerners have a pharmaceutical industry?—and to answer herself: or else they smuggle it in. Or trade with the Union via the Amerindian Federation.

Catherine listened to this inner conversation with utter detachment. As so often happened, she felt perfectly lucid, weightless, freed by the fever from extraneous things: polite behavior, uncertainty, caution. Eyes closed—she felt somewhat dizzy, another sure sign—she heard someone come in and guessed that it was the man. She waited, curious as to what he would do. After a moment he sat down in the armchair.

"Am I a prisoner?" Catherine asked point blank, without opening her eyes.

Silence—surprise? She opened her eyes. He seemed more embarrassed than angry.

"No. Not exactly."

An interesting pause. Catherine closed her eyes again, forgoing his facial expressions, which were difficult to discern in the shadow, and relying on intonations. "Who are you?"

"Simon-Pierre Le Guével. You can call me Simon." Another pause, then a concession. "I'm an old friend of Joanne's."

Suddenly the dream of the fight replayed in Catherine's head, a single flash in her memory, the words, the omissions, what those omissions might contain. Still in the same light voice, without apparent curiosity, she said, "You aren't a friend now."

Silence. The creaking of an armchair, a body settling itself. "Differences of opinion." An old anger, an old sadness. More softly, to himself, "She left, I stayed."

A distant echo reverberated in Catherine's memory, but she put it off until later. There was a thread here she mustn't lose. "Why am I here?"

Silence. Longer this time. Body stirring in the armchair. Was he uneasy? "Joanne told you nothing." Another statement, a tired, almost routine irritation: he expected Joanne to say nothing. He cleared his throat. "It's difficult to explain." A sigh. More creaking. "There are ... differences of opinion in the Realm about people like us."

"Like us."

A small, inarticulate noise, annoyed, tongue against teeth. With an effort, Catherine opened her eyes. The man was half turned away, not watching her, head lowered, massive, angry, wounded. A pale lock of hair fell on his forehead. Catherine had a sudden desire to push it back, to see this face turn toward her, but before she could move, Athana appeared out of the shadows and took her hand.

Catherine felt tired, but curiosity sustained her. The man had lifted his head when Athana arrived. He was leaning against the back of his chair, a retreat. She asked gently, "What's so disturbing about Athana?"

Joanne's voice broke into the quiet room, too loud, ironic. "She'll be a lot more disturbing for those fine people on the Council." The Métis advanced into the lamplight and sat on an arm of the chair, preventing the man from rising (from escaping?) as he had been about to do.

"One anormal ultimate infant might be acceptable, but not two."

Catherine didn't even try to hide her stupefaction. Joanne and the man looked at each other. He nodded with the shadow of a bitter smile, as though he were resigned to his role in the conversation. "And with the two of *us* as well, it would be dreadful. Too much is too much."

"Totally disorienting for those poor separatists," replied Joanne with swift sarcasm. "You have unique visions, Catherine, but they don't correspond to what tradition prescribes for the female infant. Anyway, the male infant would still be missing."

"So they'd be obliged to consider the possibility that *she* was the ultimate infant, and that the ultimists had been right all along," said Simon with a dry laugh.

"Except that you don't correspond to the descriptions of the ultimate infant," said Joanne. "You *are* a woman, aren't you?"

The question was clearly rhetorical, but Catherine murmured, "Yes," while her mind, with amazing efficiency, churned out the meaning of the words, complete now with capital letters. Separatists: one of the dominant sects among the Believers; the Infants must remain separate from one another in order to achieve the Liberation and wake the Deity. Ultimists: the male and female Infants must fuse into an Ultimate Infant, either androgynous or hermaphrodite, while for the subsects the Ultimate Infant is to be either male or female.

"Or else it's the female Infant that wins out," continued Simon, taking up the thread. "But why would she have a past history, or a name? Why these lapses of memory? And why would her Coming be like this? Tradition is completely off the mark, I'd say."

They weren't talking to Catherine, but to another or to some absent audience. Their alternating voices had taken on a special quality, that of an exchange of arguments known by heart, too old really to annoy them now, but too threatening not to need defusing, and both had chosen the compromise of irony.

"The girl would be a more likely candidate for the Ultimate Infant," said Joanne. "Young, innocent, appears out of the blue, is easily forgotten, even has a certain plastic quality, since she seems to have grown since I first saw her. But the disturbing element in all this is you. Why is she following you? You ought to be following *her*, at least. And then she really is too innocent. Tradition has never said that the Ultimate Infant would be simple-minded."

Catherine glanced at Athana, but the girl was listening with a detached curiosity, as though they weren't speaking of her.

Simon's face darkened. "In any case, *we* are still here. If either this child or you is the Ultimate Infant, it's the result of a fusion of the two Infants, and we shouldn't still be here. You ought to have taken them to Chicoutimi, Joanne. If only to see the expressions on the Council members' faces. To see them squirm as they tried to explain these two away."

Irritation had got the better of irony. He rose.

Joanne sighed, as though suddenly weary of pretending to play a game, and slipped from the arm to the seat of the chair. "It would be pandemonium, in any case." Her voice took on a doomful tone. "The End of the World is at Hand!" She shook her head and leaned suddenly toward Catherine. "No. Keeping you here was the only thing to do. To give us time to breathe, to think. To give you time to recover, too." Joanne laid a hand on her forehead, smiling almost affectionately. "We shouldn't overwhelm you with all this. You ought to rest. We'll talk about it when you're feeling better."

Catherine was about to say, "But I'm fine," when a fit of coughing shook her. She stifled it with difficulty, and opened her eyes to see Joanne staring at her in alarm. A sense of urgency swept over her, and she managed to stammer, "They think . . . that you two are the Infants?"

"They did think so," growled Simon. "Long enough to make our lives miserable."

"Because you had . . . different visions?"

"In my case, yes, in the South," said Joanne. She apparently didn't want to talk about it anymore, and finished vaguely. "All sorts of things."

"But aren't there other explanations?"

"Other than religion?" Joanne laughed without humor.

"No," said Simon brusquely. "There's no explanation at all."

He turned and walked out of Catherine's field of vision. Joanne gloomily watched him go. Then she seemed to master her disappointment, leaning over to arrange Catherine's pillows, sheets, and fur blanket, and holding her head as she gave her something to drink. "We'll talk about this later," she said gently. "Get some rest."

The dream envelops Catherine like a cocoon, molding itself to her body, but not touching her. Sometimes she almost feels pain, but the cocoon absorbs and diffuses it, makes it fade away. She ought to go out, perhaps. Or should she stay? Go out of what? Stay where? It seems to her that she *did* know, once.

Inside. She is inside, but inside is nowhere. Something neutral, white, perhaps, or slightly bluish-gray. There is no shading to indicate a possible depth in the field, no sound. She opens her mouth and gives a shout she doesn't hear. She'd like to move her arms, but it's as though she had none. She tries to put her hands on her body, but she has no hands because she has no arms—logical. She isn't too sure about the rest of her body, either. She can see, that's all. She feels an insidious sense of anguish and tries to hold on to it with all her strength, not wanting the cocoon to absorb and diffuse it. It's the only focus the dream gives her. The anguish becomes sharper: all this is familiar. Different but familiar. There should be movement, a race, a chase. The space should be a sphere that will close in on her, a sphere that she'll burst. There should be . . . the Presence, that's it: the Dream of the Presence. But the Presence has won, the Presence has caught her!

Suddenly she repossesses her body, the sensations that were her body. A victory. But it's a painful body, a short-lived victory. Pain wretches her from herself, and her awareness is scattered once more. But the cocoon has returned to reassemble the fragments, and strangely enough, the pain, instead of concentrating in this tiny space, wanders off once again. Now that her head is clear, she's able to think. If the cocoon is a condensation of the Presence, would she be able to see it by condensing herself? She gathers all of herself in her eyes, the only sense left her. And little by little, patterns appear, creating a space, faint phosphorescent lines that all lead to a concave surface, also luminescent: the cocoon. A more luminous line dances above her belly, made of a number of braided threads, like a rope, but a living rope, silvery-blue. It's the main link. If she tears it out, perhaps she'll still have a chance of escaping the Presence, but how can she do it without hands? A crushing sense of despair—which the cocoon carefully eradicates. Now, calm and detached, she looks at the rope: the Presence is sucking her through it. She notes the rhythmic pulsating that must propel her substance upward as her sheath of skin is emptied.

Yet she doesn't feel weaker or less whole. In fact she feels almost better, almost a body once more. Arms, hands, breasts, a belly, legs, a face, and without the sharpened pencil of pain to puncture their contours. She can move. Stretch an arm toward the rope, close her hand around it. . . . She gathers her forces to tear it out, she's going to do it, she must do it. She sees better now: the substance passing through this umbilical cord isn't flowing out; it's not her substance that's being greedily sucked out, it's the substance of the Presence that's being poured into her, contaminating her, displacing her. But a terrible doubt assails her at the very instant of tearing out the rope, suspending her horror and her action. Contaminating her . . . or feeding her? Displacing her . . . or giving back what she has lost? If she breaks the contact, will she escape or will she trigger a hemorrhage that will kill her?

What an odd idea: why would the Presence protect her, and from what?

Or else, for reasons that escape her, they have concluded a short-term pact, and she'll begin running away again when she's feeling better.

But the Presence won't ever let her go, now that it has her in its grip!

For a brief moment, the cocoon fades away. Totally. There is nothing but Catherine's body, free, with dawning pain. Then the cocoon envelops her again, soothingly.

Perplexed, she thinks: Yes, you'd let me leave?

A segment of the phosphorescent network linking

Catherine to the cocoon condenses and strokes her cheek, like a cool but timid hand.

Was that a yes? Then there really is someone there, all around. Who hears me, understands, responds. It should be even more terrifying, but the cocoon apparently absorbs the terror because Catherine isn't particularly afraid. Instead she thinks, with an absurd desire to laugh, that she has never yet tried to tame a nightmare, but that maybe this one wants to be tamed.

How does one go about it? She'd have to persuade the Presence to situate itself in space, give itself a body. . . . No, the Presence is so immense that it would probably take on the body of a giantess, and then how would she communicate with it? She'd have to clamber up, crawl along its body to yell into its ears, it would be dangerous, and maybe the giant wouldn't even hear her. Stay in the cocoon and speak to it without words, as she's doing now? Tell it stories, perhaps? Or rather, since speaking is apparently impossible, think it stories? Once upon a time?

Once upon a time there was a garden.

That wasn't Catherine's thought. Anyway, if someone thought it, it's no longer a thought but a place. Catherine recognizes the paths of the Sergines garden, paths and borders that try to look well-groomed but in fact are thronged with yellow cowslips, starry primroses, and once-neat clumps of pansies now running wild, smaller but hardy, popping up here and there, wherever the winds have carried the seed. Catherine smiles. All right, there was a garden. And in the garden there was a little girl. . . .

The garden seems a lot bigger, the trees, too, and the grass and flowers are much brighter. Catherine is wearing her blue apron and red leather sandals, and her braids are looped in two thick coils on either side of her head, held in place with barrettes. There was a little girl . . . who was tired of being all alone, despite the flowers in the garden, despite the cherries to be eaten, sitting astride the branches in the company of sparrows. . . . So, to while away the time, she observed the anthill on the terrace behind the kitchen. She had tried to dig neat little roads for the ants, but the ants didn't follow them, they were stub-

born and pretty stupid, the ants, because their roads were
a lot longer than hers. . . .

From somewhere that is everywhere, Catherine
watches the little Catherine seated crosslegged on the terrace in the shadow of the blackcurrant and raspberry
bushes. And she senses that someone else is also watching
curiously, that the whole garden seems to be suspended in
this curiosity.

. . . But the little girl didn't know there was another
garden in the garden, an invisible garden, a fairy garden
that occupied the same space, with a little fairy girl in it
who was also bored. . . .

Suddenly the garden seems deeper, as though another,
much larger garden quivered translucently, like a mirage
at the limit of her vision. Catherine is delighted. Now to
make the little fairy girl appear. . . .

And she is there, even before Catherine starts describing her: a little girl with long curly hair, brilliant red, and
white skin dotted with freckles. She's wearing a pair of
black overalls and an apple-green blouse. She has large,
tawny, almond-shaped eyes, a round, dimpled face with
fossettes, and a turned-up nose. Catherine is sure she's
never seen her before. Then why does she seem to recognize her? She's called, she's called. . . .

Lila, like lilac, but without a c.

And Catherine recognizes the voice—her own—this
phrase—her own—this given name—the one she had
thought of for her daughter, the daughter she would
surely have one day, perhaps even with François, or so she
thought at the time before realizing he would never be the
kind of father she wanted. It would be a daughter;
strange, during all those years she had thought she'd want
a boy, and now she wanted a girl, could actually remember when she'd changed her mind: after the child who had
left before even arriving, whose sex she'd never know,
their error in timing. The child she hadn't let live, something she'd never regretted in itself—but now she *did* regret never being able to have a child to replace it. She'd
thought she would, someday, half laughing, a little scared,
although less than she'd imagined, at the prospect of becoming a mother one day, at last.

A child she regrets, with a sharp, poignant regret,

now that she sees her, now that the child is being shown to her, but what right has the Presence to show her the child? The Presence, invisible in the garden, who *is* the garden—for, frightened by Catherine's anger and chagrin, it slips away, and the garden trembles, becomes transparent, as does little Catherine under the raspberries, and little Lila. . . . And Catherine finds herself back in the cocoon even before she can think, "No!" Even before she can think, "It's nothing, it's not your fault."

She must begin again. With another little fairy girl, that's all. A little girl . . . blonde, with blue-green eyes, an elfin face, that would be better for a little fairy girl.

The garden surges up around her again with the warm smells of earth and fruit, the whine of crickets, the sharp whistling of the swallows above the attic roof, the distant cough of a tractor on the hill opposite the house. The child Catherine is leaning over the ants as they hurry to and fro. Floating above her is a slender little girl, half transparent, with long, tawny blonde hair, wearing a short blue dress. Catherine feels she's seen this child somewhere, too, but the curiosity of the Presence nudges her, and anyway she can't stop to explore this already fading echo. She must find a name for this small fairy girl.

Italie.

She's called Italie? Catherine smiles with amusement. All right: Italie it is.

3

For several days, Catherine thought she would get the better of her cold. The fever stayed within reasonable limits, and her sneezes and coughs weren't too violent—luckily for her broken rib. On the fourth day she even felt strong enough to be distinctly bored. When she had gone to the bathroom, helped by Joanne, she'd been able to see something of her surroundings. Simon-Pierre Le Guével might be a hermit, but he was certainly comfortably ensconced. The house was a small geodesic dome, three-quarters sunk in the earth and rock. The rooms all opened onto a tiled platform, which was the last in a series of wide steps that surrounded the central depression. Here, big easy chairs were arranged around a fireplace that was more for decoration than heat, since there was a hot water radiator in each room. The bathroom had hot and cold running water, as well as all the other supposedly modern conveniences. The kitchen was beside the bathroom and appeared to be a more rustic affair, as far as Catherine had been able to see, with a wood stove for cooking. Simon must be a gourmet cook, nonetheless, judging from the number of dishes and utensils visible on the shelves and the kitchen table. From her bedroom, she could see the living room and an enormous bookcase, curved to fit the opposite wall.

No electricity, although there were candles and gas

lamps. ("Methane," Simon had commented dryly, seeing Catherine examine her bedside lamp.) The wooden furniture was simple but elegant, as was the wooden panelling and the parquet floor that covered everything but the bathroom and kitchen. All handmade, and visibly by the same hand, Simon's. Sometimes she could hear the noise of sawing and hammering coming from the basement up the stairway beside the main door—the noise of pottering at a workbench and of electric engines.

Joanne confirmed her deduction: electricity worked below ground level. Did all Northerners live half buried? The irony of Joanne's little smile was again lost on Catherine. "No. But there are those like Simon—much worse than Simon—who rough it completely."

Were there others who didn't rough it? But she hesitated to ask Joanne questions, partly because she knew the Métis was reluctant to answer them, and partly because of a persistent cautiousness, a fear of her questions revealing too much. And another fear: discovering new gaps in her knowledge or, on the contrary, acquiring too much upsetting information. Observe and reflect, yes, but not too much. Her injuries, the threat of flu, the demands and weaknesses of the body, all this had given her a sort of reprieve, a period of grace in which she could let herself float a little before trying to gather together the suddenly sparse bits of her life—the bits she knew about, at any rate. She had no desire to add too many new pieces to the puzzle. The possibility that the citizens of the North and the worrisome "Council" might consider her and Athana to be incarnations of supernatural creatures was more than enough!

To get her ideas in order, she'd have had to write them down, but it was impossible to do this discreetly. The best solution, and one that would take her mind off her boredom and the dull but everpresent pain in her leg and chest, was a book. She would have asked Athana for one, but wasn't sure of being answered. The girl had agreed to a camp bed rather than the armchair, but spent most of her time sleeping or eating. During the brief moments when she was awake and not eating, she was distracted, almost uneasy, and didn't talk to Catherine or answer her questions. Catherine therefore made her request to Simon about it when he brought breakfast that day.

"A book?" he said, looking skeptically at his curved bookshelves. He passed his hands through his hair. "What kind?"

"Pick one at random."

He seemed to stiffen. "Are you an adept?"

She realized after a second that he meant "an Adept," and smiled. "Of books with a small *b*, yes. And of chance, sometimes."

This earned her a genuine smile, a pleasant rarity from a man who was always frowning. He picked a book at random off a shelf, then gave a small exclamation, although it was impossible to say whether he was surprised or irritated. He came back with the book.

"*The Book of Steps*, by Pierre-Emanuelle Manesch." Good, an author she didn't know! The book had been read often. She let it fall open and read the first paragraph on the right-hand page. " 'The revelation develops on several different levels of complicity, which accounts for the inadequacy of what is said—never completely said—in relation to what is perceived—never completely perceived. . . .' "

" '. . . so that the revelation is written in what is expected, forgotten, found, and lost again,' " finished Simon with one of his half-amused, half-bitter smiles. "It's a family book: Manesch was my grandfather."

Catherine flipped through the book, a collection of thoughts or very short essays, sometimes poetic texts—a fragment jumped out at her: Example of the tree/We will reach the haven of the earth/Each of us dies anew through what opens us to joy. "A poet?"

"Poet, writer, philosopher. . . . Prophet."

The tone had hardened. Catherine decided not to ask her question and instead let the book fall open at another place. She read aloud again: " 'It is always through fragmentation that the incommensurable totality can be read. Therefore, it is always in relation to a fabricated totality that we approach the fragment; the latter representing, each time, the part of totality that is accepted, exalted, and at the same time, by a renewed contestation of the origin, by substituting itself for this origin, becoming itself the origin of all possible, discernible origin.' I think this author is going to interest me. Has he written anything else?"

"No."

"Did you know him—your grandfather?"

"No." Even more abrupt, now. "I was born the year of his death."

He put the breakfast tray on Catherine's lap, and Athana's tray on the armchair. The girl was still sleeping. It would be useless to ask him anything else: the moment of grace was over. Catherine put the book down beside her on the bed and began to eat.

Simon seemed more affable when he came back for the trays. "Do you like duck? I thought I'd do duck today."

"What's today, anyway?"

"January first."

Catherine smiled. "Happy New Year."

He seemed a little taken aback. "Oh, yes. Happy New Year."

A quick calculation: the accident had happened on the night of December twenty-sixth. What had Joanne told the guards and the doctor at the frontier post to explain their departure? Did anyone know that Joanne was now with Catherine and Athana? Simon had said they weren't really prisoners. Was the famous Council aware of their presence? Or had Joanne actually kidnapped them? And in that case, what had happened at the frontier post?

"I've nothing against duck," she said as all this was running through her mind.

"And the child?"

Athana was awake now, and busily downing her breakfast. Catherine smiled. "Oh, she seems to eat anything."

"All right, duck it is," said Simon, turning on his heel. "With blueberries."

Curious how Simon and Joanne talked about Athana. They never called her by her given name, never actually spoke to her. In the beginning, they had both appeared to view her with suspicious reserve. Then Joanne must have decided to consider her as a piece of furniture—Athana was always "the girl." Simon usually called her "the child," and treated her like a sort of pet, often with a slightly amused indulgence. Had they given themselves a period of respite before deciding what to do with their guests? That would imply they could afford it, that no one was aware of Catherine's and Athana's presence, or would bother to check out Simon's place. After all, why would she imagine that the whole Independent Realm of the North would be buzzing like a hive gone berserk because she and Athana were now within its frontiers? Perhaps only Joanne had built God-knows-what crazy theories about them, and as far as everyone was concerned, they'd just be ordinary refugees.

Charles-Henri. Charles-Henri knew a lot. If he were questioned. . . . But was he really in Chicoutimi, as Joanne had said? Suddenly worried, she asked Simon this when he came out of the kitchen.

"He's probably reached Chicoutimi by now," he answered with a mixture of irritation and embarrassment, no doubt aimed at Joanne more than at her. "Joanne wrecked the frontier post's communication system. By the time Central got worried and came to check, what with the blizzard and all. . . ."

"Do they know we're here?"

A sigh. "I don't think so. I hope not. For your sake and the child's."

"Not for you?"

The thin lips widened. "Oh, they've given up on us. And of course we may yet be revealed as the Infants, right? We could've turned the Realm upside down, and they wouldn't have lifted a finger."

"But you didn't."

The pale eyes rested on her appraisingly, then turned away. "No." Simon straightened up with a small scowl. "Don't worry. You're in good hands. Or the least possible bad hands, given the present situation." He went back into the kitchen.

Catherine picked up Manesch's book again. It wasn't easy to read. As she progressed, it seemed that each passage, even the poetry, must refer to a vast body of knowledge or beliefs that the author considered a given, but about which she knew nothing. She didn't share in the "complicity" mentioned in the first extract that she'd read aloud, and as for the "totality" referred to in the second passage, it left her puzzled, as did many other passages in the book. Was he speaking of the total reality of the world? Or of the author's consciousness, a consciousness that might also have been collective? Some fragments seemed to show Manesch as a slightly twisted Adept. For example, "Everything that can be grasped frees itself as soon as it is apprehended, for it becomes gradually involved in a network of contradictory relations that, although they reduce it to its function as a symbol, an image, or a sound—a sign among signs, an image among images, a sound among sounds—free it, at the same time, from the oppressive dictates of sense, the tyranny of the Totality."

Or in another passage: "First, one great liberty: that of not submitting to the real but choosing an *unconditioned* reality." This could be interpreted in an anti-Adept sense, though.

Other passages seemed to refer to a more traditional approach to spirituality: "Having attained these limits, what desire would dare present itself as desire, if not the infinite desire, the untouchable heavenly summit at the foot of which our desires and limitations expire like wavelets on the shore; if not the azure enamored of the azure, beyond horizons?"

But this fragment went off on an almost obsessional tangent about a "visage," no doubt of the deity, "the unidentifiable visage through which ours has access to the truth . . . an image to which we are eternally dedicated, like the blue of the air to the blue of the sea; a visage from before the first dawn, smooth, and becoming smoother still with each manifestation, with each ephemeral metamorphosis, until the total, final transparency."

This might at least refer to the Deity of the North, which was sleeping and must be wakened by the Infants, its infants—its incarnations? "Prophet," Simon had said. If this grandfather had been the inventor—sorry, the revealer—of the Northern religion, there would be other written works, the sacred texts of this religion. She'd have to ask Joanne. Simon didn't seem to care much for his grandfather.

Actually, Catherine preferred the poems, or at least the poetic fragments. She found them more accessible than the prose works, however paradoxical that might seem. Plenty of allusions could be read into the poetry, nevertheless; references to the cold and the snow, for example: "Imagination, emanation of the ice/a godsend to me." Or: "Choosing frost/Like virgin lips/Gleaming/Giving me character." Or this stanza from a poem that had held her attention for a long time. It was called "South/North": "Snow in a harmonic line/Meant to be black, yet blue."

Was the reference to blue meaningful? It was a color mentioned throughout the book, in both poems and fragments.

Also, there were passages that could be read as allusions to the Infants, always in the form of references to the second or third degree. . . . It was clear that if Manesch had experienced a transcendental revelation, he was incapable, as were most mystics, of expressing it in normal, everyday language. It needed the language of the night—poetry, for example.

"No," remarked Joanne when asked. Her sardonic smile resurfaced. "It's because he could only write in code. There are no sacred books in the North, nor religious books. 'Books would unduly hinder the dynamic movement of the Quest.'" This was clearly a citation. "Why do you think there are so many sects? Anyway, the word sect is incorrect. The religion of the Realm is not an organized religion. There are no priests, no church, no dogma—or else just one: the Deity sleeps and must be awakened so that the world may at last exist in reality. Awakened by the Infants, or an Infant—almost everyone agrees on this point, too. As for the rest, each is free to follow his or her own quest."

"What about *The Book of Steps*?"

"I can't believe Simon gave it to you." Joanne still seemed surprised.

"I told him to pick one at random."

Joanne burst out laughing. "Poor Simon! But it's not supposed to be a book about religion. It's Pierre-Emmanuelle Manesch's spiritual testament; it wouldn't have been published otherwise. Copies of it are very difficult to come by these days. They've gradually stopped circulating. Don't ask me why." She seemed to have a pretty good idea, though. "Excuse me, I've got to get the meal ready."

Joanne took care of midday meals, Simon of breakfasts and suppers. They appeared to have fallen into a familiar routine, although most of the time they passed each other without speaking or even looking at one another. After lunch on this day, the Métis announced that the weather was now good enough to clear the road. "We might as well make use of the snowcar while we have it."

Simon grudgingly got dressed for the outdoors. Apparently it took two to clear the road. How did he manage when he was alone? He had horses, and perhaps they pulled a snowplow? But Simon and Joanne were already outside, and these questions remained unanswered. Puzzled, Catherine listened to the faint hum of a motor. No electricity functioning on the surface. Did they have steam engines, then? No, it didn't make the right sounds. Some chemical engine? She promised herself that she would ask them when they came back.

The house was quiet with the sort of inhabited silence characteristic of houses built with a lot of wood. In the fireplace on the other side of the room, the embers of Joanne's fire still glowed, shooting up sparks every now and then. The sun poured in through the uncovered sections of the dome, giving a golden glow to the wood floors. The daylight was controlled by a mechanical system of blinds, although in Catherine's room the ceiling panels blocked out the sun permanently.

No electricity above the surface. Something kept tugging at Catherine's memory: the tinkle of a telephone slammed down on a hard surface. She hadn't dreamed that fight between Joanne and Simon—only mistakenly shifted it to her childhood, where such fights had been all too familiar. Had there really been a telephone? That knot of energy seen through her hyperceptions. . . . But it was a dream, wasn't it? Or a vision. In any case, influenced by the dream after the accident, the dream of that radiant garden. That emerged from my subconscious—Sarah notwithstanding. It must have something to do with Mama. It was *her* garden. She made vegetables grow there, good nurturing mother that she was. She was also the one who wanted to plant pretty-by-night on the terrace behind the kitchen. I used to stand in front of the bushes at dusk and watch them. These flowers were more alive than the others; you could see them *move*. Time-lapse films of plants blooming were a movie trick, but in the garden it was *true*, I could see it with my own eyes, catch nature in the act. Good old Mother Nature.

Yes, Sarah, mythico-symbolic dreams, "psychoanalysis," the analysis of the psyche.

As far as dreams were concerned, it was hard, in all honesty, not to give in to the usual terrorism of psychoanalysis, you-can't-know-what-you-know-you-don't-want-to-know. Furthermore, with Joanne and Simon in the picture—including their comments about the infants and so on, even if their ideas seemed highly improbable, not to say ridiculous—she must keep an open mind about the possibility that her dreams and visions had very little to do with her subconscious. But with what, then? A collective unconscious? Belonging to a culture about which she knew almost nothing? Unfortunately, the collective unconscious was still a hypothesis. . . . Or she could fall back into the paranoid delusion of The Great Machination, of all-out mind control, but she couldn't take that seriously, either. The desire to escape the complexity of this world, imagining it to be deliberately organized by a superior power, whether benevolent or evil—no, it was too easy. Various scientific credos also fell into that trap, credos hardening into an all-encompassing principle of explanation. No, you had to keep an open, flexible mind. She hadn't enough facts at her disposal to back up any theories.

Catherine gingerly changed position. Facts. If there really were a telephone in the kitchen. . . . Could she get up? No, she didn't have the strength.

"Athana?"

The girl was awake and seemed to be meditating, staring into the distance. The blue-green gaze turned questioningly on Catherine. At least Athana seemed to be in a communicative mood today.

"Do you know what a telephone is, Athana?"

After a moment's thought, the blonde head nodded.

"Would you go into the kitchen, and if there's a telephone. . . ." Disconnect it and bring it to me? Too complicated. ". . . show it to me?" She could always put the second request once they'd established the existence of a telephone.

But it was impossible to foresee Athana's way of interpreting things. She returned from the kitchen holding what seemed to be a cellular telephone. Catherine flicked the switch and listened to the dial tone in amazement. Before she even thought about it, her fingers were dialing Christine's number and she was listening, her heart beating fast—but there was no sound, now, not even the dial tone. Whatever energy the phone used, it couldn't get past the barrier. She looked in her bag—had she dragged it all this way without realizing it? Wonderful thing, the feminine reflex. Yes, there it was, the metal nail file that she carried everywhere. She took it out and began unscrewing the casing.

If there were batteries, she couldn't recognize them as such. Just a small, silvery pellet. Spherical. Detachable. Catherine took it out of its compartment and weighed it in her hand. Warm. It must be made of metal, although it wasn't very heavy. A radioactive capsule would be heavier, would be sheathed with lead, wouldn't it? Could the process of controlled fusion be contained in a pellet that size? Impossible. *E pur si muove.* And yet it worked. Therefore, this must be the source of energy. She examined it more closely. There was no middle line indicating that two halves had been soldered together. . . .

The pellet exploded in her fingers. A small but intense bluish light, almost white. Paralyzed, Catherine stared at the tiny fragments lying on the bed in front of her, more delicate than an eggshell. Her brain struggled to think. She must have squeezed it too hard; the pellet had been hollow. The little flash—sublimation? Had the energy source volatilized?

"Blue," said Athana; she sounded puzzled. With a finger, she turned over the pieces lying on the sheet.

The main door opened, and Catherine flinched, feeling ridiculously guilty. Simon was coming in, taking off his outdoor clothes, would almost certainly turn to look at the bedroom to see if all was well. Catherine resisted the impulse to hide the phone under the sheet. Simon frowned and skirted the dome to the bedroom.

"I wanted to see how it worked. I think I've broken it."

He picked up the telephone and examined it, then put it on the night table. "It's not serious," he muttered. He didn't seem really angry. "It can be replaced." The intonation was strange, almost resentful.

"What's the source of energy?"

"A source of energy."

"That's a little tautological, isn't it?"

He surprised her by giving a wry laugh. "Very. Completely tautological."

There was some undercurrent here, but she was still unable to fathom it. Annoyed, she gathered the bits of shell in her palm. "It's made here, in the North?"

"If you like."

"I just want to understand!"

"And what do you think *I* want?"

They glared aggressively at each other. Catherine controlled her irritation, however. "Tell me," she said, "is it usual for cadavers to disappear in a blue flash?"

"Yes," said Simon very stiffly.

"At the moment of death, the bodies become volatile and sublimate in a flash, leaving behind only the clothes?"

Contrary to Catherine's expectations, he seemed to relax a little, perhaps because of the surprise she'd unwittingly displayed. He sat down in the armchair by the night table and wiped his forehead without making the slightest difference to the persistently tumbling lock of hair. "Not necessarily at the moment of death. It could be after a while—it varies. Some become volatile all at once, others exude. Here in the North, they usually exude."

"Exude? Exude what?" asked Catherine.

"Blue. A blue . . . light."

"And why is that?" said Catherine. She suddenly realized that the word uttered by Athana when the pellet exploded was the same word she'd spoken in the tavern when the policeman died: "Blue."

Simon shrugged, then said mockingly, "Chemical phenomena, maybe?"

It was useless to continue this line of questioning.

"And does it happen more often in the South? Most of the time? And does everyone know about it?"

Showing surprise was definitely a more effective way of eliciting information. "No," Simon said, "they generally don't know. It doesn't happen until the body is in the coffin or at the crematorium."

"And if there's an exhumation, doesn't anyone wonder where the body has gone?"

"They know that some bodies decompose faster than others."

Simon's good will was running out. Catherine tried once more. "Is it the same for animals?"

"Yes."

"And it's always been this way."

"Yes. Not so often now, depending on where it happens."

He was annoyed, but like someone facing a familiar enigma, not an importunate curiosity.

Catherine took a chance on the telephone again: "The barrier absorbs energy, but not this kind of energy. What produces the barrier?"

The thin lips kept on smiling, but the genuine amusement had gone. Simon nodded with ironic approval. "No doubt the same kind of energy as in the sphere—that's what we call those little silver pellets. Ah, but what kind is that? Go back one square and miss a turn."

"Oh, but it's very simple." Joanne's sarcastic voice reached them from the main door. They hadn't heard it open or close. "It's the will of the Sleeping Deity."

Simon turned brusquely toward her, biting his lips. "I know that I know nothing!" he snapped finally. He stood up, knocking against the chair as he did so, and disappeared into the kitchen. Soon the clatter of dishes could be heard.

The Métis took his place in the chair. She still smelled of the outdoor cold and of balsam.

Catherine looked at her for a moment, then sighed. "And you, what do you know?"

Joanne gave her a calculating half-smile. "Try this for size: the Realm is an artificial creation, an experiment on a human scale in brain manipulation. There's no way of knowing what exists behind appearances, the data we possess are manipulated, people are conditioned not to be surprised by contradictions or impossibilities."

"A perfect description of the South," Catherine said. Oh, no! Not the Great Manipulation again! But perhaps it was too early to be disappointed: a gleam of satisfaction had shone in Joanne's eyes in response to her remark.

"The same manipulators are experimenting on the North and the South, then, trying different parameters—politics on one side, religion on the other, plus various economical and technological forms," Joanne said.

"But who could these manipulators be?" Catherine countered. "To secure the degree of control that you're postulating, they'd have to possess a highly developed technology, far beyond what we know." She was sure Joanne was going to say that we only know the technology *They* permit us to know, and the argument would have come full circle.

"What if it involved extraterrestrial, nonhuman technologies?" asked Joanne.

The great Extraterrestrial Conspiracy? Catherine had trouble not laughing, but the image of a leonine head silhouetted against a sky spangled with unknown constellations pulled her up short. But that was merely an anticipated memory of imaginary creatures on an imaginary planet, fabricated by a local artist! "Even if the Marrus did exist, that doesn't necessarily. . . ."

"The Marrus don't exist. No one had ever heard of them before those posters appeared in Quebec. We haven't even begun to explore our solar system."

"What about the moon? Come on!" protested Catherine. "Are you saying we haven't been to the moon?"

"What's the moon?"

Catherine tried to control her voice. "The Earth's satellite planet."

"Earth has no satellite," said Joanne, and then, more slowly, "*My* Earth, everybody's Earth, has no satellite. For you, it has one?"

Catherine was petrified. When had she last seen the moon? In her recent Garden dream. But in the sky, the real sky? She couldn't remember. Should there be a moon in the sky? Everything in her cried out, yes, there should.

No new "memory" suddenly popped up to tell her that earth had no moon.

Joanne was staring at her with puzzled interest. "The Marrus were *your* vision. No one ever had it before. A solid vision, durable, shared—by the whole damned city. You're a new parameter in the experiment."

Catherine refused to panic, tried to regain control of the conversation. "Create an entire world for an experiment? Just what are these extraterrestrial beings of yours, anyway? God?"

The young women leaned over her ardently. "Not an entire world! Not 'a world.' " Maybe the world doesn't exist. I mean, there are ourselves, here, the Realm, the South, Montreal, and—well—Quebec, broadly speaking. But not the rest."

"Joanne!" exclaimed Catherine with a forced laugh. "There are radio and TV, newspapers, airports, planes! I was in France last May!" Her voice cracked in spite of herself. "My father *died* in France last May!"

The young woman looked at her pityingly. "That's what I told myself, too. I tried to get on the plane to Louisiana, you see. Several times. Each time all sorts of things prevented me—'objectively' prevented me. I couldn't even get to the airport, Catherine. It was the same with the train, or trying to drive or hitch a ride. West, south, no matter where outside Quebec, it just didn't happen. And at the time it didn't seem at all odd. Radio, TV, those things can be simulated. And as for traveling. . . . You remember going to France. The same way you remember the moon, the same way you don't remember all kinds of things that suddenly come back. Have you undeniable proof of having gone to France?"

Catherine looked at her, suddenly gripped with compassion. Joanne was crazy. Delirious, although logical, as with most cases of genuine delirium. Once you decided that everything was an illusion, fabrication, simulation, it all hung together, you could account for everything. That's what had stopped Catherine from being tempted to think this way. If an explanation leaves absolutely no loopholes, it's suspect. "Perfection is the proof of the nonexistence of the determinist world," as said by . . . who was it? "And imperfection is a proof of the existence of the random world." Not a totally scientific precept, but she would stick by it.

It was probably useless to try to reason with Joanne, but Catherine couldn't help herself. "All right. Most of my memory lapses were filled fairly fast, it's true. But on the other hand, why would your extraterrestrials go to so much trouble? Why would they keep up the illusion of an entire world existing outside Quebec? Why give me a life history in which Europe plays an active part? And I'm certainly not the only one. Just think of the micromanagement it would take! The number of people and machines involved would be gargantuan! For if everything we perceive is an illusion, you're still implying that there's another reality behind it, aren't you? The reality in which your manipulators are manipulating."

Joanne shook her head, her expression one of sharp distress. She wasn't playing games, now. "I don't say that everything is an illusion, Catherine. I'm not saying that all this exists only in my head and that *you* are an illusion! I'm simply saying it's an experiment, implying the existence of real people, real things, an objective reality, if you like, but which we perceive in a twisted way, and to which our manipulated perceptions add another layer of reality. Visions, for example. Once they're directly manipulating our brains. . . ."

"Directly manipulating our brains." Easy to say! Especially if one postulated an "objective reality." There were limits in objective reality. Immutable physical laws. Planck's Constant. The speed of light. $\frac{1}{2}$ of mv^2. All that. Memories, perceptions, all are electrochemical processes that can be traced in neural matter. How would "They," these extraterrestrials, manage to intercept such things "directly"? With implants, possible—why not? But I have no implants. And you'd have to explain how these implants would receive electric impulses here in the North, or at least above the surface, since the barrier . . .

. . . absorbs specific electrical frequencies, suddenly said the other Catherine, popping up in her head. Not solar energy frequencies, for example, or bio-electrical frequencies. And the barrier could very well not interfere with the implants, provided they operated on a frequency that wasn't absorbed.

Well, no need to look for extraterrestrials, a human agency would fit the bill!

"You don't believe me," said Joanne with resignation. "I have trouble believing myself, too—but it's the only explanation that takes everything into account."

Catherine sank back in the pillows, her face twitching slightly with pain. *No use getting excited, it doesn't agree with my ribs. How can I make her understand that explaining enigmas with some totalitarian mystery is no explanation at all?*

But Joanne apparently didn't want to be convinced. "What do you think those spheres were?"

She had a point there. The hyperceptions didn't seem to show up anything recognizable—Catherine caught herself up: *she wasn't about to consider her . . . perceptual visions as a reality, was she?*

And why not? They seemed to correspond to known and legitimate manifestations of energy. *For the moment, let's accept the idea that hyperceptions were a reality; they had certainly shown the "blockage" of the electricity produced by the underground generator. What had the hyperceptions shown about the sphere that powered the telephone?* Some kind of stable, self-perpetuating reaction. *Even supposing it was something that They wanted her to see, what did it evoke?*

An answer suddenly surfaced—supplied by the other Catherine, no doubt.

"It could be a form of plasma," she said, not opening her eyes.

"A plasma?" Joanne seemed a little lost.

"What I saw in the spheres." While she was at it, she might as well talk about her hyperceptions. "Sometimes I perceive things—how can I express it?—more broadly. Sometimes I can see in the infrared and ultraviolet wavelengths. And see infrasounds, ultrasounds, electromagnetic waves. I saw the energy in the sphere the other day. It reminds me of a sort of plasma."

The quality of the silence made her open her eyes. At the limit of her field of vision, she could see Simon's silhouette leaning against the wall that separated the bedroom from the bathroom. In the interval Joanne had picked up the phone and had been systematically demolishing it. Now, however, her hands were still. She was looking at Catherine with a speechless stupefaction that disappeared just as Catherine became aware of it.

"Broader perceptions," said Joanne tonelessly. There was a pause. "Are you also telepathic, by any chance?" Crushing sarcasm. Without giving Catherine a chance to react, she stood up, threw the demolished telephone on the bed, and strode out.

Simon, walking in, considered Catherine with grudging approval. "You annihilated her grand theory?"

"Not really," sighed Catherine. "Unless the notion of hyperceptions is an argument that could knock it cold—but I knew nothing about it."

"The notion of what?" asked Simon, coming over to her.

"Perceptions that are . . . different. I have them. I think. Seeing infrareds, ultrasounds, that kind of thing."

Simon stopped abruptly beside the armchair. He looked as dumbfounded as Joanne.

"What is it, for heaven's sake?" She jerked with sudden irritation, and a searing pain shot through her right side. She repeated weakly, "What?"

He kept looking at her, clutching the back of the chair so hard that his fingers bit into the upholstery. "According to tradition, this is one of the characteristics of the Infants," he muttered. "Neither Joanne nor I have ever possessed it. Other things, yes. Being able to block out physical pain, a sense of orientation, and—well, I call it an internal clock. Knowing exactly how much time has passed without needing to look at a watch. But not multivision. Nor the rest—at least, I don't think so. Telepathy, precognition, telekinesis, and what else? Too much is too much! All the sects differ on the subject, anyway! It's probably happened in the other direction: people found they had these capacities, and attributed them to the Infants because it made for a better story! Tradition! Old wives' tales, that's all."

Catherine was looking at him, unable to say a word, when she noticed a blur on the other side of the lower level of the living room. There was someone there, by the bookcases. But the shelves were different, straight instead of curved, and now she could see several fine old glass-fronted cupboards made of dark wood. A man was standing there reading. He was three-quarters turned toward her, a fairly massive figure, wearing a garnet-colored velvet smoking jacket with gold silk button-loops. The lamps lit up his white brush cut and imposing square beard, also very white. Even with the gold-rimmed pince-nez, his resemblance to Simon was striking. Catherine was about to speak to him when he turned toward her, smiled as he put a finger to his lips, and disappeared.

Simon had noticed nothing; his back was turned to the living room, and he hadn't been looking at Catherine. "My grandfather . . ." he murmured. "My grandfather had perceptions of this kind, apparently. This multivision. Until the last time he came back from the Far North."

Catherine glanced at the bookcases, feeling overwhelmed. All was as before, with the warm light of the late afternoon sun pouring in. "Your grandfather?" she finally managed to say.

"Manesch," said Simon, slumping into the armchair with a sigh, unaware of Catherine's dismay. His eye fell on the wrecked telephone, and he straightened brusquely. "The bitch!" he hissed between clenched teeth.

"Your grandfather, Pierre-Emmanuelle Manesch," Catherine repeated in an almost normal voice.

"He's the origin of the barrier, the spheres," murmured Simon. "He prayed, and the Realm awoke with the barrier. After that he had a revelation, and he brought the first energy spheres from the Far North. And finally, he organized the Pilgrimage." He was examining the broken telephone, piece by piece, as though unable to believe his eyes. "Joanne has always been against machines fueled by the spheres—except when it's convenient for her. . . . But I have none, except this phone! They forced me to take it, it was their condition for letting me go. In a way, they were right. If something should happen, I've no radio, nothing."

Catherine sat up, suddenly more alert. "Officially, what's the point of the ritual pilgrimage in the Far North?"

"To restore substance to the Sleeping Deity in order

to comfort it while the infants seek their name." Another citation, spoken with dark sarcasm.

"Joanne said the spheres were . . . the will of the Deity?"

Simon shrugged and gave a snort. "That's what they say here in order to explain how the spheres work. Explain! The spheres are fragments of the Deity that It is supposed to give us in exchange for those we give back to It. It does this to help us. Nice Deity. Energy in exchange for corpses!"

Catherine took a deep breath to try to calm her rapidly beating heart, and immediately regretted it, but the pain didn't matter. Energy for corpses. The blue flash that volatilized the policeman in the tavern. Athana saying, "They come back." Corpses, in the North and the South. But energy spheres only in the North. What was missing for all the elements to click together? Render unto the Deity its substance . . . fragments . . .

"Your grandfather wrote his book after his revelation?"

Simon had placed the dismembered phone on the bedside table. He sighed. "It was found after his death. They'd wanted to turn him into a prophet, even one of the Infants, but he would never have any of it. In the end, he went on a final voyage to the Far North. When he came back, he had changed. He died shortly afterward. They published the book: a spiritual testament, they said, out of respect for the memory of the Prophet, and all that. But they never knew how to interpret this book. In fact, it was always an embarrassment to them."

Now she understood Simon's feelings about his grandfather better: Manesch's path somewhat prefigured his own. A man invested with an unwanted sacred character, despite his objections. But also a man who had instituted an exchange that Simon refused to accept. An ambiguous figure, arousing ambivalent emotions. And who had left this book. Was it an esoteric description of the revelation?

Simon touched the bits of telephone. "Joanne never accepted it—the tradition, the Pilgrimage, the spheres." His voice seemed distant, tinged with an old regret. "But it's impossible to get anything moving here. I told her so. And finally she left for the South to verify her theories."

"Which you don't share."

He leaned his elbows on his knees and folded his hands, obstinate once more. "It doesn't make sense. Extraterrestrials and what else? It's crazy. Even if we were cattle, if the purpose was to recoup basic organic material, it would be done on a much more systematic basis, with organized massacres. But the Pilgrimage is voluntary, and everything has been codified to avoid abuses. You can't kill someone to obtain spheres, for instance, it won't work—the corpse won't be accepted in exchange. And the distribution of the spheres is strictly regulated."

"Joanne would say we can't fathom the motivations or acts of nonhuman creatures"

Simon straightened up with a disdainful little laugh. "But it is *not* unfathomable. There is a very human logic at work here, a very stupid human logic. Religions, ideologies. Power, repression, violence or nonviolence, all that is very human. If there is manipulation, it's ordinary human manipulation, intoxication, propaganda, disinformation. A so-called religion here, another kind of ideology in the South. Established powers wanting to hang on to power and secure their control over their populations."

This was pretty much what Catherine had thought, but it wasn't a decisive argument. Still, she could see why Simon preferred this theory: without answering the how, it more or less took care of the why. If you explored the picture more closely, however, it began to get fuzzy.

"And what are Athana and I, in that case? Northern agents? Southern guinea pigs who've broken through our conditioning?"

"Of course not," snapped Simon. "You have no implants, and in any case they don't function here. And we recognized you."

"Recognized us?"

"Yes, of course. You thought you knew me—and Joanne. The same for us, with the girl. Or for Joanne and me when we met the first time. My grandfather was the same. Another of the so-called characteristics of the Infants. And there are others who ... detect us. The 'sages.' Those who are 'in resonance with the Deity.' Most of the Council members, among others. What can you do against a setup like that? My father. Joanne's mother. . . ."

He fell silent. Catherine studied him, suddenly feeling sorry for the man. Since they'd been children . . . especially Simon, no doubt, the grandson of the "Prophet." Pushed not only by their families but by a whole society to assume a role they didn't want, and unable to deny the fact that they possessed special faculties, although they didn't understand them. If others could "detect" them, did that mean that these people had similar but latent faculties? A mutation? Catherine closed her eyes, suddenly weary. Genetic manipulation of humans, on top of everything else?

When she opened her eyes again, she found Simon watching her with a mixture of curiosity and alarm.

"You could have explained sooner," she said rather more drily than she intended.

He shrugged, stubborn once more. "Told you what? We don't really know your role in all this. Joanne wanted to keep you in the South. But you had to come to Quebec-City. And apparently the child follows you around like a dog."

Catherine glanced at Athana, who was sleeping the sleep of the just—or the innocent—curled up in the arm-chair on the other side of the bed.

"Joanne thinks that Athana and I are new parameters in the experiment," she remarked, watching Simon's reaction.

He leaned back in his chair, hands behind his head. "You're certainly important to Joanne," he said, suddenly derisive. "You and your unique visions. That exhibition in Quebec. . . . Impressive. But you won't do her much good if you stay here. She has always thought the solution lay in the South. She's never really been able to prove it, but she prefers the South anyway. Cleaner, she says." He folded his arms, his expression darkening. "On one hand, I understand how she feels. I've always thought that polit-ical oppression was more honest than religious oppres-sion. And they don't use spheres in the South. But she doesn't realize what she's become down there. All these machinations. . . ."

"She works for the North, doesn't she?"

A small, bitter laugh. "She works for herself. Sometimes that coincides with Northern interests. You never know which Joanne you're dealing with. She has a finger in every covert organizational pie going—left, right, center, every which way! And of course she uses her prestige as a possible Infant with the Believers when it suits her. But in point of fact Joanne only works for her one-track idea."

"Where do I come in?"

"People who have unorthodox visions are put under surveillance and generally arrested. According to her, they're considered 'resistant to manipulation,' individuals who threaten the established order, who are dangerous for the Canadian government. Which means, still according to her idea, dangerous for its secret manipulators. She's always been very disappointed with the people she kept out of the CNP's clutches. Either their visions became normal, or they no longer had any visions at all. But I understand her interest in you: you're one hell of a case."

More than you know! Thinking of the dreams about which Joanne and Simon knew nothing, Catherine swallowed her absurd irritation at his remark and kept silent. Come to think of it, what was the status of dreams in relation to visions in the North? And what did they do to people with heterodox visions?

"And you've never had visions?" she queried.

He looked at her, as though hesitating between anger and amusement. "No," he said finally, still hovering between the two. "I've never left the Realm, and people don't have visions in the Realm."

It was exasperating. Catherine started to laugh, but not too hard, mindful of her ribs. "I had one not five minutes ago!"

"What kind of game are you playing?" he exclaimed, stiffening.

"And you?" protested Catherine, a little too energetically, for she was obliged to lie back on the pillows. She grimaced. "I saw someone standing by the bookcases in the living room just now, after Joanne had left. An old man, wearing a garnet-colored smoking jacket and pince-nez. Except that the bookcases were different."

Simon's face was ashen. "It's not true," he murmured, getting up and stumbling against the armchair as he backed away. "It's not true. People can't have visions here. It's never happened. You're lying, trying to make me, of all people, believe you're an Infant! Do you take me for a fool?"

"But it's true," stammered Catherine. "I swear to you. . . ."

"Enough!" he shouted in desperate fury. "Leave me alone! I was at peace, beginning to forget all that, and now Joanne is back, and here you are with your crazy stories, and that child—but I've had enough. Leave me alone, all of you!"

He almost ran down the steps, crossed the living room, grabbed his parka, and rushed outside.

4
—

Catherine waited for a moment, hoping Joanne would re-
appear to see what all the shouting was about. But nothing stirred in the house. The sky was turning dark blue,
and dusk rose in the dome like an incoming tide. The fire
was probably out. Catherine turned to look at Athana.
The girl was still sleeping.

She tried to find a more comfortable position, but it
was impossible. This half sitting, half lying gave her a
pain in her lower back and the nape of her neck. And her
throat was dry with the rising evening fever. She stifled a
cough and drank a mouthful of water directly from the
carafe. It was tepid. She balanced the carafe on her stomach and watched the refractions from the last rays of the
setting sun. The story so far: our heroine is in the middle
of nowhere, with a broken leg and rib, being held *incom-
municado* now that Joanne has destroyed the telephone.
She has just alienated her only two possible sources of information. Bravo. And now what? Hope, or fear, that the
famous Council will learn of my presence and come to get
me?

Gloomily, she stroked the fat, round contours of the
carafe. What had she learned from her grudging "sources
of information," anyhow? Disconnected and contradictory facts—with the nature of the overall structure remaining stubbornly elusive. A few brief glimpses of

Joanne and Simon's past. A paranoid theory that explained the whole but ignored the details, new details that complicated the whole without explaining it. Corpses exchanged for energy. A grandfather who had visions—no, people don't have visions in the Realm, and it's true that Simon said "revelation," not "vision." But I certainly had a vision just now, and I bet it was Simon's grandfather! Who had hyperceptions just like me, or at least "multivision." "Trying to make me believe you're an Infant." Infants are supposed to have visions even in the Realm? Curious: the South seems to function "normally," but visions are a common occurrence, whereas the North functions magically, but there are no visions. It's all topsyturvy. Does everyone from the North who is transplanted to the South have visions? Joanne did, it seems.

Catherine closed her eyes, feeling despondent. She had to admit the theory about an experiment in manipulation was the most plausible, at least on a partial basis—in fact it *had* to be partial, because when setting up an experiment you could control the original parameters, but after that you let things follow their course in order to see the results. Except that in this case there definitely seemed to be specific changes in the parameters. Bad science, that! All right: these experimenters are rotten scientists—which would prove that they're human? Probably. Small comfort: I'm being manipulated, but not all the time. It would be more comfortable to envisage total manipulation, in a way. You'd have no choice but to let yourself go with the flow since all your actions were programmed, no matter what you did. But how could you tell where a partial manipulation began and ended? When am I free? When am I *me*?

She squeezed her eyelids shut to keep back the unexpected tears. Mustn't cry. It's fatigue. But the question kept echoing in her head, proliferating in wild reverberations that almost drove her mad. When am I myself, what am I, anyway? How do I pick out the false from the true memories? Did I go to France last May? Have I ever gone to France? Does France exist? Did my father die last May, did I have a father, a mother, an ex-husband in Louisiana, does Louisiana exist, or the rest of the world? The photographs in the box at home in Montreal—what were they, fakes? Did I imagine the box, the house, Montreal?

With trembling hands she reached for her wallet in her bag. The two photographs she carried everywhere: the lush summer garden within the four walls of her house in the Enclave, and the little sepia photo that she'd taken from the old passport, the precious passport with which her mother had been able to escape the incestuous adopted father, the precarious Indochina of the postwar period. The passport in which the timid young girl with her braids cut still bore her native name: Nguyen Thié Té. Were these proofs? It was all she had left, along with her unreliable memories. How was she to know? To choose? Her hands were twisting convulsively, like two blind animals. She forced them to be still, but she couldn't stop the questions or silence the broken voice that protested within her: these memories, these bitter experiences, these lessons so painfully learned, which were illusions, lies? And what am I, then, if not the sum of my memories?

She stopped trying to suppress the sobs that rose from her chest. It hurt less to let go, to cry aloud, with huge gulping sobs, ignoring the dagger-thrusts of her broken rib, careless of who heard her—but there was no one here, had there been anyone here, did here even exist?

Cool hands on her hands. Athana. Her blue-green eyes, worried, forlorn beneath the tangled golden hair. Catherine put her arms around the girl and buried her face against her neck, holding her tight, so tight it hurt her rib, yes, the pain was real, just that, at least that. Athana stirred a little, but it was better to rock her, stroke her, yes, it felt good, these gentle fingers on her face, her eyebrows, her mouth, like a sad benediction, it was good to hold and be held, to feel this warm body encircling hers, so that the pain spread like a sonorous fog, losing its sharpness and becoming almost comfortable, like one of those fuzzy woolen blankets people knitted for babies, in which you could lose yourself, forget.

"But if you forget, I won't exist anymore," says Italie reproachfully.

Little Catherine shakes her head vigorously, making her braids whirl. She has unrolled them for greater comfort. "I didn't call you the first time. You came all by yourself."

Italie looks skeptical. "I'm not sure about that."

"Then you're not sure of the opposite, either," says little Catherine reasonably.

They are seated on the low wall along the terrace, beside the stone trough with a tap used for watering the plants and washing the dog—and the teddy bear when the dog rebels. The water glimmers, dark and green between the mossy walls of the tank. The light falls in slanting rays, apricot-colored: the afternoon is drawing to a close. On the hill opposite, the cows meander along the old path beside a wheat field dotted with field poppies. The garden is alive with summer noises: swallows, bees, crickets, and the distant lowing of cattle. The stones on the little wall are rough but warm beneath the little Catherine's bare thighs.

"I'd rather you didn't forget," Italie says, twisting a lock of hair.

The little Catherine turns to her, hands on hips. "Look!" She closes her eyes. She opens them. "You saw me close my eyes?"

"Yes," says the fairy child, disconcerted.

"Well, I couldn't see you anymore. You no longer existed for me. But you existed for yourself, didn't you? If I forgot, it would be the same. You would continue to exist for yourself. But no matter what happens, I won't forget, I tell you." She slides off the wall, scraping her thighs. "Come on, let's go and see the little calves by the fence at the end of the garden. When you go, 'Moo,' they answer. They think you're their mother."

Italie obediently climbs down from the wall. Sometimes she is transparent, and you can almost see through her to the trees behind. Sometimes she trips on a clump of grass. She's not used to it—having a body of flesh and blood is a lot of work.

The summer afternoon goes on and on. The light gets warmer, the sky deepens in color. Clouds float by and gather into shapes that are fun to recognize. There, that's a dragon . . . an owl . . . a lynx . . . a bear standing on its hind legs . . . a face, a woman's face, wait, I'll recognize it in a moment, it's Mama when she was little, no, I know,

don't tell me, it's . . . Joanne. Nasiwi. The worried face of
Joanne Nasiwi, the hand of Joanne Nasiwi on Catherine's
forehead, her voice saying, "She's burning up!" Catherine
would like her to meet Italie, but the fairy child isn't there
now, she must have stayed at the bottom of the garden
with the little calves that had been trying to lick their
hands through the fence. Catherine turns her head to call
Italie and laughs in surprise: there's an armchair on the
path with someone sleeping in it, a big, blonde girl, curled
up like a cat.

"Catherine?" says Joanne. It can't be suppertime already, can it? It's broad daylight. Joanne makes her drink
something. If she drinks it, can she stay in the garden with
Italie? "Of course," says Joanne in a funny voice, and
Catherine agrees to drink the slightly bitter liquid.

After a while, the fever drops a bit. Catherine opens
her eyes. It's dark. Beside the night table, the circle of
lamplight shows the outline of someone in the armchair,
quite close, a man sleeping, his head tilting back a little,
the mouth slightly open, and a lock of hair falling over his
forehead. Why does Catherine feel she's seen him sleeping
like that already? Why this twinge of sadness? She's
thirsty. She says ". . . thirsty," but it's just a murmur.
Which is enough to wake the man, nevertheless, Simon-
Pierre, there, she remembers and smiles at him. He smiles
too, a little hesitantly. "Catherine?"

He hastily fills the glass, lifts her head to help her
drink—she would like to say "No, don't bother," but in
fact when he lets go of her neck she feels her head fall
back weakly on the pillow.

"How are you doing?"

He is worried and she would like to reassure him, but
she realizes that she feels pretty awful. Thoughts form
with exasperating slowness in her brain and reach her
lips. ". . . the flu. Got me."

He nods. Another shape looms in the half light,
above the back of the chair. "Is she conscious?" says Joanne's voice.

Catherine would like to say, "I was unconscious?"
but the idea of talking exhausts her, and she is content
merely to think it. To think, "Organism weakened, not

fighting well. Flu? Pneumonia? No hospital here." Too tiring to worry. She closes her eyes.

To see Italie, who comes running from the bottom of the garden, all excited at having found a gilded scarab. They go and sit on the terrace, near the pretty-by-nights that are still closed like little upside-down umbrellas, with their white-veined, blue and purple petals. They put the scarab on a leaf. It falls. They put it back, again and again, until the insect consents to hang on to the leaf. But soon it unfolds its outer wings and flies off with disdainful brusqueness. They laugh. Afterward, Catherine shows Italie the roads she made for the ants.

"They aren't following them. They're stupid," remarks Italie.

But now Catherine, who meanwhile has thought about the irritating behavior of the ants, has another view on the subject. "No, they prefer their own paths."

"But theirs are full of pebbles. It's harder for them to carry stuff that way."

"Maybe they find it more fun." She thinks of a word she's learned recently. "More sporty." She explains the word to Italie, who looks doubtful.

"The ants build underground passages and bring food home; they haven't time to be sporty or have fun."

"What do you know about it? You're not an ant."

"But I'm much bigger than an ant. I'm much wiser. I must know better than they do what's good for them, don't you think?"

"I'm bigger, too, but I think they have the right to use whatever path they like, as long as they're doing what they have to do." As she says this, Catherine has something very clear in mind: she knows her parents are listening from the open kitchen window, and that they don't want her to stay so long in the garden with Italie. But she's done all her chores, the dishes, brushed the dog, even tidied her room. She has the right to amuse herself as she likes, now. Just because they're bigger and older, they can't always decide everything for her, can they?

Italie watches the ants hurrying back and forth. She rolls and unrolls a lock of blonde hair around her finger. "I could crush them if I wanted to."

"But you mustn't!" protests Catherine, appalled and

a little frightened. She has just imagined a huge foot falling from the sky.

"Even if I can make them as good as new afterward?"

Catherine is about to say, "But you can't," when she remembers that Italie is a fairy child. Intrigued, she asks instead, "You can?"

"Of course," says Italie. Before Catherine can say, "No!" Italie has put her leather sandal on the ants' path and lifted it again. The little black dots don't move. She leans over, picks up several between the tips of her fingernails, puts them in her palm, and shows them to Catherine. Fascinated and horrified, Catherine sees that some of the ants are still waving their feet.

"They're still alive!"

"I can heal them and make them as good as new."

And the newly resuscitated ants frantically explore Italie's hand, which she shakes so they'll fall off and join their companions.

"You see? Well, if I can make and unmake them, I have the right to decide for them, haven't I?"

Catherine thinks this over, frowning. She hadn't looked at it in this way. But no. No. Her parents made her, didn't they? Nevertheless, she doesn't feel the least desire to let them decide for her, in particular how long she can stay in the garden with Italie. She hears their voices floating from the kitchen window. "But we can't keep her here in that condition!" says Papa's voice. Mama would like her to stay and says stubbornly, "Everything will work out, she's strong." Papa's the one who doesn't want it. "I'm not prepared to run the risk! I've done your bidding for long enough. If she shows no improvement between now and tomorrow morning, I'm taking her. End of discussion."

Tomorrow is a long way away. Reassured, Catherine goes back to Italie's question. On one hand, Italie isn't wrong. When you do something, you have the right to undo it. Card houses, block pyramids, paper birds, for instance. But it doesn't apply to people, surely! Suddenly Catherine feels a vague anxiety. Just because her parents made her, they can't have the right to unmake her, can they?

But if they could make her over again?

Catherine stares at the zigzagging black dots. It's impossible to tell which ones were resuscitated. "Did you make the ants the way they were. Exactly the same?"

"Yes. I could make them different, but it wouldn't be . . . well, it wouldn't be right."

Catherine smiles at her, satisfied to find they agree on this point. All the same. If you don't make them different, what's the point of unmaking them in the first place? Might as well leave them alone, let them go about their business and not interfere at all.

Italie thinks about this for a while, chewing on her hair, and finally concedes, "Yes. . . ." She doesn't seem completely convinced, though.

They watch the ants for a while without speaking. The insects run along their silly roads carrying their inhuman burdens. "But we're not ants at all," says Catherine suddenly. She's still thinking about her parents. "It's different for people." She checks to see that her parents are no longer at the window, and continues, "I'm little and my parents are big, and I do what they tell me, but not all the time. And they don't always get angry. Because one day I'll be big, too." That's what Mama tells her sometimes; she lets her choose when Catherine doesn't know which dress to wear to school, or whether she'd rather play or do her homework first: "When you're big, you'll have to make up your own mind."

Oddly enough, Italie seems to have been thinking the same thing because she says, "But what if you're much, much bigger than your parents, even when you're very small?"

Catherine stares uncomprehendingly. "Bigger," Italie repeats, miming with her hands. What, are fairy parents smaller than their children? That doesn't make sense. But Italie is very serious about it, even a bit distressed. Catherine decides to believe her. Grownups smaller than their children? Silly, but amusing. It would be useful, too. When she didn't want to listen to them, she would put them in a box and. . . . No, she couldn't do that. Too bad. She shakes her head with virtuous assurance. "After all, they'd still be your parents. And if it works one way, it must work both ways. If they can't always make you do what you don't want to do, just because you are smaller, you can't do it to them, either. It wouldn't be fair."

"Mmmm," says Italie. She, too, seems to think it's rather too bad, but she understands. They smile at each other. Catherine thinks about what they will do, now that the ant question is settled. There are other things she'd like to show Italie, other games in the garden where the sun never sets and the cows are forever walking on the hill along the horizon, going back to the farm. But Italie seems preoccupied. "I'll have to go," she says.

Not so soon! But Italie insists. "They're right. You can't stay here."

Did Italie hear her parents, too? But it's only for to-morrow, Papa said, and with the way the day is going, to-morrow won't be here for a long, long time!

"Tomorrow will come soon," says Italie rather sadly. She holds out a hand and touches one of Catherine's braids. "I'll come back. You promised not to forget me."

Catherine makes a show of beating her with her other braid. "I told you that it wouldn't matter if I forgot! You can make ants come alive again, so you're certainly able to make yourself exist!"

Italie tilts her head dreamily. "Perhaps. I don't know if it's the same. I'll think about it. Goodbye, Catherine. Thank you."

The pretty-by-night bushes begin to appear through the fairy child's body, and it's true that their flowers are beginning to open. Night is coming. Italie's smile lingers a moment, a transparent smile superimposed on a spray of mauve flowers, and then she is gone.

5

Catherine opened her eyes and during a moment of calm acceptance looked at the pale ceiling, then at the opposite wall with its large window opening onto the blue sky. Colors, the warm smell of mechanically circulating air, the texture of sheets on her skin, the pillow under her head. A hospital room. She had been sick and they had taken her to a hospital. No, she'd had an accident and. . . . An accident, and then she'd been sick. No. . . .

She kept herself from sitting up abruptly as memory returned, like an elastic band snapping her in the face. She was no longer in Simon's dome-house. He'd brought her to a hospital. In Chicoutimi? Probably. She turned her head to look around the room. Spacious. She was alone. Surprising, a bit disappointing: she'd expected to find Athana asleep in an armchair beside the bed. It was a pretty room, luxurious for a hospital. To the right of the bed, on the night table that could also be used for meals or writing, stood a water carafe, a plastic glass, a cylindrical alarm clock/calendar showing that it was 2:34 pm on January 7, 1989, and a small black box with buttons that looked like a TV remote control, except for the wire.

Catherine reached out gingerly to pick up the box, noting that her ribs felt better. A pictogram showed how each button worked. She pressed the call button and examined the box while waiting. The wire wasn't there to provide electricity. It was attached to the night table so that the patient could pull the box closer if necessary. There was a small compartment underneath the box that opened easily. Catherine looked at the silvery sphere without touching it, and replaced the cover just as the door opened to admit a middle-aged woman in a nurse's uniform. She smiled at the nurse, who was identified by a clip attached to her blouse as one Marielle Dumais.

The nurse smiled hesitantly back and said in a rather too jovial voice, "So we're awake." Without once looking Catherine in the eye, she went through the usual examination routine with what seemed exaggerated thoroughness. She then showed Catherine how to manipulate the bed with the control box, which also worked for the TV-radio combination, as well as the lighting, air conditioning, and window blinds.

Does it serve as a telephone as well?" asked Catherine, amused.

"No." The nurse cleared her throat. "But we'll certainly install one if you wish." She seemed almost embarrassed at this oversight, having taken Catherine's remark seriously. Somewhat disconcerted, Catherine assured her it wouldn't be necessary, and tried to joke about it in a sufficiently obvious way—she didn't need a telephone, who could she possibly call?

The nurse cleared her throat again. It was beginning to seem like a nervous tic. "Your friends," she said, and the tone was slightly questioning. Totally impervious to humor, she stared fixedly at the pillow beside Catherine's head.

It took Catherine a minute to understand. "Joanne Nasiwi?" she asked at last. "Simon-Pierre Le Guével?"

More throat-clearing. "We informed them that you were awake, when you rang."

"Oh," said Catherine. And as the woman seemed to be waiting for something more. "That's fine."

The nurse went out, apparently in a great hurry to leave the room. Catherine looked at the ceiling inquiringly, and suddenly the explanation was clear. She gave a little laugh, more surprised than amused. Her reputation had preceded her. Or accompanied her, rather, in the persons of Simon and Joanne since they had both apparently decided to leave their retreat to bring her to Chicoutimi. If the nurse's behavior was any indication, perhaps it wouldn't be so terrible. Comic, more likely. Her smile faded. After a while it must become downright unbearable! She's have to make these people understand that she was no Infant!

And where was Athana? She should have asked. But she wasn't going to bother the nurse for that. Simon and Joanne would tell her when they arrived.

She picked up the control box and turned on the television—it was as good a way as any to get to know the natives. A figure-skating competition. Regional. Commercial for a snowmobile manufacturer. Local. A program of small ads, also regional. Three local channels. Logical, since the barrier would block reception from the South. Radio? Light pop music—no difference from the South there—classical music. Two local AM stations. On FM— one . . . two . . . four stations, two with more modern classical music. Not bad for a population of. . . . She realized that she had no idea of the number of people in the Realm or its capital.

She felt a bit dizzy and switched off the set, put the control box back on the bedside table, and closed her eyes. Disappointed? Why? Because it wasn't different from the South? But why would it be different, anyway? She realized that she had in fact built up another image of the Realm, an unlikely mixture of an archaically puritan society and a pastoral utopia. (At minus forty degrees centigrade? Be serious, Catherine!) The first descriptions she'd heard of the North used words like pacifism, ecologism, and nonviolence, words that triggered in her a response conditioned by the Events of '76. Then Joanne had alluded to people who "roughed it," although she had seen for herself how Simon lived. The image had altered again, without too much concern for its own contradictions, when Simon and Joanne had talked of the absurdities of Northern beliefs, winding up with the barbarous exchange of corpses for energy. But one thing didn't change: by definition the North wasn't the South. It had come into being to oppose the South and even consid-

ered itself, or was considered, the enemy of the South.
And so, yes, it would be a ridiculous irony, although very
logical, if North and South were really pretty much the
same!

The door opened, interrupting her thoughts.

Three strangers filed in with a solemnity that was all
the more awkward because they were trying to hide it.
First a majestic old man, the kind who gets his features
carved on a cliff face after his death: white hair, beard and
mustache, rather too short and narrow-shouldered to be
God-the-Father, although he was making praiseworthy efforts in this regard. The second was a pureblooded Amerindian, as far as Catherine could judge, black braid on
either side of that type of fine Asiatic face worn smooth
by life, making it difficult to tell whether it belongs to a
man of thirty or sixty. And the third was a stern-looking
individual in her fifties, a Métis woman whose face
seemed familiar to Catherine, but no more than that. Both
men wore the same outfit: dark blue tunic and slacks
without any decoration whatsoever, and the woman's
clothes were the same, except for a long skirt instead of
slacks. Catherine felt her image of Northern society shifting toward the puritan again.

Introductions were similarly without flourishes. The
Noble Elder was Frédéric Manesch, mayor of Chicoutimi,
Simon's father (he must be eighty at least, but well pre-
served . . . absolutely no family resemblance, though). The
Noble Indian was Councillor Kiwoe Tchitogama, and the
Mother Superior was Councillor Alta Nasiwi. "Joanne's
mother?" The woman inclined her head with an expres-
sion of studied neutrality.

The silence that followed seemed to indicate they
were waiting for her to say something. Desperately, she
said with a somewhat forced smile, "Catherine Rhymer.
Pleased to meet you."

Manesch cleared his throat (not another one!) and
said, "I hope everything is to your satisfaction. The doctor thinks you're off the critical list now. You've had
pneumonia." A curious intonation, as though the man
hadn't been sure of his information—more precisely, as
though he didn't quite believe it. So, Infants weren't supposed to get sick? Excellent!

"The room is very nice," said Catherine. "I'm sure I've been very well looked after. Your hospital seems very modern." She felt as though she was reading stock sentences from a foreign-language textbook.

"It's perhaps a little premature to touch on the subject," (cough) "but do you know whether you're planning to stay in the Realm?" (Cough, cough.) "Complex procedures must be initiated and. . . ."

"It certainly is a little premature," said Catherine, interrupting with what she hoped was a charming smile. She noted with fascination that Manesch managed to keep his majestic bearing, despite his uneasiness. "I'll think about it," she added. It was time to take the initiative. "I've very much appreciated your son's hospitality. I hope I'll see him again, as well as your daughter, Madame Nasiwi."

They nodded after exchanging a rapid glance.

"One of my friends was with us when we crossed the frontier, Charles-Henri Neveu. I think he's in Chicoutimi as well. Are you aware of this?"

"He's staying with the Fortin family," said Tchitogama. His voice didn't fit the role. Catherine had imagined it as being low and gravelly, but it was a fine, light baritone that suddenly took years off him.

"We'll tell him to visit you," added Manesch.

All right, let's see what happens now. "I also had a young companion, a girl, not more than twenty, blonde, long hair. Her name is Athana."

They knew whom she was talking about—their faces betrayed the fact. Manesch cleared his throat yet again and said, "We don't know where she is at present. She came to tell us where you were, and . . . well, she disappeared."

Catherine nodded. Typical Athana. But at least they had seen and remembered her. She would no doubt show up when the fancy took her. However, Manesch had such a hangdog air that Catherine felt obliged to say, "It doesn't matter. She'll come back."

Her three visitors didn't look as though they relished the idea, and she remembered Joanne's remarks about Athana. With the glut of possible Infants currently available, Ultimate or otherwise, having Athana around didn't help. They'd probably be glad if she stayed away. Perhaps that was also why Manesch was so interested in her own intentions. Maybe they'd be just as glad if she left, too! Interesting. So this is how would-be Messiahs or their equivalents in the Northern religion are welcomed?

Looking at it from another perspective, since these Messiahs are supposed to herald the end of the world, it's understandable that their presence might be less than desirable—even if, according to tradition, a better world is to replace the old one. I shouldn't be taking this interview so lightly, though, and I ought to put myself in their place. It isn't just a question of human respect, but of good common sense and prudence. However absurd their beliefs may be in my eyes, they're real enough to them, probably rule their lives. And their actions. I'll have to be more subtle, not reject these things as a block, otherwise the block might fall on me!

Perhaps she might take a less compromising, more concrete approach? "I don't know how your medical system works. I've very little money on me, and I'm afraid I won't be able to withdraw the funds I've left in the South."

"No, no," said Manesch hurriedly, visibly relieved, "it's the least we can do, considering the risks you took. Unfortunately, it's too often the case with our brothers and sisters of the South. . . . No, to begin with, we assume all expenses. Later, you'll find work and get settled, and it will be different. But," (he cleared his throat yet again) "you haven't decided whether you'll stay or leave."

"Is there a deadline?" said Catherine, careful to make her voice just hesitant enough. "Time to get back on my feet. . . ."

"Yes, certainly," Manesch assured her. "If you like, you can stay at my place when you get out of hospital. Simon and Joanne are already there."

Catherine took this in without batting an eyelash, smiled, and gushed the expected thank-yous. Joanne and Simon both staying at the same place . . . so that they could be kept under surveillance more easily? And she herself staying with them, too. Interesting.

"Will I have to stay in hospital long?" she asked.

Manesch seemed to hesitate for an instant. "Actually, according to the doctor, you could probably leave today."

"Would it be a bother if I went to your house now?"

"No, not at all."

It was hard to gauge the old man's expression. He glanced at Alta Nasiwi, who gave the briefest of nods.

"It is the custom here, when we receive new ..." (more throat clearing) "visitors, to offer a gift. Allow us. ..."

He took a small wooden box out of his tunic pocket and handed it to Catherine. Alta Nasiwi and Kiwoe Tchitogama did the same. The boxes were of different sizes, but otherwise identical, round, with the same pattern carved on the cover: a sprinkling of little stars, with a space in the center for a blue-and-gold circle divided by a wavy line in the form of an S. Catherine forced herself to keep a straight face, although she was both amused and disconcerted. Not gold, incense, and myrrh? No, in fact. Manesch had given her a copper bracelet engraved with a geometric pattern; Tchitogama's box contained a leather-and-ivory necklace with animals carved in intricate detail; Alta Nasiwi had given her a lovely belt decorated with small blue beads. Catherine thanked them profusely, and when she got dressed made a point of wearing all three. Her visitors seemed satisfied. Were they relieved? These were all objects used to hold or attach. Had they exorcised her without her knowing it? Was she supposed to writhe and shriek, and disappear in a cloud of dust?

Or perhaps it was truly the custom, and they were pleased to see that she was willing to be treated like any other new arrival.

Chicoutimi was laid out on three levels of hills rising fairly abruptly from the south shore of the Saguenay, which narrowed at this point. The hospital was a large complex, clearly made up of all sorts of buildings from different periods, with three highrises of different levels, giving the overall impression of a rickety fortress. It sat on the second level, between the port installations and the college campus higher up. The latter was a vast snowy stretch dotted with trees and crowned with a building that immediately brought to mind the religious architecture of a preceding century. The comfortable, not to say luxurious, car in which Catherine was traveling with Manesch and the others sped eastward, according to her sense of orientation (apparently it had activated itself unbidden). The car glided through elegant residential sections and winding streets that must be following the indentations of the cliff overhanging the river. At last the road became a lane leading to a small stone mansion two stories high, flanked by two wings disguised as towers. Pure nineteenth century, like almost all the homes in the area. Catherine watched the trees slide by the car window. Chestnuts? Five hundred miles north of Montreal? But the car stopped in front of the main entrance, and she kept her astonishment to herself.

Tchitogama pushed the wheelchair through the door. The interior of the house corresponded to the exterior: a handsome residence belonging to a bourgeois family, sure of its antecedents and its wealth. A large, high-ceilinged hall with a crystal chandelier and a staircase with a carved bannister. Marquetry floors, paneled walls, smooth, dark wood, portraits of ancestors. Facing the main door was a full-length painting of a man in early nineteenth-century dress; the resemblance to Simon was obvious, despite the ancestor's mustaches and bushy sideburns. Catherine took it all in at a glance, thinking of Simon's semi-rustic dwelling.

The whole household had assembled in the hall to welcome the new arrivals. Frédéric Manesch introduced the half-dozen people ceremoniously. Mathilde, his youngest daughter, had a rather soft, oval face—a woman in her forties, with dark clothes and hair pulled back in a bun that did nothing to lessen her age. Véronique, Mathilde's daughter, was seventeen or eighteen, redheaded and lively, looking as though she'd just stepped out of a Montreal discothèque. Her clothes and haircut were the last word in fashion—a total contrast with the others. She knew this, judging by the aggressive smile with which she greeted Catherine.

"You know Simon already," said Manesch with a

slightly forced joviality. "Madame Georgette Otchiwey, our excellent cook-housekeeper," continued Manesch, "and Monsieur Clément Martel, my secretary."

There were also Grandbois and Étienne, two sturdy-looking men, both professionally self-effacing, whose role was not specifically referred to. Catherine nodded rather coolly when introduced. Bodyguards, probably police-men—that answered one of her questions. Madame Otchiwey was a plump little woman in her sixties, more of a cook than a housekeeper in appearance. Catherine felt immediate rapport with her, as the cook was the only one who shook her hand and looked her in the eye, as well as putting an end to the rather theatrical introduc-tions. "Come, I'll show you your room. You mustn't overtire yourself."

Catherine prepared to follow her, wondering all the while where Joanne could be, when a sarcastic voice floated down the stairway. "Catherine. How kind of you to come. If Athana was here we could play a rubber of bridge."

Joanne had stopped in the middle of the staircase. She was wearing a fluorescent-orange track suit and her braids were undone, for once; she had knotted her hair in a loose pony tail that flowed over one shoulder. She didn't look as though she were prepared to come down and join the others, who were staring at her as though turned to stone.

"I don't play bridge," said Catherine with a smile, "but I wasn't going to refuse Monsieur Manesch's gener-ous hospitality. I hate hospitals, even ultramodern ones." Good: she'd got just the right tone of light sincerity.

Madame Otchiwey caught the conversational ball with a deftness that raised her yet again in Catherine's es-teem. "Yes indeed. Come and see your room: it may not be as modern, but it's just as comfortable."

The household fell in step behind them, which rather detracted from the spontaneity of the situation. Catherine made a point of not noticing them, and in any case most of them stopped at the elevator at the back of the hall—a feature that came as rather a surprise to Catherine. Only Tchitogama, who pushed her chair,

Manesch, and Madame Otchiwey stepped into the elevator with her.

Catherine's room-to-be looked westward. The high French window, showing the golden sky of sunset, attracted her immediately. It gave out onto the back garden, a large space dotted with snow-covered bushes and trees, sloping toward the edge of the cliff. Beyond that was the river, a frozen expanse that opened out toward the western horizon. Across the river was another cliff where immense slides had revealed the naked rock, pink and gray.

"It's magnificent," said Catherine, turning her chair around and smiling with genuine sincerity at her host, who still stood beside the door. "Really. Thank you so much."

Catherine got out of the wheelchair and onto the bed, annoyed at not being as strong as she'd hoped. She let Madame Otchiwey pull up the sheets and blanket, as well as a light but cosy eiderdown in a satin cover. She sunk her hands into its softness, smiling in spite of herself.

"Warm enough?" asked Madame Otchiwey.

"Just fine. I prefer being cool."

There was a short silence. Then Manesch, still standing by the door where Tchitogama now joined him, cleared his throat. "Well, we'll let you get some rest. Madame Otchiwey will bring up your supper in a while." He stroked his beard nervously. "Good evening," he said, and the two men turned and paused, finding Simon standing in the doorway. With perfect coordination, they walked around him, one on each side, and disappeared into the corridor.

"If you need anything, you'll find a buzzer there, on the night table. Don't hesitate to call me at any time," Madame Otchiwey said. She slowed down as she passed Simon. "Don't tire her out, now."

He closed the door, then walked over to the bed, hands behind his back.

"The family mansion," said Catherine, trying a bit of humor.

He nodded, frowning. She gave up the attempt and sank with a sigh into the pillow. Its softness was just right.

"I was going to bring you here," said Simon. "I was getting you settled in the snowcar when the helicopter arrived."

He was staring at the wallpaper just above the bed. She tried to think of an answer, but found only, "I know," which seemed to satisfy him. He'd only come to tell her this, obviously, and was already turning away when someone knocked on the door. Joanne walked in without waiting and marched over to sit on the edge of the bed. "Well, what do you think of the ancestral pile?" she said nonchalantly.

"Very ancestral," said Catherine.

"And well guarded, as you'll see," added Joanne.

Simon waved impatiently. "Joanne, please. . . ."

"My room is on the other side of the hall," continued Joanne, as though she hadn't heard. "Simon is at the end of the passage. His old room." She gave Simon a sardonic smile that provoked a smothered oath. He strode out of the room.

When Joanne turned back to Catherine, she seemed a little upset. "I'm glad you've recovered so quickly," she said apologetically. "It's just that this house gets on my nerves. I hate being shut up."

"Prisoner?" said Catherine with an economy imposed by the fatigue that suddenly weighed on her.

"No. But it's hard to get out without someone tagging along." Joanne straightened up. "Anyway, the main thing is that you're feeling better. We were about to take you to the hospital when Papa Manesch and Kiwoe arrived."

"They told me. About Athana."

Joanne narrowed her eyes as she studied Catherine. "The morning before, she just wasn't in the house anymore. I looked around outside with Simon, but there wasn't a trace. And she got to Chicoutimi pretty quickly. She told them about you herself that very same morning. After that, she disappeared."

She was visibly expecting some comment, some reaction. But what was there to say? Catherine closed her eyes. "Perhaps . . . special vision . . . my guardian angel," she murmured with a faint smile. She heard Joanne give a small, skeptical grunt, felt a finger touch her cheek. "Get some rest."

Footsteps walking to the window, the sound of curtains being pulled, the door opening and closing. For a moment she listened to the strange noises of this strange house as she breathed in the smell of clean sheets and the citronella fragrance of the room. Athana, where are you, what are you doing? But thinking was impossible, and at last she let herself sink into sleep.

The morning after she'd settled in at the Manesch's, Catherine received a visitor, Charles-Henri. Who gave her a bear hug and had to catch himself to avoid squeezing her broken rib, but still held her for a long time, saying nothing. When he finally let her go, she saw he had tears in his eyes, as she had. He sat on the edge of her bed for a moment, saying nothing and looking around the room, then gave his characteristic, huge laugh. "In Frédéric Manesch's house! Imagine that!"

"It seems I might be an Infant," smiled Catherine, although she really didn't feel like smiling.

"They told you that?" He was serious again.

"No. Well, Simon and Joanne warned me, but not. . . ."

"Yes, of course," he said. She was watching him, trying to find the best way of getting the most information out of him. She looked away, overcome by the realization. This was Charles-Henri, a precious piece of her inner landscape, and yet at the same time she no longer knew who he was, she was no longer sure of anything. The inner landscape was in ruins, bombarded, marked off limits by signs that warned, "Attention: land mines!" She allowed a few seconds for the distress to subside into irritation, then, controlling her voice carefully, said, "Tell me what happened to you."

He made a face. "Not much. Help came two days later. They came because the frontier post no longer responded. They took me to Chicoutimi. They interrogated me, of course. They had a pretty good idea Joanne had taken you to Le Guével's place, but I don't think that bothered them much. I was taken in by the Fortins, the family of Marc-André, someone I used to know in Quebec. He arrived a few days later, without difficulty. There were no roadblocks anywhere along the way."

"Christine and Dominique?"

"They were released, as usual. Things seem to have gone back to normal."

Back to normal. Catherine lay back on the pillow and closed her eyes. Quebec, Christine, Dominique, these few words, Charles-Henri's voice, and suddenly the events that had brought her here were playing back in her memory. But all these memories had a curious patina, as though they had happened months ago, not a mere three weeks. So little time, yet it seemed like an unbridgeable gap separating her from her former life. Was it possible, really—"a former life," with the road back cut off forever? She made herself take deep breaths to calm herself, and opened her eyes again to look at Charles-Henri's dark, worried face.

"It must be hard for you," he murmured.

She suddenly saw the crushed rear of the van, and murmured, somewhat ashamed, "And for you."

The black eyes went dim and turned away. "But I knew who Antoine was," said Charles-Henri softly, after a while. He took one of her hands, stroked it rather awkwardly, then said more loudly, "And I know who I am. And then I always thought I would end up here. For you . . . it's different. Very different."

She snatched her hand away. "And what do you think I am?"

He took back her restless hand, holding it more tightly. "You are Catherine. My friend. Whatever else you are. If being one of the Infants canceled out everything you were before . . . I wouldn't believe in it."

She stiffened. "But you believe in the Infants?"

"I still don't know. Since I've come here, I realize I was pretty ignorant. Half the facts I'd learned were false.

And I didn't know many details about the Infants." He laughed, once again the old Charles-Henri, glad to be astonished. "There are lots of things I've never even heard of!"

"Such as?"

"The Manesch clan. The first Manesch, the second—the role they played in transforming the North. The spheres, the nature of the Pilgrimage. The status of Simon and Joanne." He became serious again. "The North is a lot more complicated than I thought. The religion, the sects, well, of course. But the sects don't exist in a vacuum. There's all the rest: history, politics, the economy. Since the spheres have come on the scene. . . ."

"Since the revelation of Pierre-Emmanuelle Manesch."

"You know about it?"

"I read bits of his book. Simon talked to me about him, but he didn't say much."

Charles-Henri nodded. "It's difficult to be part of a dynasty like that," he murmured.

"Dynasty?"

"The first Manesch, Louis-Raoul, was the founder of the Realm. In 1851. Didn't Simon tell you?"

Catherine gave a big, weary sigh. "No."

"You mustn't hold it against him."

"I know!"

"The Father of the North was also an inventor of genius, it seems," added Charles-Henri pensively, after a while. "He'd developed a whole series of machines that functioned with steam and compressed air and were the basis of Northern industrialization before the barrier." With a slightly sarcastic smile, he waved his hand at the luxurious room: "It was a great success."

After he'd left, someone knocked on the door. It was Joanne with lunch. "I saw Charles-Henri downstairs. It seems he's given you a little history lesson?"

"It seems I have to be completely re-educated as far as the North is concerned. Or educated," said Catherine, not sure whether to be amused or depressed by the prospect. She sat up to receive the tray. It smelled good, and she was starving.

"You're in the right place." Joanne sat on the bed and lifted one of the covers on the tray. "I recommend the chicken with wild mushrooms—one of Georgette's specialties. If you want to find out things, the Manesch library is the best in the Realm. In fact, it's the only real library in the Realm." She stood up. "Ring when you're ready. Twice. I'll take you to the holy of holies."

The library was in the north wing and occupied the whole ground floor. As she pushed Catherine's chair, Joanne gave her a lively but mocking rundown of the family history since the first ancestor, Gaétan Manesch, had come to the Saguenay region from Quebec-City in 1758. Louis-Raoul Manesch had built the house in the nineteenth century, and his museum now occupied the entire ground floor of the south wing. He was the subject of the imposing portrait hanging in the front hall opposite the main door. A more modest portrait of the young Frédéric Manesch hung in the passage leading to the library, as well as that of a young woman who looked like Mathilde, but more smiling. It made all the difference: the woman in the painting was pretty. "Marie Le Guével," said Joanne. "She died three years after the birth of Véronique."

"Simon took his mother's name?"

"When he came of age. He had his name changed officially."

"Was everyone scandalized?"

"No. One mustn't thwart the Quest of the Infants, right?"

It was strange to be so suddenly brought back to a context so foreign to this house and its evocation of a Balzacian bourgeois epic. But after all, Balzac loved fantastic fiction and was himself a slightly mad visionary. He would probably have liked Louis-Raoul Manesch, the inventor, and his visionary son, Pierre-Emmanuelle.

"Isn't there a portrait of Pierre-Emmanuelle?"

"Yes, in the library. The library is his creation. You might say it's his own museum, in a way, except that the public isn't allowed in. Few people are allowed in, actually. Make the most of it."

When she went into the library, Catherine automatically put her hands on the wheels of her chair to stop it. She wasn't really surprised, however. It was the library of her brief vision. Judging from the painting in the front hall, the man in a jacket who was looking at her was the same one she'd seen, although much younger and without pince-nez.

"Impressive, isn't it?" said Joanne, who'd misunderstood Catherine's reaction. "There are over ten thousand books."

Catherine had regained her composure. "Not all on the history of the North?" she exclaimed with a horror only half feigned.

"No. On all sorts of things. Literature, the sciences, geography, history, the North, the South, the world as it is supposed to exist elsewhere. Pierre-Emmanuelle Manesch was a curious man."

The emphasis on the word "curious" was odd in itself. "Do you mean curious-weird?"

"That too. In a way, I've always regretted that Simon wasn't more like his grandfather. Where would you like to begin? The history of the Realm is on the left of the central bookcase. The history of the South is on the right-hand wall, first and second bookcases. The rest of the world is in the remaining shelves." She waved her arms as though directing traffic.

"Simon isn't weird?"

Joanne paused, then lowered her arms. "Simon isn't curious," she said abruptly, then added more aggressively, "Well, what do you want to look at first?" She walked up to one of the glass-fronted shelves, opened the door, and read emphatically, "*The Exodus, 1755–1800*. Volume one of the august work of Henri-Martin Faucher, *The History of the Independent Realm of the North*. Dated 1900. Recommended. Not exactly side-splitting but fairly informative. Volume two covers the history of the Northern Confederation; volume three, the appearance of the barrier and its consequences."

Catherine sighed. "That will do to begin with, I suppose. And there's nothing on religious history?"

"Not really. Allusions here and there, when politics and religion clash, which does happen. Particularly at the end of the nineteenth century and the first half of the twentieth. By the way, there's an easy method of getting your bearings, religion-wise: until at least the fifties, you can tell that people were orthodox Believers if they have a double-barreled name, of which the second is a feminine form, grammatically speaking; those with two hyphenated masculine names are Ultimists who lean toward a male Infant; men with two given names with feminine endings, or names that can apply to either sex in French, like Claude or Dominique, are Ultimists of the other kind. It's a little more complicated for women, but here as elsewhere, it's men who write history."

"You know this library well," hazarded Catherine.

Joanne gave her a knowing smile. "Yes."

"You've lived here?"

Joanne sighed and took out a chair from the central table, sitting down and resting her elbows on her knees. "From the time I was old enough to understand what was going on, I wanted to meet Simon. I lived in Mistassini with my parents at the time, at the far end of Lac Saint-François. He was still living here in Chicoutimi with his wife."

Catherine started. "He's married?"

"Was. Divorced. Two girls. They live with their mother in Alma. The oldest is married, with children. They're all very . . . normal. I was sixteen when I met him." A small, joyless smile. "I upset him a lot."

"And he let himself be upset."

"With him it's cyclical," murmured Joanne after a short silence. "I came at the end of a cycle. Fifteen years of marriage and pretending to be normal toward and in spite of everybody. He broke down."

"And so did the marriage."

"No!" Joanne burst out laughing. "Don't be so melodramatic. I went back to my parents after two days, terribly disappointed because this so-called Infant had no answers for me, while I had been ready to idolize him. And for his part . . . well, Simon is the deep, silent type. Nothing shows on the outside, and then all of a sudden he explodes. It took him three years. And then the marriage fell apart. And it took another two years for him to come and get me."

"You were expecting him?"

Joanne didn't answer right away. Her face darkened, and she looked away. "Yes," she said at last.

"And you lived together here?"

"I wanted to have access to the library," Joanne said carelessly. She stood up abruptly. "Would you like other books? If not, I'll take you back to your room."

Catherine didn't insist, and allowed herself to be wheeled out of the library.

A man runs down a corridor, a blond man whom Catherine knows, although she can't remember his name. He should be younger. Or older. In any case, he's desperate, terrified, as a loop in his memory replays the sequence of events—a hand shaking him, a voice saying Talitha had knocked out the monitor on duty and locked herself in the Bridge room. He knew it—the crisis that hits aspirants metamorphosed by the operations. She was having trouble controlling her new perceptions, she wasn't ready for the operations, he should have known!

He runs down the stairs. The unconscious monitor is slumped against a wall and someone is looking after his bleeding nose. The door to the room is closed. It doesn't matter, the emergency circuit can be activated, it's provided for. But the important thing is what is happening on the other side of the door. Someone behind him says, "The Bridge hasn't yet been activated." Thénadèn. Over the intercom. At Central.

He presses the intercom. "You can see her?"

"Yes. She's in the capsule."

But she hasn't destroyed the communication system, she has left an opening, in spite of everything.

He presses the other button, the one that activates the intercom to the room. He thinks of the acoustics of all those hard surfaces against which the sound rebounds and shatters, of what Talitha will perceive if he speaks. But he must establish contact. He speaks slowly, spacing his words so that their reverberation across the metamorphosed perceptions of the girl won't deprive them of all meaning.

"Tali, it's me, Egon. You can't leave alone, Tali. You need someone to close the sphere."

Has she forgotten? The aspirants are told often enough. The Bridge didn't always work this way; the process was developed in the light of mistakes and after many deliberations. The Voyagers leave when they want to—but someone must be there to close the sphere of the Bridge over them: a final failsafe measure, the ultimate appeal. Once the sphere is closed, the aspirant can push the green button that sets off the automated process that no one can stop, not even the Voyager. There is another button in the capsule, a red one—to open the sphere. Each button prevents the other from working once it has been pressed.

"Let me in, Tali. I want to help you."

A voice behind him, a murmur. "What's she doing?" And Thénadèn's voice, "She isn't . . . yes, she's coming out of the capsule!"

"Help me?" Talitha's voice, at some distance from the intercom.

"Yes. Open the door."

"She's not moving," murmurs Thénadèn from the station. "We could open the door from here."

Egon shakes his head. She must open it of her own accord. Thénadèn must know this!

"She's climbing down the ladder. She's missed the last step. She's fallen."

Talitha's distant voice on the intercom, muttering intelligible words.

"She's getting up—walking over to the console."

Talitha's voice comes through clearly now, as she gets closer to the intercom. A language Catherine doesn't understand, but the intonation is clear: rage, sorrow, desperate terror.

"I'll help you, Tali," says Egon again. "Open the door."

Somebody in Central heaves a sigh. The door slides into the wall, revealing the brilliantly lighted room, the open sphere, and beside the command panel at the back, Talitha. She turns toward Egon with the slow movements of a swimmer, her face ashen, her body gleaming with sweat. She is young, barely twenty years old, hair closely cropped. Her left knee is bleeding.

He walks toward her slowly, very slowly. She holds out her arms stiffly, hands rigid, in a defensive gesture. She staggers a little.

"I'll help you, Tali," he says softly. "Get into the sphere. I'll close it for you."

She stares at him, squinting as though trying to gauge his sincerity with the twisted perceptions she must have of him. At last she says, carefully spacing the syllables, "What for?"

He mustn't weaken, show relief. Must keep the contact. "Because it's up to you to choose, Tali."

"Ha!" she says, with a grimace meant to be sardonic.

It isn't what she wants to hear, perhaps, but he can't say anything else. Fascinated, he watches the girl's arms fall slowly to her side, as though they were completely independent of her conscious mind, while she repeats, "Ha," and adds, in a voice that is too loud, as though immersed in an invisible storm in which she can't hear herself, "Never."

"You chose to come to the Center, Tali."

"Didn't . . . choose," she said, still speaking with exaggerated care. "Nowhere. Never."

"This isn't nowhere. It's the Center, Tali. Nobody forced you to come here, did they?"

She nods her head jerkily. "Forced. Yes."

He keeps doggedly on. "Who forced you, Tali?" But he knows she followed him, that she's here because of him. If she says it, admits it, that would be a beginning. . . .

She waves her hand vaguely, staggers, and grabs the command console. "The Bridge," she says with deliberate clarity. "I am ready."

She totters over to the sphere. Climbs the ladder awkwardly, lies down in the capsule. He follows her, deeply anxious, and leans over the capsule. "The Bridge won't kill you, Tali. It will send you somewhere else, and you will have to begin all over again."

At last she looks at him, frowning. "Begin?"

Speaking at random, trying with increasing desperation to get through to her, he keeps talking. "Perhaps. Other Egons will be there."

The black eyes close, the eyelids squeezed tightly. The head rolls from right to left on the upholstered surface. "It's not true. Close the sphere," she hisses between her teeth.

"You won't die," he insists, trying to sound calm, assured. "You don't want to die, or you wouldn't be here. You wouldn't have chosen to come to the Center. You know it."

She opens her eyes again and stares wildly. "I don't want to . . . begin again," she murmurs finally, a note of almost childish protestation in her voice.

"The only way not to begin again is to stay and finish what isn't finished. You aren't ready, and you know it."

She continues to gaze at him. "Finish?"

And he knows it so well, knows she isn't thinking of the training, knows she's thinking of him and her, yes, that too, Tali, if you stay, there will be a chance for us—give us a chance to end it properly! He takes a deep breath and plunges in. "I'm going to close the sphere, Tali. It's up to you to choose. No one can oblige you or prevent you. You will choose. Remember."

He clambers down the ladder and goes over to the console, hears Thénadèn say worriedly, "Egon—" at the very moment that he pushes the button.

The sphere closes soundlessly.

He slides to the ground and leans against the console. His head is spinning. The intercom is quiet, except for the breathing of attentive presences on the other side of the door. The lights are too bright. He closes his eyes, his mind a blank.

And Thénadèn cries, "No!" and he knows he's lost his gamble, that Talitha has pressed the green button. He hunches over, covering his face with his hands, his heart is breaking, she is leaving, she is lost! The long, useless flight of this young Talitha flashes through his mind and he tries to tell himself that in other universes there are other Talithas who have pressed the other button, but it's no good saying this, it will never be any good, he is in this universe here and now, and she will soon be gone, he couldn't love her as she needed to be loved, he could do nothing for her here. And as he is helped up, Catherine understands, like him, that he'll never really forgive her.

7

It took some time for Catherine's reading habits to be re-established. At first she still had trouble concentrating for long periods. Joanne was only too glad to advise her and supply her with a list of books to read. By the end of the first week, however, Catherine could move around pretty much on her own with her wheelchair, and she felt the need to explore the library catalogue more thoroughly. Joanne was puzzled: why should Catherine go and fish for dusty old books that nobody had ever heard of?

To tell the truth, Catherine didn't understand her own motives very clearly. After reading Faucher's three volumes, she'd felt a diffuse uneasiness that kept on growing. Something was wrong. And it wasn't so much that she saw the proof of a deliberate, nonhuman manipulation in the curious gaps in chronology as in the apparent arbitrariness of certain key events. She had the impression of incoherence, yes, but deeper, more general, and especially more random than Joanne seemed to think. To begin with, there were very few documents on the early settlement of the North. Too few. Not even registers of births and deaths, which was amazing. Another curious fact was that no oral tradition had survived. Henri-Martin Faucher's first volume of history was more a hypothetical reconstruction than a relation of facts.

The fugitives had left the South in the wake of the

English Conquest, which had led to persecution because of their beliefs. Visions and dreams seemed to have already been common occurrences, and were repressed with the most severe intolerance by the Catholic as well as the Reformed Churches, which viewed them as evidence of witchcraft. The fugitives were welcomed freely by the Algonkin tribes in the region, among whom they found a cult involving the Sleeping Deity and the Infant that offered striking resemblances to their own, still embryonic beliefs.

Very well. But *how many* of these first fugitives had there been? There were no hard facts. The total population of the Realm now numbered over two million. Even taking into account increased fertility, it implied a large number of refugees in the beginning, or a considerable number of Amerindians. However, the Manesch library happened to contain the censuses for the francophone population of the whole of Quebec, before and after the Conquest, from 1657 to 1795. The figures didn't jibe.

And then how to account for the absence of the South in all this? It was possible and probable that after the Conquest, the British might have decided to leave the North to take care of itself, even if it served as a refuge for fleeing francophones. The inhospitable climate, the absence of desirable resources, a population that was difficult to keep track of—why try to maintain power in a region where the cost of control would be greater than potential income from taxes? Later, during the confrontation with the young American Union, it was normal that the North be ignored. Southern resources had been concentrated along the Union's frontier and in the threatened Canadian plains. But the two remaining Canadian provinces had become independent of the British Crown after 1890. That Eastern Canada hadn't tried to take advantage of the Northern mineral and timber resources at that point was inexplicable—and unexplained.

All the more reason, when you knew the Confederation (or the Realm, as it already seemed to be called at this period) had no army. Faucher and the others made no mention of one. There was a police force, but no army.

Catherine's sense of uneasiness continued to focus on the barrier, nevertheless. It had appeared at exactly the period when electric power had begun to spread, making potentially frequent North-South contacts much more likely. Neither Faucher nor the others had much to say about the circumstances leading up to the installation of the barrier. Pierre-Emmanuelle Manesch had been forty-five at the time. He was a councilor in Chicoutimi, a very pious man who was worried about the growing materialism in Northern society. He'd announced publicly that the barrier was the answer to his prayers—the Deity's way of protecting Its creation. The people believed him.

Catherine could only speculate on the various upheavals that the barrier's appearance and Manesch's declarations had caused among the Realm's theologians (among all Northerners, if she'd understood correctly!). Economic upheavals could well have been minimal, taking into account, for example, the fact that nonelectric industrial technologies developed by Louis-Raoul Manesch were still far more widespread than more modern technologies. But the resurgence of religious questions seemed to have dealt a blow to the progress of contemporary industrialization. At this date, a schism had developed. On one side were partisans of what could be called a para- or proto-capitalist system; on the other were those connected with a way of life closer to nature, however harsh nature might be in Northern latitudes. The energy spheres had brought about some changes, of course, although these didn't appear at the same period as the barrier. Apparently the Sleeping Deity hadn't wanted Northern technology to regress too far: its favorite creation might thus pollute its environment to the point of no return. (This was one of Joanne's preferred arguments in proving outside manipulation: in the South there was a great deal of careless pollution.)

But Catherine was still fixated on the apparition of the barrier and its consequences. Or rather, the absence of some predictable consequences. No scientist from the Realm seemed to have studied the barrier: you couldn't submit divine intervention to a scientific examination, now could you? But why hadn't the *South* sent hordes of scientists? There was no mention anywhere of the names of the great European scientists, either at the time or later, when the scientific world should have been constantly poring over the barrier to elucidate the mystery! Einstein, de Broglie, Rutherford, Heisenberg and all the others, none of them had been known to speak of it, and the rest of the world had never heard of it! (Perhaps the rest of the world didn't exist, Joanne emphasized.) And during all this time, why hadn't the South surrounded the Realm with a blockade and at least established a permanent military presence? No official document mentioned it, in any case. As far as the South was concerned, it was as though the barrier didn't exist.

What one saw appearing in Southern works of the period, on the contrary, was the fact that communications with the North had been cut off and no one knew what was happening there, although this didn't hamper the first descriptions of the North as a tyrannical state, the first talk of a Bolshevik revolution, the first calls for vigilance—if not for a crusade.

Joanne, of course, saw all this as evidence of the same secret control being exercised on Northern and Southern minds, but merely with regard to different data. Catherine was incapable of explaining to her why she still felt uneasy, unable to put into words the strange feeling that came over her when she looked at the data as a whole, the feeling she'd already had in Montreal and Quebec, although never so intensely. Seen as a whole, it looked like a puzzle that was at once too consistent and too patchy. As far as she was concerned, it couldn't be entirely accounted for by outside manipulation, human or otherwise.

But why was she suddenly so attentive to detail? Or was it rather the fact that unconnected details kept jumping out at her, linking up to sketch an overall structure in which the gaps or contradictions were blindingly obvious? Where did she get these deductions, these ideas for avenues of research, for correlations? She hadn't been trained as a historian, nor a sociologist, nor a demographer! She hadn't been trained as a geographer, either, and yet suddenly, in studying an economic map of Quebec, she'd been startled to find there were coal mines in Alma, fifty miles from Chicoutimi, and oil wells in Chibougamau, a hundred and fifty miles further to the northwest. She

296   ELISABETH VONARBURG

looked for a geological map to check whether this was likely.

And then she made a curious discovery: Pierre-Emmanuelle Manesch's library contained maps that were incompatible with one another. On one of these maps, the geological strata justified the existence of oil deposits in the Chibougamau region. Another map contradicted this.

Fascinated, she had continued to study maps without really knowing what she was looking for, and had stumbled on one showing the levels of terrain along the banks of the Saint Lawrence. Still without understanding why, but conscious of a sharp sense of hidden discordance, she had carefully noted the levels at Montreal and Quebec. Then suddenly it flashed upon her: if Montreal had canals at the level of Rue Sainte-Catherine, the whole Lower Town of Quebec should have been under water at the corresponding level. The present shoreline development in Chicoutimi wouldn't exist, moreover. The hospital ought to be at shore level instead of being halfway up the hill. Either the elevations shown for Quebec and Chicoutimi were wrong, or else sea level was thirty yards higher at Montreal than at Quebec or Chicoutimi.

Absurd. Impossible. Perhaps, if she'd been in the college library in Montreal, the erroneous map would have metamorphosed beneath her eyes. The thought brought a nervous laugh, but things didn't happen this way in the Realm, and the two maps in front of her maintained a stoic sameness.

The most exasperating factor in all this was her inability to explain to herself—and even more to Joanne—why all these details didn't seem to fit the Great Manipulation theory. It simply seemed as though the different versions of certain aspects of reality had existed at different times. But why play with data and minds in this way?

Joanne shrugged and said stubbornly, "I don't see what the problem is. The data have always been manipulated. You're getting hung up on details." She paced the room, obviously irritated. This wasn't the first time they'd been at loggerheads on this subject. Joanne was disappointed, it was understandable. But Catherine had found nothing to confirm Joanne's theories once and for all. Nor did she have another explanation. She felt powerless before all these new data and the inner certainty that kept doggedly repeating "something is wrong."

Joanne came back to the table and sat down, stifling a yawn. Catherine removed her glasses and rubbed her eyes. It was very late—they'd spent part of the night going over the available elements and arguing yet again about their relative importance.

Joanne was looking at Catherine, eyes half-lidded. "Have you decided what you're going to do?" she said suddenly.

Catherine raised her eyebrows. "Do?"

"You're fit to travel, now. We'll have no problem getting you through to Ontario, and from there to Louisiana."

Catherine listened to Joanne's words reverberating within her, astonished at the automatic refusal that rushed to her lips. Why didn't she want to go? Did she want to stay here, in the North? Lose all chance of going back to a normal existence? She felt a chill settle over her. What guarantee had she of leading a "normal" life in Louisiana? What guarantee had she that Louisiana even existed? While she'd been absorbed in the contents of Manesch's library, she'd forgotten about all that. It was as though the timeless and familiar action of reading, coupled with the intellectual challenge of solving all these old enigmas, had numbed her awareness of the here and now. But she *was* here, now, in the Realm of the North, in Chicoutimi, in the Manesch mansion. She had to deal with what these people thought about her, had to make decisions. One decision. Leave or stay.

"Didn't you tell me you've never been able to leave Quebec?"

"I've never tried to do it from the North."

Let's try it together, that's what Joanne was suggesting. An interesting experiment, surely. Why wasn't she more interested, then? Was it because, if the experiment failed, they would have to come back to Chicoutimi in any case and confront all the unanswered questions? Or was it because, if the experiment succeeded, the same questions would still be asked and might even—depressing thought—

lead to new questions? She might as well stay put. Anyway, was she going to leave without having seen Athana?

No, it was useless to argue about it; she was merely rationalizing her initial reflex. She simply didn't want to go. How could she tell Joanne? But why did she want to coddle Joanne, anyway?

"I think I'll stay here for a while."

Joanne got up. Her face was expressionless. "As you like. Goodnight."

Catherine remained alone in the silent library, the books scattered on the table in front of her. She sighed and began sorting them into piles. Idiot. What had she expected? The only reason Joanne had been friendlier than usual was that she'd hoped to convince her—the Métis really was obsessed with her theories. She'd probably back off now. A pity, she was so charming when she wanted to be. . . . Even though they sometimes disagreed, at least Joanne was partially aware of the problem, and you could discuss it with her. Charles-Henri . . . Catherine didn't dare broach the subject with him, too fearful of encountering his lack of comprehension and of what it might do to their relationship. The other members of the household were obviously out of the question. No one had come into the library. No one had visited Catherine in her room, either, except Frédéric Manesch, who came as regularly as clockwork every three days for conversation carefully restricted to small talk. Apart from Georgette Otchiwey, everyone studiously avoided her. While she was still confined to her room, Joanne had brought up her meals. One evening, she'd felt better and had decided to join the family. Joanne had given her a crooked smile. "Really? I'll go with you, then." Simon hadn't been in the dining room. He always had dinner in his room, and in any case she hadn't seen him since her arrival. The flustered reactions of the others and the constrained atmosphere of the evening had dissuaded her from trying again. The only person who'd spoken to her without embarrassment had been the young Véronique.

"A modern young girl," Joanne had said with a smile when Catherine had remarked on this. "She doesn't put much stock in these stories about Infants. Not as far as Simon and I are concerned, anyway. She thinks people ought to leave us alone. When she was little, she wanted us to get married. How shocked Mathilde was! Véronique's a child of her time: 'Infants, a Deity to be wakened, all right, but not in *my* lifetime, thank you very much.' "

Joanne, when she forgot her obsession for a moment, was a storyteller with a great sense of humor and an acute eye for people and things. She had read a lot, liked music, had brought Catherine a CD player and had ransacked the impressive Manesch CD collection for her. But now Joanne would have nothing to do with her. All of a sudden, the thought of staying in Chicoutimi seemed less attractive. How would I earn my living if I stayed, anyway? Teach, perhaps. . . . And how would I get rid of my reputation as a presumptive Infant? Take the bull by the horns, find Frédéric Manesch and say, "I'm not *that* sort of woman"?

The thought of the old man's expression made her laugh.

"I didn't know Pierre-Emmanuelle's library had anything funny in it." Simon, wrapped in a blue dressing gown, stood, sandwich in hand, at the kitchen door opening into the library.

"Not funny, necessarily, but curious," retorted Catherine.

He munched a bite out of the sandwich as he walked over to her. "And you're curious."

Catherine wondered how long he'd been in the kitchen. Anyway, hadn't she had this conversation with Joanne at one point? Were Simon and Joanne carrying on a conversation through a third person? "It would seem you're not curious enough."

Simon shrugged. "I used to be. You can't spend your whole life asking questions without answers."

"Joanne has answers."

"That's her way of no longer being curious."

"And you?" He took another bite of sandwich. She thought he wouldn't answer, but finally he murmured, with unexpected irony, "I try not to think of it more than an hour a day. Why do you want to stay here? Do you think you'll find answers?"

Catherine took this change of subject in her stride. He'd overheard her talking with Joanne. "I'm not sure. My journeys have a way of taking strange turns, these days. I'm not ready to leave yet. Maybe I need more time to recuperate. To take things in. What do you do around here all day? You're invisible. I was wondering where you'd got to."

"I was waiting until Joanne had finished with you. Or you with Joanne."

He'd surprised *her* this time. She hid the fact with a smile. "You really *are* curious."

"I choose my curiosities, that's all."

She sighed, conceding the point. "Do you always discuss things in attack mode? It's almost midnight."

He took yet another bite of sandwich and sat down on the table, pushing aside a pile of books. "Sorry," he said at last. "Joanne's training."

"You hadn't seen her for over ten years, if I'm not mistaken."

"But I lived with her for a long time. It's like riding a bicycle: you don't forget. It's enough for her to be in the neighborhood. But really, why do you want to stay, since you don't believe in her theory?"

"Correction: I don't believe in total manipulation, nor in the work of extraterrestrial beings. But I think it's difficult to deny that partial manipulation is going on."

"Human."

"Certainly human. But if you also believe it, why haven't you ever tried to find out more? Joanne is still trying, in spite of everything."

"Joanne is young."

"About the age you were when you went to her."

Simon didn't react—and therefore must be aware she knew about this episode. He chewed on his sandwich, frowning. The lock of hair had fallen over his forehead again. "But we found nothing," he murmured wearily, after a moment. "We didn't even find each other. What do you think you'll find here?"

Catherine gave an impatient little wave. "I told you, I don't know what I think or hope I'll find. I just don't want to leave right now." She thought of one of the inner arguments she'd used and was surprised to find it true: "I want to see Athana again."

"Athana," said Simon after a short silence. He smiled wryly. "She's wandering around the region. Several people have seen her—at Lac Saint-François and around Chibougamau."

"And they remember her? How is she, what's she doing?"

"Little Bo-Peep has lost her sheep," sang Simon sardonically. "She's wandering around, that's all. She talks to no one and seems to be in good shape."

"What do people say about her?"

"What would *you* say if you thought the end of the world was near?"

"It's that bad?"

He finished his sandwich and wiped his hands on his pajama pants. "No, not quite. They're more or less aware that Joanne came back with you, which makes for too many Infants. But it doesn't help, really."

"And would it help if I left with her?"

He glanced at her, surprised. "I didn't mean that."

"It wouldn't suit you if I left?"

He looked at her for a moment, tilting his head to one side and automatically pushing back the lock of hair. "It would suit my father and no doubt the rest of the Council. As for me . . . well, it's your decision, in any case."

"You don't care whether I stay or leave."

He hesitated, then suddenly gave in. "I didn't say that," he continued, looking her in the eye then turning away.

"But?"

"It would be better . . . I think you ought to stay." He lifted his head and eyed her uncertainly. "You, me, Joanne, Athana. After a while, when nothing has happened, they should begin to understand. . . ."

"That the Infants don't exist, that the Deity doesn't exist?"

He nodded, lips tight. It occurred to Catherine for the first time that perhaps his continual frown was less a sign of anger than of pain.

"Is there"—she couldn't help smiling—"a sect of atheists in the Realm?"

There was a pause, then Simon smiled, too. "Yes, Joanne and myself. You want to join?"

She digested this bit of information for a moment. "Just you two," she murmured. "But how can you be sure?"

"In the days of . . . our crazy youth, Joanne and I conducted a poll. The subject was religion, but no one would have dared fail to respond. All the questionnaires came back duly completed. The existence of the Deity and the Infants was the one certitude shared by the whole Realm."

Joanne was right, then: the mind control was as strong here as in the South. Much stronger, even! The question was, why were Joanne and Simon exempt from such control?

And myself.

Was it a psychosocial experiment on the phenomena of belief? With Joanne and Simon as stimuli? But how are Athana and I involved in this? It seems quite redundant! Or perhaps the experimenters think there's a quantitative threshold? What are they expecting to happen? Mass hysteria, a sudden epidemic of disbelief?

And wasn't there another essential question? If the experiment was drawing to a close in any case, what would be the fate of the subjects? Clean out the cage and begin again with others? No, that's the simplistic horror version. There's the possibility of horror on a more sophisticated level: use the same subjects, brainwash them, and begin another experiment. The visions and maybe some of my dreams could be a botched brainwashing— maybe we're palimpsest-guinea pigs used too often and wearing out.

Time you went to bed, Catherine.

Simon was looking at her with a slightly worried curiosity. "What?"

She tried without much success to laugh. She was beginning to realize what this man's life must have been like, must be like now, and Joanne's—and they've lived like this for years?

"It's hard not to become paranoid," she finally admitted.

He didn't smile but reached out awkwardly and touched her shoulder. "You mustn't, though."

That night, Catherine dreamed.

It was the first time she'd really dreamed since coming to Chicoutimi. There'd been what she called blender dreams, a jumble of incidents and images brought to the surface of her consciousness by the dip-net of the subconscious. But that night she dreamed of the garden—the espaliered shrubs, the trees, the berry bushes, the lawns, the straight rows of the vegetable garden, everything flowering and fruiting at the same time with benevolent luxuriance. But underneath the snow. And if not snow, a white substance that outlined each fruit, each blade of grass, each pebble in the alleys, but thicker and softer than frost. The contrast made the summer colors oddly vivid. Everything was silent. There was no one in the garden. Catherine herself was floating, a bodiless consciousness, somewhere above the cherry trees, waiting a little anxiously.

At last, footsteps appeared in the alleys, the sign of an invisible walker, seemingly the prints of a child. They traced the invisible being's trajectory along the main alley, past the honeysuckle, and around the bottom of the fennel plant, as tall as a small tree with its leaves and their intricate patterns delicately emphasized by the snow, then along the trellised walk with the espaliered pears and into the other alley, leading to the main lawn.... Suddenly, Catherine felt these weren't footprints, but fingerprints, the tips of a gigantic hand walking in the snow, imitating the feet of a child, and she looked up at the sky, prepared to see the shadow of a palm, and behind that the contour of a face. There was nothing. And yet she hadn't really been frightened. You couldn't be afraid of a hand that played at drawing fake prints in the snow, could you, even if it were invisible?

Joanne disappeared one day at the beginning of February and came back a week later, from which Catherine deduced that the voyage west had failed. She only stayed a

few hours. More as a challenge than by way of information, she came to tell Catherine, "I'm going to see what
Athana's up to. Any message for her?"

"I'd like her to come back and see me," said Catherine, caught a little off guard.

Joanne nodded and walked out before Catherine
could ask her to stay.

When Catherine had told Frédéric Manesch that she
intended to remain in Chicoutimi, the old man hadn't
shown any particular emotion, but she was used to this,
now. He offered to speak to the college and university administrators. There'd certainly be room for a literature
professor from France, he said. The academic year ran
from September to the end of May, with a month's break
at Christmas. Catherine wasn't very surprised to be hired
by the university on a full-time basis for the following autumn, nor to find everyone very understanding about the
seven months separating her from her job and salary. The
Realm Bank agreed to a loan with a ridiculously low interest rate, and Manesch insisted she continue living in his
home. She knew better now: when she'd begun going out,
first to hospital physiotherapy sessions for her leg, then to
do errands and visit the city, she'd become aware of the
extreme solicitude shown by Grandbois and Étienne. One
or both of them would insist on acting as driver, guide, or
porter. Nevertheless, she accepted Manesch's renewed
hospitality. She hadn't finished going through the library,
and to tell the truth she didn't feel ready to live on her
own. This sudden weakness annoyed and worried her, but
on the other hand, Simon had been right: she must try not
to be paranoid, and it was easier if you weren't alone.

No one had prevented Joanne from leaving. It seemed
Manesch or the Council felt it unnecessary to keep all the
potential Infants under the same roof, now that Catherine
had decided to stay (or for some other reason that escaped
her). She'd thought Simon would go home, but he was still
there. Nevertheless, she decided to look for an apartment
for far-off September, and it was Simon rather than Grandbois or Étienne who came along on her outings. February
and March were deep winter at this latitude. There were
almost no snowfalls, and it was bitterly cold, with winds
whipping up the existing snow in blinding clouds and of-

ten sending the thermometer plummeting to minus fifty. The downtown area wasn't much affected by this, since most of the shops were underground—more so than in Montreal or Quebec. This subterranean city had wide malls with shops and offices on either side. Small vehicles (Catherine no longer cared whether they were powered by electricity or energy spheres) ran up and down these underground avenues. There were even underground residential sections along the river, and Simon had advised Catherine to look for her future lodging here. But she felt somehow repelled by the idea of living underground. She must at least have something partially aboveground, like Simon's house. A house, in fact, not an apartment. She wanted to be in her own home. There were houses for rent near the university, but they were considerably more expensive.

"I might get a good deal," said Catherine, half joking.

"Don't fall into that trap," said Simon, frowning.

Catherine looked at him gravely, aware of the strength Joanne and he had needed to resist being spoiled. Potential Infants could do what they liked, even deny they were Infants, since that might be part of their Quest. That revolt itself was tolerated as part of the system must have been the most devastating of all. And neither of them had given in to it. Bloody but unbowed, as the saying was. Forever isolated in their opposition. Joanne had left, finally. But what had she gained? Her frenetic wanderings had led nowhere. Maybe Simon's decision—to stay on the fringe, but to stay—had been wiser.

"I was joking," she said with an absentminded smile. She was thinking of other things. Leave, stay, come back, why did these words and their complex mixture of emotions and images reverberate within her like the echo of some former conversation—but with whom?

Outside the big window, the cement promenade had been swept clean by the storm and the March wind was whipping up white snow-serpents. She was sitting with Simon in a downtown restaurant with a room aboveground. At first, he hadn't much liked being seen with her in public, but now he appeared to have come to terms with this. Today, he hadn't even been annoyed when people carefully avoided looking at them as they chose a table and the waiter made a point of being as lightly jocular with them as with his other customers.

"It's easier when there are two of you, particularly if you aren't on the defensive," Simon had said when she remarked on his equanimity. She'd let the subject drop, not wanting to emphasize, either for herself or him, the parallels or differences between their present relationship and what might have been his relationship with Joanne. She preferred to discover him without comparisons. In the last few weeks, he'd relaxed and shown a surprising, rather timid kindness, a fund of common sense and the occasional flash of unexpected humor, as well as a fair mastery of the art of understatement and ellipsis. Confidences that were restrained enough not to cause embarrassment. Comfortable silences that didn't need to be filled. Attentive silences that made it easy to talk.

He fluttered a hand in front of her eyes. "Hypnotized by the snow?" She came back to him with a start, and smiled.

Toward the beginning of February, Charles-Henri left for Lac Saint-François to attend some sort of religious retreat. Just before leaving, he came to see Catherine at the Manesch mansion, accompanied by a brown-skinned, doe-eyed young man whom Catherine recognized with amazement as the boy in the Greenburg Center, the one who'd read a message of supposed danger in the shop signs. Of real danger, as it had turned out. Catherine felt a slight shock at the sudden realization. Did the Adepts really have a case?

The young man was called Marc-André Fortin. At first he was timidly silent—probably one of those who would like to think of her as a potential Ultimate Infant, thought Catherine, annoyed. At one point in the conversation, however, Charles-Henri leaned toward Marc-André to emphasize something or other and touched him with a characteristic gesture that made her think of another reason for the young man's timidity toward her.

"Are you going on this retreat too, Marc-André?" she asked kindly.

"Yes," he said, rather hoarsely.

She guessed from Charles-Henri's expression that he might have been a little worried about her reaction, so soon after Antoine's death, and she winked amicably at him. "Are Adept teachings completely esoteric, or have you the right to tell me about them?" she asked.

"Oh, no, we can talk about them!" said Marc-André. "Maybe you'd like to come one time? Charles-Henri told me"—he blushed, but had to go on—"you have interesting dreams."

"Not really, not since I've been here," she said. Her only so-called interesting dream had been about the garden in the snow with a few blender variations thrown in here and there. The visions had stopped completely. If the painted countenance of Pierre-Emmanuelle Manesch hadn't met her each time she entered the library, she would have thought her vision in Simon's house had been . . . a dream, a hallucination, an illusion? These terms had now taken on such a special meaning that it was difficult to use them lightly. "Is this retreat about dreams?"

"If you like. We have . . . we call them dreamers' circles. We tell each other about the dreams that have impressed us most, and we try to understand them as a group, to understand their relation to the life of the dreamer within the scope of his quest, but also their possible importance to the community. For us, they're signs in the Book, like all the other signs we see around us, everything that seems to have meaning or should have a meaning. . . ."

He was less timid now, no doubt buoyed up by his faith. Catherine smiled at him. It sounded like group therapy, but in a religious setting. It also dovetailed with local Amerindian tradition. Why not? Everything depended on the interpretation.

"And you're going on this retreat to take part in one of these circles?"

"Yes," Marc-André replied. "You don't find the right circle all at once. There are different kinds of dreams and dreamers. You learn by trying, by participating in several different circles, until you find the one that suits you best. The circles change, people come, go, come back—it's a delicate balance. . . ."

"Antoine has asked me to participate in his circle," concluded Charles-Henri.

Under the circumstances, this was both a proof of confidence and a test. Catherine watched Charles-Henri, not hiding her curiosity. "Have you had special dreams since you were here?"

"Yes," he replied, a little embarrassed. "But we only talk about them in the circle."

"Well," smiled Catherine, "perhaps I ought to try a circle myself, one of these days."

Charles-Henri visited her as soon as he came back. He had lost weight, but seemed to be blooming. His smile had always been a little nervous, but now it had a peaceful glow. Catherine, after giving him a hug, held him at arm's length. "Don't tell me. You're a convert."

He laughed—at least his laugh hadn't changed—and said, "I think so."

"The answer to all your questions."

She couldn't help moving off a little. He looked at her gravely. "Some answers. But mainly new ways of asking questions."

She raised a skeptical eyebrow. She didn't always agree with Joanne's extreme theories, but she no longer doubted the mind control exercised over the North. What kind of questions was one allowed to ask?

"Mainly about our relation to the Quest. Our conduct in the world, the way the world speaks to us, and the way we respond."

She'd talked about it a bit with Joanne, then with Simon, but both had been shy about giving her a detailed account of the Northern religion, and for the same odd reason: they didn't believe in it, they'd said. And Charles-Henri, who believed in it, wouldn't mind talking about it? No, she suddenly realized, because the Northern religion was transmitted in this way, orally, from person to person, with these manifold subjective nuances that were exactly what prevented it from ever hardening into dogma.

"But the world doesn't really exist, does it?"

"A world exists," said Charles-Henri, "but it's incomplete. Influenced by other potentials, other manifestations of itself, of its future state. States, I should say. Only when the Deity awakes will the Infants find their name and be able to tell It Its name. . . ."

"And only then will the world exist in its definitive version?"

"If you like. One reality will become the whole reality."

Catherine thought of the strange maps collected by Pierre-Emmanuelle Manesch. Were they simply artifacts concocted by the Adepts to illustrate or support their theories? Or else, inversely, had the Adepts built their theories on just such a basis?

"What about the dreams?"

"Dream are the signs of potential realities. Like visions in the South."

"And the Infants are supposed to have visions, even in the North, is that it?"

"Yes. They have a deeper relation with creation. They can see its virtual manifestations everywhere."

But I didn't *dream* about the library and Pierre-Emmanuelle Manesch! And they weren't part of a future or potential reality!

Catherine kept her protest to herself, however. She studied Charles-Henri, amazed at not being more upset by his quiet conviction. He hadn't come back a fanatic, in any case. He was simply talking about what was for him a reality. His reality. A purely spiritual one, as true for him as the dark political reality of the South was true for Joanne—frustrated demands, repression, manipulation, secret wars. . . . As true as anything—or as false? All of it had seemed to evaporate at the moment the van had crossed the barrier, and Catherine had to remind herself of the bullet that had killed Max to prevent herself from wondering whether the South was either nonexistent or no longer existed. In any case, she had the greatest difficulty imagining the North plotting an invasion of the South or the overthrow of the Canadian government. The North barely existed as a political entity and didn't even seem to have a central government! If the North was truly the source of agitation in the South, she would have to theorize that people like Manesch or the other councilors in Chicoutimi (it was the "capital," after all) were capable of more deviousness than she was prepared to postulate.

No, the image of the North that fed the paranoia of the South and its policies was clearly false. The Canadian government had probably fabricated this image as a pretext, a smokescreen, to hide ... what? Its terror in the face of unfamiliar or incomprehensible things such as visions—a reality that escaped it, that its narrowly rationalist ideology couldn't account for? Maybe even the covert struggle with the Enclave and its francophones was just a diversionary tactic, unbeknownst to the actors, aimed at that which stubbornly refused to bow to the logic of common sense, at these visions that kept on *resisting*.

Because the visions, the dreams, all these things really happened. The metaphysical and religious concepts of the North had evolved to account for real facts. Wasn't that better than the South's trying to erase visions through violence, deferring to the lethal fantasy of a world order with no disorder, no loose ends? What better than the Northern concept of a somehow virtual world to make room for the plasticity of visions and dreams?

Yet according to the Northern myth, the virtual world would become real one day. Did this express a deeply-rooted human desire for permanence? Or something as real as visions and dreams? One mustn't succumb to the temptation of symbolism. Simon exists, and Joanne, and Athana. And myself.

"Tell me about the Infants, Charles-Henri. Are they really of this world, incarnate? And since their liberation is such a topic, what do they have to liberate themselves from?"

The black face smiled—a grave smile. "Incarnate in the world, prisoners of illusion."

"Illusions like having a civil status and memories, for instance?" said Catherine, troubled by her sudden spurt of aggressiveness.

"Possibly. But mainly the desire for power, control."

"Aren't there more specific illusions? Where do these so-called illusions come from, anyway?"

"From the Infants themselves, of course. They think they, not the Sleeping Deity, have created the world. They don't think It has created them. They believe they're fighting each other to determine the shape of the world to come, when in fact they're fighting against themselves so they can fuse."

And the South was in actual fact fighting against joining the North, then? The Infants' Quest transposed into a collective endeavor? But Catherine kept this thought to herself.

"Are the Fortins Ultimists?"

"And Adepts. Yes. But I don't think I am."

"You're a Separatist? The Infants have to remain distinct?"

"Yes. You know how I've always liked contrasts."

She smiled, reassured by this flash of the old Charles-Henri. It was true he seemed more like his "old" self than when she'd been in Quebec. Was it a good sign? Did it have to be a sign? Why not simply enjoy having him back?

"You ought to try going to a circle, you know," he said. "With the kind of dreams you have. . . . Just to see."

"But entering a circle in a spirit of scientific inquiry, wouldn't that be sacrilege?"

"Not at all, Cat. In fact, that's what convinced me. There's no question of sacrilege in a circle. Nor in any of the forms of the Northern religion."

"That's what makes the circle's therapy so effective," remarked Catherine, watching for his reaction.

He burst out laughing. "Yes!"

Catherine looked at him for a moment, then gave up trying not to smile. "Well, I must say it's tempting, the way you put it. If I start having more 'interesting' dreams, I may drop in."

That evening, as she recorded this conversation in her journal (again on diskette, since there were at least three computers in the Manesch household), Catherine felt something nagging at her. As though she'd forgotten to say something to Charles-Henri, but what, on what subject? Should she worry about it? Was mind control suddenly being exercised over her as well? She finished her summary of their discussion and reread it, searching for the element that might crystallize her vague feeling. The illusions of the Infants. The dreams. Her dreams. These were the points that caused her the most uneasiness, gave her the sense that it was on the tip of her tongue, whatever it was. The "illusions" of the Infants. Her own illusions? She certainly felt threatened: if her memories weren't her memories. . . . But she'd more or less overcome that initial terror. The dreams, then. The highly detailed memory she had of the Marrus, more detailed than the exhibition. What did the explanatory plaques say about the Marrus, anyway? Something about the relationship between the development of the young Marrus and the place where they stopped in their voyage. . . .

Voyage. Well, what about "voyage"? The Marru's journey, an initiation (and a hormonal trip, don't forget!). A quest for identity, like the life of the Infants in the world. But she wasn't going to interpret this dream as a circle would! By definition, she couldn't do it all by herself, anyway. But the word voyage did ring a bell, somehow. Why had the Marrus made her think of the Infants? Yes, the young Marrus were also infants, children. Were there Marrus who refused to leave? What happened to them? Did they remain childlike all their lives? Or were they unable to resist hormonal changes, voyage or not?

Here she was, going on as though the Marrus actually existed! But hadn't she decided to consider her hyperceptions real, at one point? If her dream had been the cause of the Royal Museum exhibition—the collective vision offered by the exhibition—and not the reverse. . . . If there was a link between imagination and these visions (whatever Sarah might think), then that was a degree of reality worth considering, wasn't it?

Just how many degrees of reality are we talking about? The journey of the young Marrus from the red sea to their villages, with the flowers, the forest, and the white beast—how was that *real*? If it was a mind trip brought on by the changes of puberty, then how many embedded realities are we dealing with?

But in her dream the flower and the white beast had been so very real! And in her other dreams, or in the reality of her visions, the hyperceptions—those metamorphosed perceptions—were also very real. What switched them on? Hormones? Certainly not the hormones of puberty in her case. But it was a bit early for menopause, wasn't it? And then no hormonal process could possibly explain the mental map of the underground network in Quebec's Old Town, even if hormones could explain what happened to the young Marrus—this voyage of metamorphosis, by metamorphosis. Young metamorphosed voyagers. . . .

Metamorphosed voyagers.

After a moment, she realized with a start that the automatic screen saver had taken over her text. Geometric patterns were telescoping, dizzyingly changing from one into another. Voyagers. Metamorphosed. The dream, the dreams of the Bridge. She'd forgotten! Egon, Talitha. How could she have failed to recognize them. . . . No, she could have, but something had made her forget.

Or else something had just invented them for her?

She curled up in her chair, hugging herself in sharp, icy distress. Everything had seemed so normal here! It was because of this house, the bookcases in the library, the ancestral portraits, everything seemed to tell of a past so ancient, so certain! Or else it was her fault, yes, hers; she was still all too ready to indulge in her desire for order and control, that's why it was so easy for her to grow roots anywhere! Make up a place to go back to, even if she was exiled forever, a home, a fake normality, whatever the cost!

Leave, come back, stay. Voyagers. The many Egons and Talithas. Those who stayed, those who came back. Why would she forget, especially that? The Talithas who resembled her mother, the Egons who resembled her father!

On the screen, a series of squares ballooned and shrank, turned inside out, and shivered in a frenzy of metamorphosis through a series of triangles and circles. Catherine wrenched herself away from their fascinating convolutions. She hesitated, hands suspended above the keyboard. Her head was a jumble of rushing ideas, images from these dreams—were they dreams? Memories? No, not memories. Even though she'd shared the thoughts and feelings of those Egons and Talithas, she'd never identified with them as she'd done with the young Voyager Catherine; she had somehow seen them from a distance, like . . .

characters, yes, characters in a story that *she* wasn't telling.

And not dreams either. Did visions sometimes happen in dreams? These fragments of stories had the same solidity, the same texture, the same *reality* as the visions. . . .

And yet, if I were in a dreamers' circle or on an analyst's couch, what would it tell me—the resemblance of these Voyagers to my mother, to my father? Symbolic, obviously! These Voyagers, this Bridge that might never bring you back. Travel, leave, cast the old self aside. You turn the fatal corner of forty, your parents die, you recognize your own mortality, and all that claptrap. A warped variant of my Mother-who-shrinks Dream. Die, shrink, or slow down your molecules to around absolute zero in the Bridge and disappear: these must be interchangeable in the modeling clay of imagination. Why else would the young Egon have walked in Mama's garden with the other monitor?

The Garden-under-the-snow Dream; is there a connection? Footsteps. Invisible in the snow. Invisible. A child's footsteps, or an imitation of them. A gigantic hand, invisible.

A variant of the Dream of the Presence? But what's the connection with the Egons and Talithas? And why does this last name suddenly seem so familiar? Talitha, Talitha . . . Thalia, the Greek muse of comedy. Theater. Athalie, good God, we're onto Racine and seventeenth-century tragedy, now! What's Athalie doing in the picture? Ah, yes, the figure of the devouring mother. Athalie—an unhappy daughter and a murderous mother at the same time. Athalie: Talitha. Yes, maybe. The young Talitha was very unhappy in the dream, but the older Talitha wasn't murderous, she'd merely left, while poor little Egon drank the cup of sorrow to the lees. . . .

Italie. Athana.

She stared at the cursor blinking after these two words, then turned the computer off, her mind a blank. Her body vibrated with an electric tingling, as if her thoughts had been pulverized into a myriad of darting, quicksilver droplets. She went to bed, moving like an automaton, and tumbled straight into sleep as though switching off the light had somehow switched her off, too.

It's winter. She's in one of the large buildings in Montreal-City. The architecture is very complicated, the decoration overly ornate in the vaguely organic style of the early twenties, somewhere between the fiddlehead of a fern and the honeycomb texture of lung tissue. There are brilliant blue tiles everywhere, spiral staircases, frescoed ceilings impossible to see clearly, and chandeliers or perhaps spidery sculptures of metallic netting. She enters a vast exhibition hall with a gleaming floor of pale varnished pine. It contains food, clothing, all kinds of objects, particularly Japanese, a whole collection of armor resembling fearsome insects, exquisite plates, enchanting kimonos, but also severely simple ultramodern objects with no obvious useful purpose.

She goes over to a window offering a panoramic vista of the snowbound city. Among the people moving along the city's arteries—for the window overlooks a boulevard with wide sidewalks—some women stand out strangely. They are very beautiful, dressed in magnificent clothes, and much more real—clearer, brighter—than the other pedestrians. They walk as in slow motion, dreamily.

The building begins to move: the landscape outside the window is changing. As long as she's looking at the boulevard, she can almost accept the idea, particularly since all her senses confirm it beyond a doubt. But now the building glides down the small, close-knit streets of a picturesque older quarter, the Old Town of Quebec. The building is really a bus with large panoramic windows of smoked glass. She's full of curiosity, and as the bus slows down to stop at a small marketplace, she decides to get off.

She takes a few steps on the uneven paving. A shape appears, outlined by strokes of silvery-gray, a bit like a photographic negative, but more like cinematographic trick film, since the shape slowly moves toward the bus and passes through the people standing in the marketplace, apparently without their noticing. It reaches the bus, grabs the railing beside the bus steps, and climbs aboard, becoming one of the strangely real and beautiful women who were walking on the boulevard a little earlier.

She understands. The occupants of the bus and the building don't belong to this world. They visit it or occupy it without being perceived. She herself must be like this, because people she passes don't see her. Suddenly frightened, her heart beating faster, she realizes she shouldn't have gotten off the bus. She runs toward it, stumbling on the paving blocks. She almost makes it, but the bus is picking up speed. She runs alongside it, waving to the driver, who sees her and slows down. Saved! But her fingers slip on the railing and the bus moves off, looking poignantly real, along a street that is now a little bleaker, a little paler.

She tries to hold back the tears while constructing an explanation to calm herself. There is another dimension of the world, and she has fallen into it by accident. She has been transformed, but not enough: she no longer belongs to her original world, but she doesn't belong to this one, either—a world resembling her own but distinct from it, since she first saw the beautiful woman as a ghost, and only later in her true form, when the woman touched the railing, the giver of reality. If she has seen strange, beautiful women walking slowly along the boulevard, it's because she was looking at them through the windows of the building, which is also the bus, and which also belongs to another dimension, the slow dimension. Now she'll have to wait. Wait to see other sketchy, silvery-gray silhouettes, or another bus that may never come.

Branches grow out of the market stalls, grass springs up on the paving stones, the alleyways stretch out, the street breaks up and rises to become the terrace with the pretty-by-night bushes behind the kitchen in Sergines. And while she looks around, not certain she should feel reassured, the roofs and the acacia in the next-door schoolyard slide slowly away and disappear to the left, down the length of the garden. The hill comes closer then also slides away, slipping under the garden.

The garden is moving! The garden is traveling! She dares not stir at first, feeling terribly dizzy and at the same time exultant. Then, with careful steps, she goes and sits on the low wall. She sees nothing beyond the garden; she must be in the sky, the garden is flying! While she watches, a thick white layer begins to form over the espaliered apples on the trellis in front of her and over the whole garden. She feels a sudden anxiety. It's cold high up in the air. Will the garden die? Then the answer from some indefinable source: no, because it's traveling northward and it's April, the time of the Pilgrimage—the garden must get ready for northern latitudes, the snow growing on top of the grass and trees will be like protective clothing. She herself is covered with snow, and it really is warm and soft. She touches it, it doesn't melt, it's silky, like fur.

A violent shock suddenly knocks her off the low wall. The garden and the sky crack, as though she's inside a shell, a sphere that's breaking up. She closes her eyes, afraid to see the gigantic hand that's crushing the sphere.

She wakes up.

8

The Fortin family lived on the southeast side of Chicoutimi, where the first escarpments of Laurentide Park raised their stark black-and-white slopes toward the sky. The architecture of the Fortin house was typical, according to Simon, who'd insisted on driving Catherine there in the snowcar. The house stood at the edge of one of the many small lakes dotting the region, a low building, seemingly very small, with a humped roof that kept the snow from piling up. This was all that could be seen of the house, which was actually underground. Catherine now knew that religious choices in the Realm often corresponded to a particular lifestyle. Most Ultimists, especially the Adepts, were city dwellers—probably the reason why they figured among the clandestine proselytes who now lived in the South. Catherine even wondered whether the sect hadn't been born in an urban setting, where its obsession with signs might have more flamboyant fare than could be found in the depths of the country. She hadn't been surprised to learn that the Nasiwi family were Adepts as well. Joanne had merely transposed their basic credo—seeing signs in everything—into a great unified theory about manipulation. The Separatists, on the other hand, tended to avoid towns and cities, shunning the complexity and the stresses of urban life.

"You've only met atypical types so far," Simon had

joked. True: the city-dwelling Maneschs were Separatists, the country-dwelling Fortins Ultimists.

The Fortins welcomed Simon and Catherine with a smiling, unforced kindness. "I'll get Charles-Henri," said Josiane, a pretty, plump brunette. She was Marc-André's sister. Aurèle, the father, began preparing a hot toddy: the snowcar had been fairly well heated, but the wind had been strong. He chatted to them as he busied himself around the kitchen. His wife worked in the Chicoutimi hospital, the two younger boys in the Jonquière pulp mill. The oldest had taken over the small family business—treating furs and skins—where Marc-André now worked, and where Charles-Henri would join him once Aurèle had initiated him into the secrets of the art. Josiane was finishing her education as a speech therapist at the college.

Catherine sipped her drink with a painful feeling of strangeness. All these details seemed normal to the point of banality, these lives laid out in clear lines, this tranquil family setup, unquestioned in space and time, everything settled, right down to the soft glow of the polished furniture, the small hand-embroidered napkins that Josiane had given them to hold their burning-hot glasses, the spot of ketchup on Aurèle's shirt, everything seeming to stand out in absurd relief. The day before, the false security of the routine she'd constructed for herself since Joanne's departure had evaporated, leaving her lost, adrift. How could people like the Fortins, or all those people like them in Montreal and Quebec whom she remembered in such detail, exist in the same universe as visions, dreams, Sleeping Deities and amnesiac Infants?

But she mustn't give in to that temptation, either. The fact was, they did exist, they were very real. They *coexisted*. That's what she had to understand, surely?

A shape appeared in the stair from the basement: Charles-Henri, wiping his hands. "Cat! Excuse me—I was up to my eyes in dye, or almost." They hugged each other. The black eyes studied her attentively: Charles-Henri had immediately sensed something was wrong.

"You must show me what you're doing," she said, her smile too brilliant. He indicated the stairway with a small bow.

The workroom smelled of leather and glue, as well

as the harsh, pungent odor of dyes and solvents, although not as much as she'd expected—there must be excellent ventilation in these underground houses. He made room for her and half sat on his worktable. Although he'd lost weight, he still had the broad-chested torso of a swimmer, and his face was as round as ever. She smiled at him, annoyed with herself for her sudden tenderness. She hadn't come here to cry on anyone's shoulder, for heaven's sake!

"Got a problem?" said Charles-Henri.

"Dreams."

"It's a bit difficult to hold a circle for only two," he said after a moment.

"I don't want a circle!" She lowered her voice carefully. "I just want to talk."

"Simon won't do?"

"No."

"Mmmm," he said, rather sadly, then added with a small shrug, "Okay. Shoot."

She hesitated to begin with the dreams of the Bridge and the fairy child. Why? Did she want to test him first? Yes—she had to admit it, and it made her feel horribly lonely, the pain of it so sharp that she couldn't speak for a moment. Then, in a rather hoarse voice, she told him about the Bus Dream. He remained silent for a while after she'd finished.

"A voyage," he said at last. "You're in Montreal, then Quebec. And then the garden that flies northward. . . . Did you know that the Pilgrimage for the spheres took place last week?"

"Yes." She'd thought it was one of the blender elements in the dream—she'd heard Madame Otchiwey mention it the day before. But a voyage to the Far North? She hadn't thought of that.

She stiffened. She hadn't thought? Or someone hadn't wanted her to think. The dream had ended so abruptly. Come to think of it, all the Garden-in-the-snow dreams had something hurried about them, as though they'd been sequences insidiously spliced between two ordinary dreams, there being no time to let them expand to their true dimensions; she didn't feel anxiety while dreaming them, more a feeling of urgency.

No, she wasn't going to adopt a paranoid view, back off from the complexity of what was happening to her, as she'd reproached Joanne for doing. *They* hadn't necessarily wanted to prevent her from thinking about the dream. Maybe *she* hadn't wanted to think about it—another journey, leaving, again—of course she didn't want to think about it! Of course she didn't want to admit that everything was pushing her northward. This was what she'd come for, in fact: a confirmation. Not very fair of me to get cross with Charles-Henri for telling me what I wanted to hear. Feared to hear. And he said it without even having heard of the other dreams.

She suddenly realized how far she'd come. She was actually ready to consider her dreams as oracles! True, she'd always paid attention to them, noting them down, but that wasn't the same! She used to think of them as symbolic. The story didn't count, or counted for something else, was intended more as a smokescreen for the figurative meaning. . . .

And now it's the opposite. I feel it's the symbols that are the smokescreen. But what do they hide? What story?

You know what story, Catherine. You do have a story to explain all this.

Charles-Henri watched her patiently. She took a breath, and without looking at him began to recount her other dreams, the changing dreams of the Presence, of the fairy child—and the dreams of the Center, the Voyagers, the Bridge.

When she'd finished, she made herself look up. Would Charles-Henri's expression be skeptical, or, far worse, ecstatic? But he was frowning, thinking, had no answer to give. Not even the one she'd finally become resigned to hearing?

"I think I'm a Voyager," she said, more for herself than him, just to hear it said.

He nodded, still thoughtful. "But it wouldn't explain everything."

She relaxed. "No, but a good part of it. The dreams of the Presence especially. I am the Presence. Fighting myself. A little like the Marrus: stay on the edge of the red sea, or the lake, or in the forest. Or go back to the villages."

"Leave a finished stage of your life?"

"Leave, anyway. Get out of this world. One part of me wants to stay. Something in this world appeals to me profoundly, calls to me. The monitor said it quite clearly: the Bridge doesn't send Voyagers just anywhere."

"It sends them to worlds that resemble them, that say something to them, yes," murmured Charles-Henri. Of course this aspect of the dream corresponded to his own beliefs. "And these two Voyagers resemble your parents. But are you sure? I mean, were your parents really like that? Something's happened to your memory, that's obvious—all the more so if you're a Voyager and have forgotten the fact."

"Voyagers have total mastery of their memory. Under certain circumstances, if they want, they can make themselves forget certain facts. That's what I must have done to help me stay here, a sort of self-conditioning, which is in the process of unravelling."

"You would have supplied yourself with a complete biography, then. How can you decide what's true or not? If these Voyagers are like your parents, wouldn't it be a reason to think you'd invented them?"

Catherine slumped a little. Invented those memories, so clear, so painful? The death of her mother, of her father? But why would she have invented such suffering for herself?

"I don't know," she murmured stubbornly. "The fact is, they resemble my parents."

"And the rest?" said Charles-Henri after a moment. "Us. I mean this world, here. You're implying this isn't the Earth that you left, but an Earth in another universe."

"That's why some of my memories don't jibe. Why my visions don't jibe either. Through the gaps in my self-conditioning, I recall another Earth."

"But that doesn't explain the visions, Cat. You aren't the only one to have them. Or dreams. There are people who dream of other worlds here, just as there are visions of other worlds in the South . . . worlds you didn't recognize in Sarah's book. As far as I know, there are two very specific categories of visions in the South, aren't there?"

Catherine sighed. It was inevitable that it would come to this. "Because there are two other Voyagers here. The visions are theirs. Come from them."

"But how?"

"I don't know," she replied. "Since you don't have visions in the North, I suppose the Southern visions are transmitted by a . . . traditional energy." And your vision of Manesch in Simon's house, Catherine? But there had to be a simple explanation for it: a single exception to the rule surely couldn't count for much! "In any case, if they possess that kind of technology, they may also have a Bridge. Somewhere in the Far North."

Charles-Henri said nothing for a minute. "The spheres and the barrier are their doing?" He didn't seem upset by this mundane explanation.

"Yes," said Catherine, smiling gratefully at him.

"I see. But it doesn't answer my question just now, Cat. This world. Us. The North, anyway. Why have a barrier? And Cat, they've been having visions in the South for nearly three centuries. Are your Voyagers immortal?"

She sighed. "Not as far as I know. They aren't even particularly long-lived. It's a gap in my reasoning, I know." She pulled a little face, annoyed to feel the conversation becoming a sort of intellectual speculation for her, almost like a game. On the other hand, it was less threatening this way. Anyhow, she mustn't take these new theories too seriously or she'd end up like Joanne.

"A big gap," retorted Charles-Henri. "It's too bad, in a way. It might have explained the Infants."

So he'd thought of this, too? She gave him an affectionate smile. This was the old Charles-Henri, ready to question anything, even the things he took most to heart.

"The Infants' characteristics are definitely those of the Voyagers, Charles-Henri."

"You don't believe it could work some other way?" he said gently. "If the Bridge really sends Voyagers to worlds resembling them in a symbolic way, couldn't they send them to worlds where someone literally resembles them? Has resembled them for all eternity? The Voyagers aren't immortal, but the Infants are, Cat."

She considered him for a moment, feeling troubled. This implied the Infants really existed. Which implied that all the rest existed, right up to the Sleeping Deity? Absurd. Such creatures could only be mythical. Symbolic. But on the other hand, if she really was a Voyager. . . . If the Marrus actually existed, for instance, then her experience among them hadn't been a dream, but real—including the flower and the white beast, although they'd lent themselves so well to a symbolic interpretation.

"And most of all, Cat, if they have a Bridge, why would they still be here, not taking into account their life-span, I mean?"

"Perhaps this world is too suited to them," said Catherine obstinately. "Perhaps, one way or another, they've found a means of prolonging their existence here, and they stay because they feel comfortable and because it pleases them. . . ."

To play with you. She fell silent, surprised at what she'd almost said. The Voyagers as Great Manipulators? An adaptation of Joanne's theory? But Voyagers *could* have the required technology: people able to build a Bridge should be able to do much more, especially if they had the time. Let's admit their hypothetical longevity, then, although that's a pretty big step! It would explain the whole situation so well—the religion of the North as well as the religions of the South, the historical development of both North and South, their political and economic differences, the impossibility of getting out. An experiment, yes. An experiment conducted by Voyagers would explain so many things.

Too many. It was plainly a variant of Joanne's theory. Based on data Joanne didn't possess, certainly, but rendered suspect by the actual theory of manipulation—after all, if I've forgotten these dreams and suddenly remembered them, how does that prove they relate to any reality? This was the latent defect in the theory of absolute manipulation: the elements that could prove it might themselves have been manipulated. *Regressio ad infinitum.*

And in any case, the dreams weren't all the same:

there were the dreams about the Garden and the fairy child.

But the Garden dream is the transformed dream of the Presence, isn't it? And if I really am the Presence, symbolically speaking. . . .

Something was still wrong.

"There are a lot of gaps," said Charles-Henri at this point, as though he'd been following a parallel train of thought. "And too many odd details. Why do some bodies disappear in a flash, and others not? What's the connection with the content of the spheres? And then there are Joanne and Simon. They have some of the same capacities as you. Don't tell me they're the Voyagers? Could the Voyagers be here and in the Far North at the same time?" He straightened up. "And above all, there is Athana. Italie. Your Garden dreams. The Presence is there, too, isn't it? Your invisible hand in the snow, or the hand that destroys everything at the end of the Bus dream. . . . What's the link between the Presence and Athana?"

Especially if I'm the Presence! He's right, of course. Exasperating, but right. Catherine hunched in her chair. "Have you another explanation?"

He laughed, but stopped when he saw her defeated expression. "No, Cat."

"You still believe in the Sleeping Deity and the Infants."

"The arrival of Voyagers, now or in the past, wouldn't be enough to disprove their existence, would it?"

She had to admit the truth of this.

He stood up. "But you know, somehow they don't seem mutually exclusive to me." He leaned his head to one side and smiled hesitantly. "You really should come to a circle."

"But I don't believe in them, Charles-Henri," she said wearily. "The basic premise of a circle is to believe, isn't it? I don't believe in the Sleeping Deity. I don't believe in the Infants. It would undermine the whole thing."

He sighed. "Perhaps. Or perhaps you'd find new avenues for reflection. You'd choose which avenues suited you, you know."

They looked at each other for a moment. "In any case," Catherine said gloomily, "there's something in the Far North. I've got to go to there."

Charles-Henri bowed his head gravely. "And we must find Athana."

Catherine laughed. "It will probably be easier to go to the Far North!"

9

Joanne reappeared a few days later, without Athana, which didn't particularly surprise Catherine. Joanne moved back into the Manesch household. After a first, somewhat difficult breakfast in the library with Simon and Catherine, the atmosphere seemed less tense. Joanne wasn't as abrasive as before. Was it because of her fruitless hunt for Athana? "The more you seek her, the less you find her," she'd remarked. But she didn't tell Catherine why she'd been hunting Athana. And Catherine didn't explain to Joanne what she'd concluded about Athana, if conclusion was the right word for the rudimentary idea that if she found the key to the enigma of Athana, it might open other doors. She hadn't talked to Simon about her rediscovered dreams, and she had no intention of telling Joanne either. Sometimes she studied them covertly as they sat on each side of the table, telling herself the three of them were more united in what they didn't tell each other than in what they revealed.

They often had occasion to go into town together, now. The return of the pilgrims marked the official start of spring, and there was a two-week celebration, despite the lingering snow. Concerts were given in the evening, along with plays and balls. In the daytime there were numerous sporting events—skating, cross-country skiing and snowshoe races, dogsled races. Catherine's fears didn't materialize, however. Joanne didn't use their outings as an obvious reminder of their status as potential Infants. She appeared to appreciate the chance to rediscover simple joys. In the large park beside the river, where most of the festivities took place, she showed Catherine how to eat maple syrup poured on the snow and quickly rolled onto a stick. There were sugar maples at these icy latitudes? "Why not, when there are chestnut trees?" replied Joanne with a conspiratorial little smile. The other Joanne was still there, but she'd apparently decided to lay down her arms for the time being.

"What are you going as, Catherine?" Joanne asked. The three of them were standing in front of the poster advertising the May Day costume ball that would close the celebrations.

Simon frowned in astonishment. "You want to go to the ball again?"

"Of course. Don't you?"

"I remember the last time."

"I've grown up since then."

"Really?" he murmured.

Joanne didn't give the retort Catherine was expecting, just a simple "Yes." She and Simon stared at each other in a silence devoid of aggressivity.

Simon sighed, and turned to Catherine. "Do you like masquerades?"

"Why not?" she replied, looking from one to the other, intrigued.

Simon must have decided to observe a truce, too, or else, like Joanne, he rediscovered some of the innocent pleasure lost with the years as he showed the spring festival to someone for whom it was new. Above all, he and Joanne seemed to have rediscovered each other in Catherine's presence, as though she'd been a catalyst, but with a positive effect—not like what happened at Simon's or at the beginning of their stay in the Manesch household. Nevertheless, as time went by she had the feeling they expected something from her. But what? She was quite happy being led around by either one, delighted that they got on so well, wanted it to last—at least until the end of the festival. She'd decided to tell them about her plan to travel to the Far North immediately afterward. She welcomed this respite. Her decision would certainly throw cold water on their relationship.

She chose to go to the ball dressed as a gypsy. She'd been five years old the last time she'd done it—for a children's dance organized with enormous difficulty during the Occupation. Her mother had sacrificed a pair of curtains to make her costume. She remembered that a photograph had been taken—it was now in the shoebox in Montreal. But she refused to let the thought sadden her.

Joanne had decided to be an Oriental dancing girl. Her costume included a gauze blouse and harem pants strewn with sequins, multicolored veils, a richly embroidered satin bolero, and an impressive quantity of tinkling bracelets and necklaces. "A gypsy and a dancer go well together," she'd said. "Maybe we could register for the group contest. The Magician and his Slaves."

Simon-Pierre would go as a magician, in accordance with his first given name, or so he said. He responded to Joanne's suggestion with an eloquent grimace. But Véronique, who was going as Puss in Boots, was enthusiastic.

"Oh, yes, you could do magic tricks! You used to do them!"

"I've lost the knack," he protested weakly, and finally agreed to practice a few sleights of hand. Catherine and Joanne would be his assistants. The finale of the act would feature bouquets of flowers.

"The ladies always like flowers," remarked Joanne with a wink. "If we don't win first prize with this, I give up."

The first of May was an exceptionally mild day. After months of minus thirty-five degree weather, a temperature hovering around zero centigrade seemed positively warm, and Catherine wasn't surprised to see people out walking in pullovers or just plaid shirts. Bigger crowds turned out for the final part of the festival, especially as most of the children's events had been scheduled for this day. Merry-go-rounds had been set up along the waterfront, and a huge snow castle of winding toboggan runs had been built with the snow cleared from the street—clean snow, as there weren't much traffic and what there was brought very little pollution. Clowns and acrobats roamed along the midway, and actor-dancers performed pantomimes on small stages erected between the food stands and shooting galleries. These performers re-created the legends and myths linked to the creation of the world and the adventures of the Infants on their Quest. The symbol of the Deity was displayed everywhere—the same one as on the boxes given to Catherine when she woke up in hospital.

"Did you see that?" said Simon to Joanne. "The Warrior-Woman."

"And the Vagabond," agreed Joanne with the same amused smile as Simon, almost tender. She turned to Catherine. "The last time I went to the fancy-dress ball, I chose the Warrior costume."

"Véronique was the Vagabond," added Simon with a little laugh. "Of course, no one ever chooses those costumes for the masquerade."

"The Vagabond is the Ultimate Infant, male version, and the Warrior-Woman is the Ultimate Infant, female version," continued Joanne. "We arrived together for the costume contest, around eleven o'clock."

"And made quite an impression," concluded Catherine, amused in turn.

"Several people fainted," said Simon.

"I was leaving for the South the day after," said Joanne. "I wanted to mark the occasion." She and Simon looked at each other with rueful affection. "Come on," said Joanne, slipping an arm through Catherine's and leading her over to a shooting gallery. "I'm sure you have a pressing need for a stuffed teddy bear. I want to see if my aim is still good."

The owner of the shooting gallery was an old man with apple-red cheeks. When he saw Joanne he shook his head, threw up his hands, then handed her a big white bear.

"No, no, we must go by the book," laughed Joanne. She nonchalantly picked up a gun and shattered the seven clay pipes as required. Only then did she accept the stuffed bear.

"I'd like a panda better," said Catherine in a little-girl voice.

The proprietor handed her a panda in exchange for a bear.

"And now a stick of barley-sugar, maybe?" teased Simon.

"No, a ride on the merry-go-round!"

The largest carrousel was built for adults as well as children, with chimerical animals painted and decorated with frenzied detail—unicorns, dragons, sphinxes—alongside the more traditional horses, lions, and swans.

"Hey, a two-seater dragon!" exclaimed Simon, jumping onto the carrousel and holding out a hand to Catherine. She slipped into the seat, between two wings. The beast's ferocious air was belied by its mauve coat and green polka dots. Joanne mounted on a lion behind them, an improbable beast with a red-and-black-striped pelt. The carrousel began to move to the sound of a pseudo-Strauss waltz that Catherine couldn't place, and the animals suddenly began to twirl on their poles, swinging from side to side as they rose and fell. Catherine gave a surprised little cry and instinctively grabbed Simon's arm. He slipped an arm around her shoulders with feigned solicitude. "There, there, you mustn't be afraid, they're just little wooden animals."

She looked at him, about to protest, then saw the gleam of amusement in his pale eyes. They both burst out laughing.

Later, going back to her room after a quick lunch at a stand featuring regional food, she found her costume laid out on the bed. Madame Otchiwey had put the finishing touches to it during the afternoon. Catherine took her time dressing and put on her makeup carefully, amused but also annoyed at being so excited. Costume balls always had this effect on her. It was the idea of being someone else for a few hours. She didn't need a costume; the simple fact of getting dressed up and putting on makeup "like a Real Woman" had the same effect, even in normal life, whether she was going to a show or to meet someone. She'd learned too late and too little from her mother, and afterward from her school friends, of how women were supposed to behave and think. The actions and attitudes attributed to women were like a foreign language she would never really master, an imitation that could fool others, but not her. She liked disguises, though, and that was why she'd always liked to speak English—an adolescent habit she'd had to shed in the Enclave. She would have loved to speak even more foreign languages. English or Latin, woman talk, university talk, all of them disguises. She always felt a little anxious in public, and no wonder, considering she was always something of a fraud!

Yet she had good reason for feeling a little anxious tonight. She thought apprehensively of the little magic show in which she'd be Simon's assistant. They had rehearsed every day since the beginning of the week and it should go well, but you never knew. Any one of his tricks could go wrong. Or she might have a vision in the middle of the show! It was a little odd, coming up against the concept of magic in its most prosaic yet most illusory sense. Because the way the barrier worked, or the spheres. . . . But these things were part of daily life for the people of the Realm, things that no one ever questioned. They had nothing to do with magic.

She smiled at herself in the mirror. Joanne had found her a wig that wasn't so black, something closer to her real hair color. All in all, the gypsy costume became her, gold and purple with splashes of emerald green and turquoise blue. She knotted the medallion-trimmed scarf around her head and pirouetted before the mirror. *Let's play ball!*

The ball was being held in the city hall, a large, gray stone building with two wings flanking a square tower. The guests climbed a wide staircase to the first floor and entered a long, high-ceilinged hall with a fine waxed floor. The band was perched on a small stage in front of dark-blue velvet curtains, playing a nonstop medley of old and new dances and switching deftly from violins and accordions to electric instruments—or did they say "spheric" instruments here? A row of narrower, higher platforms had been set up against one of the longer walls, no doubt for the costume contest.

Everyone was in fancy dress. Looking at the lavishness of some of the costumes, Catherine realized this ball must be one of the social events of the Chicoutimi year. It wasn't a masked ball, however, and she was able to recognize Frédéric Manesch in the black-clad *gentilhomme* with the lace jabot who greeted her at the door. Catherine smiled at him. She had a weakness for eighteenth-century male garb, which set off handsome masculine buttocks and legs to advantage. For a man his age, Frédéric Manesch was still remarkably well equipped in that department. Kiwoe Tchitogama was there, too, wearing a samurai costume that hardly looked like a disguise on him.

They exchanged a few friendly words, although Joanne was unable to restrain a dig concerning the previous evening's Council meeting—traditionally a rather clamorous gathering, since this was when the spheres brought back from the Pilgrimage were allotted to individuals and communities. Out of the corner of her eye Catherine saw Alta Nasiwi, looking like a galleon surrounded by crows, what with her deep purple robe and the black veils flapping about her head in the wake of her determined stride. Simon must have seen her too, for he took Catherine's arm and steered her among the dancers. They began to tango, and she was a little surprised to find him a good dancer. Trying not to think about what her feet were doing, she abandoned herself to the pleasure of his firm but supple lead. He had let his beard and mustaches grow since the previous week to create a more magician-like effect, and it had transformed him. As is often the case with fair-haired men, his beard was almost red, and the contrast was very striking.

The tango slid into a polka. The first part of the evening was clearly devoted to ballroom dancing. The young people would have their hour in due course. Catherine burst into giggles as she and Simon swept by Joanne in the arms of Kiwoe. A samurai dancing the polka! For sheer incongruity, it beat any vision she might possibly have at this moment. When the polka slipped into a waltz, Joanne came and whisked Catherine out of Simon's arms. "My turn!" she said. For a moment, Catherine felt vaguely ill at ease and wondered why, since it was completely normal for women to dance together—and men, for that matter. Perhaps it was Joanne's way of leading, so

different from Simon's, who held you without enveloping
you, who respected your space. But Joanne was a good
dancer, too.

Manesch, Kiwoe, a few unknown men and women
who introduced themselves, but whose names she instantly forgot—the word seemed to have gone out that
she mustn't miss a dance, perhaps as a way of showing
gratitude for her benevolent integration into the social
fabric. She recognized a few faces. Véronique in her
seven-league boots, her mother Mathilde dressed as the
Marquise de Pompadour—a revelation, that. With a
quiver, she realized she was still looking for a blonde
head, a face with blue-green eyes, but Athana was nowhere to be seen.

A black face, a rotund torso swathed in yellow and
green taffeta embroidered with gold thread, with a small
ruff round the neck. "Don't tell me, Charles-Henri:
Othello! Does Marc-André make you jealous?"

A guffaw, and, "No, but I wasn't going to come dressed
as an African chief. You know how I hate redundance."

They danced two paso dobles in a row, Charles-
Henri's great specialty, and then Simon took firm posses-
sion of Catherine once more. She was getting tired,
however, and declined an extra waltz in favor of a trip to
the bar. It was in a neighboring room overlooking a terrace. The French windows were open, no doubt as a gesture of encouragement to the gods of spring. After the
heat of the dance, the night air would probably be quite
bearable for a brief moment. Most of the snow had been
cleared away, and Catherine walked over to the parapet
on the edge of the terrace. It was too soon for the city's
summer lighting, as it was called. In winter, only the strict
minimum of lighting was used in the almost deserted
streets. The sky was a black vault strewn with stars. Catherine's glasses fogged up as she stepped out. She wiped
them on a veil, put them on again, looked at the sky . . .
and froze, her hands clutching the parapet. The stars.
Constellations in unfamiliar patterns. Here and there, colored points of light she'd never seen before.

The sky faded as her glasses fogged again. Catherine
snatched them off, wiped them, and put them on again.
No, this was the familiar sky, the square of Cassiopeia,

the pot-bellied triangle of the Great Bear, Orion with his red and blue beacons. . . .

A step behind her—Simon, very close, misunderstanding her stance and putting his hands on her shoulders as he murmured, "You're cold. . . ."

Something in his voice made her turn. He still held her. In the backlight from the bar, his face was a grid of indecipherable shadows. He murmured, as intensely as before, "Catherine." It took a second for her to realize what scene they were playing; she wanted to withdraw, but he was already kissing her with lips warm and soft amid the silky beard and mustaches. She let it happen, feeling paralyzed with panic, yet half wanting to laugh. Simon held her close, a hand on her neck beneath the wig. "Catherine . . . would you . . . I'd given up hope. . . . It's been so long. . . ." He too was unable to speak, but for other reasons. She tried desperately to regain her composure. How could she have failed to see this coming? She should have remembered Joanne's warning: "He says nothing, then all of a sudden he explodes." She hadn't thought about it, she never thought about it, and for the last six years she'd been sure all that kind of thing was over for her! Not with Simon, in any case—definitely not!

She pretended to shiver. "Let's go in, Simon, I'm cold." And, with an attempt at kindness, she added, "I'd rather talk more . . . quietly. Later?"

He hesitated, then let his hands fall. They stood for a moment looking at each other. The shadows on Simon's face creased in a slightly forced smile. "Later. All right." He looked mechanically at his watch, saw that it was indeed on his wrist, and detached this anachronism, slipping it into the pocket of his long magician's robe. "You're right, this isn't the moment. Are you ready for a little sleight of hand?"

"Already?"

Yes, time for the costume contest. The platforms had been moved to the middle of the ballroom to make a runway. A small set of stairs had been placed beside the now-deserted musician's stage so the contestants could walk onto the runway from the wings. Catherine went to find Joanne, who was giving a final touch to the magician's equipment.

"Nervous?" asked Joanne with a smile.

"It's the first time I've ever done this."

"It'll be fine." Joanne examined her critically, gave a tug to the knot in her scarf, fished in her little handbag for some lipstick, and carefully applied it to Catherine's lips.

Catherine felt herself stupidly blushing: she'd wiped her lips as she came back into the ballroom, and Simon must have done the same, since his lips bore no trace of red.

"There. Perfect," said Joanne. "And don't forget, whatever happens"—she pulled back her lips to show her even teeth in a jovial, skeleton grimace—"*smile.*"

A sharp drum roll announced their turn, and Simon moved into the patter of his act, accompanied by a series of fast-paced but simple tricks. Catherine felt a stubborn lump in her chest but kept smiling as she handed him the various accessories passed to her by Joanne, one by one. It all seemed to be going like clockwork. The audience was delighted, possibly at seeing that Simon and Joanne had more or less willingly rejoined the family. Now they were at the last trick before the finale with the flowers. Catherine set up the large target against the curtains, behind which Joanne had disappeared, while Simon showed the revolver to the audience, twirling the barrel. "Real bullets, ladies and gentlemen, as I'll prove to you. . . ." That was the signal for Catherine to stand in front of the curtains beside the target, holding a fat little red china teapot at arm's length (the cover had been chipped, and Madame Otchiwey had let them have the pot). They'd broken it and glued it loosely together again. All Catherine had to do was press it slightly, and it would explode convincingly.

Simon turned as he talked, aimed the revolver, and pulled the trigger.

Catherine felt something brush her cheek and she jumped, squeezing the teapot. It exploded. Simon continued his patter, shooting at the target now. Behind the curtains, Joanne was working the mechanisms that blew up balloons, sent up showers of confetti, and finally produced a little stuffed animal. Catherine had nothing to do but stand beside the target, smiling. She thought her face muscles would freeze in this position forever, and missed the signal from Simon, who walked over to get her as though it was part of the act and led her onto the platform, producing bunches of flowers from various parts of her body and throwing them to the audience. Laughs, applause, bow, bow again, all three bow together now, and they were back in the wings to let the next contestants go on.

"Well, that went well," said Joanne. She seemed suddenly exhausted.

"What's wrong with your cheek?" said Simon, brushing Catherine's face lightly.

He looked at the smear of red on his fingers. Catherine felt unable to say a word. Simon's face went pale, and he turned to Joanne, who was tossing the props into their box. Abruptly, he jumped to the end of the platform to examine the curtain, then came back to Catherine.

"Joanne, you loaded the revolver. . . ." His voice hesitated between a statement and a question.

"Yes. Why?" asked Joanne, surprised and a little weary.

"The first bullet wasn't a blank. Catherine has a scrape on her cheek, and there's a hole in the curtain."

Joanne was beside Catherine in an instant, examining her. "I put in blanks!" she protested incredulously.

"If this is one of your jokes. . . ."

Joanne's expression changed to anger. "What do you take me for?"

"Sshhh!" hissed one of the contestants from the stage.

She lowered her voice. "Have I ever played a trick like that? Someone switched one of the blanks. Anyone could have got at the box! I could equally well say *you* had done it. You took out the first bullet to show it to the audience. You could have switched it. What do you say to that?"

They glared at each other, their faces ashen. Catherine had recovered her composure, and took them each by the arm, separating them. "It's certainly a bad joke," she said. "Whoever it was must have known Simon would never touch me, since he was aiming at the teapot." But the bullet had grazed her cheek. . . . A fluke. Had Simon missed her? But what was she thinking of! He was white as a sheet, his eyes glinting with anger.

"Who? Who knew? You, me, Joanne. . . ."

"Véronique, Madame Otchiwey, Clément, your father, the whole household. Calm down, Simon."

"We're going home," he said through clenched teeth.

"We have to wait for the results of the contest," protested Joanne.

He hesitated, the tension of his overwhelming fury almost palpable. Then, making a visible effort, he bowed his head. "But we go home right after."

They won the trophy for group presentations. Joanne went up to receive it—Simon would have been incapable, Catherine too. They slipped away immediately, escaping with a brevity bordering on rudeness from people who wanted to talk to them. As they were walking toward the exit, they passed Charles-Henri. He turned around to catch up with them, asking worriedly, "Everything all right, Cat?" He hadn't seen the graze on her cheek, but he knew her too well not to sense something was wrong. She shook her head, still unable to speak. He seemed to understand, and said softly, "I'm staying over tomorrow with friends of Marc-André's, the Morins. Will you call me?"

She nodded. He squeezed her hand. She squeezed back with a kind of desperation, and walked off with the others, conscious of his eyes watching her go. She was exhausted. Two small glasses of alcohol were enough to make her dizzy, now! Her feet hurt, her head ached, and in her chest a hard knot of anguish refused to untangle itself. Simon went to get the car, one of the mayor's limousines for the occasion, and they went home without exchanging a single word.

In the elevator they were silent and uncomfortably close. When they stepped out, she hesitated. Would they come to her room? But Simon muttered, "I'm going to get out of these things first," and Joanne agreed.

Catherine heaved a sigh at finding herself alone, half relieved and half exasperated. She walked over to the mirror to examine her cheek. It hadn't bled much.

She stared at herself, even more wearied by the idea of the scene that would surely follow. She tore off the wig and scarf and rubbed her scalp, feeling the small bumps of the scars. Why would Joanne put a live bullet in the revolver? She must have known Simon would be shooting to one side. And if he'd switched the blank bullet with a sleight of hand not planned in the program, why would he have missed? She'd seen him shooting during the afternoon; he was as good a shot as Joanne. And Joanne certainly hadn't shot at her in the tavern in Quebec, either, because she wouldn't have missed. None of it made any sense. A joke, a bad joke, that's what it was. Maybe Véronique had talked to her friends about the magic show, and one of the young iconoclasts had decided it would be a good prank to put a real bullet in the gun. Any other explanation was absurd. Especially after the two weeks they'd just spent together. And especially after the interlude on the terrace with Simon!

She went into the bathroom and splashed her face with water, looking wistfully at the bathtub. All she wanted was to have a good hot bath and go to bed, and above all not argue, nor hear the others argue—or fight.

Vain hope. There was a knock at the door. She wrapped her bathrobe around her and went back into the bedroom. "Come in," she called, sitting on the bed.

In came Simon and Joanne, one behind the other, he in his blue dressing gown, she in a mauve-and-purple house dress, braids hanging down over her chest. They both looked drawn. Simon sat down in the chair by the small desk, and Joanne sank into one of the armchairs.

Might as well take the initiative. "Listen," said Catherine in the most reasonable voice she could summon, "it can't be anything but a joke. One of Véronique's punk friends, maybe. It would be just like them, wouldn't it? Let's not make too much of it."

Simon looked at his feet, a stubborn expression on his face. "I don't know."

"Really, Simon!" protested Joanne. Her voice was almost imploring.

At last he said regretfully, "You never were one to share."

Catherine stiffened. No, not *that* scene! Because of

jealousy? Joanne? But jealous of whom? Of Simon? Or me? The way she'd behaved throughout the evening. . . . The whole preceding week. The feeling they were vying for my attention. Was that what they wanted, to have me choose between them like *that*?

Joanne was sitting straight up in her chair, now, pale with anger, her nostrils dilated. "How dare you. . . ."

"It's not important, in any case," Catherine heard herself say. "I'm leaving for the Far North soon."

She hadn't wanted to tell them this way, but perhaps it was the most appropriate moment. They forgot their budding fight and turned toward her simultaneously.

"For the Far North?" breathed Simon, incredulous and already hurt.

"On a pilgrimage?" said Joanne, and she laughed, shocked and angry.

"For the Far North, because I think part of what puzzles me must have an answer there," said Catherine. It was a good thing she'd sat on the bed. It was higher than the chairs, and they had to raise their heads a little.

They remained silent for a moment, then Simon exploded. "But for God's sake, if there were answers in the Far North, don't you think we'd have found them?"

Joanne said nothing. They must be in agreement, for once.

"I'm not asking the same questions as you."

"But what other questions can one ask?"

She ran her fingers through her hair to mask her hesitation. "It would take too long to tell you. It's late. We're all tired. Why not get some sleep?"

"If you say 'tomorrow is another day,' I'll scream," said Joanne drily. She stood up. "Well, I'm off. It seems you have a lot to talk over between you."

She walked out without slamming the door, but she would clearly have loved to do it.

Catherine allowed herself a sigh of relief. One down, one to go. But she'd better not make a joke of it. She owed it to Simon to hear him out, even if it would be more painful without humor. The silence stretched out. Was he going to speak first?

He surprised her. "Your decision is definite? You made it before tonight?"

She ignored the implication. "Yes."

"You're sure there's something in the Far North?"

"Yes." Time to change her answer; it was getting a bit monotonous. Ask me something else, Simon.

"You haven't told me everything."

"No."

A longer silence this time, then, "And you don't want to tell me."

Not a question, not a plea, not a reproach. Just a statement. She envisaged several answers, put them aside, and opted for the truth. "Simon, the very idea of starting to explain everything exhausts me." And now hers was the voice that held an imploring note.

He seemed to hear it. He looked at her for a moment. Nodded. "When?"

Nice economic speech. I won't be able to equal that. "I don't really know. I have to get everything ready."

"Do you know what to do? How to go about it?"

She stared at him for a moment, stupefied. Was he going to suggest helping her? She'd thought Joanne would have been more likely to offer. "No. But I'm capable of finding out what's needed."

He rose. "I'll see to it."

She couldn't suppress a little smile, although she was both amused and annoyed. Let the Man Who Knows do it. Yes, that was his style, taking charge. Not *my* style. Simon, sorry. Still, it was a kind offer. Come on, Catherine, make a kind gesture, too.

"I'd like to take care of it, but you can help if you like." Just the right amount of dryness in the final words.

He heard it—there was nothing wrong with his hearing, after all. Quite unexpectedly, he smiled. "Fine."

She suddenly realized he must have his own image of her, his own cliché: the woman too strong for her own good, who secretly aspires to be dependent. He'd be disappointed if he thought she would let herself be reduced to a cliché. "That's very kind of you. I've no doubt got a lot to learn about polar expeditions."

He turned to her near the door, impervious to her irony. "We won't have to go that far. It's in the Hudson Bay area. Good night, Catherine."

And he went out before she could react. We? What did he mean, we? Was he planning to come with her?

As she undid her bathrobe before getting into bed, she suppressed her irritation. After all, she'd need a guide. It might as well be Simon, mightn't it?

10

She opens her eyes in the shadows. The darkness vibrates with the silvery filigree of hyperceptions. Near the bed is a shape, partly visible because of its warmth, partly muffled because of its clothes—dark tights, big boots, a white parka. A hand on Catherine's arm, too. Long, pale hair. A heart-shaped face. A finger on the lips.

"Athana?"

No smile in response. The luminous phantom looks grave. Her hand brushes Catherine's cheek where the bullet has grazed it. The phantom is sad, actually. Then the hand closes over her arm, pulling it. She must get up. She gets up. The gentle pulling continues as far as the door.

"Where are we going?"

"Beyond."

Oh, tonight she's talking. "I have to dress, Athana." Athana lets her dress. This is a very rational dream, if it is a dream. Catherine can't decide. She feels so wide awake that it's suspect. She should be very groggy after the night she's just had. But the feel of the clothes seems so real. . . . Except it doesn't mean anything. You remember, Catherine, the little metal dream spoon that seemed so cold between your teeth in Dijon?

She finishes dressing. Athana is waiting patiently at the door. The hyperceptions seem less acute; it's darker. But the small hand takes her arm again and guides her along the passage, down the staircase—ah, I see that dreams don't take the elevator—through the main hall, and outside.

The moon is huge, creamy yellow, in a Waterman-blue sky. Well, it *is* a dream. Catherine feels a little disappointed all the same, but follows her guide, noting that they aren't outside the Manesch mansion but outside the Sergines house: the gravel courtyard, the big rosebushes still fragrant from the heat of the day. She shouldn't have worn such warm clothes. While Athana opens the gate, Catherine takes off her parka and puts it on the cement sidewalk circling the gravel courtyard. Definitely a rational dream.

She's standing on the main street, such a little street, where the asphalt has been patched in dozens of places. Everything is silent. No lights anywhere, the street lamps have been turned off. No need of them with this enormous moon. And the hyperceptions have been turned off too, probably for the same reason. Athana walks into the other street, on the right, even narrower, steeper, climbing toward the town hall square between housefronts with closed shutters. Catherine follows her, the tips of her fingers cold with excitement, a little anxious. It's not summer, it's the beginning of autumn, one of those fine blue and gold autumns where the heat seems eternal, but where the coolness slides in secretly during the small hours of the night, insidious, lasting longer and longer into the next morning. The last days before school starts. The last nights of freedom. This night, especially, with the incredible moon, its velvety light in the courtyard. . . . She'd suddenly had enough of standing at the window. She had dressed, opened the French windows, and dropped into the courtyard six feet below. Over the summer she'd gotten into the habit of entering and leaving her room like this, even in broad daylight—a kind of defiance. And now she's outside in the autumn warmth that the winter cold is secretly undermining. She should be in bed, but she's in the street, following Athana toward the main square.

The square is on a slope. You reach it by a set of uneven stone stairs, one block for each step, monolithic. A balustrade runs along the edge, made of thick, round metal bars. When Catherine was younger, she used to sit on the balustrade and then swing upside down, hanging by her knees, arms folded over her chest, braids sweeping the ground. She's too big now, she could never do that now. The thick leaves of the chestnut trees diffuse the moonlight in a mysterious, shadowy green. The night isn't as silent as Catherine thought: she can hear everything with astonishing clarity, even the fluting chirrup of frogs in the swampy pond just outside the village. Almost ridiculously showy trills come from the large park running down one side of the village square, surely a nightingale.

Athana starts walking again, perhaps drawn by the birdsong. Behind her, Catherine crunches over the gravel—such a strange sea sound, so far from the ocean. They walk toward the park with its high iron gate, the hedges of yew and boxwood on either side of it, and the smell of dust and resin once you slip through them. Great, shady trees, three enormous black pines, chestnuts, beeches, oaks with deeply-indented leaves. The empty fountain seems to have been carved out of chalk. Catherine walks behind Athana, passing from shadows to strips of moonlight between the trees, traversing whitened paths and lawns bleached of color. Where is Athana going? Yes, to the house. To the château.

It isn't really a château, just a late nineteenth-century bourgeois mansion that once aspired to be a manor house. Two turrets with pointed roofs covered in slate, a rectangular terrace in front of the main door, with a wrought-iron table and wooden chairs. A small colonnade surrounds the terrace, and at each corner stand large stone urns, overflowing with geraniums and mignonettes. Small-paned French windows open onto the terrace.

Catherine is in a state of high exultation: to be on forbidden ground, at a forbidden hour. Her teeth chatter in spite of herself, from nervousness and the late night chill. Athana pushes one of the French doors. It opens invitingly without creaking, into a huge salon filled with phantom furniture, divans and armchairs enveloped in white sheets—but not the grand piano with its black, uncompromising gleam. The carpets are rolled up against the walls, revealing an uneven floor of narrow, polished boards. Isn't there anyone here? Catherine is a little disappointed. It would be so much more exciting if there were someone, if the owners were asleep in a neighboring room, or upstairs. So much more forbidden to be there. . . . Well, never mind. It's already enough to be walking around looking at their things, even if these have been consigned to the limbo of objects whose owners are absent. Catherine lifts a sheet, strokes the soft velvet of an armchair. Opens the piano and runs a light finger over the quiet teeth. She'd like to be able to play, to sit down and tinkle the melancholy, obsessive notes of the *Moonlight Sonata*, perhaps, or "Für Elise," and anyone listening outside would think the house was haunted.

Athana is on the other side of the room, beside a chimney carved out of pale, polished stone. On the mantelpiece is a small ormolu clock, its pendulum stationary. No hands. The time is never. On every side are bibelots. A yellowed ivory shape, so smooth to the touch, a Japanese flute player, long and narrow, her delicately sculpted fingers on the flute, the precise pleats of her robe falling to the dark, lacquered wooden stand. A sort of small, thick plate of painted wood, dark blue, almost entirely covered with gold hand-painted characters, indecipherable, minuscule, and in the small central circle, beneath a glass cover, the needle of a compass suspended above a design showing the four cardinal points, revealing that this is no mere plate, as Catherine knows, but a Chinese horoscope machine. She picks it up and is suddenly stilled by the lightness of the object. Can destiny weigh so little? She puts it down again after watching the needle flutter on its axis and settle on the bias above a cluster of characters, a meaning and a direction she knows is north.

She doesn't touch the other objects. She recognizes them all, even if they shouldn't be there because she sold them when her father died, dispersed them to the four points of the compass, the four winds. At the same time, she knows her mother and father are sleeping in their own house on a street lower down, but it doesn't matter. She understands. It's all right.

A hand on her arm once more. Athana holds out a small half globe of glass on a lacquered black stand. Through the colorless liquid inside, she can see spidery trees, bushes, flowers, an entire miniature garden worked with incredible skill in some creamy white material, possibly ivory or wood. Above the small sphere, Catherine sees Athana's face, looking down like the moon, enormous like the moon. The hand closes over the globe, shakes it. It's snowing! Snowing in the sphere. A sparkling dust falls gently, with dreamy slowness, on the branches and flowers and earth of the miniature garden.

The hand stretches out. A gift. Catherine takes the globe in her palm, and for a moment she's afraid it will shatter in her fingers. But it's solid to the touch, the glass is very thick. She shakes it cautiously, watches the snow rise and fall once more over the garden. She smiles at Athana, pure and childish pleasure flooding through her. Athana smiles, too, turns around, and walks out of the salon by the same French door. Time to go home.

Catherine follows Athana diagonally across the village square, down the stairs, and into the narrow street, regret searing her as she goes downhill, because she knows she'll never come back to the château, to the house in Sergines, to her bedroom. She grabs on to the outside sill of the window, shins up the wall and over the window frame. She is back in the picture now, the other one, the picture of her bedroom in the Manesch house, suffused by the gleam of dawn. She puts the glass globe on the night table—somehow she'd managed to hold on to it safely while climbing in the window. She gets undressed and slips into bed. Athana is curled up in the armchair on the left in her favorite position. Her eyes are already closed. Catherine smiles at her; it doesn't matter if Athana can't see. She murmurs, "Goodnight, Athana. Thank you," and is surprised to hear the response. "Goodbye, Catherine. Thank you." When she closes her eyes, she's still smiling.

It was daylight when she opened her eyes again. Her clothes and boots were lying beside the door where she'd left them the night before, still damp. Athana was curled in the armchair. On the night table, the snow lay at the foot of the trees, in the garden enclosed beneath the glass dome.

Catherine kept her eye on the armchair as she slipped over to the door, opened it wide enough for her still to see the blonde head, and backed toward Joanne's door directly opposite. If Athana should disappear, it wouldn't be because she, Catherine, had turned her back! Everyone must still be asleep, but she didn't care. She leaned against the door and knocked on the paneling. "Joanne, wake up! Come quickly!"

After a while the door opened. "What's the matter?"

She turned then, to find Simon, with tousled hair and naked torso, looking at her. She stammered, "Athana, in my room."

"Athana?" came Joanne's voice, unbelieving. She appeared behind Simon, in the process of putting on a dressing gown.

Catherine turned on her heel and walked back into her room, with the other two behind her.

Athana was awake, rubbing her eyes, stretching with an unconscious sensuality. She smiled. "Hello." She seemed bigger, rounder—older, in any case. Her eyes didn't have the same innocence. A pensive gravity had replaced it.

Catherine turned to the others. "Stay with her. I'm going to call Charles-Henri." She didn't try to justify this, nor did she tell them not to begin interrogating Athana. For one reason or another, she was sure the girl wouldn't speak unless she was present. They didn't seem in a hurry, anyway. They were looking at Athana with a slightly fearful incredulity.

Charles-Henri simply said, "I'll be there in fifteen minutes."

She went back to her room. Joanne was sitting in the other armchair, Simon on the bed. He'd taken the time to put on his pajama top. Catherine sat in the sun-splashed embrasure of the window, mainly because it was the only place, apart from the bed, where she could sit with her back to the light. She didn't want to examine what she had to hide and from whom—except from Simon, of course. Why of course? It might be from Joanne. True, Joanne, too. Both of them. But how could she feel both betrayed and ... saved after finding them in the same room?

They weren't very talkative. Surely they weren't going to wait for Charles-Henri in this grim silence? With a slight shrug, Catherine picked up the glass globe from her night table. "Athana brought me a gift. Does this object have any special meaning for you?"

Simon took it and automatically shook it to make the snow fall. He smiled involuntarily. "No. But I've rarely seen such a pretty one. Joanne?"

"No."

Would she tell them how she came by it? No. It was better to wait for Charles-Henri, so as not to repeat the same thing twice. This object had been in her dream, and now it was sitting on her night table, just as Athana was sitting in the armchair; that was all she could say. She went back and sat on the windowsill, staring at the great white scarf of river below.

Charles-Henri arrived almost exactly fifteen minutes after the telephone call. He'd slipped a pair of pants over his pajama bottoms, and his multicolored parka over the top, hardly bothering to dress. He was panting as he came into the room, fur hat in hand, and stopped on the threshold with a relieved expression. "Good, she didn't vaporize," he said to Catherine.

"Charles-Henri," said Athana, apparently pleased to see him, or else to remember his name—difficult to say.

He smiled at her, although a bit timidly. "Athana." Then, curiosity getting the better of him, "Is Athana really your name?"

The girl said nothing. Catherine sighed. "I think she has several."

"The Vagabond, for example," murmured Charles-Henri.

"Maybe." That wasn't what she'd had in mind. Should she have thought of it? She felt what had happened that night had some other meaning. A little annoyed, she went on. "Is there a rectangular, open space in Chicoutimi, with one side occupied by the park of a small manor house?"

Surprised by this apparent change of subject, the others were slow to react.

"Not that I know of," said Simon.

"Why?" asked Joanne, almost simultaneously.

Catherine explained.

When she'd finished, there was a long silence. Simon seemed thunderstruck.

Joanne stared at Catherine, her expression tense and calculating. "You mean she led you to a real place, because your clothes are wet, a place where this object was found, but that you were dreaming the whole time." She could barely suppress her disbelief.

"Or it was one of Catherine's visions. Athana took her into the vision, this object belonged to it, and Catherine brought it back," said Charles-Henri gently.

"There are no visions here!" said Joanne with a shrug.

"She's already had them," murmured Simon.

Joanne turned on him. "What? Here?"

"She saw my grandfather in his library. Only she was in my house at the time."

He hadn't told Joanne about it?

Joanne looked imperiously at Catherine, who nodded and said, "Yes."

The Métis seemed to shrink a little in her chair, but muttered obstinately, "It doesn't mean anything."

Catherine took the little glass globe and knelt beside Athana, who smiled at her while stifling a yawn. She seemed so real, so ... ordinarily alive, a pretty blonde girl, somewhat tousled, who hadn't had enough sleep. Catherine pulled herself together and showed her the globe. "Athana, do you know where this comes from?"

"The château." She seemed full of goodwill this morning.

"You remember the château? When did you go there?"

"Last night. With you."

"Where is the château, Athana?"

A more difficult question. The delicate eyebrows drew together in a frown, and the rather too pale face took on a puzzled expression. "It isn't anywhere now," she said at last. "Or else...." With a small, timid smile, she lifted a hand and touched Catherine's forehead.

Catherine heard the stifled exclamation of Simon and Joanne, but she wanted to hold the attention of the blue-green eyes. "In my head? You know what's in my head?" Keep calm, don't frighten her.

"Sometimes. Images. They become outside."

"They come out, you mean? They are real, outside my head? Like the château last night?"

Athana hesitated. "Yes. . . ."

"Do you know what I'm thinking? Or Simon, or Joanne, Charles-Henri, anybody?"

Athana let out her breath. "Not anybody. Mostly images. Sometimes." Then lowering a guilty head, she said imploringly, "Why? Is it bad? It's only sometimes. And then it isn't really in your head. It's. . . ." She frowned again, clearly unsatisfied with the conclusion, ". . . everywhere. All around. A presence."

Catherine started. "The images . . . are in a presence?" she said slowly, uncertain if she had understood. Athana waved a hand by way of excuse, probably unable to explain it otherwise.

"You dream of the Presence, Athana?" asked Charles-Henri suddenly. "Like Catherine?"

"What's this?" said Joanne, while Simon demanded, "What?" But Catherine had no more time to waste on their disbeliefs or ignorance. Her whole attention was riveted on Athana. Who shook her head. "Not a dream. It's there, all the time. Everywhere. You . . . resonate?" The question was for Catherine, who could only raise her eyebrows without answering. How would *she* know if it was the right word? Athana continued to ponder the question with the serious air of a schoolchild in an exam, and Catherine finally gave up her precarious crouching position to sit beside Simon. The situation was too incongruous; at least she could sit in physical, if not mental comfort!

"The Presence is everywhere, isn't it?" said Athana. "Linked to everything. Everything . . . comes from there. And goes back." A sudden smile. "Like the man in the tavern, you remember?"

The blue flash? The bodies that . . . are supposed to give part of their substance back to the Sleeping Deity.

The spheres.

Simon stiffened beside her. In her armchair, Joanne burst into raucous laughter. "Hey, the kid is a mystic! Seems like a fairly harmless kind of madness, though."

"Do you see your presence, Athana?" asked Charles-Henri with contrasting kindness.

Athana responded by turning to him. "No. Or yes. Not all the time. It's . . . the blue. When it's blue. People and things. There are different kinds of blue."

"Is it more blue, less blue?"

"That depends." More concentration, then: "The man in the tavern was all blue. There were a lot more there. In Montreal, in Quebec."

"But not Antoine," murmured Charles-Henri sadly, more for himself than Athana, who seemed to understand.

"No," she said, saddened as well. "It was the difference in the blue. I thought they all came back. But you come back better if there's a lot of blue."

"What about me?" said Catherine, feeling an inexplicable chill. "Have I a lot of blue?"

"No, almost none. Less than they have." She waved slightly in the direction of Joanne, Simon, and Charles-Henri.

Catherine remained silent, unable to decide whether she was relieved or terrified.

"What about you, Athana?" asked Charles-Henri with the same gentleness. "Have you a lot of blue?"

"Oh, me," said Athana, suddenly gloomy. "I don't know. I can't see myself."

Joanne got up abruptly. "I've had enough. Continue if it amuses you, but I'm going down for breakfast." She went out without closing the door, her bare heels hammering the floorboards.

Catherine went into the bathroom, ran herself a glass of water which she drank all at one go, then splashed her face. The others hadn't moved when she returned.

"Still here, Simon?" she asked, aggressive and embarrassed at being so.

"It's my appointed hour for being curious," he said at last.

Catherine drew Joanne's vacated chair up to Athana's, and slumped into it with a little grimace: she'd danced too much last night. Her brain seemed to have turned to mush all of a sudden. Half questions bubbled up with great effort from the magma, and sank back unformulated. If Charles-Henri or Simon had coherent questions to ask, they were keeping them to themselves.

It was Athana who broke the silence after a while. "It wasn't a dream. Last night. But it isn't there anymore. Outside, I mean. What was it, anyway?"

Catherine could hardly suppress a snort. The million-dollar question. Athana had taken the small globe and was turning it over to make the snow fall. Exactly, Athana: it was a vision. That is to say, a concrete illusion. That forgot one of its fragments on my night table. But what on earth does concrete illusion mean? It's a contradiction in terms. It doesn't exist. Or only in terms— exactly: in words. A thing of language, like poetry. Like Manesch's poetry, in fact: *Traces of antimatter memory/ The ink the word/Meteor from the blackness. . . .* Was that why he'd written these poems? Were they more of a testament than the other fragment in *The Book of Steps*? It's the Word, isn't it, that's supposed to have created the world? Or at least according to religions other than that of the North. What was Manesch trying to say? That the North—or the South—is just an assembly of words? Words spoken in a dream by a Deity who sleeps, and when it awakes the words will fade away and the true reality appear?

She heaved a great sigh. It was all very well, but she wasn't going to let herself be persuaded that the pounding migraine or the aches in her body were *words*! Her body had always been too obstinate an entity to let her slide down the slope of solipsism. Let's get back to concrete things, for heaven's sake!

"Why did you follow me, Athana?"

"Because you're not the same," replied the girl without hesitation. "You're not like the other one."

"What other one, Athana?"

Athana's assurance evaporated. "I . . . don't know," she said, confused. "I just know you're different."

"Is that how you can find me no matter where I am?"

Athana hung her head, and repeated in a low voice, "I don't know." She sniffled and looked at Catherine, her expression suddenly angry. "I don't know lots of things. It's annoying."

Catherine couldn't help laughing. She leaned over to pat the girl's cheek. "Welcome to the club!"

"Why do things exist?" continued Athana, still bellicose. "Why something rather than nothing? Why *what is*, rather than something else?"

"Ah." Charles-Henri was also amused, in spite of himself. "Not a mystic, a philosopher!"

"Isn't the Sleeping Deity supposed to have created everything?" said Simon suddenly, out of his gloom. "Or is it this famous presence, which is everything, everywhere, invisible, all powerful, and all that stuff?"

He'd also made the connection. But Athana shook her head. "No, the Presence, too. The Presence . . . is something, too."

Catherine laughed again. It was all she had left, this sense of the comic absurdity of the situation. Are we now going to have a dissertation on the created and uncreated, the egg and the chicken, or to make a long story short, God and the universe?

"You mean your presence really exists?" said Charles-Henri, now more fascinated than amused. "That it . . . began to exist at a given moment?"

Bingo.

"Yes!" said Athana crossly, as one says "Of course!"

Well, Charles-Henri, what do you say to that? That's really socking it to the Sleeping Deity, isn't it? Catherine glanced at Simon to see if he was appreciating the humor of it all. He was ashen.

"Joanne should have stayed," she said mercilessly. She couldn't help it. "I'm sure she would have found this interesting."

"Joanne never stays when she could really learn something," murmured Simon hoarsely.

Catherine calmed down as well, a little alarmed at having again fallen into the trap of anger. Simon was also frightened by what he divined behind Athana's elliptical remarks—but *he* didn't attempt to hide it.

"Why are there things you can undo, and others not?" continued Athana, her voice slightly plaintive and childish, now. She had twisted a lock of hair around her thumb, then her index finger, middle finger, the other two, and back to the thumb.

In a rather dizzying flash, Catherine remembered—again. "Italie," she murmured.

They looked at each other for a moment. Athana didn't seem to understand. Catherine shook her head to straighten out her thoughts, but without much result. Italie, Athalie, Athana. Had she been taken in by mere words, after all? It had been such a clear flash of understanding: Italie, Athalie, Athana, Talitha. But instead of providing illumination, the meaning dispersed itself in all the syllables, turning them into an absurd nursery rhyme.

"Are there things you can undo, Athana?" asked Charles-Henri.

"Not just me!" protested the girl. "Everybody. Well, those who have some blue. I'm not the one who undid the château; that was Catherine. But this," she picked up the small glass globe, and the snow stirred a little, "why wasn't this undone?"

Because I didn't want to undo it? Because someone else wanted me to keep it? A glass globe. A garden in the snow.

"Because Catherine must go to the Far North," said Charles-Henri with serene conviction.

"Obviously." It was the sardonic voice of Joanne, who stood near the door. When had she come back? She had dressed in the meantime, in the usual fluorescent tracksuit. "We're all going, aren't we?"

"It's not a pilgrimage," began Catherine.

Joanne brushed her objection aside. "Of course not. You wouldn't get me on a pilgrimage alive." She giggled at her own joke and stared at each of them in turn, a hand on her hip. "You look as though you were at a funeral." She giggled again. "Sorry, I couldn't help it. We'll all go. Simon, it's already decided. Charles-Henri wouldn't miss this for anything. And Athana?" She approached the chair and leaned over the girl, hands resting on the sides of the chair, arms rigid. Athana huddled against the back of the chair. "Athana wants to come, too, doesn't she? Or else she'll follow us when she feels like it, isn't that so?"

"Leave her alone," said Simon wearily. "And if you intend to come with us in that frame of mind, perhaps you'd better forget it."

"And what frame of mind would you like?" She'd turned on him swiftly, and he too had a defensive reflex. "You're all here making angels dance on pinheads, hypnotized by this crazy kid! Haven't you any common sense?"

"Joanne," said Catherine, suddenly very sorry for her. "You can't keep on denying everything. You know perfectly well Athana isn't crazy, or else I'm crazy too, and Charles-Henri, and Simon. Are you really ready to assert that everyone's mad except you? You know very well something's wrong, that your explanations don't hold water, that no explanation does. We must stop trying to reduce everything to some simple answer, and go to the source. You speak of common sense. I say 'facts.' It's time to look for the facts. Have you ever been to the Far North?"

"No," said Joanne doggedly.

"Don't you think it would be a good place to start?"

"I've never been, either," murmured Simon.

"A question of principle, I suppose?" She gave them both an exasperated look. Really, she'd had enough of their childishness! "And is that common sense? Refusing on principle to go and see for yourselves?"

They remained silent.

The solemnity of the moment was marred by Catherine's gurgling stomach. "My opinion exactly!" she said, leaving them to decide whether she was commenting on their silence or the activity of her gastric juices. "Let's have breakfast. And you can explain to me how to organize a voyage to the Far North."

Part
Four

After the second week in May, the spring blizzards usually began to let up. There should be no major problem in undertaking the week-long journey to the still-frozen Hudson Bay and to the island where—as Catherine had learned without much surprise—the Pilgrimage ended. The roads were well cleared, and traveling would be fairly straightforward as far as Chibougamau, a hundred and twenty miles northwest of Chicoutimi, and even later, as they went another sixty miles directly north to Lac Mistassini. After that they'd be north of the tree line, with no roads. There was the Pilgrimage path, however, an ice road that was fairly well maintained until spring and that should still be usable. In any case, snowcars had been built to go anywhere, and that was what they'd be using after Chibougamau. They'd have to transport everything in a van from Chicoutimi, since the snowcar was only laid on after Chibougamau.

As she'd requested, Catherine took part in the preparations and in the purchase of equipment and provisions, noting that her intermittent maybe-Voyager memory had nothing to offer in the way of expeditions to the Far North. She also willingly agreed to the intensive physical training program Joanne advised her to take in the two weeks before they left. She was a bit disappointed to find that no new, superhuman capacities appeared, but per-

haps it was just as well—she'd have no awkward explanations to make to Joanne and Simon. She certainly had no
intention of telling them about her theories concerning
Voyagers.

The fact was, the three of them were circling each
other cautiously, maintaining a prudent politeness that
was at times painful. In the gymnasium, Joanne was im-
personally efficient, and Simon never alluded to what had
passed between himself and Catherine on the city hall terrace. He didn't seem to have resumed his liaison with
Joanne, either, despite his appearance at her door in the
small hours after the ball. They all ate in their rooms, as
before. The atmosphere in the Manesch household was
rather glum, to tell the truth. At first the reaction to the
expedition had been one of disbelief, followed by a silent
disapproval tinged with a poorly disguised anxiety.

Lonely in the company of others—a situation Catherine had always dreaded. There was no way of escaping it,
however. She had to forget she'd once hoped to have Simon and Joanne as friends. Also—and this was the most
painful of all—she had to remind herself constantly to be
cautious and always on her guard with them. Charles-
Henri had felt the need of another meditational retreat.
What would his attitude be during this journey? No
doubt he'd consider it a true Pilgrimage, and in a way this
would distance him from her as surely as the mute resentment of Simon and Joanne.

That left Athana. Véronique had lent her some
clothes, and Athana looked so incongruous in a black tunic and electric-pink tights that Catherine didn't know
whether to laugh or be annoyed. The girl spent most of
her time in the library, reading anything and everything
with equal curiosity. What she made of it was something
else. Catherine had asked a question early on, and Athana
had replied "All these stories!" in a tone that showed she
was both awed and disconcerted. Did she think they were
all fiction, or was it just the fact of their existence? Catherine had given her *The Book of Steps* to see how she'd
react. Her response was the same.

But at least she was an affectionate presence, as
graceful as a young cat. She slept in Catherine's room, ate
with her, walked with her, Joanne had suggested bringing

her to the gymnasium—a way of lessening the girl's strangeness, no doubt, as with Véronique's clothes. "I prefer stories," Athana had said with a little pout. "I must learn." Judging by her performance to date, she certainly didn't need any physical conditioning—in fact she'd coped very well with all the athletic adventures that had come her way.

This evening, as Catherine returned from the gymnasium, she found Athana seated in front of the small fireplace in their room, feeding the fire with twigs and bits of bark she'd probably picked out of the firewood box. Catherine sat down beside her and was soon equally fascinated by the fire—but not in the same way, as it turned out.

"It doesn't come back," remarked Athana after a while, looking grave.

Catherine decided to play along. "There's no blue in the wood?"

"Not in this wood."

Catherine straightened up, suddenly interested. "Because this wood is already dead?"

Athana nodded, frowning a little as she gazed into the flames. "Perhaps."

"But normally there is blue?"

"Sometimes." Athana held a twig out. They watched it catch fire.

"Athana," asked Catherine, "could you *not* follow me? Could you have stayed in Montreal?"

"No."

"Why?"

The girl reflected a moment. "It's as though. . . ." She smiled with sudden illumination. ". . . as though I were a compass. You are the north for me." Her face became serious again. "I don't know why."

"And could I have stayed in Montreal, or could I go back now?"

Athana picked up another twig and twirled it slowly in her fingers. "I think so," she said finally.

"And Joanne?"

"Less than you."

"More compelled?"

"Yes."

"And here? I could stay here?"

Athana looked at her attentively. "Yes."

During this interchange, Catherine had lost the thread of the vague intuition that had made her ask the first question. What could she deduce from these answers? That she still had some freedom of choice? Free will? How could Athana *see* that? Suddenly discouraged, she in turn threw a handful of bark on the fire. It burst into flame with a dry crackle.

Someone knocked on the door, and she shouted, without turning around, "Who is it?"

"Kiwoe Tchitogama," replied a light baritone voice.

Surprised, she went to the door, grimacing at her creaking joints. The councilor greeted her, somewhat embarrassed. "Forgive me for disturbing you."

She stood back to let him enter, repressing a sigh. She hadn't seen him since the night of the ball. "If you're trying to make me change my mind. . . ."

"No. I want to go with you."

"If you can't beat them, join them?"

His amused smile was unexpected. "No." He looked serious again. "I've never been to the Far North either. It's time I made my Pilgrimage."

"And you're a councillor?"

"There isn't necessarily a connection." He contemplated Athana, who was watching him, too, still seated by the fire, gaping with fascination.

"And what does have a connection?"

"It's a little complicated. . . ." He made a visible effort to turn to Catherine. "By and large, let's say it's because I'm a pure-blooded Amerindian."

This detail had intrigued Catherine ever since she'd realized how many people of mixed parentage there were in the Realm. The statistical likelihood of a child not being a Métis was very low. "I don't suppose there are many."

"There have been more and more in the last forty years."

Kiwoe's tone implied he was well aware of the improbability of this, Catherine suppressed her reaction, merely replying with a noncommittal, "And?"

"I was the first."

"How old are you, anyway?"

With a small smile, he said, "Forty-two, almost the same age as you."

He went closer to Athana and hunched down on his heels, holding out a hand the way one does with an animal to be tamed. The girl touched it with the tips of her fingers, her eyes wide, then smiled at him timidly.

"Remarkable," he murmured. "I hadn't met her before. I wasn't there when she came to tell us you were at Simon's."

"And you didn't give her a necklace?" asked Catherine rather acidly.

Kiwoe sat down on the floor, cross-legged, and rested his elbows on his knees, supporting his chin on his joined hands. He looked thoughtful. "I took part in dream circles with Simon and Joanne in the old days," he said quietly.

What had that to do with anything? Catherine pulled one of the chairs over to the fireplace. It was more comfortable, for one thing, as well as being strategically higher. "So?"

"I don't think they're the Infants. Nor you. The necklace . . . was to please Frédéric and Alta."

"And Athana?"

"That's something else. It's difficult to put the difference into words. I don't . . . perceive quite like the other councillors. It's one of the reasons they elected me, in fact."

Catherine leaned forward with interest. "How do you perceive?"

"The exact word is 'aura,' I think. That's not what you perceive, is it?"

"When I'm not in the hyperception mode, I sometimes perceive an aura of familiarity, but in the figurative sense. And Athana's aura is different?"

"Very. Much more . . . complex."

"The Ultimate Infant?"

"I don't know. I'd be something of a Separatist if I believed in the Infant."

"You're not a Believer?"

Kiwoe answered her stupefaction with a sly smile. "I believe in the Deity. Sleeping, well, I'm not sure. And that

It has to be awakened by the Infants, or the very idea of the Infants ... even less."

Athana had picked up one of the councillor's braids and was turning it over, visibly conquered. Catherine, annoyed without knowing why, remarked, "And all of a sudden you want to go to the Far North with us."

"The confluence of circumstances is ... irresistible, you will admit."

She stared at him, perplexed. Completely different from what she'd imagined. Or else a clever liar, who would act as the eyes and ears of the Council in the expedition? The prospect of having to keep an eye on someone else, apart from Joanne and Simon, was hardly inviting. On the other hand, Athana seemed completely won over, whereas she'd always been reserved with the other two.

"It isn't a Pilgrimage," muttered Catherine. "I don't believe in anything."

"Do my beliefs bother you?"

"No, not if they don't cause you to obstruct the expedition," she retorted rather drily.

Kiwoe Tchitogama smiled: "In that case, there shouldn't be any problem."

The journey to Chibougamau went smoothly. They arrived toward two o'clock in the afternoon. But just as the van passed the blue, snow-flecked sign that indicated the turnoff to the city, the motor began to cough, then cut out. There were houses beside the road, half hidden in the blowing snow. Simon knocked on the door of one. Three-quarters of an hour later, a towtractor came and hauled them ignominiously to the Hotel Marika, where they were scheduled to spend the night. It wasn't very serious, since they were exchanging the van for the snowcar in Chibougamau.

The snowcar wasn't quite ready, however—a problem with the caterpillar traction that would be fixed by the following afternoon. Simon shrugged. "Half a day isn't going to make any difference."

The Marika was Chibougamau's biggest hotel, boasting a hundred or so rooms, a pseudo-Hilton-of-the-Snows—fine woodwork throughout, soft lighting, mirrors in gilded frames, and attentive staff gliding over to you at the slightest sign. Early in the evening, Catherine decided to retire to her room and have supper there with Athana. She felt jarred by the sharp disparity between the aim of the expedition and this splendiferous decor that might just as well have been any grand hotel in Montreal or Quebec. The city itself—or what she could see of it through the blowing snow—was exactly like any of its Southern counterparts: an industrial city, prosperous and ugly. Kiwoe must have seen her expression when they were being towed into town, because he'd murmured, "Not many people here are in a hurry to see the Deity awakened."

Trying to forget all this, Catherine plunged into *The Book of Steps*. She'd brought a photocopy with her, and was beginning to know some of the poems by heart. It was odd how several now began to take on a whole other resonance. Sometimes it was just a line: *Frozen memory, raining.* Or an echo of Italie and the garden: *On the edge of awakening in the amorous jungle/Hands prefer the noises of children.* Or these lines, evocative of the Bus Dream and its stately, beautiful women: *The fall is an encounter/When the slow dimension/Works in the greatest wonder/For the expansion of the world.*

Maybe it's an optical illusion, no more and no less naïve than the modern adaptation of the prophecies of Nostradamus, she wrote in her travel diary, bought before leaving Chicoutimi, but I feel quite unable to resist. It seems to me Pierre-Emmanuelle Manesch is the only person I can trust. I need his phrases, his lines, as an indication, a secret signal across time, an arrow pointing to the Far North. The images of snow and ice, childhood, the color blue that runs through the book like a filigree, these constant allusions to a secret, a discovery, a revelation. . . . And now, after recalling the dreams of the Voyagers and the garden, especially after the dream or vision of the château, and above all, after those few conversations with Athana, how can I avoid interpreting these passages in this light, how can I not see them as a confirmation? *Everywhere . . . /A great, sprawling body/Inert and pure/And on its arms and on its loins/On its slow-burning body/Walk the beasts of winter.* Or: *In the sand, a million-year-old footprint/A step toward the other side of space.* And all the other prose fragments that are so insistent in personifying the object of the spiritual quest or revelation.

Of course everything points northward. The north of the North. The goal of the Pilgrimage, the source of the spheres, and all my dreams of the garden under the snow, the glass globe from the château. . . . There is something in the north, someone. The Presence of my dreams, the presence Athana talks about.

I wouldn't dare tell Joanne about this, nor Simon. Charles-Henri . . . just maybe. No. But perhaps there really is something nonhuman there, after all. Perhaps not extraterrestrial, but nonhuman. An alien. Maybe from this planet where we now find ourselves, maybe not. It's not the Earth, even if it's been partly shaped to resemble a fragment of it. Shaped how? We would have to postulate a direct way of controlling matter or some equally unheard-of power of mental projection—but since I'm theorizing to the point of delirium, why restrain myself? Both methods, with telepathy thrown in while we're at it! That would account for the dreams and visions, and for the Marrus as well as the glass globe. Not to mention any memory lapses, which may not be some kind of self-conditioning in the process of collapse, but an effort of this alien to . . . what? Control me, probably. Prevent me from going to the Far North. Then who would be sending me the dreams of winter? Well, let's just suppose.

The "blue" perceived by Athana, the blue of the corpses, the blue of the "energy" contained in the spheres, may be the trace of this control over matter. And over minds—who knows? And if I don't perceive this blue in the same way as she does, even when in hyperception mode (assuming the hyperceptions are real and I'm a Voyager), it would be normal: the hyperceptions aren't meant to detect this type of thing. I would perceive some of its wavelengths, but not the whole phenomenon.

Obviously, if I try to account for Athana, this fine house of cards collapses, or at least has no real place for her. Is Athana part of the Presence—that is, the alien? Several things seem to point to this. . . . The fact is, Athana is a knot that I have no way of undoing at the moment, which throws considerable doubt on everything I've just postulated.

But do I really take these speculations seriously?

Yes and no. Which philosophy should I choose? The law of redundancy, "extraordinary explanations for extraordinary situations"? Or the law of contradictions, "banal and rational explanations for extraordinary and irrational situations"? Or the good old variant of Occam's

Razor: "the simplest explanation for every situation"? Emotionally and intellectually, I'm wavering. All the more so because there's a hint in all this of the kind of paranoia Joanne exhibits: whatever may be the nature of this alien, it probably holds two Voyagers captive. And not only two Voyagers, but perhaps a whole segment of the reality of this planet. Imprisoned beneath forms and substances of a false Earth-like reality, there may be the forms and substances that really belong to this planet.

(But that mimic Voyagers' memories. I won't begin to ask myself why!)

And we're all prisoners of this charade—the possible indigenous inhabitants of this planet, the Voyagers, and myself only marginally less! To liberate reality, there is only one solution: go to the north of the North and confront the Manipulating Monster.

I can imagine Joanne's reaction to this theory. And Simon's.

But maybe this alien isn't a monster. The Presence did allow itself to be tamed a little (if in fact these dreams aren't merely a figment of my imagination, which is one more hypothesis in this sea of conjecture). Perhaps it can be persuaded to make a deal? It would seem Pierre-Emmanuelle Manesch did so, perhaps regarding the barrier, and certainly regarding the spheres.

Maybe when you get right down to cases, this alien is bored. *A million-year-old footprint.* Even if it hasn't been there for a million years, you'd have to grant it a certain longevity.

I can't seem to feel really afraid. Is that rash of me? I shouldn't forget that someone has perhaps been trying to kill me. (By manipulating Joanne? Simon? Someone else?)

But whoever it was missed.

A game? Now you see it, now you don't. If it was a game of hide-and-seek, that would explain a lot. The aim is as much to be found as to avoid being found, hence the contradictions, making me go to the North, preventing me. . . .

But how can I be afraid if it's a game? *On the edge of awakening in the amorous jungle/Hands prefer the noises of children.*

Except that children don't necessarily sense danger,

either for themselves or for others. And beings who are bored can also be very dangerous. Whatever I believe or postulate, desire or fear, my first rule should be not to let my guard down.

Too bad. If the end is in the means, to approach the unknown with balled fists is perhaps not the best guarantee of a positive encounter.

3

The road forked due north as they left Chibougamau.
Soon the city disappeared, its skyscrapers, derricks, and
plumes of smoke giving way to the stark monotony of
the plain, broken by increasingly low humps of spruce
beneath the snowdrifts. They were nearing the edge of
the tundra, and the spruce gave way more frequently to
immense stretches of wind-flattened snow gleaming beneath the sky. The wind had dropped and the sun was
brilliant, even though the temperature had fallen below
minus twenty-five. The snowcar was heated, but the
outside cold seemed to filter through the eyes rather
than the skin. Catherine, seated in the back with Athana
and Charles-Henri, huddled inside her parka. No one
had spoken since leaving Chibougamau. There was
something hypnotic about the relentlessly white exterior
that cut short any attempt at conversation. No one had
said much the night before, either, apart from intermittent remarks as they listened to the Chicoutimi radio
station, then the Chibougamau station. But once they'd
left the city, the radio had begun to fade. After twenty
miles it had disappeared completely. Joanne explained
with biting sarcasm that the inhabitants of the Lac Mistassini region were dyed-in-the-wool Separatists who'd
long ago rejected the most superficial manifestations of
modernity.

As they came closer to the lake, Joanne seemed to be increasingly gloomy. Did she regret having embarked on the expedition? They would be staying with her father's family at the lake. Perhaps that's what was bothering her. Judging from her few confiding remarks to Catherine in the library, she got along with her father's family no better than with her mother's. In that case, why had she arranged this stopover? Unfortunately, knowing Joanne, there was an obvious answer: out of defiance. Why regret it, then? Catherine turned toward the window with a sigh, letting herself go with the movement of the snowcar. Joanne's contradictions seemed endless.

Watching the monotonous scenery slide by made it easy to imagine occasionally that there was nothing else, that the whole world consisted of this winter whiteness, that Chibougamau, and Chicoutimi farther to the southeast, had disappeared as in a dream. Sometimes it even seemed to Catherine that the snowcar was simply not moving, while painted scenery spooled by on either side of it. She remembered having entertained such fancies when she was little, on trips made with her parents, lying on the back seat of the old gray Peugeot and staring at the interminable calligraphy of the electric wires running from one pole to the next like a word always begun but never finished. One more memory. Real? Invented? Better not start down that dangerous slope. She stared determinedly at the northern landscape. No electricity poles to ruin the scenery, anyway—one of the advantages of the sphere "technology" that she'd appreciated in Chicoutimi. Very zen, this stripped landscape, almost the equivalent of contemplating the void. The eye almost had to hallucinate in order to compensate.

She squinted against the sunlight, despite the dark visor covering her glasses. Those movements that she seemed to glimpse at the edge of her field of vision, those translucent forms too swift to be seen must be hallucinations—or else the sun's reflection on the snow. But, on the plain between the tongues of forest, the sinking sun was sending out longer, deeper-blue shadows from the clumps of spruce, revealing aspects of the terrain that had been invisible until now. In fact, the forest seemed to be thicker here, the trees taller. And they weren't just spruce. There were other trees that Catherine didn't recognize. Had she already seen these clustered trunks, slender and silvery, with sweeping branches like the weeping willow? And those squat round bushes? And other trees that seemed to be oak or walnut, but couldn't be, and yet familiar shapes rose on either side, mingled with the curious shapes of other trunks, other branches. . . .

She closed her eyes and opened them again. The snowcar was traveling through a dense, shady forest. She glanced at Athana, who was sleeping as usual, and at Charles-Henri, who was looking out the window on his side. No one had said anything. Another vision? She hunched in her corner, arms folded, resigned to silence.

At about four o'clock the snowcar stopped. When they stepped out of the vehicle, barking dogs jumped out of the snow, lending another meaning to the long shadows: a small village at the western end of Lac Mistassini, where the shores narrowed to meet the mouth of the Rupert River. The village consisted of about a dozen low houses, at first almost indistinguishable from the surrounding whiteness. A slight slope ran down to a stretch a little flatter than the rest—the lake and its shores. A shape muffled in furs appeared out of nowhere and ordered the dogs to be quiet. The voice spoke English, much to Catherine's amazement. But why would only francophones take refuge in the North? Everybody could have visions. In any case, the man switched languages immediately to greet the new arrivals and invited them to follow him. A low door between two walls of snow led to a sort of small foyer. The walls were hung with dog harnesses, snowshoes and guns. A stairway disappeared downward toward a welcome warmth.

Once he'd divested himself of his voluminous furs, James-Marian Marshall, Joanne's father, was revealed as a man of about sixty, tall, thin, and bony, a former redhead with very white skin, very British looking, his face long and somewhat lantern-jawed. Joanne clearly didn't have much in common with him as far as physique was concerned. She introduced Catherine and Athana, and Marshall shook hands without any particular comment. Father and daughter didn't touch one another, Marshall having merely nodded a greeting. He was clearly not delighted to receive visitors—or was it these particular visitors? He accorded Charles-Henri a raised eyebrow—not, as Catherine first thought, because her friend was black, but because of his double-barreled male name. She'd more or less forgotten about this detail, but it was obviously important for the Marshalls, who must be strict Separatists if the name James-Marian was any indication. She suddenly wondered whether Joanne had been Joe-Anne before shaking her heels free of the dust of the North and its beliefs. Kiwoe . . . Kiwoe Tchitogama was clearly a special case, and the only one to receive a truly warm greeting.

The underground home seemed like a vast labyrinth of corridors and rooms. Marshall didn't give them a tour, however, merely showing them their respective rooms. Catherine noticed various people as they walked along, but Marshall didn't introduce any of them. Nor did Joanne.

The rooms were comfortable, however, and just warm enough. Like the rest of the house, they were lit by oil lamps and chunky candles that threw a soft, pleasant light. The travelers had to explain that Athana never left Catherine's side. Without comment, Marshall got Simon to help him carry a second bed into the room.

The evening meal passed off without being quite the ordeal Catherine had feared. Only Marshall, an old woman (whom he introduced as "my mother"), and the visitors ate together. Damage control was the expression that inevitably sprang to mind to describe Marshall's behavior toward his guests. Conversation flagged, although the food was satisfying enough. Was this culinary largesse an effort to keep their mouths harmlessly occupied? Such discussion as there was involved safe subjects: winter, trapping, news from the South—Catherine realized with amusement that it was merely south with a small *s*, and that her host meant Chicoutimi. Then, after dessert and a bitter but fragrant herb tea. Marshall stated firmly that they must surely want to get some rest, considering the early start they'd need for their long, journey tomorrow. Catherine followed the lead of the others in standing up, thanking Marshall for the excellent meal, and retiring for the night.

Back in her room she found a bowl of good hot water awaiting her. As she was performing her evening ablutions, she heard a burst of voices in the hall—Joanne and Marshall, arguing in English.

"Don't ask me to agree with you!" Marshall was saying, "I never have and never will, you should know that by now. It's enough that I let you come up here."

Catherine couldn't help poking her head out of her door. Joanne burst out of a room at the end of the hall, near the dining room, and rushed blindly past her, jaw set and cheeks wet with tears. She slammed the door to her room violently. Catherine hesitated for a moment; then, with a sigh, she tossed her towel on the bed and headed for Joanne's room.

Kiwoe suddenly blocked her way. "Let me do it," he murmured. For the journey, he'd exchanged his formal councillor's garb for more suitable clothing. He was now wearing only leather trousers.

"You think so?" she queried, her eyes drawn to the muscular harmony of his smooth, coppery torso.

"I'm sure."

He turned on his heel, marched into Joanne's room without knocking, and closed the door behind him. Catherine waited. Nothing.

"She'll listen to him," said Simon's voice behind her. "They left for the South together."

There was soap on his left cheek, just above the red beard that he'd kept and cultivated after the ball. His expression was slightly sardonic. Well, so what? He knew more than she did about Joanne and Kiwoe, and undoubtedly about lots of other things. At the same time, this bit of information gave her pause. Joanne and Kiwoe? Kiwoe in the South?

"But he came back," she said at last.

"He wanted to see, he saw, he wasn't convinced."

"And she'll listen to him, even so?"

"With regard to her father, yes."

Catherine folded her arms and leaned against the wall. It seemed a curious place to have such a conversation, but she might as well take advantage of Simon's sudden loquacity. "The potential Infants seem to have a lot of problems with their human parents."

Simon shrugged. "It's mutual. Put yourself in the parents' place."

"You bear no resentment, it seems."

"My mother died a long time ago. My father is . . . too old, now. And so am I, I guess."

"Is one ever too old?" Catherine murmured, unable to help herself.

"One becomes resigned."

"Joanne isn't exactly the type to be resigned," Catherine said at last. Why did she want to hurt him? Surely she wasn't still jealous?

He smiled with sudden indulgence. "Neither are you."

Honest despite herself, she sighed and looked away. "It depends."

Neither of them spoke for a moment.

"Catherine, I have to tell you. . . ."

The door of Joanne's room opened and closed, and Kiwoe came and stood beside them. "She'll never learn. What did she think?" He took a deep breath.

Simon, to whom this remark was clearly addressed, nodded and said, "That ten years would make a difference."

Catherine's curiosity surfaced. "He reproaches her for leaving?"

Kiwoe gave a small sigh. "For existing, rather. He never believed she was an Infant, never forgave her for letting Alta turn her head with the whole idea. Later, when she broke with her mother, it was too late to make amends. Obviously, taking off for the South didn't help."

"She believed her work there would please him, I think," murmured Simon. "At least, that was always my impression."

"Why?" asked Catherine. She was genuinely surprised.

"Because Marshall was from the South himself," said Kiwoe with a slight shrug. "Recent refugees are usually more anti-South than anyone, especially if they're not Believers."

"I didn't think there were any atheists in the Realm," commented Catherine with a glance at Simon.

"Oh, he converted in the end. He'd had visions in the South, dreams here. But he didn't convert where it counts." Kiwoe placed his hand on his heart. "He kept his old outlook: confrontation, power. I always knew Joanne would go to the South. Alta was too much like Marshall."

There was a brief silence. Kiwoe rubbed his bare arms and shivered. "I'm going to bed. You ought to do the same. Long day, tomorrow."

"He's right," said Simon. If he'd wanted to tell Catherine something, he'd changed his mind.

She stifled a sigh and murmured, "Goodnight," as she returned to the room where Athana was waiting. Catherine had got into the habit of braiding the girl's hair for the night after Athana had complained about the difficulty of doing it in the morning. It had become their evening ritual. She loved brushing the tawny hair, crackling with electricity, then weaving it into neat braids. Childhood memories—but memories she could allow herself to indulge in, more soothing than sad, so ancient they had no sting.

This is a tamed forest with space between the trees for walking. Winter is nearly over, you can tell it by the animal tracks in the snow, you can feel it from the very texture of the snow lying along the gnarled branches or over the large, round rocks like a lazy beast. The chill lies lightly on the land, which exudes a vague smell of damp earth. The slight bulges on the branches tell of future buds. Not a sound—the cold hand of winter still muzzles the earth. And yet, somewhere, scarcely discernible. . . . Catherine slowly pivots, gazing into the dim forest light. Over there, yes, a movement. And, nearer, over there. And another. Almost imperceptible, at the edge of her field of vision, but also impossible to avoid catching. A flash of color, a dash of dancing green. She stands completely still as she detects a pattern in these movements: they are coming closer. Someone is coming closer. She forces herself to relax, to loosen the knotted shoulder muscles, let her hands hang free at her sides as she waits.

Abruptly they are there. A multitude of silent children, springing out of the undergrowth as though born from the trees. Jackets or jerkins, tights or trousers, moccasins or boots, the clothes are makeshift, made from old garments patched together just anyhow, but they are all of the same muted green. The oldest children are no more than ten. They carry lances and bows taller than themselves, quivers bristling with feathered arrows, and daggers at their waists. There may be girls among them, it's difficult to say since they all look much alike—thin brown faces framed by smooth black pageboy locks. Perhaps the resemblance is in the eyes—blue and almond-shaped, with a grave, almost severe expression. Several of them jump up on a big boulder and stare at Catherine as they lean on the shafts of their lances. Suddenly she feels out of place among them, too big and awkward; she wants to crouch or even sit in the snow so as to be less visible.

She holds out a hesitant hand to the child standing in front of her, a thin boy with a triangular face. He backs away, and she lets her hand drop. How should she speak to them? In what language? Do they even talk? There hasn't been a sound, not a murmur, since their sudden appearance.

"You shouldn't be here," says the child abruptly. "It's too soon."

She has understood, although not recognizing the language. Unsure of how to respond, and feeling ever more embarrassed by her overgrown adult body, she sticks her hands in her pockets.

The boy gives a brief yell. Distant cracks echo in the underbrush, the sound of an enormous mass approaching. She looks toward the sound with a certain anxiety, catching sight of colors before she can see a shape: black and yellow, geometric patterns on a bronze background. Then the shape of a foot with claws, and another foot, and her eye rises up a long neck, thick but snakelike, to a huge muzzle with long, needle-shaped teeth and flaring nostrils, and immense yellow eyes with vertical slits

for pupils. Some kind of translucent crest stands atop
the skull.

The beast comes to a halt beside the boy, who is no
higher than its ankle joint. It leans its head toward the
child and emits a small, interrogative grunt, accompanied
by a hot smell of sulphur. An eye as big as a shield is level
with Catherine and seems to observe her with curiosity.
She examines the scaly skin incredulously, the short wings
folded against the rounded flanks, wings that are surely
incapable of lifting this great bulk. She takes a step backward, then another, trying to see the whole beast. The
body is long and of mammoth proportions, ending in a
tail with a fork at the end. For the moment the tail is at
rest. The crest on the head runs down the neck and along
the rest of the body, splitting to make a double row along
the spine, a kind of natural howdah. The children clamber
up the folded back legs of the beast and settle themselves
between the double crest.

The boy clicks his tongue, and the dragon—what
else can it be called—spreads out its front legs rather
like a cat stretching, so the boy can climb up quickly
and sit in the hollow between the shoulders. He signals
to Catherine to join him. The scaly skin is dry, warm
and rather loose, making it easy to grab big folds of it
and pull yourself up. Catherine sits beside the boy. He
clicks his tongue again and the child-carrying dragon
begins to move.

They advance between trees and oddly-shaped rocks,
and Catherine suddenly sees that the latter are in fact ruins
disguised by the snow, sections of concrete wall, steel gird-
ers, twisted pipes, broken ceramic tiles—remnants of a city
that once existed where the forest now grows. And these
children? Are they the children of the survivors? Where are
the grownups?

Soon the forest gives way to what must be grassland
beneath the snow, and as they approach a steep slope,
Catherine shudders. Below them lies a huge orange expanse, a vast unfrozen lake with an island that appears
blue in the distance. The dragon strides majestically
through the deep snow still covering the grassland, stops
momentarily on the edge, then slides down the slope on
its belly, faster and faster, holding its front feet out while

the children scream with delight. It stops before reaching the orange water, however, swerving parallel to the shore to face a clump of trees in which a log cabin is nestled. Smoke is curling out of the chimney.

The children fall silent and stay perfectly still, as does the dragon. Finally, the door opens. Two silhouettes appear in the doorway, then come slowly forward, an elderly man and woman, blinking in the sunlight.

The boy nudges Catherine's elbow and points to the cabin. She doesn't want to get down. The boy frowns a little. "Go with them."

There is no arguing. She slides down the dragon's shoulder, sinking into the snow to her knees, and moves off. The beast turns around and lumbers along the shore.

"Hey!" cries the old man in a gruff voice—at least he speaks French. "Is that all you've got today? Couldn't you try a little harder?"

"Will you shut up?" snaps the old woman, hobbling through the snow toward Catherine. She doesn't appear to feel the cold, although clad in only a deep purple dressing gown. She stops beside Catherine and raises her head to look at her. The old woman barely reaches Catherine's chin; she must be a Métis, given those slanting lids and the sparse, still-black hair drawn back in a bun.

"No luggage?" The old woman clucks disapprovingly. "Well, we'll try to fix you up. Come along, child." They walk past the old man, who is still looking at the receding dragon, his hands deep in the pockets of his garnet smoking jacket. "They could have made an effort today," he mutters.

"They've brought us a guest: that's something. Come inside now, Father."

The old man follows her inside, grumbling as he goes. He limps a little with his left leg. He isn't very tall, although fairly sturdy for his age, with a rugged face and thin lips. Clearly a white man: despite the half-closed, slanting lids, he has pale eyes.

She follows the old people into the cabin and is nearly suffocated by the almost tangible heat radiating from the fat stove in the middle of the single room that serves as kitchen, dining room, and bedroom. A dressmaker's dummy stands in a corner, displaying a long evening dress in mauve satin and velvet—the sleeves are full, the military collar and yoke are embroidered with sequins and tiny, shining beads. Beside it, a dinner jacket stands at attention on another dummy.

Catherine sinks into a chair. The old woman is rummaging in a large trunk, muttering, "At the last minute like this! What on earth can I do for her?" She turns around, holding a long-sleeved white blouse with a large lace collar, a tightwaisted jacket of black brocade, and a long, black, silky-looking skirt with a double frill. "Black and white always looks dressy. What size are you? Medium? More like large. It should fit. All the same, I can't perform miracles! Try this on." She holds the clothes out to Catherine, who obeys, dumbfounded.

"Bah!" grunts the old man, "you're giving yourself a lot of trouble for nothing. *They* don't care. If we didn't go to their party they wouldn't even notice."

The old woman turns around, shocked. "It's the least we can do, after all we've done to them!" She becomes less shrill. "Listen, Father, we're not going to argue on the day of the party, are we? You know how they hate it when we fight."

Catherine tries on the blouse. It's big enough. The skirt has an elastic waistband. It'll do, too. The jacket is tight in the sleeve, however. The old woman advances on Catherine, brandishing a pair of tiny scissors, and begins snipping at the seams under the arms.

"Couldn't I take it off?" asks Catherine, drenched in sweat.

"There's no time, child!" exclaims the old woman, rapidly snipping away. "Good, there's some material there, we'll be able to let it out. Stand still, will you? I don't want to make a mistake with these scissors."

"What's the party?" asks Catherine, trying to turn her thoughts from her discomfort.

"The children's party," says the old woman gravely, as best she can with a mouth full of pins.

"But whose children are they? Where are their parents?"

"We are their parents!" says the old woman in rather shocked tones. "Who else? Raise your arm."

Catherine obeys. She's almost nauseous with the heat. "Couldn't we open the door a little?" she begs timidly.

"Do you want to catch your death?" protests the old woman. "It may be spring, but it's still very cold, you know."

"But I'm boiling!" Catherine hears herself whine, like a small, spoiled girl. But she can't help it.

"You're just imagining it because you've been outside."

The old man is sitting in a rocker, swinging back and forth with sullen energy. "A guest," he grumbles. "Since when do they bring us guests? We don't even know where she comes from!"

"I teach literature," says Catherine, feeling rather vexed.

"You see, Father, she's a teacher. That's very good."

"Ha!" snorts the old man. "Those teachers are such chatterboxes!"

"You shut up, Father!" orders the old woman. "Where are your manners? I'm sure this young miss is an *excellent* teacher."

"I'm not miss, I'm madam," says Catherine, rather to her amazement. She doesn't have to prove anything to these old people! Suddenly she's utterly sick of being treated like a child and takes off the brocade jacket despite the old woman's protests, slips out of the blouse and skirt, and pulls on her traveling clothes. "I'm not obliged to attend this party. I don't know these children. I have better things to do, you know!" She stalks out of the cabin, slamming the door behind her.

The cold is balm to her face and hands. She leaves her jacket open to take advantage of it. Is it night already? No moon, anyway, but thousands of stars. She looks along the lake for the children's campfires: she should really go and tell them she won't be coming to their party. There: reddish points of light in the phantom shadows of the snowy landscape; she need only follow the dragon's trail.

She is shivering and has buttoned her jacket by the time she reaches the children's camp. It consists of low, round huts made of stretched skins. There are more children than she'd thought, perhaps a hundred, and they seem impervious to the cold, gathered in small groups around fires and sinking their little teeth into fish cooked on sticks. They say little to each other, and always in the language Catherine doesn't understand. The fish smells delicious, Catherine's stomach contracts. She walks forward, studying the children as she goes, not sure she'll recognize the boy who rode the dragon with her this afternoon. The children fall silent as she walks by, and when she reaches the big bonfire on the shore, the only sound is the crackle of the flames. One of the children rises as she approaches, but he lets her come right up to him. It's the boy of this afternoon. He stares at her, his disapproving expression rendered abstract by the shadows. A little to the left an enormous mass moves, blocking out the lake, and two green mica gleams fix on Catherine, the eyes of the dragon reflected in the glow of the braziers.

"It was too hot," she finally explains. "They wanted to disguise me." She lowers her head and slips her hands into her pockets to keep her countenance. And finds a smooth, round surface.

With a hesitant smile, she hands the globe to the boy. He frowns and takes it between two fingers, as though anxious to avoid all contact with Catherine. The movement shakes the snow inside, and the brilliant flakes swing lazily over the miniature garden. The boy watches the flakes, then looks at Catherine with a new seriousness. Keeping his eyes on her, he lifts his hand, and the globe shines with sudden brightness in the flames. A murmur of respectful surprise runs around the circle of children, condensing into words that come back to her and the boy. "The ordeal."

He takes her by the hand and she follows. Once she is outside the circle of firelight, her eyes again become accustomed to the shadows: a wide path curves along the lakeshore over the snow, packed hard by many comings and goings. The boy heads for a small point of land closest to the phantom whiteness of the island. The waters of the lake give off a vague phosphorescence, and despite the lack of wind they quiver with strange little waves and eddies, rather like mercury. Without knowing why, Catherine suddenly feels very afraid: are they going to throw her in the lake? She stops, refusing to budge when the boy pulls her hand.

"What ordeal?" she asks.

"The river," replies the boy. "You mustn't be afraid."

Reluctantly, she starts walking again. She feels all the other children behind her, a silent, compact mass, and still further behind, like a strange shepherd, the dragon whose heavy footfalls crunch the snow. She scrutinizes the landscape, looking for a river, but there is none. The boy halts in front of a gigantic pile of rocks; she stops. The boy holds out the globe to her; she takes it. He points to the rocks, and she moves forward.

There is a hole in the rocks, a black, vertical slit. Too small, too narrow, she'll never get through that! She leans over and sticks her head through, trying to penetrate the shadows, then turns back to the boy in distress. There's just enough light—the gentle blue light of the garden in the globe—to see him smiling. She leans forward again, holding out her illuminated hand. The slit is perhaps wide enough to get a shoulder through, yes, and a head, and the rest of the torso, by dint of wriggling a little, there, and now the hips, then one leg after another.

She walks forward holding the garden aloft and slowly lifts her eyes to the smooth facets of the rock vault above. How high and wide it is on the other side of the slit! Vast, silent. If there's a river, shouldn't she hear the roar of furious waters? She pivots, trying to catch a sound, and finds the children have followed her. They are all there behind her, eyes reflecting the blue light of the globe. They cluster around her, leaving an opening to her left. She begins to walk in that direction.

The vault lengthens into a tunnel that becomes increasingly low and narrow, and soon Catherine has to crawl on all fours. Fear hovers again: what if the passage gets narrower? But she's reassured by the bluish light of the garden in her hand. The tunnel can't be the whole ordeal; it must lead somewhere, to the site of the true ordeal. And in fact the tunnel doesn't get smaller; a distant light shines in response to her tiny blue garden, comes nearer, turns into a round orifice. Catherine wriggles through. . . .

And stops on the edge of nothing. She has emerged into a stone slipway, long but fairly narrow, dropping steeply to . . . is it a river, that silent glow of thousands of lights on the walls of the cavern? Catherine straightens up on her knees, then stands up, feeling dizzy.

The river stretches away beneath a wide, low roof. Immobile. Frozen. Radiant with a steady light rising from its depths. Is it ice or a low flow of unpolished diamond gleaming with all the colors of the rainbow? The river lies motionless yet rushes on, an immense force held in suspense. Catherine opens her mouth to breathe, as though this powerful, static thrust had sucked away all the air molecules beneath the cavern roof. There should be noise, a deafening, cataclysmic sound, yet there's nothing but this even more crushing silence.

Catherine tries to shrink against the wall, but the children are behind her, standing shoulder to shoulder on the stone slipway. Once again, there's only one way to go: down to the frozen river. There's something on the shore, a round flat rock or an enormous tortoise shell. . . .

It's a large shield of ice or translucent stone— Catherine touches it, feels neither heat nor cold, and when she runs her hand over the figures carved in relief she still feels nothing, as though her fingers were just above the surface. She tries to study the carvings but can't seem to see them—they refuse to yield to her curiosity, and all she can do is glimpse them out of the corner of her eye: letters, runic inscriptions, perhaps. But she senses the waiting children behind her. She puts the garden globe down at a safe distance from the river, then turns the shield over—it's as light as a feather—and begins to drag it toward the glowing surface of the river. She comes back for the garden, then climbs gingerly into the overturned shield. It wobbles a bit, then steadies itself.

The boy and two of the other children come down and push the shield onto the frozen river.

Instantly the river carries the shield off, silent, immobile, vertiginous. Catherine clutches the edge of the shield, trying to catch her breath, eyes half-closed as the razor-sharp wind cuts her face. She could curl up in the bottom of the shield, thus offering less resistance to the wind, but she wants to see: see the walls and ceiling of the cavern rush by above her head, perilously close, see the diamond waters race by on either side of her vessel, endowed with illusory mobility by the speed—is it the shield that's sliding along or the river moving so fast that it appears immobile? Catherine soon ceases to wonder, drunk with the rush of speed, exultant, fulfilled. She doesn't know where the river is carrying her, but it doesn't matter, it's the movement that counts, the movement, the passage.

4

The road stopped at the village on Lac Mistassini. After that, they would be traveling over the lake itself, following its northeast shore, then on to Lac Sakami. At the northernmost tip of this lake was the last human outpost, Nakiakami, after which they would follow the ice road to Hudson Bay, to the point where the pilgrimage stopped and where the exchange of bodies for spheres took place. They were now above the tree line, crossing a flat, white plain. Floating in the sky above the distant horizon were the round hills of Labrador. *The mountain is like a dream above the horizon,* Pierre-Emmanuelle Manesch had written. *My beautiful dream/Father of all rivers/Which do not reach the ocean/Father of all clouds/Which do not see the other side of the sky/Never cease to retreat/Mountain.* They would never reach the mountain, for the trail forked west after Nakiakami.

Kiwoe sensed the approaching blizzard in the changing sky and light while they were in the middle of Lac Sakami, with a hundred and twenty miles still to go. They stopped just in time to set up the protective plastic cover. The wind and snow began tearing at them with full force as they snapped together the last buckles and hurried back into the vehicle. The snowcar would keep warm without any danger of the passengers begin asphyxiated— one of the many advantages of the energy spheres—and they had enough to eat. The snowcar was fairly spacious and would serve as their living quarters during the last part of the journey. It even had a tiny, enclosed toilet where travelers could, with a number of contortions, answer the call of nature.

Everyone lowered their seat backs and prepared to wait out the storm. Athana rolled herself into a ball and went to sleep, her head on Charles-Henri's thigh. Simon got a miniature chess set out of his bag and started a game with Joanne, Kiwoe and Charles-Henri watched them for a while, then Charles-Henri folded his arms and closed his eyes for a nap, or to meditate, while Kiwoe came and sat beside Catherine. She had taken out her copy of *The Book of Steps* and opened her notebook when she saw that no one was watching her. Now she stopped writing.

"I'm bothering you," murmured Kiwoe regretfully.

She didn't want to lie to him, nor did she want to discourage him. "Writing is something . . . very intimate to me."

"And if I don't watch you?" He smiled.

She smiled back, but closed the notebook. "It won't do."

They had left a window slightly open to make sure there was some air circulating. They could hear the wind roaring and the spattering sound of snow granules on the plastic cover. The lamps were lit inside the snowcar, but the daylight, even though muted by the storm, filtered through the green plastic with a vaguely submarine effect.

"*The Book of Steps,*" said Kiwoe quietly. "You must have played the little game of clues?"

"Everyone does it, I suppose?"

"No."

"But you did?"

"Of course. Particularly after meeting Joanne."

"Joanne raises a lot of questions," remarked Catherine, carefully neutral. "And a lot of passions."

Kiwoe smiled as if she had said something else. "We've never been lovers, which is doubtless why she still listens to me from time to time. But she let me play the question game by myself."

"And what did you conclude?"

"Not much." He sighed. "It isn't really certain whether Manesch left coded information in his book—at least, not information about his experiences in the Far North. Or at least not"—he gave a low chuckle at his successive modifications—"anything other than strictly personal impressions, which is admittedly the subject of most of the book. Poetry, that's all."

Catherine laughed too, but for a different reason. " 'Poetry, that's all'? But poetry is a perfect vehicle for all sorts of interlocking codes. Poetry doesn't have to mean only one thing."

Kiwoe's smile became a grin. "Point taken. I was describing Joanne's approach. I prefer yours, however. Poetry, then, and something else."

"Poetry *is* something else. Everything else."

He shook his head. "I was forgetting you taught literature."

"Well, even so—I know I'm also tempted to see something else in the book; it's impossible not to be. But I don't want to give in. That would be slipping into mania. Did Pierre-Emmanuelle Manesch have a mania about codes?"

"No. He had a deep faith and was very humble according to what we know. You might argue that faith is a code, but it's an unequivocal one, isn't it? I don't know whether he was still such a believer toward the end, or believed in the same way after his last voyage to the Far North."

"Would he have written *The Book of Steps*, in that case?"

"I'm not sure the language of poetry is compatible with the language of faith, even in as flexible a religion as ours. Poetry is a religion in itself."

Catherine looked at Kiwoe with renewed interest. "A form of spirituality, not necessarily a religion."

"The religion of words, no?"

She looked doubtful. "The passion of sense, more likely."

"Of senses?"

"Of the possibility of meaning, any meaning."

Kiwoe settled himself more comfortably. He was seated on the floor facing Catherine, leaning against the next seat back, with his feet on the seat cushion between herself and Athana.

"The desire for meaning." He smiled. "Our words stem from our body and thus give us an incomplete apprehension of the world: true reality is inaccessible to us, and if we postulate its existence even so, how can we avoid being frustrated?"

Catherine gave a little laugh; this conversation was taking an unexpected turn. "By adopting a solipsistic outlook, for example? Nothing exists outside my brain?"

"That's sometimes a satisfactory answer. But it's too difficult to uphold in the face of overwhelmingly concrete contradictions."

Although Kiwoe smiled, she felt he was serious. Perhaps they weren't having the conversation she supposed. "You become paranoid, then," she said, entering into the spirit of the discussion. "Reality has a grudge against us, or is playing with us or else continually giving us signs we must either decipher or be damned."

"Or you become a mystic: we can only reach toward reality asymptotically, that is, we can come ever closer, but never quite touch it. Nevertheless, there is a secret bond between reality and ourselves, and it's in ourselves that we can find the signs, in our consciousness and the language that embodies our consciousness."

"You mean we become poets."

They smiled at each other.

"And what do you make of science in all this?"

"Ah, science," said Kiwoe, clasping his hands, stretching his arms, and cracking his knuckles. "Science is another form of consciousness, isn't it?"

"As poetry is?"

"From another angle than poetry—complementary, maybe. Science as well as poetry satisfies our need to make sense of things."

"Science has always seemed to me more . . . totalitarian than poetry."

Kiwoe smiled again. "But it seems to me the true scientist and true poet are humble people. People whose hands are outstretched, not to grab but to receive."

She stared at him for a moment. "Tell all, Kiwoe. Have you ever written poetry?"

"I also tried to understand the spheres—the energy of the spheres, if not their music."

"You went to the South."

"And I came back. Under the circumstances, poetry was more satisfying."

"Lots more possible stories," Athana chimed in.

They turned to her in surprise. She must have been awake for a while, but they hadn't noticed. Kiwoe laughed softly. "Yes, more possible stories."

5

The blizzard began to blow itself out toward the end of
the afternoon—enough to enable the travelers to re-
move the plastic cover and set off once more. They had
been driving for nearly two hours in the growing dusk
when Joanne, who had replaced Simon at the wheel,
gave a muffled shout. Catherine felt the snowcar halt.
She and the others stood up to see what was happening.

Within the circle of light blazing from each side of the
vehicle streamed a tumultuous sea of brown bodies—
rumps, bony backs, antlers.

"Moose?" said Charles-Henri. "Caribou wouldn't
surprise me. But moose?"

The animals did seem like moose, but a second look
revealed the proportions were wrong. The legs were too
short, the body too massive, the branches of the antlers
too numerous. But it was a herd, an interminable herd,
hundreds and possibly thousands of animals. They trotted
past unhurriedly, paying no attention to the snowcar. And
kept on passing. And passing.

Joanne sounded the horn and started the snowcar
moving again. It crawled forward, but the animals
wouldn't veer from their path. Joanne swore under her
breath and backed up. She turned to the right to drive to
the back of the herd. After five minutes, they found
themselves confronting another living wall, and Joanne

turned right again. The quasi-moose streamed in front of them there, too, heading south. What about the left? Same thing. The herd had divided on either side and had encircled them, as Catherine had vaguely expected it would.

Joanne stopped the snowcar again. They watched the animals going by.

"Caribou herds can migrate for days on end," murmured Kiwoe.

"Have you ever heard of such huge migrations in this region?" said Simon. "But these aren't caribou. Did you ever see animals like these? Where do they come from? Spring hasn't even begun here."

"Wait," said Joanne philosophically. "We've housed, warmed, and fed, we can certainly afford to wait."

The animals kept streaming by, undeterred by the headlights. Other animals or the same ones? Catherine suddenly wondered, feeling slightly hysterical. If these animals wanted to block the snowcar's progress, why had they cut off its retreat as well?

The headlights flicked off and the motor stopped.

"Oh, no!" exclaimed Simon.

Was that an answer? How long would it take for the heat inside the vehicle to dissipate? Would the blizzard start up again, just for good measure?

Simon put on his parka, pulled back Athana's seat, and opened the trap door to the motor housing. An icy blast of air rushed in. Simon crawled into the motor compartment while the others quickly put on their warm clothing. Catherine was mentally going over their reserve equipment. There were gas stoves for cooking (Joanne wouldn't hear of using stoves fueled by spheres), but these wouldn't last forever. Neither would the herd, perhaps. But how could they move forward or go back if the snowcar wasn't working? It wasn't very logical, even if some force didn't want them to go on. Unless it wanted them to die here. But she couldn't believe their death was the real aim. Was this denial? If the way back was also cut off, then. . . .

She shivered. Athana had sat down beside her, half on her knees, while the seat was pushed back to free the trap door. Now the girl put a warm hand on Catherine's cheek. "You're cold?"

"I'm afraid," admitted Catherine softly.

Athana put her arms around Catherine's neck and held her close. "You mustn't be afraid. It's just some blue going by."

Catherine registered this information with a certain interest, in spite of everything. "Some blue going by." In the animals' bodies, perhaps. Had there been a sort of short circuit in the sphere because of the proximity of all this blue? But she mustn't forget: there was meaning in that blue, a will somewhere.

"Some blue that prevents us from moving. And it has stopped the snowcar. If the car won't start, we'll be very cold and finally we'll die." Perhaps it was rather too short a summary; they could probably backtrack to the village on Lac Mistassini; after all, they had snowshoes and two emergency tents. But if something really wanted to stop them. . . .

"If we die, we'll come back," said Athana, although she suddenly seemed rather uncertain.

Catherine sighed. "I don't know about that, Athana." And I'd rather not have the opportunity of finding out. Athana nestled against her once more. After a moment, she murmured something Catherine didn't understand. Something in a plaintive but obstinate tone.

"What did you say, my love?"

Athana sniffed: "I don't want you to leave."

Simon's head reappeared through the trap door. "Everything looks all right. I'm going to replace the sphere. You never know." He hitched himself up into the snowcar and went to the back to rummage through their stores.

Without the heating, a thin layer of ice had formed on the windows. Catherine scratched the window on her side, and saw the herd still streaming by. There seemed to be no end to it. It was snowing more heavily, but the wind seemed to be dying down. Occasional gusts of blowing snow whirled through the whitish dusk. Catherine squinted. The whirling snow looked rather solid. With a start, she realized the eddies were moving toward the snowcar alongside the herd—white, compact forms leap-

ing forward on four paws, with black holes for the eyes,
gaping maws and pointed ears.

"Wolves!"

"What?" said Simon from the bowels of the snowcar.

"Look!" Kiwoe whispered.

Wolves, some twenty of them, were running in front
of the snowcar, snapping at the animals' shins, leaping at
their throats, and howling at the top of their lungs, so
loudly that it could even be heard through closed windows. The herd still streamed by, but the animals at the
outer edge had become aware of the wolves and were trying to veer away. Little by little, an empty space formed in
the steady flow.

Simon hitched himself up from the motor compartment once again and closed the trap door with a click.
"Try it now!"

Joanne pressed the starter. The motor roared into action as the beams of the headlights shone out on the wild
dance of the attacking wolves. The vehicle moved forward
slowly, pushing into the hollow that grew apace as the
park drove deeper into the herd. Some of the wild-eyed
prey jumped over the wolves or passed behind them,
skimming the snowcar, but most swung away in a huge
crescent so as to bypass the wolves and keep up with the
herd.

And suddenly it was over. In front of the snowcar lay
the flat surface of the frozen lake beneath the snow. They
all turned as one to look at the dark line of the herd that
had closed ranks behind them and the white shapes of the
wolves now running along the edge, like sheepdogs.

"Well," said Joanne finally, "it looks as though we're
continuing on our journey, after all." Catherine wasn't
taken in by the sarcastic tone. Perhaps Joanne wasn't, either.

When they reached their destination, the wind had
fallen and the sky was a stark black vault splashed with
stars above the plain. Nakiakami, like the Marshalls' village, was mostly below the surface. Although the ancient
natives had never lived underground, in other respects the
three village families lived in the traditional way. They
had no guns, almost no metal, and most of the subterra-

nean installations seemed more like burrows than bunkers.

The travelers were greeted with enthusiasm and a certain amount of surprise, as individual Pilgrimages were fairly rare. When Simon then mentioned the time of their departure from Lac Mistassini, their hosts were astounded that it had taken so long to cover two hundred and forty miles. Catherine remarked that with the blizzard. . . . But there'd been no blizzard, said their hosts, more surprised than ever. She caught Charles-Henri's eye: of course, there had been no blizzard at Nakiakami. With unspoken accord, the travelers said nothing about their encounter with the quasi-moose and the wolves. Their hosts already seemed fairly impressed at the thought of having Simon, Joanne, and Kiwoe as guests, although they appeared to find nothing special about Catherine or Athana, which was just as well.

Catherine was the first to wake next morning. She wandered into the common room, yawning, to check the temperature. Through the transparent roof above ground she could see a wall of blowing snow. She went to tell the others that the storm had caught up with them. Somehow it simply didn't worry her, and not just because they were safe underground. When she returned to the common room, Athana was already there. The children of Nakiakami—there were about thirty of them, of all ages—seemed fascinated by her blonde hair and white skin and had clustered around her, almost climbing over one another in their eagerness to show her their toys; Athana seemed equally fascinated, more by the children than by the toys.

Catherine watched them for a moment, then went to sit in a corner with *The Book of Steps*. She didn't undo the bundle of photocopies right away, however. Instead, she pondered her reaction to this new delay. Aggravation, yes, tinged with indulgence. If they were going to be allowed through anyway, what was the point of all these childish tricks? Wasn't it now understood that they would continue on their way? The alien had been around long enough to comprehend human nature! But maybe the alien wasn't a bored child, but a senile old man? There were all sorts of disquieting possibilities in such a theory.

And why should there be just one alien? Perhaps there were several. A whole boatload of aliens, a vessel shipwrecked in the tundra—it was anybody's guess.

In the group surrounding Athana, a child let out a rippling, exultant laugh. Catherine shook herself. She wasn't going to let herself slip into paranoia now! What she had told Joanne after announcing her intention of going to the Far North still held: no more speculation, just facts. No trying to bolster up her lack of knowledge with theories, upsetting or not. Anyway, no matter what's in the Far North, I'm going. I want to know. So much that I'm willing to die? Yes. She examined this sudden certainty with astonishment, then admitted it. Perhaps I'm more free to go to the Far North than Athana, Joanne, or even Simon, in relation to the possible alien who is calling me, but I'm not free in relation to myself. I *have* to go. I want to know. So be it.

She leafed through the package of poems. Other fragments took on new meanings—she wanted to give them new meanings. *Then the syntax builds a rhythm/To harbor the proffered moment/My surrender to the razor's edge/The only bearable tenderness.* Surrender could even be far less tense. "Hands outstretched, not to grab but to receive," Kiwoe had said. Wasn't that what she'd done in the dream, by letting herself be carried away on the river? *Today I play the earth creature/I wait for my chance/As for a stranger/Sensing the exception made there/Oblivion/The one excess.* In all this, there was an exchange between her will and the will of another—more than a game: a delicate equilibrium to be preserved; more than strategic moves: a conversation in which only some of the words were spoken, and to which she must remain attentive.

6

They had to stay a whole day at Nakiakami, after which, as Catherine had foreseen, the blizzard petered out. They thanked their hosts and set off the next morning on the last leg of the journey, about another two hundred and forty miles north to Rivière-à-la-Baleine, then due west to Hudson Bay. The ice road used for the Pilgrimage was in excellent condition, and this last stage would take only six hours. "Unless there's a migration of terrestrial whales," teased Joanne, half-serious.

It was still the same austere landscape, although the sky was now blue—a minimalist painting in which a few indigo shadows indicated the rare change in ground level. And yet there were moments when something fluttered at the edge of Catherine's field of vision, like a mirage: suddenly the snowcar was driving through the forest of the green children. It was only for a few seconds, but she could have sworn she saw them running through the undergrowth alongside the snowcar, with the astonishingly agile mass of the dragon passing through the trees like an animated building. She gave an involuntary cry the first time, and the others asked her what was the matter. Nothing, she replied, just thought I saw a wolf. After that, she bit her tongue each time she saw the mirage—or vision.

And then Athana cried out, pointing to the window,

"Look, more green children!" and everybody said, "What?"

They saw nothing.

Catherine listened to Athana's description and wondered whether she ought to corroborate it—Simon and Joanne were reacting rather negatively although both Charles-Henri and Kiwoe seemed fascinated, but with a hint of disbelief. After the incident, the silence in the snowcar took on a different quality. Catherine closed her eyes and leaned back in her chair, rather despondent. She felt the same aching disappointment each time the others unwittingly reminded her they really weren't her friendly allies. Would she never stop being a sentimental idiot? Athana came over and snuggled against her, as though she perceived her sadness. Catherine stroked her cheek, but she had no real sense of peace. Athana's affection and fidelity were even less justified than the mistrust or reserve of the others. She wasn't and couldn't be a real friend, either. Like Joanne, like Simon, she was part of the problem, not the solution. Beyond the blonde head resting on her shoulder, she suddenly met Charles-Henri's eye, attentive and . . . understanding? There is still Charles-Henri, after all. And possibly Kiwoe. But it doesn't console me. They're not the ones I want, that's all. I want Joanne's and Simon's friendship, but why? Is it the intense impression of familiarity I always feel with them? But in that case I ought to want Athana for my friend as well.

Suddenly seized by an incomprehensible feeling of compassion, Catherine stroked the young girl's cheek and kissed the blonde hair. Poor Athana.

But why "poor Athana"? She has what she wants. She has me.

Toward the middle of the morning, the storm returned. "Damn!" muttered Joanne, which pretty well summed up the general feeling at the sight of the first flakes of snow spiraling in the wind. It wasn't enough to stop the snowcar, however. They moved slowly but surely westward along the frozen bed of the river. Snow, ice, wind, white sky. . . . Sometimes Catherine wondered what they could have seen beyond their field of vision if they'd been able to be both inside and outside the snowcar at the same time. Had a corridor of whirling storms been created for their exclusive use? Not bad as far as controlling matter went: microclimates at will. On the other hand, there were all these halfhearted attempts to stop them. Perhaps whatever it was didn't want to convince them, either.

When the snowcar stalled, an hour after the blizzard had begun, Catherine couldn't stifle a brief outburst of nervous laughter. What treat was in store for them this time? Joanne's migration of terrestrial whales, perhaps? But after an hour in the motor compartment, Simon hadn't found the source of the breakdown, and finally used their third and last replacement sphere. It didn't help.

Once Simon had climbed back up and shut the trap door, they all remained silent for a moment. "All right," said Simon wearily at last, "we can wait until it clears, and continue on snowshoes. It's three miles from here."

So near? Surely no one meant to kill them so close to their goal? Unless out of sheer sadism? But she wasn't going to base her decision on that kind of reasoning!

"And if the storm doesn't die down?" she heard herself ask.

They turned toward her, looking mystified. How could she explain? She was suddenly certain they mustn't stay in the snowcar, that they must continue without the machine. Now, without delay. A test. Did she believe in her dreams that much? But what else was there to believe in?

"Three miles. In a straight line." She looked at each of them in turn, taking in Joanne's sardonic expression, Simon's frown, the hesitation of Charles-Henri and Kiwoe . . . Athana's smile. Had she the right to do it? Athana would surely follow her.

Was she herself up to it physically? Yes. Perhaps it was the Voyager who spoke, or the memory of what she'd already been surprisingly capable of doing, but it was a certainty.

"I'm going to continue on snowshoes. Now."

"What?" said Simon.

"It's not a real blizzard," she insisted. "It's . . . like

the herd and the wolves, except this time it's up to us to get through on our own."

"A test?" said Charles-Henri, suddenly illuminated.

"You're absolutely crazy!" Simon was furious now, not with her, but with everything implied by Charles-Henri's comment.

"Maybe she's right," said Joanne, an unexpected ally.

Simon turned brusquely. "Of course you'd say that!"

"You saw the wolves just as we did, Simon."

"Predators always follow herds."

"Just to open the way for us? Simon, there are limits to being disingenuous, even for you!"

"I didn't say we were all going to continue," said Catherine calmly, in order to keep tempers from flaring. "I said *I* was."

"As though we could let you go on alone."

"I'll go," said Joanne.

"I think I will, too," murmured Charles-Henri.

"In any case, it can be done," said Kiwoe. "Especially if there are several of us."

"You can stay if you like, Simon," said Joanne.

Simon shrugged violently and went off to get the snowshoes and other necessary equipment from the storage bay.

Catherine helped Joanne fill the backpacks, bewildered. She hadn't really thought they'd follow her or that she would be assuming this kind of responsibility in deciding to continue. Risking her own life was one thing. Risking theirs was something else. She couldn't bring herself to believe their lives would really be threatened in those last three miles, but what grounds did she have for this feeling, after all? A cluster of elements that she found totally convincing as a whole, but if she looked at each one separately. . . . Dreams! Poems!

Spheres. Athana.

White wolves, clearing the way for them. No, Simon might deny it, but it couldn't be a coincidence.

They tied themselves to one another, Simon first, Charles-Henri, Kiwoe, then Joanne, Athana, and Catherine. Joanne had taken charge once more, and decided who would follow whom and carry what. Since Catherine was the strongest of the women, she would carry one of the tents. Athana would carry the kitchen utensils, Joanne some of the provisions, and the rest would be divided between the three men. It was almost one in the afternoon when they walked away from the snowcar. They had the wind at their backs—possibly a good sign, remarked Joanne. Simon growled something incomprehensible and set off, supporting each stride with an angry slash of his poles at the snowdrifts.

After a while the snow seemed to get thicker, although the wind didn't increase. Through the visor covering her somewhat steamy glasses, Catherine could barely see Athana's form three steps in front. Joanne and the others were invisible. At least she could feel the constant pull of the rope. Even with snowshoes, they sank to their calves in the powdery surface. Catherine forced herself to walk rhythmically, controlling her breathing. The backpack straps were beginning to dig into her shoulders, despite her thick parka. At times, when she let a thought break through her physical concentration, she wondered what she was doing here. It was like another dream, slightly more absurd than the others—this slow determined marching from nowhere to nowhere over a surface blown indistinguishably flat by the wind, through snow that her visor colored strangely yellow. The shrieking wind seemed no longer a sound but a dimension; if it stopped she would suddenly topple, as though deprived of the support of an essential component of space. How long had they been walking, anyway? One hour, two hours, more? Were they really walking? It was impossible to shake off the constant feeling that they weren't making headway. Despite the gloves, the parka, and all the layers of clothing separating her from the cold, she could sense her body becoming numb. She leaned more heavily on her snowshoes from time to time, waiting until the slack on the rope tightened so that she could feel the pull and remember she was really walking, had a body for walking, that there was a fixed surface in the constant swirl around her, a direction in the formless space. A sharp anguish had coalesced in her chest, slowly becoming a hard ball, heavier and heavier. She tried to make it go away, but it also acted as a point of equilibrium, a center around which she could regroup. Then she would forget to think, would lose herself in the regular swing of arms and legs, in the shock of her heels hitting the gut snowshoe strings, in the animated, obedient matter that was her body, carrying her toward her destination.

Suddenly she bumped into something. Athana had stopped. Her face was invisible beneath her visor and the hood of the parka, but there was something strange in the way she stood, so utterly still.

"What?" shouted Catherine.

Athana lifted a gloved hand. She held the six feet of rope that had tied her to Joanne. One end of it had been neatly cut.

Catherine, hunching against the wind, was speechless for a moment. Finally she yelled, "When?"

The wind whipped away the first syllables of the answer. ". . . know!"

The snowshoe tracks were probably already blown away, anyway. They had a tent, two burners and some pots. The others had the provisions and the two compasses. No way of knowing which was the right direction. The wind was still in their backs, but wind can turn.

Joanne! Joanne had cut the cord! The searing thought suddenly burst through the succession of calm, practical observations Catherine had forced herself to make. It was Joanne, every time. Catherine had been so hypnotized by the blizzards, the herd, and the wolves that she'd forgotten about the breakdown of the van and later the snowcar. And all the rest: the live bullet instead of the blank, the shot in the tavern. . . . Joanne had missed, but this time the blizzard would do her work. Joanne really wanted to kill her. Joanne had cut the rope.

Catherine felt her knees buckle. Sit down in the snow, that would be better, more protected from the wind. She could curl up, hug her knees to her chest, tuck her head in between her knees, coil into the small circle of her own threatened warmth. . . .

Firm hands grasped her under the arms to keep her upright. Athana had raised her visor and was looking at her sternly. "Beyond," she said. "Not much farther."

Had Athana shouted? Catherine only knew she'd heard her voice very clearly above the suddenly greater howling of the storm. She straightened up, feeling curiously lightheaded. "Not much further." How did Athana know? But that was the wrong question. She shouted in the wind, "Where?"

Athana pointed into the maelstrom of nonspace.

Catherine eased the straps of her backpack, then lowered Athana's visor over the blue eyes. "Lead on!"

Athana bowed her head, turned around, and began to walk northward.

7

Three hours later, as night began to fall, they arrived on the shores of the frozen sea. The ice had taken on the shape of the water's wavelets and currents at the moment of being seized by the cold. Blowing snow had polished the surface to a steely black, silky in the dusk. Catherine stopped, and Athana, halted by the rope linking them, turned around.

"It's that way," she said, pointing to the sea. The wind had dropped enough to make it possible to talk without shouting. Catherine hesitated. The idea of walking on the sea made her uneasy. It was solid on the edges, but out from shore it might not be so safe.

Athana wrapped the rope twice around her wrist, and Catherine grudgingly allowed herself to be pulled forward. "Don't be afraid," said Athana. "It's not very far, now."

Catherine had felt herself slip into Voyager mode just after setting off behind Athana, once they'd discovered the severed rope—there was no other term to describe the sudden resolution that had gripped her. But now this energy was beginning to dissipate and she stumbled on the frozen wavelets in the growing dusk.

"Athana, wait!"

The girl stopped and looked back. Catherine rummaged in one of the compartments of her backpack.

Weren't there ... yes! Cyalumes. She took one and shook it to activate the chemical reaction. A bluish-green light began to glow in the baton, lighting up Catherine's gloves, making Athana's eyes gleam now that she'd lifted her visor, and glancing off the uneven ice around them.

"Does it burn?" asked Athana, awed by the spectacle.

"No. You can hold it."

Athana took the cyalume gingerly and examined it, then, with a delighted laugh, held it high and twirled it around to light the ice field. "Cold fire!"

"Forward march, O bearer of light," said Catherine, smiling in spite of herself.

They set off once more. The bluish gleam of the cyalume shone in huge, liquid pools over the ice, and created moving reflections below the surface. Perhaps it hadn't been such a good idea, after all. Catherine realized she was waiting for a cracking sound, the rush of suddenly liberated water, and the fall. A fragment from *The Book of Steps* kept running through her mind. *The ice is thin above....* Athana strode forward fearlessly, her boots pounding the ice, one arm raised to illuminate the night. *A thread stretched in my space....* Surely, if the ice could support Athana, it could carry Catherine, couldn't it? But the sense of anguish wouldn't go away. It was too strong for her, and she couldn't help imagining the dizzying space separating her from the sea floor. *The ice is thin/ Below/The shoulders of the waters rise....* Stem the flow of images, just put one foot in front of the other, live in one dimension only, the horizontal. Look forward, forget even the existence of the sky beyond the blue light of the cyalume, advance and keep looking ahead, toward the dark line unfolding that would soon become the island, that *was* the island, yes, a pile of sharp-crested boulders barely covered with snow, rough slabs hewn by some giant axe, where the light held high by Athana threw fuzzy shadows.

And where another light responded: a round, orange-colored half sphere—no, a translucent membrane behind which she could see other shadows stirring, human shapes. They had pitched their tent in the shelter of the rocks. Someone must have seen Athana's light through the tent wall. There were exclamations, the sound of a zipper being hastily opened, and Kiwoe burst out.

"Catherine!"

He had taken her by the shoulders and was shaking her as if to make sure she was truly real. Simon, who had followed him out, pushed them both toward the tent, along with Athana. "Get in, quick." They shook off their backpacks and crawled into the tent.

Charles-Henri must have been sleeping and now propped himself up on one elbow, eyes wide. Catherine let herself fall beside him and he hugged her, unable to speak. The light of the cyalume mingled weirdly with the glow of the torchlight and the heater, throwing the interior of the tent into sharp focus. On the other side of Charles-Henri sat Joanne, her knees drawn up to her chest, staring at Catherine with disbelief. More than disbelief. Relief? Joy? She had a dark mark on one cheek.

The tent was too small, but for the moment it was enough to be together, crammed comfortably against one another. Then Kiwoe asked, "Did Athana guide you?"

"Yes," said Catherine without taking her eyes off Joanne. The Métis lowered her eyes, then her head, and rested her chin on her knees. The mark on her cheek must be the result of a blow. Simon, maybe, when they realized. . . . What had she told them? Impossible to make them believe it was an accident. Had she said that Athana had cut the rope?

"Why, Joanne?"

"I don't know." The voice was low, hoarse.

Catherine flexed her face muscles and rubbed her tingling cheeks. She was beginning to get warm. Until now she hadn't realized how cold she was. Athana had put the cyalume on the ground at her feet. Kiwoe was kneeling by the stove preparing something, probably soup from a cube, but Catherine wasn't hungry. She was exhausted, yet at the same time she was suspended in a crystalline patience, beyond her body. "Why, Joanne?" she asked again.

"I don't know!" A strident, terrified cry, this time. Simon, who was seated next to Joanne, put an arm around her shoulders. She collapsed against him. Catherine stared at them for a moment, puzzled.

"I tried," murmured Joanne. She straightened up, as

if the contact with Simon had given her a little courage. "I tried to resist. I didn't realize it was happening, at first. I rationalized it. Even in the tavern. And taking you to Simon's after the accident, considering the condition you were in. But afterward. . . . The night of the ball. . . . I loaded the revolver, I knew what I was doing, and at the same time. . . . I didn't know." She repeated in a whisper, shaking her head, "I didn't know. The rope—it was the same compulsion. Too strong for me to resist." She struck her chest with her fists, letting out a broken scream of despair and rage. "Too strong!" She fell sobbing against Simon, who held her close, his face twisted with pain.

"For me, too," he said finally. He made a visible effort to look Catherine in the eye. "But I was aware of it. The night of the ball. That's why I went to Joanne's room. On the terrace—it wasn't me. Not really. I saw myself doing things, heard myself talking, but it wasn't me. Do you understand?"

Catherine nodded, wondering when her calm would evaporate.

"I was going to ask you to live with me, to leave Chicoutimi and come back to my place. But I wasn't really the one who was asking, and I knew it."

And he'd decided to go north with her because something had tried to make him prevent her from going. Because now he believed there really was something there, a someone, a will that wanted to take over his will.

"You realized it, but not Joanne?"

He sighed, while Joanne slipped out of his arms and furtively wiped her cheeks. "It wasn't the first time it had happened to me," he murmured. "When I was younger, around fifteen or sixteen, I got strange ideas. A crusade against the South. To be the new prophet. I would totally believe it, and then, thinking about it, I would find it totally ridiculous. And so, each time I felt like going to a Believers' meeting to give an impassioned speech, I resisted. In the end it was an actual physical battle. Crises, like epilepsy. The hardest was to hide them from everyone."

Joanne was staring at him, thunderstruck. "And you assured me there were no manipulators, no experiments, nothing?"

He lowered his head, a stubborn expression on his

face. "It could be . . . well, I don't know, split personality syndrome. With the upbringing I had. . . . You weren't brought up to be an Infant, not the way I was. You can't know what it was like."

Joanne moved away from him. "You're really unbelievable!"

Kiwoe held out a steaming bowl to Catherine and broke the awkward silence by saying, "Is this what you've come to look for? Manipulators?"

"I don't really know," she murmured. "But it's here. And it went to a lot of trouble to prevent *us* from coming here."

Kiwoe handed another bowl to Athana. He watched her blow on it and then take several cautious mouthfuls. "Without much success," he remarked.

Catherine nodded. Her eyes closed of their own accord—Superwoman was fading fast. "Joanne never managed to kill me, either."

After a while, Kiwoe stood up as best he could and said, "Come on, Simon, we'll pitch the other tent. We can't all sleep in this one."

8

The next afternoon they set off with lighter backpacks for the place where the Pilgrimage ended, beyond the small rock hill beside which they'd camped. There was a fairly wide path with most of the stones removed, usually used for the convoy carrying the coffins—the packed snow still showed caterpillar tracks. It was a beautiful day, almost as though a point had been conceded in making no further attempt to discourage them. When they reached the summit, Catherine contemplated the small clover-shaped lake below. It wasn't frozen, and it sent up an orange gleam.

She followed the others down the hill. It wasn't what she had expected. She had imagined there'd be buildings, a covered place where the exchange of bodies for spheres took place. But there was only the lake in this rocky landscape, with a white streak of snow here and there. And at the end of the Pilgrimage the coffins were emptied and the naked frozen bodies put into the lake one after the other. They disappeared in a blue flash. The pilgrims camped on the edge of the lake, spending the night in prayer and meditation. The next morning there were thousands of spheres of all sizes on the shore, like pebbles carried in by an invisible tide.

Catherine crouched down on the shore, intrigued. As in her dream, the liquid looked more like mercury than water. She was about to touch the surface when Simon stopped her. "That may not be wise," he muttered. He was probably right. She threw a stone into the lake. It floated. She picked up another and examined it. No, it wasn't pumice, but good old pink granite. Which floated on water. Not water, obviously. A colloidal substance?

She turned around. "Now what?"

"You're the one who wanted to come here," said Simon. His tone bordered on the hostile. He was standing with Joanne and the others, as far as possible from the lake.

She turned to Charles-Henri and Kiwoe, who threw up their hands in ignorance. With a sigh, she sat on a rock and looked around. The scenery was vaguely familiar—probably the effect of the orange surface of the lake and the rocky promontory. With an involuntary half smile, she remembered that the globe with the garden and the snow had been left in Chicoutimi. But she could still hear the boy's voice, the unknown syllables that had clearly meant, "You mustn't be afraid." A bit of dream that probably had no connection with anything this time, unlike the orange lake. It was the same thing with her memories: if any of them corresponded to genuine reality, she had no way of knowing which. If signs were being given here, she didn't know which to follow.

Something moved. Athana leaned against her and took her arm. Catherine hadn't done her braids the night before, and wisps of hair were now loose from the hood of her parka. Athana looked around with amazement. She seemed anxious.

"And you, Athana," said Catherine without much hope, patting her hand reassuringly, "do you know what must be done now?"

"No." She pressed her forehead against Catherine's shoulder and whispered, "But there is blue everywhere. Especially down there." Her gloved hand waved toward an outcrop of needle-toothed rocks sticking up about a hundred yards to their left.

Well, it was worth a try, since there didn't seem to be anything else to do.

Catherine walked toward the outcrop. The others followed, apparently under the impression she knew what she was doing—and yet as she approached the rocks the feeling of déjà-vu increased sharply, perhaps because of the new angle from which she now saw them. They were the rocks to which the green children had led her, the rocks beneath which ran the diamond river. There should be a gap so that she could slip inside, shouldn't there? She circled the rocks, but there was nothing. An idea occurred to her, but she shrugged it off: surely she didn't need the glass globe! What a stupid idea. Why not "Open Sesame" while she was at it?

She came back to her starting point and stood staring at the rocks, hands on hips, uncertain what to do next.

The gap was right in front of her, between two angles of rock, exactly where it should be but where it hadn't been an instant before.

She closed her eyes and opened them again. The gap was still there. She glared at the pile of rocks as if it were a face, more annoyed than relieved. Will that be all? Any more tricks for us today? But the rocks preserved a stony silence—naturally. Catherine gave a little sigh and walked toward the gap. It was comfortably wide, and she slipped into the blackness beyond. A blue light suddenly sprang up behind her. She turned with a start, but it was only Athana who had just come through the gap holding a lighted cyalume.

No slipway, no river. Simply an underground passage roughly hewn from the rock, with a fairly steep slope disappearing into the darkness. "Due north," remarked Kiwoe quietly, at the very moment when Catherine thought of it. She took the cyalume from Athana. The rest of Manesch's poem had come back to her since she'd been on the ice, and was ringing in her head. *And I on the ice immobile/Await the great rending of crystal/The coming of the true depth/That which turns over in the sun.* But there was no light at the end of the underground passage, just the luminous baton in Catherine's hand, throwing its bluish light on the dark rock. The passage was interminable, going on and on without branching off, getting neither bigger nor smaller, but only deeper and deeper into the mineral silence where their footsteps and breathing aroused no echo. It was neither cold nor hot, and Catherine could barely feel the movement of air on her skin. She suddenly realized that the hand holding the cyalume was trembling with fatigue, and she switched the baton to the other hand. Her thoughts were nebulous, without origin or direction, tinged with a vague anguish. Put one foot in front of the other, watch the walls moving by within the lamplight, walk, advance in this immutable landscape. They might as well have been immobile.

Immobile.

She stopped abruptly, felt her companions do the same behind her, bumping into one another. For an instant she let anger flood in, washing away the anguish, then she dumped her backpack on the ground and sat down cross-legged, resting against the passage wall, with the cyalume beside her. Athana sat down, too.

"What's the matter?" asked Simon grumpily.

She shrugged, discouraged at the thought of having to explain. "Sit down. We're going nowhere." And knowing it was absurd to raise her voice, yet unable to help herself, she shouted, "We'll stay here."

The underground passage disappeared.

A great fire crackled in a rustic hearth in front of them. On their left, in high-backed wing chairs, sat an old man in an outmoded suit of garnet velvet and an old woman wrapped in a black, fringed shawl over a long mauve dress. She wore a crown of thick white braids.

"Well, we were almost kept waiting." The old man smiled as he quoted the Sun King. Another wing chair materialized on the other side of the fireplace.

"Sit down, sit down. Make yourself comfortable!" he added.

Catherine hesitated, then put her pack on the floor and sat down, staring at the old man. Seventy, perhaps, but sturdy, with head held high and fine hands negligently draped over the arms of his chair. White hair in a brushcut, a snowy beard framing the square face with its benevolent wrinkles, and pale blue eyes partly hidden by slightly slanting eyelids. Catherine had worked for hours in the Manesch library beneath this serene, slightly amused gaze. The voice was that of the old man in the cabin where the green children had taken her, but without the whining tone. Instead, it was deep and serious, yet affable and assured. Indulgently, he let her look him over then turned to the others. "Please, do sit down."

Four more chairs materialized, arranged in a half circle opposite the old people. There was a pause, then Kiwoe put down his pack and sat next to Catherine, soon followed by Charles-Henri. Simon and Joanne stood paralyzed, their hands gripping the straps of the backpacks.

"Manesch!" muttered Simon.

The old man nodded. "Among others, at your service. Won't you sit down?"

Simon dropped his pack and moved to a chair like a sleepwalker.

"At our service?" said Joanne, who remained where she was. Her chin was raised, but it wasn't really anger than made her voice quiver. "Surely not. We're surely not here thanks to you!"

"But yes, my dear child. Thanks to me, precisely." He glanced at the haughty old woman, who hadn't moved since their arrival and who was watching them with an inscrutable expression. "It's a rather long story. Wouldn't you prefer to hear it over a good meal? It's nearly six o'clock, and you must all be hungry."

"No, here and now!" said Joanne. She shrugged off her backpack and dropped into the remaining chair, folding her arms.

"Dear, dear, the children demand an explanation, Mother," said the old man, turning to his companion.

The old woman frowned. "Don't call me that."

"Now," said Simon gruffly.

The old man leaned back in his chair and crossed his legs, resting his chin on two fingers. "Let's see; where shall we begin?"

Catherine felt a hand slip into hers: Athana, who had sat down at her feet, there being no chair for her. She seemed terrified.

"You're not Pierre-Emmanuelle Manesch!" protested Simon huskily.

"Well, yes and no. We should perhaps reverse the question. Was Pierre-Emmanuelle Manesch *me*? In fact I've always had a weakness for reproduction—natural reproduction, let's say, but all things considered, you and I could be relations. However, my dear Simon-Pierre, you wouldn't be my grandson, but my great-grandson. I began with Louis-Raoul."

Catherine glanced around her. They were in a large, well-proportioned room, without doors or windows, but with a high ceiling and walls filled with large, glass-fronted bookcases, very similar to those in the Manesch library. Some odds and ends were also displayed in softly-lit glass cabinets—she preferred not to look too closely. In one corner a computer was standing on a large translucent desk whose ultramodern but harmonious lines blended imperceptibly with the rest of the decor. A decor. A stage set. She mustn't forget that.

"Louis-Raoul?" stammered Simon.

"Of course. All that is part of our little game, you see. By and large, she has the South"—he waved a careless hand at the old woman—"and I have the North. Our creative techniques are ... different, shall we say? I always like to leave a little something to chance. Your beard is red, for example. A detail, but that's the spice of life. My companion, on the other hand.... I don't think you consider yourself the mother of our little Joanne, do you, my dear?"

"No," said the old woman with disdainful irritation.

"What game?" demanded Simon, gruffly.

The old man sighed. "You see, my dear boy, we've been here so long that it sometimes gets dull."

"Couldn't we skip all this?" said Catherine to no one in particular, leaning back in her chair with studied boredom. "Is it really necessary?"

"You came here looking for answers."

"I came to find the real player, and you're not the one." She couldn't help looking at the ceiling, although it was a pointless gesture. "Let's do away with the simulacra, all right? Why don't you show yourself as you really are?"

There was a brief silence. No one moved. Then the old woman straightened in her chair. "Simulacra? Is she calling us simulacra?" She burst into scornful laughter. "Ha! That's rich!"

The old man waved a mollifying hand at his companion as he looked at Catherine, amused and very indulgent. "Explain your interesting theory to us, my dear child."

"I don't think I'm obliged to, by the rules of the game."

"What on earth are you talking about?" exclaimed Simon.

Catherine hesitated. Kiwoe was giving her a puzzled look, and Joanne was frowning. They didn't know—and of course they were impressed. The fake subterranean tunnel, these majestic old people, the old man's resemblance to Pierre-Emmanuelle Manesch. . . . She sighed and waved at the room. "All this doesn't exist. It was entirely created for our benefit. So were they. Mouthpieces. Puppets. The real creator is somewhere else. The creator of the spheres and the visions. And the blizzards and herds of pseudo-moose. Someone who controls the matter around us, or the matter in our brains, making us see what he wants us to see. An alien. You were on the right track, Joanne. An alien from this planet, which isn't Earth. Or from somewhere else, it doesn't matter. It's hiding. We're here, we've passed the tests. So why continue this silly game?"

The old woman stood up, pushing her chair back roughly so that it grated on the wooden floor. "Puppets? So we're puppets?" She dragged Catherine from her chair with astounding strength, considering she was a head shorter, and pulled her toward a door that suddenly appeared between two bookcases. Catherine instinctively resisted, then let herself be pulled along, resigned, and conscious that the others were following her.

They strode down a corridor, passed through a door that opened without the old woman even touching it, and emerged into an immense, rectangular courtyard, paved with black and white herringbone tiles. It seemed to be an interior courtyard bordered with rather blurred facades. In the center was a large pool surrounded by a path of colored pebbles, a sort of square basin filled with the same substance as the orange lake.

"There's your alien!" The old woman let go so brusquely that Catherine almost lost her balance and stumbled toward the raised edge of the pool. "And don't touch it. Simulacra are very susceptible." The old woman emphasized the word "simulacra," and when Catherine turned to look at her she picked up a pebble and threw it into the pool, where it disappeared in a blue flash. Catherine heard Athana give a terrified cry behind her. The old woman snickered. "Simulacra, yes. Copies. Puppets. Your very own expression. Do you remember the blue flash of the dead bodies? Well, it's the same with lives ones. So don't touch it!"

The old woman sat down abruptly on the cushions of a white cast-iron loveseat that suddenly materialized behind her. She folded her arms and looked at them, eyes glinting. The old man walked up to her, shaking his head regretfully, and sat down in another chair that sprang from nowhere. A low little table appeared with similarly accommodating suddenness, complete with a large basket of fruit, glasses, and a big pitcher of what looked like orangeade. He poured a glass and handed it to Catherine. She took it, pleased to see that her hand wasn't shaking. The orangeade was just sweet enough, just cool enough. She put her glass down on the table.

"And to what do we owe this interesting demonstration?" she asked.

The old man observed her, smiling. "Not impressed, I see."

"Not when someone's so obviously trying to impress me."

He laughed and turned to the old woman. "Ah, Tali, she's a real little jewel, this one!" Then he became serious again. "You see, in a way the situation is as ... unexpected for us as it is for you. You will excuse my awkwardness, I'm sure. In fact I'm going to show you, if you don't mind. All these explanations are a bit tedious, and it seems a picture is worth a thousand words."

A large screen appeared on his right, floating in the void.

"What did you call her?" asked Catherine, wishing her voice wouldn't quaver.

The old man gave her a lopsided little smile. "Tali. A diminutive. I'll let you guess the full name. Surely you and your friend Charles-Henri can figure it out?"

The white screen dissolved into black space—the blackness of space, strewn with steadily shining stars around an orange-colored sphere. The sphere grew—they were approaching it. The orange dissolved into vapor layers, slowly swirling as the sphere turned from right to left on the screen.

"The orange thing isn't the atmosphere, but it occupies a considerable part of it. Please understand that this is a re-creation," remarked the old man. "I don't know if it's exactly like the planet on which we now find ourselves."

Now they were piercing the cloud, the vapor gradually turning into bigger and bigger particles, living cells, in which they could distinguish the flutter of electrochemical exchanges as the cells bumped against one another and stuck together or split.

"Life can take many forms. Here, it's taken the form of this cloud made up of organic particles."

The screen pulled back from the planet. Now they saw the cloud slowly swirling around the sphere. There was a sudden condensation in one spot: the orange became brighter, and waves of color rippled out with ever-increasing speed over the whole surface. Then the deep spot of orange faded and the waves disappeared.

"And we both arrived on this planet—an event that must have acted as a kind of trigger on the cloud. Because when we awoke—Voyagers are always unconscious when they arrive—we each found ourselves in separate, familiar surroundings."

More images. The pounding of Catherine's heart thudded in her ears and throat. She recognized the little village square that ran down to the cold, gray water with the bobbing masts: it was there that the young Egon used to walk with his Talitha. And another image: a view through an open window of a promenade along a cliff, where tall, feverishly green trees wave above a sparkling sea. She felt suddenly weak, and a cast-iron chair obligingly appeared behind her. She slumped into it. Voyagers. Not simulacra. Not prisoners. Her very first theory had been the right one. Players controlling a game. A Talitha who is surely not the one this Egon had been seeking, since this isn't the Egon desired by this Talitha. What had they thought when they met? That they'd found one another at last? And when they're realized they were wrong, what then?

"After some mutual checking, we realized that we had apparently arrived at the same time, which. . . . Oh, but I forgot: Catherine didn't deem it advisable to tell everyone everything." The old man looked at his amazed audience with an almost impish smile. "There is a machine, you see, which makes it possible to transfer Voyagers from one universe to another. Not more than one Voyager to a given place at a given moment. Or so we believed. Tali and I didn't arrive exactly in the same spot, but we did arrive at the same time. I don't know whether the arrival of a single Voyager would have been enough to trigger the cloud's mimetic tropism, but in fact we very soon became aware of their existence and explored their possibilities."

The last image disappeared from the screen, to be replaced by another. Joanne gasped. It was Simon as a young man. He was sitting pensively in a chair in front of a low little table. He said, "Glass of water," and something appeared on the table—a curiously blurred drinking glass. No, not blurred: it was a liquid glass, a glass made of water. The young man laughed. "No, a glass of cut crystal." He appeared to concentrate. "A glass made of cut crystal, with water in it," The glass was now more solid, with a stem, the diamond-shaped bevels acting as a prism to the water. The young man smiled, picked up the glass, and drank.

"The cloud had a tendency to be pretty literal, in the beginning."

"That's what responds to your request—the particle cloud?" murmured Catherine.

The old man looked doubtful. "At first we thought there was indeed an intelligence responding to ours. Unfortunately, that's not the case. There is life in this cloud, but it isn't conscious. It's . . . a plastic life. That takes on the forms imposed by us. A sort of response, yes. But like a reflex action."

Catherine tried to think, tried to verbalize objections. All she could say was, "By remote control?"

The old man nodded with the satisfied air of a master whose pupil asks the right questions. "Even if they aren't always visible in the lower atmosphere, we are surrounded by these particles and the force field that links them. As far as the particles are concerned, our bodies are simply a slightly more dense arrangement of matter. They perceive what we call images, or desire, or so many highly specific electrochemical impulses, which they immediately imitate."

"Visions," murmured Kiwoe.

The old man turned to him with a look of slight surprise, as though he had forgotten about the others. "Visions," he said finally, "aren't very different from all the rest, except for the length of time they last. We've developed an extremely exact control over the whole process. It's become second nature to us, so to speak."

Charles-Henri murmured huskily, "The world. You created the world. You are the Infants."

The old man gave another crooked smile. "That's right."

"The Infants?" murmured Joanne, who was standing near the pool.

The old man bowed his head, still smiling. "I know we seem old, but that's a sort of . . . reverse vanity, if you like. In reality. . . ."

The man sitting in the chair was in his prime, his hair and beard were blond, but the resemblance to Simon was still obvious. And in the other chair sat Joanne's double—who gave a vexed little cluck and became once more the old woman of a second before. She glared at her companion.

A second later the white beard and hair were back, and the smiling wrinkles. "We haven't aged since we arrived here. No doubt a consequence of the particular circumstances of that arrival. In any case, after a while it gets . . . how should I put it? Annoying. Disconcerting. Sometimes we feel like looking our age, you see. But sit down, my dear child; you look as if you need to."

A chair appeared behind Joanne, nudging the back of her knees, and she sat down without a word.

"Simon?" said the old man more amiably.

Simon shook his head like a punch-drunk boxer. "A game . . . you talked earlier about a game. What game?"

"South versus North, various social and political theories to be tested. . . . You know. It's already occurred to both of you."

"But Joanne is from the North, not the South," murmured Kiwoe, rather confused.

"A development of our . . . friendly challenge," said the old man. "You see, each of us has perfected our own methods for controlling the cloud, and we each have our own ideas about our creations. Tali prefers to generate visions, for example, and I prefer dreams. Well, to be brief, Tali bet me she could do with Joanne what I hadn't been able to do with Simon. And things didn't turn out quite the way we expected."

The old woman stiffened in her chair. "We don't have to give them explanations, Egon!"

"My dear, as Catherine pointed out, they've got this far; the least we can do is give them something in return."

Catherine looked from one to the other, thunderstruck. Simon, Joanne: Egon, Talitha. Her ambivalent feelings about Joanne, and about Simon—who looked like her father. The point about a blind spot is that you can't see it, isn't that right, Catherine? She hadn't seen the resemblance between Joanne and her mother, either!

She'd been prevented from seeing it.

"What was I supposed to do in the Realm?" asked Joanne, almost inaudible but still mulish.

"You were supposed to be Simon's adversary, my dear child. Or to goad him into becoming a religious firebrand, I must admit I've never really understood your plan, Tali. As for me, I had . . . abandoned this line of action, but Tali seemed to think she could succeed where I had failed. The least one can say is that the result wasn't exactly conclusive. But she kept at it." The old man laughed. "That's the difference between us: I don't want the sinner to die."

"How dare you!" exclaimed the old woman.

"Come now, my dear, you're the one who kept egging on poor Joanne. After all this time, you could at least accept responsibility for your actions."

"For my actions, yes, but not yours!"

"Admit it: because you created Joanne, you've always considered you had the right to. . . ."

"Catherine as well?" said Kiwoe.

Catherine jumped when she heard her name. The two

old people turned to Kiwoe, equally surprised and a little annoyed.

"Another kind of experiment, of course," said Egon. "Wasn't it, Tali?"

"Yes," said Talitha, smiling, but her liquid black eyes didn't smile. "Another type of creation. One has to vary one's pleasures a little."

"Like with her," added the old man airily, jerking his chin in Athana's direction. The girl was sitting on the ground beside Catherine again. She hid her face against Catherine's thigh. She was shaking.

There was a long silence, undisturbed by any bird cry, any buzzing insect. Catherine had closed her eyes; her head was spinning and she could have fallen asleep then and there in the cast-iron chair.

The amiable voice of the old Egon pierced her fatigue. "You must all be exhausted. Come, we'll show you to your rooms. A meal will be brought to you."

9

She was awake but unable to move. There was someone in the room, a heavy, quivering presence she could sense through her closed eyelids. At last, with a convulsive gulp of air and a wrench of her whole body, as if pulling herself from a bed of mud, she opened her eyes. The terror dissipated like an electric current that is suddenly grounded.

She sat up, realizing she hadn't even turned down the covers and had slept in her clothes. The final moments of the previous evening were blurred. She remembered coming into the room. There had been a tray of hot food on a table, and she had eaten. After that she couldn't remember anything. Had she really been that tired? Perhaps it was the result of the forced march in the blizzard. Or perhaps her fatigue had been encouraged.

She frowned and stood up. Daylight filtered through the window. She went to pull the curtains and to her surprise found herself looking down on the courtyard with its orange pool. The bedroom was on an upper floor—but she had no recollection of climbing a staircase. Despite the brightness of the courtyard, the sky seemed to be an expanse of even light, curiously near. She studied the view for a moment, trying to pinpoint the source of her uneasiness. It wasn't the façades on the other side of the courtyard, which were as blurred as the night before, nor the square pool and its enigmatic orange-colored substance, nor the geometric pattern of the black-and-white tiles. . . .

There wasn't a bit of green anywhere. Not a tree, not a lawn, not even potted plants. There had been no birds or insects either, the previous day. Did this inorganic landscape reflect the two Voyagers' mentality? They'd made it like this. Did they hate life so much, even when it was fake?

A familiar odor made her turn toward the table, where a steaming red teapot now stood. Earl Grey. Toasted bagel slices in a small basket, a little jar of butter, an assortment of jams, and a white bowl containing a perfectly ripe orange and banana.

She went over to the tray and picked up the orange. A navel orange with delicate skin. She sniffed it. Fragrant drops spurted out as she split it open. Perfect. True as life. Better than my dream vanilla ice cream and the little steel spoon, in any case.

She closed her eyes, suddenly overcome by dizziness. All this, and the room, the courtyard, possibly the entire island, reproduced by the cloud. Subjected to the will of two humans. Were they still human? Two immortal Voyagers.

And they created me, too. She created me.

That's what they'd said, wasn't it, just before sending their visitors to bed like children that had stayed up too late? She was an experiment. Like Simon, like Joanne.

A simulacrum. A local condensation of the cloud, maintained by the caprice of her creator, a woman who could let Catherine's particles disperse whenever she liked. And what about all the rest, the North, the South? All those people, all those landscapes, all those objects, so clear in her memory—illusions, perhaps slightly more durable than visions?

Catherine's knees were shaking. She leaned against the table, felt for the chair, and sat down like an old woman. She stared at the teapot, at the thread of steam rising from its spout. The fragrance of the tea was so intense, so real, the red glaze of the pot so brilliant, as though it had been lacquered. . . . It had a familiar look, this fat, red teapot. Of course: it resembled the teapot that

424   ELISABETH VONARBURG

had been sacrificed in the magic show. But this one had a cover, and naturally it was brand new. Not a teapot to be broken and reglued. It would be a shame. You'd need a live bullet to break it.

Joanne had loaded a live bullet into Simon's revolver.

Catherine stiffened. This was a clear idea, incisive, like a lighthouse beam piercing the dark despair that had enveloped her. A live bullet. Joanne had tried to kill her. Joanne had cut the rope in the blizzard. But not really Joanne, since Joanne was a creation of the old woman. It was Talitha who'd tried to kill her. And yet she's the one who created me. Or maybe it was Egon who tried to kill me. They were blaming each other yesterday—why would they do that? Who were they trying to convince, and why? Why try to kill me if I'm one of their creatures, since they can unmake me as easily as they made me? An experiment. What did this experiment consist of? Were they trying to see if I'd get here, despite all obstacles? And who placed these obstacles in my way? If they're playing. . . . It's one against the other. One wants me to succeed, the other wants me to fail. But why make me come—or prevent my coming—to this particular place?

Catherine forced herself to breathe slowly and deeply. This sudden rush of questions was intoxicating, the intoxication of high mountains that fills you with energy, even if it quickly fades. There was a thread here she mustn't lose. Thread, rope. Joanne cut the rope. She had missed her mark the other times, but this time. . . . Or else the one who'd foiled the other's attempts had succeeded in protecting me again? Athana saved me.

Athana. They created her, too. They said so. And she was afraid of them. Athana. Poor little Italie who was afraid of being unmade. . . .

But no. Surely Italie wasn't afraid of being unmade. She had re-created the ants, hadn't she? She was just afraid of being . . . forgotten. To cease to exist if she were forgotten. The Presence. . . . It was the Presence that created the garden and Italie, wasn't it?

Where was Athana? Why wasn't she curled up on the bed or in an armchair? She'd nearly always been there when it mattered, and now she wasn't. What had they done to her? How thoughtless the old couple's behavior toward the girl had been, providing no chair and remarking carelessly that she was also one of their creations! And yet she must have been an essential pawn in their game. She had saved Catherine several times—after the accident, at the frontier, and when she went to tell the people in Chicoutimi about Catherine being at Simon's. And she had given Catherine the glass globe with the garden in the snow.

Who had really given her the globe? Why? As a clue to the entrance to the underground cavern? But the underground cavern didn't really exist, did it? The dream about the green children, all those garden dreams. . . . But there wasn't even a blade of grass in the courtyard! Moreover, she'd received the globe in a vision, not in a dream. Who controlled the visions? Old Talitha; the other preferred using dreams. But I had both. They both manipulated me, then.

But if one of them wanted to prevent me coming here, there should have been visions or dreams that would turn me away from the North. There had been none. The only terrifying dream was the one about the Presence, and it had changed when Italie came into it. Italie-Athana.

Who was afraid of being forgotten and of ceasing to exist as a result. Who was much, much greater than her parents, but still small.

There was a meaning there, she sensed it, but it still eluded her.

She finished splitting the orange, divided it in four, and ate the sections deliberately, one after the other. The substance of the cloud, nourishing another condensation of the cloud. But all things considered, was that so very different from what happened "normally," according to the laws of physics—such as she knew them, in any case? There was no magic at work here. And she was hungry. But this wasn't the only cause of the tightness around her heart. There was something else, an emotion she recognized with a sort of satisfaction: anger. She thought of a terrified Athana, and she was angry. Anger was like a purifying bath: her memories of the previous evening came back to her with fresh clarity, and she saw the whole thing differently—the theatrical production, the phony decor. They'd wanted to impress their visitors. But why? If they were the quasi-gods they pretended to be, why would they want to impress their wretched creatures? Oh, it was subtle, neither lightning nor thunder. They could have presented themselves as young immortals. Or appeared immediately to Joanne and Simon as their perfect doubles. That would certainly have been impressive! But not in the right way: it would stimulate too much terror, horror maybe, aggressiveness. Less controllable emotions. It was more to their purpose to choose just enough physical resemblance with the appearance of age to activate fearful obedience.

They'd done the same thing for her, as well. She, possibly even more than the others, had listened, accepted without question all the revelations as absolute truths. The elderly Egon and Talitha looked like her parents, and her childhood reflexes had come into play in spite of herself.

Her hand closed over the last orange quarter, crushing the pulp. Her childhood, her memories were nothing but images imposed on her mind, a failsafe mechanism to make sure she would obey! Her parents didn't exist, had never existed!

Why these particular images, though? Why show her the different stories of the alternate Egons and Talithas—who were human, far too human? And in the dream about the green children, the guilty old couple living in isolation. . . . Was that how Egon and Talitha saw themselves? Was that what they really wanted, the reason they had finally allowed her to reach their retreat? Did they want to be judged by their creation? But in the Northern myth, the Deity was to be awakened, not judged. . . .

Oh, they had plenty of ready answers, they overwhelmed us with revelations—to keep us from asking the real questions. Why should we believe them, anyway? Because they created us? Or maybe that's why they invented this whole ridiculous scenario from the start, to see whether their creatures were capable of rebelling against them. To see whether the ants wanted to follow their own paths. Except that in the dream, it was Italie that could make or unmake the ants. Italie. Not an Egon, not a Talitha, but a little fairy child.

I must find Athana.

10

She came out of her room and found herself in a very ordinary hallway with various doors. She knocked on the nearest, and after a moment the door opened to reveal Kiwoe. His room was identical to hers, including breakfast on a table. He gave her a wry smile. "Our hosts are very attentive."

"You're not impressed?"

"Not when people try so hard to impress me, as someone said yesterday."

She looked dubious. "But I let myself be impressed in the end. I forgot."

"Me too, until this morning, and then the questions resurfaced. Athana isn't with you?"

"I was going to ask whether *you* knew where she was."

They looked at each other for a moment and then, with one accord, walked down the hall, each knocking on another door. Simon opened to Catherine. He was dressed and Joanne wasn't with him. Again the same room, the same breakfast on the table. Very attentive, their hosts, but not very inventive. Charles-Henri joined Simon and Catherine while Kiwoe went to knock at the remaining door. Joanne appeared in turn, visibly having slept in her clothes like the rest.

None of them could remember going upstairs to the

bedrooms very clearly. And no one had wondered about Athana until now.

"She wasn't with you?" asked Simon in surprise.

Catherine nodded, her sense of anxiety growing. She tried to remember the last time she'd seen Athana. It was more a tactile than a visual memory, the feel of Athana's face pressed against her thigh, of the girl trembling. After that they must have stood up to follow Egon and Talitha, but she remembered nothing about it.

She took a deep breath, feeding the flame of anger that had just rekindled itself. She turned to walk away, but had only gone a few steps before she realized she had no idea where she was. It didn't matter. In this silly decor, all roads must lead to their beginning!

Suddenly she was standing in front of the library door. A long table of dark wood now dominated the room. The old people were having breakfast, each at opposite ends. Large silver candelabra illuminated the elegant china laid out on damask table mats, but there were no flowers. Egon smiled amiably at them, patting his lips with a pristine napkin.

"Ah, there you are. Did you sleep well?"

"Where is Athana?"

There was a slight pause, then the old man put down his napkin. "How would I know? I don't watch for every fallen sparrow."

"She was afraid. She always stays with me, and now she's gone. What have you done with her?"

Egon lifted a white eyebrow rather haughtily. "But my dear child, are you accusing us of something? That's a fairly . . . impertinent thing to do at this hour of the morning."

"I'm asking you a question, and I'd like an answer."

Talitha gave a dry little laugh from her end of the table. "Do you think we're obliged to answer?"

"You let us come here. It surely wasn't just to offer us breakfast. Nor to let us play guessing games. You must have tons of extraordinary revelations to make, mustn't you? We're all ears."

Too aggressive, far too aggressive! But she couldn't help it.

Old Egon smiled: "What? You haven't yet found the

answers to your questions from what we told you yesterday? Can't you do it on your own? You disappoint me, my dear."

The voice, the intonation were so familiar that Catherine had to dig her nails into the palms of her hands to keep from swallowing the bait. It was the voice her father would use during those endless adolescent discussions. Her imaginary adolescence. No matter. It was the intonation of her imaginary father, the tactic he used when he didn't know how to answer one of her imaginary arguments. She mustn't let herself be taken in.

"Where is Athana?"

"Again? You're becoming a bore, little one."

"Where?"

The old woman slapped her hand on the table. "Do you really imagine you can demand an accounting? It's unbelievable!"

"Is that so? Why don't you prevent us, then? Make me dumb, and the problem will be solved."

Talitha sniffed disdainfully. "I wouldn't gratify your sense of importance."

"You don't want to, or you can't?"

The old man intervened. "Sit down, you young folk. I'm sure we can work all this out with a minimum of good will."

Catherine sat down, astonished and disquieted by the rage that had seized her with Talitha's reply. What was happening? Couldn't she stand this new confrontation with these echoes of fictional parents without shielding herself with anger? Or were they manipulating her in order to make her lose her self-control?

"And what other pressing questions have we?" asked Egon indulgently.

"Where is Athana?" replied Catherine stubbornly.

A look of irritation crossed the old man's face. "Really, does it matter?"

"If it doesn't matter, why did you send her to me right from the start? She saved my life several times. You know perfectly well why she matters. Where is she?"

"Ask me a more interesting question and I'll answer you."

He didn't know. Catherine stared at the old man with

a feeling of incredulous triumph. Neither of them knew. They had lied about Athana, because if she were their creation, they must know where to find her. What else had they lied about, in that case?

"The dreams," she said. "Who sent me the dreams?"

She saw Egon look at the other end of the table, and swiveled around to observe Talitha. "You? You sent all the dreams? Why? I thought you preferred visions."

The old woman shrugged. "I'm the one who made you, and I control you better. And you had to be given a few clues, as you couldn't have found us on your own."

"Clues to what? Clues to lead me here? Why should I come here? Or not come here, for that matter?" She turned to Egon again. He was buttering his bread with considerable concentration. "Why did you try to kill me?"

"It was Joanne who tried," he retorted without even lifting his eyes. "You ought to understand I wasn't the one who pushed her to it."

"In that case, why did you send me dreams about the North and the Voyagers, and then try to prevent me from following them? And the dream about the green children? It doesn't make sense!"

She saw the look that passed between the two old people, the identical expression of both: questioning, mutually accusing. They didn't know. They hadn't sent her the dream about the green children.

She stood up, both hands flat on the table. "You lied. You're lying now. About Athana, about the dreams. You didn't send all the dreams."

"Oh, really?" Egon seemed amused. "I can give you the list. The Presence. The Ruined Garden. The Garage-with-the-hole-in-the-earth. The Hyperceptions. The Garden-in-the-snow. The Implants. The Voyagers. The Marrus and the Shingèn. The Bus. And the Green Children, of course."

"And the dream about the Fire Brigade?"

"Yes, of course. I almost forgot. There were so many. . . ."

Catherine's laugh was exultant. "I never dreamed of firemen! I made it up this very minute! You're lying! You know about the ones I mentioned in my journal, and those that I told Charles-Henri about, and the green children because I've just mentioned them. Tell me what's in that dream, and I'll believe you!"

"Children dressed in green," said the old man with a shrug, "with a dragon, in an exotic forest."

"That's because Athana saw them and talked of it to the others. But what's in *my* dream?"

The old man buttered another piece of bread. Catherine brought her fist down on the table. "You don't know. Neither of you. You weren't the ones who sent me that dream. And maybe you didn't send the other dreams. Or the visions. Then who? Who else sent them? Who wanted me to come to the North?" She suddenly saw a light. "And why were you so afraid that you tried to kill me? Athana saved me from the storm. Where is Athana? Who is Athana? Do you have the slightest idea?"

Talitha tossed her napkin on the table. "This is absolutely intolerable! Who do you think you are? You're nothing but simulacra, and we can make you disappear whenever we want!"

Catherine leaned across the table. "Do it."

"No!" It was a frightened cry from Joanne.

"Do it," repeated Catherine. "If you can."

The dining room disappeared. They were now standing in the courtyard, all of them, near the orange pool.

"No, not that. Make *us* disappear. Make *me* disappear, if you can."

The old woman's eyes glinted with rage, but Catherine suddenly felt herself to be invincible, as she had on the day when her father raised his hand to strike and she said, "Go ahead, hit me!"—another false memory, but why that one, why now?

"You can't. You can't because you didn't create me. Because I'm not a simulacrum, I'm a Voyager, and you have no power over me!"

They glared at each other, and Catherine knew, was sure, the old woman would be the first to look away.

With a growl, Charles-Henri suddenly shoved Catherine toward the pool.

She tripped and grabbed him in stupefied panic. He pushed her toward the orange substance, wild-eyed, his face twisted. Over his shoulder she saw Kiwoe running toward her, but he suddenly stopped and fell to his knees, as though he'd hit an invisible barrier. The others hadn't moved. Simon and Joanne looked on, terrified. She saw it all in a flash as she tried helplessly to stop the slow but inexorable force pushing her toward the basin.

It stopped so suddenly that she felt herself topple forward. Charles-Henri held her. His breath came in short gasps, like sobs, his black skin gleaming with sweat; he clung to her, trembling violently, and now it was she who held him, feeling him ready to crumple. She sat him down on the ground and crouched beside him. She was trembling, too, and gulping for air.

"Do something, Egon!" gasped the old woman.

But Egon didn't move. He was gaping at Charles-Henri—Charles-Henri, who should have pushed Catherine into the pond to be destroyed in a blue flash, Charles-Henri who had resisted the will of Talitha or Egon, it didn't matter which: he had *resisted*.

Catherine rose slowly to her feet. Something vibrated within her, swelled, and suddenly burst. She opened her mouth automatically to breathe, as though the inner explosion had deprived her of air. Now she was standing in front of Talitha, grabbing her by the wrists, dragging her, and hurling her into the pool.

The old woman disappeared in a flash of blue.

In some deep recess of her mind, Catherine was stupefied by her action, but the uncontrollable rage that had seized her refused to fade, driving her toward the old man. He was frozen to the spot, his eyes bulging.

"And you?" she snarled. "Do you want to try, too?"

Egon backed away, tottered, and fell to his knees, still staring at the pool.

A shape had risen over the raised edge. Old Talitha, her face still contracted with terror, then astonishment. She looked at them, then slapped her hands to her face, her chest, and finally gave a horrified groan: "No, oh no!"

They all remained motionless as the old woman collapsed, crouching on the ground and sobbing.

"And you?" the old man suddenly growled in a voice full of hate, turning to Catherine. "Prove to us that you are anything more than a simulacrum! Go on—jump, you little idiot! A true Voyager, eh? Well, yes, there is another

Voyager, and she's the one who made you! You shouldn't have come here!"

She took a step toward the pool, then another. Someone shouted, "No, Catherine!" Kiwoe. Another step. She couldn't think; her mind was too taken up with fury, strident, unbearable, and something else, something unnamable squeezing her chest with a vise-like grip as though she were about to cry, but her eyes were dry, the burning rage went beyond tears. They were simulacra. They could control the orange substance up to a point, because they were made of it themselves. But it was the alien who maintained the real control, the alien who had made them. They were lying. She *was* the third Voyager, not a copy. She climbed onto the ledge of the pool, put a foot in the orange substance—no, *on* the orange substance, rubbery, impossible to penetrate. She tried with the other foot, lost her balance and felt herself falling. There was no time for fear. She was lying full length on the surface.

And then she sank slightly. She felt suddenly exhausted, weak around the hands, the neck, all those parts of her skin that touched the orange substance. She recognized the sensation and closed her eyes with faint despair, as in a dream. This was it, she was going to die. Not in a blue flash, but little by little, noiselessly. Disappear, be drained. The Presence had won at last.

A great voice spoke. "Not you. You haven't enough blue. I made you almost without blue. You won't leave in this way, either."

She opened her eyes, and suddenly the garden materialized around her in a silent explosion.

But it is a ravaged garden. A lurid light hangs over it, stormy, threatening. The grass is too green, the flowers too bright. The raspberries are garish beneath their sharp-toothed leaves, too shiny, their texture somehow perfidious—if they are picked, they will burst with soft explosions. An odor of acrid smoke pervades the garden. Between the stumps and the few doomed, yellow-leaved trees still standing, Catherine can see an orange flickering in the central lawn, surely the funeral pyre of all the dead trees. And yet it is a steady glow that spreads over the grass instead of twisting upward. An orange spring is spurting out of the middle of the lawn. Gradually, in fits and starts, it gulps one clump of grass after another in large, turgid bubbles that burst silently, like lava. It is very hot. The humidity rises in white veils from the ground, almost solid, obliterating the bottom of the garden. Catherine is finding it difficult to breathe. Her glasses are fogging up. Only three steps and sweat is running between her shoulder blades.

She raises her head, but the sky is a silent turmoil of clouds rolling and unrolling at unbelievable speeds, steel-gray draperies edged with a sickly, sulphurous light. And hanging above the garden like a cold sun is a sphere that Catherine recognizes: the sphere of the Bridge. There is a sort of blinking, pulsating effect—one moment it appears solid, metallic, and shining, the next transparent, a glass bubble, and Catherine can see a human shape, naked and still, a butterfly caught in amber. Just not for long enough, just too far away to be recognizable. But is there any need to recognize it? A woman; the other Voyager.

The sphere beats like a heart, the sky undulates, the orange stain spreads, the bushes twist and turn. All this movement and not a sound. Catherine backs away, turns and hurries up the path, even though she realizes that the garden stops at the flat space in front of the kitchen, hemmed in by a seething fog. She sits on the little parapet, far from the raspberry and blackcurrant bushes undulating furtively in the still air. She tries to forget the pulsating sphere suspended above her head, tries not to look at the broken branches on the trellis in front of her. She counts her heartbeats, the only reliable measure of time in this lunatic landscape. She tries to think. To hear again in her mind the voice that spoke to her. Feminine, masculine? Impossible to say. Immense, in any case. And angry. "I made you almost without blue. You won't leave in this way, either." Almost without blue. That's what Athana had said, wasn't it? Meaning that Catherine was freer than herself, or Simon, or Joanne.

Catherine gathers her forces and calls, "Athana?" The sound of her voice makes her start—she wasn't sure the garden would let her speak. No answer. Or else the answer is the orange-colored explosion that has just devoured one of the stumps at the edge of the lawn, again without a sound. The orange swamp gets wider, climbs toward Catherine. But she has been allowed to speak. It's a sign, perhaps an invitation.

"You are the cloud? The Presence is the cloud?"

After a moment, as though with regret, the voice thunders, "I am."

"And you are the blue as well."

"I am."

A curious way of putting it. But the voice is willing to converse. Catherine settles more comfortably on the parapet and rolls up her sleeves. "Why don't you want me to leave?"

The voice passes like a gust of wind over the garden. "You are mine. I made you, you must stay."

"But you made me almost without blue, you said. If you are the blue, I don't entirely belong to you in that case."

Another explosion on the inundated lawn. "But I made you, all the same. You have no right to leave."

Catherine contemplates the sphere. The Bridge. A simulation, no doubt.

"And you don't want the Voyagers to leave, either?"

"They tried. They jumped into the pool. But I remake them every time. As for her, she's been sealed in the sphere since the beginning. You're all mine."

Is the voice less resonant? It no longer seems to be coming from everywhere at once. As she tries to localize the voice, Catherine suddenly understands what has just been said to her, and stands stock still. *I remake them every time.* How many times have Egon and Talitha tried to end their captivity? How long has it been going on?

"Do they know?" she murmurs with horrified compassion.

"They pretend not to know. But they have to be made exactly the same each time, otherwise . . ."

The voice breaks off, and it is like a silent thunderclap. The garden undulates with shock waves. Catherine is overwhelmed: "They pretend not to know." No, they don't *want* to know. The only possible escape was into madness—a voluntary madness. Somewhere along the way, between one re-creation and another, they understood what was happening and took refuge in their ability to forget absolutely, the reverse of the Voyagers' total recall. They forgot the truth. They replaced it with a bearable lie—not enough to stop being afraid, but still bearable. They weren't lying, yesterday or just now: they are living in their own reality in which they are all-powerful gods and the cloud an obedient *thing*. But it isn't a thing. It's the Presence, it is . . . an entity. *I am.*

"What would happen if they were different? What would happen if you let us leave?"

The only response is a new series of orange explosions that swallow up the strawberry bed.

"Why should I believe you? You say you created me, but it's the third Voyager who created me, as Egon and Talitha created Simon and Joanne! They used you to do it, but you don't really have any say in the matter, you obey their will, produce the images they've imposed on you!"

The sulphurous glow behind the turmoil of clouds vanishes in an instant. Silent geysers burst through the gloom, engulfing the terrace and the fruit trees. And suddenly the false sphere of the Bridge drops from the sky and tumbles into the orange swamp, disappears in a large blue flash—and at once reappears, with its prisoner immediately hidden behind the casing that again becomes opaque.

Catherine is crushed, forces herself not to move, not to heed her instinctive urge to back away from the orange liquid. The other Voyager is a simulacrum. The simulacra created by the cloud can manipulate their creations at a distance, as Egon and Talitha did. Her memories, visions, dreams, they came from the other Voyager, she's the one who wanted Catherine to go to the Far North, while Egon and Talitha tried to prevent it. But it wasn't this other Voyager who created Catherine.

"I believe you," Catherine makes herself say. Perhaps she doesn't even need to speak; the entity must know her deepest thoughts. "You created me."

The garden ceases to writhe. The light reappears. The orange liquid stops rushing forward. She must forget the other garden of peaceful conversations between the little Catherine and Italie. This entity is not peaceful. It is barely reasonable. Mad, perhaps? Terrified, maybe. The Presence was afraid in the dream, wasn't it? Athana was afraid the previous evening. The fairy child was also afraid.

"Tell me how it all came about."

She's in the cloud. She *is* the cloud. It's a bit like the Dream of Hyperceptions, but the sensations are almost all internal. It's not a question of her body and the world; her body *is* the world. She can't really see, but she can feel all the directions of space, sensing the slow rotations of the dense mass that is her center as well as those that define her own movement around this center. And there is also the swirling of the billions of particles that make up the cloud, the crackling of their exchanges, their dynamic dance as they fuse and divide over and over again.

Little by little, she learns to recognize other directions, to perceive other spaces: there is the energy ricocheting within her own immensity, and an energy that surrounds and nourishes her. She understands: this energy comes from somewhere else, from a world beyond the world. Little by little she learns to feel the attraction of the star from which the energy comes, and the movement of the star on its axis, and of its orbit in space, its subtle balance with the other planets that it illuminates, the other, cousin stars, and the slow spiral of the galaxy to which it belongs.

The other movement of this nascent awareness is inward: the spherical mass in her center has an existence distinct from her own. If she wishes, she can separate herself from it, surround it without touching it. But then the sphere seems as though it has faded away, so pale, so slow. . . . Curious, she sends pseudopods toward the sphere: there is an exchange of energy on contact, and interesting transformations take place. She wraps herself tightly around the sphere again, and everything that has begun to develop on the surface disappears on contact, providing her with a pleasant surge of nourishing energy.

Now and then something dives in from outside and buries itself in her, a condensation of matter rather like that of the sphere in her center. She's accustomed to it now. Most of the time these are rather small and can be immediately absorbed. But one day something enormous plunges into her, so enormous that it takes a moment for her particles to react, to decompose the intrusive matter into nourishing energy, and the meteorite has time to open a fissure in her substance. For the first time, briefly, her continuity is interrupted, she's open. It's a new sensation, this momentary hiatus between her particles. Intrigued, she copies it, putting space between her particles. More. And more. The energy forms in new patterns to accommodate the break in continuity.

And now the sphere in the center is partially uncovered, bathing directly in the energy from beyond. And transformations occur spontaneously on the surface of the sphere!

This time, the entity doesn't descend to absorb them. She really doesn't need them for nourishment, and now she understands better: the internal energy of the central sphere isn't enough; the sphere needs external energy. Only then can these new structures develop on its surface, these condensations of energy in matter that obeys laws similar to those that the entity has learned to recognize in herself, but far faster, with very different results. She watches them. From time to time, she goes down to absorb some of them and tries to imitate their increasingly complex patterns.

Time passes, the entity of particles swirls about the planet, letting in the light of the sun here and there, and life on the planet spreads and diversifies.

Until the day when something totally new happens. Two minuscule intruders materialize inside the entity. They haven't come from the exterior. They weren't there, and suddenly they are. And an instant later they have disappeared again, dispersed among the particles of the cloud, which has absorbed them instantly.

And yet something is there that wasn't there before. Strewn about, broken up into myriad particles, but at the same time kept intact by energy patterns that the entity doesn't recognize as her own, different even from those that she sometimes seeks on the surface of her center. The shock wave that transmits the information reverberates from one particle to another at the speed of light, but it isn't only information that's transmitted, it's a will. These strange things try to condense of their own accord, try to gather the particles of the entity in patterns unknown to her! She's irritated by it—a physical irritation that reverberates from one particle to another, and sets off curious metamorphoses. But at the same time, the strange things offer her so many new models to imitate—an almost infinite number! After a moment, she gives in to her tropism: she copies them.

For a long time, she copies them.

And at the end of another eternity, she understands. These things are ... miniature entities. Much more condensed than she is, like the sphere in her center, but equipped with shifting energy patterns, as she is. A little like what moves on the surface of the planet, but much, much more complex.

She then reconstitutes the two minute entities, puts them on the surface of the planet, and watches them as they re-create around themselves, without even realizing it, the patterns most familiar to them. After a time she helps them, all the while continuing to study their resonances in the energy patterns of her own particles. She can understand some of it: hunger, curiosity. ... As time goes by, she learns to find her way around the multitude of minipatterns twinkling in the great network that constitutes the entities, multidimensional structures of dizzying complexity and minuteness. She discovers images and sounds, odors, tastes, textures. She learns words, the relationship between words and sensations. And because the matter/energy of the minute entities and her own are the same and are in constant resonance, she learns what they didn't know they knew, she sees what they don't want to see. She learns suffering and anger. She learns fear. She learns death.

And everything else, of course, which she gradually begins to grasp: the existence of the Bridge, the way it works—the pseudo-death by cold for the Voyage, the tri-

umph over a nothingness always close but never admitted—
and the existence of the Voyagers. She learns to recognize
these Voyagers, this particular Talitha and this particular
Egon. The woman, fleeing the risks of life, too frightened to
risk a real death. The man, pursuing an illusion, too stubborn to let it die. Both of them persuaded that the Bridge
would make them masters of their destiny, masters of the
universes into which they would be projected, universes that
existed, so they wished to believe, entirely in relation to
their will.

And aren't they right? Aren't they here on this planet
where the cloud shapes itself in response to their whims?
Can they not make and unmake the condensations of her
substance at will? With them, all can exist. Without them,
there is nothing. If they stop or leave, everything will disappear. They're profoundly convinced of it. How could
the entity not be convinced too?

With a brusqueness that almost makes her lose her balance, Catherine finds herself seated on the parapet. The
orange swamp is no longer at her feet. It has retreated to
the lawn in the middle of the garden. Catherine looks
around. Is it less hot? The humidity seems less heavy, too,
and the light less resonant with storm rumblings. She
can't help asking, "Are you still there?"

A breath of cool air passes by her. A good sign? She
thinks about it for a moment, still overwhelmed by her
experience. How can one talk to a being of such immense
age?

A being with a consciousness that is almost new, as
well. Just think of Italie—or Athana.

"You've told me a fine story," she says slowly, "but I
think you're wrong. You existed long before they did.
They're not the ones who created you. They can't unmake
you."

A rush of air swirls dust along the alley, carrying
bits of grass and dead leaves. The light grows lurid
again. The Presence isn't convinced. Of course they
can't destroy her physically, but she doesn't fear for her
substance, she's afraid for her consciousness. It was in
imitating them that she gained self-awareness, or so she

believes. She's persuaded that the disappearance of her models will plunge her into unconsciousness once more. And as for them, they don't even believe she's conscious, that she truly exists! They don't want to know, because that would mean admitting their status as simulacra and everything else—a terror too deep to be admitted. Yet isn't this stubborn will to exist proof of her conscious existence, this will to exist against all the certitudes, even those of her "creators"?

But how can she be made to realize this?

"On the contrary, it's you who created and re-created them. And although you made them exactly the same, if they've forgotten they weren't the originals, that makes them different, doesn't it? And yet, each time you re-create them, the world doesn't begin from scratch, does it? It is preserved, it goes on. You make it go on. You don't really need them." She remembers the books and conflicting maps collected by Pierre-Emmanuelle Manesch: yes, almost everything has been preserved. . . .

The garden seems to be suspended in a state of supernatural immobility. Then the voice echoes through it again, tinged with a vaguely interrogative note of resentment. "But they won't admit it."

The voice isn't as strong as before, nor does it seem to come from every direction. It's beginning to take on gender, as well. And now it has a more definite location, somewhere to Catherine's right. She almost smiles, a smile of understanding, of compassion: the entity wants to be acknowledged. Her creation isn't valid unless its connection with her is recognized. In a way, the entity's human creations have sucked in her personal myth along with her blue milk: the Sleeping Deity that created the world in its sleep, the Infants that must awaken It to give It its name and thus enable the world to truly exist. But the Deity isn't sleeping: it's already awake! Only waiting to be told. . . .

The myth has been transformed and adapted by its creatures: isn't that proof of their autonomy? But Catherine knows with whom she's dealing now, and this kind of argument may be a little too complicated for a child.

"If you remade these two Voyagers one last time, exactly as they were in the beginning, with all their memories intact, then they would have a chance of acknowledging you."

"They didn't before."

Yes, the voice is getting younger and younger, more and more feminine.

"But that was before. Now it's different. Conditions have changed." She decides to take the risk, and adds, "You are there, Athana. You gave yourself a name, even two, Italie! You don't need them in order to exist. You *are*. It wasn't they who created you, and they know that very well." Otherwise they wouldn't have neglected her so obviously last evening; they don't know what she is, just that she exists, and they're afraid.

But a wave of dark distress rolls over the garden, and after a while the voice says, "They know it was *you* who created me."

Catherine is once more the entity, somewhere above the planet. The ambience is curiously different. Before, the consciousness was diffused throughout the whole cloud of particles; now it tends to become condensed occasionally into temporary formations. The orientation of this consciousness has also changed, it is no longer centrifugal but gathers itself around the central planet. When the new Voyager suddenly materializes in the cloud, the assimilating tropism acts immediately, the shock wave spreads as quickly as it did the first time, but now there is a consciousness that can react, take over these new energy patterns, this new psychic matrix that has impregnated and reoriented its particles.

This new matrix is too different. In the binary universe that the entity reconstituted as best it could around Egon and Talitha, based on their respective worlds, there is no place for a third pole. This intrusion of a third universe imposes almost unbearable stress on the cloud's substance, for it hasn't even finished assimilating all the data from the first two Voyagers. The reaction is much more violent—and not only on a physical plane. There is stupefaction, disbelief. And fear at this confrontation with the

alien, guilt, too, at having so involuntarily assimilated
her. . . . But there is a curiosity as well, the desire to inte-
grate all these new images, new emotions, new concepts.
The automatic impulse to imitate is irresistible, but it in
turn arouses the entity's anxiety: what will the first master
say? Won't the entity have betrayed them by abandoning
itself to the alien? The cloud swirls as powerful conflicting
impulses struggle within it, and the particles' gyrations are
a far cry from their usual dance.

And suddenly there is the flash, the condensation,
something springing from a depth the entity didn't know
she possessed, and this something streaks toward the
planet, carrying within it all the contradictions, the suffering, the fear: the self-awareness. It abandons the cloud to
the powerful but confused writhing of preconsciousness.
But this new creature is almost without memory. All that
it possesses are images of unknown provenance. Slowly,
with growing insistence, a need grows, orienting the creature toward a particular condensation of matter/energy
somewhere in this new world that it now inhabits. It
doesn't know why, only that the resonance is stronger, desirable, and sweet. It finds what it is looking for without
having really searched. And now the need takes on meaning, a name, "Catherine." And the newborn creature finds
a name in response: Athana.

The garden gradually reappears around Catherine.
The false sphere of the Bridge is still hanging above the
main path, but the fog caused by the heat has disappeared. The air is cool. In the smooth and quiescent orange pool, trees unfold one after another and stretch out
limbs that are slowly covered with pink-and-white flowers. Catherine feels someone is near, and she knows who,
without even turning her head.

It isn't quite Athana, however. It's the little girl of the beginning, the girl of the Botanical Gardens, the fairy child
in the dream about the peaceful garden. Athana, Italie.
Born of three parents, she has nevertheless made up her
name from fragments shared only by "Talitha" and
"Catherine." No father, Athana? Perhaps this is normal:
at her rudimentary level of consciousness the role of Egon

in her genesis hasn't managed to counterbalance the presence of two female Voyagers. But the fact of having invented names isn't sufficient proof of her existence for her, naturally: if the others don't call her by name, don't acknowledge her, how can she exist?

"I recognize you," says Catherine gently. "Italie, Athana, I know you are truly real. And even if I closed my eyes, you'd continue to exist. The Voyagers may have been the stimuli, but nothing would have happened if the cloud hadn't already existed as an entity."

The little girl says nothing. Catherine studies her veiled eyes and pouting mouth. How can she make her understand? The child has given herself names fabricated from the names of others, and she thinks this is a sign of her subjugation when it's only a sign of her provenance. This is how beings are created, and consciousness: by assimilation and integration of what went before, in the flesh and in the mind, by successive separations and re-creations, a chain without beginning or end. One mustn't be afraid at the moment of separation—and suddenly Catherine realizes what she's saying to herself—because this is the order of life. To separate oneself from the larger consciousness is neither to die nor to kill. Something must stop for something else to begin. That's the way it is.

"But what will it be, the something else that begins?" asks the little girl with hesitant curiosity.

"We don't really know: that's what's so beautiful about it. It's a gamble, a game—the unknown."

"I'm afraid," whispers the little girl, the girl who is the cloud, the entity, the Presence. But it's easy not to think about this: Catherine sees and hears only a human child.

"We are all afraid, all the time." Catherine smiles. "We feel pain all the time. Neither peace nor joy could exist without contrasts. And it's normal, it's even a good thing as long as it doesn't prevent us from living and doing things. It didn't stop you, did it? Think of all you did so that I could come here."

The child looks doubtful. "I didn't even know it was me, before."

"But you know now. And when you understand, you can control things better, can't you?"

The child ponders this thought for a moment, rolling and unrolling a braid around a finger. "It was often the other Voyager who controlled your visions and dreams. She tried, anyway. They tried, too, but they're even less able than her to resonate with you, and it was easy to stop them. I slipped in through the chinks." She smiles timidly at Catherine. "But there were bits in your dreams that came from no one."

Catherine understands: fragments that belonged to her, Catherine, to the part of herself that wasn't made with blue (but with what, in that case?). To the part of herself that had been left to evolve on its own, that had been neither pushed toward nor attracted to the North, that had made its own way through the conflicting desires and fears of others in order to find its own true north. And yet, as with South and North, her dreams have been a collaborative effort: the interplay of human memories, myths and fantasies with those that the entity has developed.

"I wanted you to go to the Far North," says Athana—she's almost an adolescent, now—"but *it* was afraid." She points her chin at the rippling orange liquid.

"*It* is you, Athana."

The adolescent Athana kicks her heels rhythmically against the stone balustrade, a rather stubborn expression on her face. "But it always wants to . . . grab everything. Like in the beginning—you know, in the Dream of the Presence? Grab, swallow up. It always wants to have its own way. They were the only ones who could control it. They got really mad when it wouldn't obey them. It scared me." She thought a minute, and added, "They scared me, too. I was in the middle, and I was scared."

Catherine suppresses a smile at Athana's use of the past tense. "And now you're not?"

Surprised, Athana ponders this, and finally says, "Not so much."

Because the substance of the cloud is part of you, the rebellious foundation of your power. And the Voyagers are also part of you. They're the source of order, but they have no real sense of where to draw the line, either. *You* hold the balance, you're the one who keeps things in proportion when fear and desire meet, you are the center, the crucible.

Athana bows her head pensively, although Catherine hasn't spoken aloud. "Maybe."

Catherine smiles at her. "Well, shall we join the others?"

A worried gleam traverses the blue-green eyes. "But what will they say? I haven't been . . . nice."

"Neither have they," sighs Catherine. "They'll understand. Everything will be all right."

After a moment Athana murmurs, "But what must I do?"

Catherine stifles a nervous laugh. Advisor-to-Quasi-Gods, Inc. But she can't, she will never be able to see Athana as anything but Athana. Neither cosmic creature nor thundering goddess, just a small girl, rather lost, who is trying to grow up. And Athana probably won't be able to see herself any other way before a lot of time has passed. Catherine smiles at her. "We must be sure to remember that everything can't necessarily be good for everyone at the same time."

"Does everything have to be put back the way it was before?"

"What do you think?"

Athana sighs. After a moment's reflection, she says. "It wouldn't have been worth the trouble, then."

A good way of putting it. Later, Athana will understand that not only must things *not* be made to revert, but that it's impossible, even for her—particularly for her, because she's changed—the cloud, the entity have changed irreversibly.

And Catherine knows very well that she herself doesn't want to revert to what she was before, either. What would it mean, anyway, "before"? She didn't exist "before." There was only the young Catherine of her dreams, before.

But all I've learned, all I've done since I've been created, and even what there is of the young Catherine in me—her dreams and memories—now belongs to me, *is* me.

"What about just them? Make just Egon and Talitha like they were before?" Athana frowns. "But they'd keep their memory of everything they'd done since, even so." There's still a tinge of resentment in her voice, and Catherine wonders whether she should be amused or saddened. Both, probably.

"It would be a beginning."

Athana seems lost in contemplation of the latticework on the trellis. At last, with a sigh she says, "You think they'll want to leave?"

Does she mean "leave" or "die"? Maybe they're the same thing for her.

"Will you let them leave?"

A silence. Then a regretful whisper. "I must, mustn't I?"

Catherine nods, her throat suddenly constricted. She thinks of her parents, and it doesn't matter if they were the young Catherine's parents, it's the same thing. She let them go with such difficulty, caught up in her pain, her guilt, her resentment, that she couldn't even help them die a better death. Let go. Open one's hands, accept loss, the hardest thing of all. And yet how can one continue to receive with closed hands, hands that cling desperately to what cannot be held? But it will no doubt take Athana longer to understand this. She can hold on for longer. The cloud, the entity—what is its life span? The name Athana, the name she chose for herself, doesn't it mean something like "deathless"? But she's only at the first stage of learning: keeping is killing.

But to let go, to lose . . . no, it doesn't necessarily mean to die oneself.

Catherine stands for a moment, contemplating the resuscitated garden in the warm afternoon light beneath the blue sky—the cherry trees heavy with red clusters, the path lined with yellow-and-purple pansies, the trellises with their ripening fruit. A last look at the velvety raspberries, the black shiny bunches of blackcurrants, and beneath the bushes, between the pebbles, the ants hurrying to and fro. And when the snowflakes begin to fall gently on the garden, a light snow that won't freeze anything, she smiles at Athana. "Let's see what *they* want."

Everything would have to be explained to them. She sighs at the prospect, but Athana says, a little timidly: "I showed them everything at the same time as you. Do you think that will help?"

Catherine can't help smiling at the adolescent Athana. "I hope so."

11

When Catherine saw the others, she realized that only a few minutes had gone by for them. Kiwoe was helping the old Talitha to an armchair. The old Egon was where he'd been standing when he challenged Catherine to jump into the pool. Simon and Joanne hadn't moved. They looked thunderstruck.

Charles-Henri was still sitting on the ground beside the pool, his head in his hands. He stood up hastily when Catherine and Athana appeared beside him, and she guessed from his expression that he was making an effort not to shrink back from them. She smiled at him, grateful and a little sad. The dark eyes glanced at Athana, then back to her.

"Don't be afraid, everything will be all right," mumbled Athana, embarrassed. Other chairs appeared in a circle around Talitha at the same low table as the evening before, this time with glasses and a large carafe of water. "Why don't we sit down?"

No one moved for a moment. Then, with a low laugh, Kiwoe sat down and began to pour water into the glasses. The others sat down slowly. Simon and Joanne as far as possible from the old people. As Catherine sat down she noticed there was one chair too many, just opposite her. But no, of course there weren't too many chairs. Someone was sitting there now, carelessly draped over the chair in a manner belied by her tense expression. A slender young brunette wearing a white jumpsuit. Catherine watched, hoping the girl would look up, but the young Voyager stared studiously at her hands folded in her lap.

"She's called Katrin," whispered Athana, handing Catherine a glass of water. "In two syllables, with a *K* and no *e*."

Catherine nodded. This wasn't the only difference between them.

After the glasses had been handed around, the group fell silent. Catherine sighed and was about to speak when Athana touched her arm, "No, *I* must do it," and stood up.

"I would like to ... set everything right. Or better. But I don't know what to do. First you must tell me what you want."

"To leave," said the young Katrin impassively.

Athana sat down again, looking rather taken aback. "Right away?"

"As soon as possible. As soon as there's a functional Bridge."

"But ... she can't leave," said Simon, sitting up slightly in his chair. His voice grew stronger. "If she leaves here, she'll disappear. She's a copy."

The young Katrin stiffened. Yet it must have occurred to her.

Athana seemed perplexed. "I don't know," she said slowly. "If I continue to exist without them, they must be able to exist without me. Isn't that so, Catherine?"

Catherine sighed. She would have been glad to forego this public role of advisor. Could they exist without the entity? Earlier, in the garden, she hadn't really envisaged the possible reversal of the proposition. It was Athana who had to be convinced that she'd continue to exist even if her models disappeared. Catherine felt a little stab of anxiety; even after knowing herself to be a simulacrum, she had still taken her own continued existence more or less for granted. On what had she based this grand certainty? She felt she existed, she believed she existed, therefore she existed? A bit elementary in the circumstances. And yet the human body was a local condensation of matter/energy, and the cloud had imitated exactly the organic matter of the human body. What difference was there?

The blue, the cloud's particular form of energy. When someone died, whether in the South or the North, the energy returned to its source. If this was what maintained the cohesion of the entity's creations, then how far could this invisible cord stretch? Could it be broken? If Katrin were propelled into another universe, surely the contact would be severed?

"I could remake her completely," proposed Athana hesitantly. "Without any blue. Like Kiwoe."

Catherine started. "Kiwoe?"

Abruptly, a tall, slender creature stood naked where Kiwoe had been. Beneath his bronze-green skin she could see the long oddly-arranged muscles of his torso. The hands gripping the arms of his chair had only four fingers and no nails. The green eyes were placed frontally, in a very human way, deepset, with a round iris and pupil. The nose was slightly hooked, and the mouth large, with full curved lips.

Catherine hardly had time to react before the familiar Kiwoe reappeared. He sat completely still for a moment, then lifted a hand and stared at it. He let it fall. With horror? But the other Kiwoe hadn't been horrifying. Catherine realized, with a thrill of astonishment and pleasure, that she wasn't repelled, but fascinated.

"There is indigenous life on the surface of this planet, remember?" said Katrin in her precise voice. "Distinct from the cloud. She has learned how to use it—she would have spread her own substance too thin, otherwise."

At the risk of disappearing by scattering her energy. Hence the ritual of the Pilgrimage, which restored. . . No, it wasn't the entity that had started this ritual, but Pierre-Emmanuelle Manesch. And yet, if the blue energy returned spontaneously to its source, then why. . . . Something must be lost in the process, all the same. The cloud had a very long life expectancy, but it was affected by entropy like everything else.

"Indigenous life," said Kiwoe, his tone altering slightly. "How long has she been using it?"

"From what I've been able to gather, some forty

years," said Katrin. She met Catherine's eyes, and looked away. "You are a first version, a trial version. With a bit of blue. For others like him, now, she rearranges the existing organic matter."

It was confirmed, then: "You didn't create me."

Katrin resumed her falsely relaxed posture. "I made a copy, of course. She . . . replaced it."

"And the visions, the dreams?"

Katrin gave her a lopsided smile. "We must suppose she wanted to let me contact you. In any case, there was always interference."

Catherine turned to Athana.

"I told you how it was with the dreams and visions," said the girl.

"But you didn't tell me you'd *re-created* me, or how."

"It wasn't really me. I wasn't really me, you know it!" She sat up very straight. "Anyway, it means you're more *you*."

Catherine looked at her. *Me*. Somewhere at the interface between the entity and the young Katrin, the appearance of a third, autonomous consciousness? "All right," she said at last. And thank you, I suppose.

"I don't want her to re-create me on the basis of a native of this planet," said Katrin calmly—but her pupils were dilated, her body quivering in taut stillness.

Catherine raised her eyebrows, but it was Kiwoe who asked, "Why not?"

The young Voyager didn't answer immediately. "Because they are . . . what they are," she said stubbornly, "and I am what I am. I don't want a mixture."

"It wouldn't be a mixture," remarked Charles-Henri. "A human being is made of organic matter with a certain type of structure. Athana would simply reorganize the slightly different organic matter on the basis of your structure."

"And would she ask the opinion of the slightly different organic matter?"

"It wouldn't necessarily be *people*," protested Athana.

A horrified expression had flashed across Katrin's face. This was the real reason for her refusal, not a question of morality: the irrational fear of otherness, the fear of being soiled. *I don't want a mixture.* But who am I to judge her? thought Catherine. I had this reaction to the Presence in the beginning.

What am I saying? *She* had this reaction to the Presence. . . .

We had this reaction to the Presence, and afterward I was less afraid, and able to meet Italie. Young Katrin hasn't come this far. She's still afraid. We're really not the same.

"There has been enough interference with the original life of this planet," said Katrin, stubbornly clinging to rationalizations. "I don't want to add to it."

Of course she had a point. But was there a moment when the native life of the planet had existed without interference? It had begun to exist because of the cloud's interference. One might argue that this had happened when the cloud had *ceased* to interfere with the solar energy, but the distinction was fairly theoretical. All in all, interference was perhaps one of the inevitable features of life.

Catherine looked at the anxious young Voyager. "You would be willing to risk leaving by the Bridge as you are now?"

Talitha's weary voice rose in the silence. "The Bridge re-establishes physical integrity."

"That's a reasonable risk," added Egon.

The old Voyagers had lost their aura of vaguely menacing power and sovereign assurance. They were seated side by side, slumped a little in their chairs, a tired old man, a tired old woman. Yet they seemed more real, closer. Because they'd been defeated? Catherine looked away, feeling a little ashamed.

"You want . . . to leave by the Bridge, too?" murmured Athana.

Egon didn't answer immediately. He turned to his companion, and she put her wrinkled hand over his. They exchanged a sad smile.

"No," she said. "No. We should never have used the Bridge in the first place. It's a bit late to realize it, but. . . ."

Catherine turned to Athana questioningly, and the girl replied without taking her eyes off the old people. "Yes, I gave them back all their memories." And, with a note of defiance, "I didn't have to ask their permission, did I?"

They probably wouldn't have given it, anyway. "What you can ask them," said Catherine, "is what they want to do now." If Athana was as much in resonance with them as with herself, there was no need to converse out loud—but perhaps it was some required ritual, for her as much as for them, and Athana had become human enough to need it.

"What do you want to do now?" Athana's question had begun aggressively, but ended on a slightly fearful note.

The two old people looked at each other, and Talitha sighed. "Stop. Let us die. Really die. Can you do that, Athana?"

A look of horror dawned on Athana's face. Catherine understood at the same instant: they were asking her not to reintegrate their substance into the cloud, to let their energy dissipate along with the insubstantial matrix from which they were re-created. They wanted to renounce even the relative immortality of the particles in the cloud.

"Nothingness. . . ." Catherine's voice faded.

But old Egon shook his head gently. "No, Catherine. No more and no less than when one leaves by the Bridge. It's merely another Voyage, but one you can't begin again."

There was a long silence, then Athana murmured, "Now?" Her eyes were turned away.

Egon and Talitha looked at each other again. "No," said Talitha. "We need to have a little time . . . together. And a little time for each of us. We'll tell you when we're ready."

She got up with an effort, and so did the old man. She took his arm, and they walked across the courtyard with short, slow steps, dragging their feet a little. Behind them, the white-and-black tiles faded one by one, to be replaced with rocks interspersed with clumps of grass and yellow-flowered bushes resembling broom. By the time they passed through the door into the house, the courtyard had vanished and the pool had become a pond surrounded by small, twisted trees with shiny leaves. The pond water was green and clear, rippled by a light breeze.

Beside Catherine, an insect with iridescent wings plunged toward the surface and skated over it like a water spider. The light had changed, the temperature too: it was cooler. Thin clouds streaked the blue sky.

Catherine turned to Athana. "Who's doing all this?"

"That's the way it is, here. The island is like this." And quickly she added, as though on the defensive, "They put it back the way it was."

"So far north, and at this time of year?"

Athana chewed her lips. "It isn't so cold. I mean . . . the real world. The planet. And we're not all that far north, either."

There was a real world, then, beyond the frozen enclave of South and North. A world that was neither Egon's nor Talitha's—nor the entity's. Catherine picked a blade of grass and examined it closely: astonishing how it resembled grass! And what would happen to the North and the South, now that the Deity had been awakened?

Joanne must have had the same idea, for she asked in sudden horror, "Has everything been transformed, everywhere?"

"No, not everything," said Athana reassuringly. "They created things, and me too. But"—she glanced gratefully at Catherine—"many things have become . . . true, as they evolved by themselves." And to Catherine, with a little less assurance, "I don't quite know what to do, now."

"Do you think you have to do something more?"

Athana reflected for a moment. "Maybe not." She gave a hesitant, conspiratorial smile. "Let them all go their own way."

Catherine smiled back. "Yes, perhaps."

But North and South weren't going to remain eternally isolated from the rest of the planet. And without dreams and visions, without the arbitrary machinations of the two old Voyagers, they were probably going to change radically.

"But it mustn't happen too fast," murmured Athana.

"What?" said Joanne, who had been following the conversation without understanding it. She seemed to be recovering from her successive shocks, however.

"The changes in the North and South," said Kiwoe.

"Now that the Deity is awake," murmured Charles-Henri. The echo made Catherine smile.

But Joanne didn't smile. "Are you going to tell them. . . ." She bit her lips.

"We can't!" protested Simon. "Not right away, not all at once!"

"That's what I meant," remarked Athana reasonably.

Charles-Henri was pensive. "It depends what you want to explain."

Toward the middle of the afternoon they ran out of words at last, and Catherine realized what a shield words had been. When they had lost the animation provided by arguments and counterarguments about how to tell what to the North and South, they all seemed to retreat into an individual stupor, alone once more with all that had just happened.

After a while Joanne stood up brusquely. "I'm going for a walk."

Simon followed her after a moment's hesitation, but with a slow step: he didn't really want to catch up with her. Then Kiwoe rubbed his face and, with unconscious grace, undid his braid, shook the hair loose, and massaged his skull. "I think they're right." He stood up, followed by Charles-Henri, and looked inquiringly at Catherine. She shook her head. It suddenly seemed to her that the least movement would diffuse her substance in space, like dust shifted by the wind. The shock was catching up with her, too. The curious thing was that she could still think—indeed, she felt she was extraordinarily lucid—but moving was quite beyond her strength.

After a moment, Katrin's voice was heard. "Well, here's looking at you, kid." Catherine stared at her, absurdly glad to find her capable of humor under the circumstances. If the young Voyager was in a state of shock, it didn't show. But she had something to support her, it was true: her obsession about leaving.

She didn't look at Catherine, though, but at Athana. The girl nodded with a little sigh: the sphere of the Bridge appeared on their left without even stirring the air. The capsule was open. Katrin must have had the same sense of unreality as Catherine, for she got up and touched the metal shell, letting her hand rest on it for a moment. Then she turned to Athana. "Does it work the same way?"

"Yes."

The young Voyager seemed to hesitate. She met Catherine's eyes. Catherine immediately understood: someone was needed outside the Bridge to activate the capsule's closing mechanism. The Voyager's face relaxed, and she began to take off her jumpsuit. She was naked beneath it, the same strong slender body that Catherine remembered from her dreams—the body that had never been hers. Katrin climbed the ladder, slung one leg over the edge of the capsule, then the other, and lay down.

Where was the button? In the dream—the memory—there had been a control panel, but not here.

"You have to climb up," said Athana. "It's near the hatch."

Catherine climbed up. Inside, Katrin waited, her hands on her stomach, the tips of her fingers interlaced—a posture so familiar that Catherine froze.

Katrin made a face, a little annoyed. "I'm ready."

"Really?" murmured Catherine in spite of herself.

There was a short silence, then Katrin asked, "You're not by any chance afraid you might disappear once I'm gone?"

"And you?"

Katrin's sardonic expression became stubborn. "I've decided to take the risk."

"Is it that important to go back?"

"You ought to know."

Catherine accepted the rebuff. "I do know. But not in the same way as you." There was a pause, then she added, "I know you can't go back, even if you return. Have you thought about that?"

"Yes. And it doesn't matter. I was torn away from my home against my will. I want to go back. That's how it is."

"Will going back wipe out your having left, and everything that's happened since?"

The Voyager rose up on one elbow. "Do you want to help me or not?"

They were very close, and Catherine contemplated

the strange, familiar young face, suddenly gripped by sad compassion. "I would very much like to," she murmured.

Katrin blinked. "Listen, you are you and I am I. You know that, too, don't you? The resemblance is . . . fortuitous. The entity could have made you totally different."

She didn't really understand, then, this young Voyager. "But she didn't," Catherine said softly, "and she gave me your memories, your dreams, everything."

The Voyager stared at her. A muscle quivered in her jaw. She seemed to sag a little, and looked away. "Not really." Suddenly she sat up and leaned against the wall of the capsule, hugging her knees. "I'm not married. And my parents were . . . are still alive. I mean, in my universe." She glanced at Catherine, who was staring at her in amazement, then looked straight ahead again. "Your marriage, their death. . . . You invented all that. Or she did— your Athana. Or you did it together. Difficult to know who's doing what, isn't it?"

Catherine gazed at her, not really understanding. Invented? Then she became aware that Katrin was stiff with tension. The contact between them had worked both ways: Katrin had shared her invented memories. Invented? Extrapolated, rather. It was . . . a possible or alternate future for Katrin, which terrified her. Failed loves. Lost loves.

Finally, in a slightly husky voice, the young woman said, "I sacrificed everything to the cause—the Revolution."

She lifted her head, at last looking at Catherine with an honest pain that softened to something like hope. "If I go back, there are a lot of things I'll try to do differently."

There was a lump in Catherine's throat. She said gently, "Why not do them differently on the way, as well?"

The Voyager thought a moment, then smiled slightly. "Perhaps." She became serious again, and now there was no aggressiveness. "But it's my own path, isn't it? After all, the Bridge is about that, too. I don't suppose I sent myself here for no reason."

She hesitated, lifted a finger to touch Catherine's cheek and showed her the tear that trembled on the tip, then put the finger on Catherine's lips. "Your glasses are getting fogged up. Time to go."

Catherine couldn't help laughing, even as another tear rolled down her cheek. She leaned back and looked for the button. It was true: her glasses were fogged up. She took them off and wiped them as best she could.

"Catherine," said Katrin.

She leaned over the capsule again. The Voyager smiled up at her, once again slightly sarcastic. "I didn't know what would happen if you came to the North. I didn't know if you'd even come. It was just a gamble, trying to make you come. And it was better than doing nothing."

You've always been free of me.

Catherine smiled, accepting this offering and bending over to kiss the girl's forehead. "Happy travels."

She straightened up, pressed the button, and watched the translucent hatch slip over the capsule. After a while, the cryogenic substance began to fill the chamber, dimming the peaceful features of the sleeping Voyager.

Catherine climbed back down the ladder, step by step, face to face with her own distorted reflection in the curved shell of the Bridge. Then she went and stood beside a white-faced Athana, who was staring at the sphere, chewing her lower lip.

They waited in silence, side by side, for what seemed a long time. Catherine was aware of the warm light of the setting sun and the cries of nameless birds flying back and forth over the pond. Yet at the same time she was suspended in a moment without end. Then Athana said very softly, "She has left."

Catherine felt herself instinctively go tense, waiting for something, some shock, the progressive dimming of all sensation. But nothing happened. She still sensed Athana beside her, still saw the shining sphere of the Bridge, and beyond it the sky turning a soft blue-green.

"She has left," repeated Athana in a different tone.

Catherine had no need to turn her head to know that the girl was smiling.

12

Catherine was in the library when Egon and Talitha came looking for her. To her surprise, *The Book of Steps* had been on a shelf. She had let it fall open on her lap without looking at it. Everyone else was still sleeping, and she had woken early. They had eaten the rations from their backpacks and gone to bed early last night, without further talk. Athana was also sleeping when she left the room, but after a moment the girl had appeared at the door of the library, one braid undone, hands behind her back. Catherine had waved at her to come in. Athana had said nothing, had simply sat down to wait by the blazing hearth opposite Catherine in her armchair. But Catherine was no more inclined to talk than to read. The events of the previous evening were finally sinking in, as though sleep had provided the necessary space for them to assume their true dimensions. She didn't remember dreaming, but there was a memory of incoherent emotions swirling about, unable to become thoughts—wonder, panic, uncertainty, curiosity, and spurts of anger that were too absurd not to subside quickly. When the two old people entered the room, she understood what Athana had been waiting for.

They drew two armchairs up to the hearth. She made no move to help them, because she understood that doing this was a kind of penance for them. They sat down slowly, taking care not to strain their knee joints. Athana hadn't made them exactly "like before," Catherine suddenly realized. She had given them an age more in keeping with their long memory.

They stared at the fire. Catherine watched the flames etching shadows on those faces whose familiarity was so poignant—yet knowing, with a strange and painful discordance, that they weren't those whom they resembled. Should she speak? What could she tell them?

"We were afraid," said Egon suddenly in a gruff voice. "I hope you understand."

She nodded, feeling somewhat choked herself.

"We're still afraid, in fact," remarked Talitha, almost amused. "But in a more . . . normal way." A pause. "I'm sure you understand." Leaning toward Catherine, she turned over the book on her lap. "Oh." She looked at her companion with a candidly mischievous smile: "Manesch."

Egon snorted. "Bad poet. Too abstract. And too many fine words."

"You're exaggerating a little."

Catherine stared at them both, incredulous. Had they come to discuss poetry?

"You were Manesch," she said, aware of the aggressive note slipping into her voice, but unable to control it.

"Ah, you're wrong. Louis-Raoul, yes, but not Pierre-Emmanuelle. Don't you remember? I told your friend Simon." The old man considered her from under his frowning eyebrows, then sighed. "You didn't believe me, obviously."

"But the book is from you, all the same? He came back here, and when he returned to Chicoutimi, he wrote this book."

The old man's gaze focused on a distant point. "No." After a while he added dreamily, "He came to ask the Deity to take away his powers. His Voyager-like capacities. I wasn't so angry with him, then. After all, he had done what was needed, although reluctantly. I granted him his wish."

"The poor man was so unhappy," murmured Talitha.

"But he was happy in the end. Because of writing the

book." The old man gave a puzzled grunt. "I've never really understood why, but he was content."

"Because he was free," said Catherine after a moment.

There was a brief silence. Old Talitha nodded. "We should have begun to realize, then. That they all really existed, I mean."

"Yes," sighed old Egon.

Athana shifted nervously at Catherine's feet, and they looked at each other.

"Well, time to go," said old Talitha.

Catherine almost cried, "No!" looking for something else to say, something other than insignificant phrases that spoke of other things. Then she saw the black eyes of the old woman resting on her, filled with compassion, and she slumped back in her chair, forcing herself to relax. They were really not speaking of anything else. It was their way of talking about it, and she'd probably have to accept it.

Egon fumbled in his pockets and brought out a round medallion that he held out brusquely to Catherine. "We wanted you to have this."

"It's something that was made, not . . . created," added Talitha. "He made it for me. We thought—" Her voice broke a little. "There's at least one universe in which you are our child, isn't there?"

"We wanted to leave you something," concluded the old man, almost fiercely.

Catherine took the medallion. It was made of silver and engraved with the same Deity motif as the boxes given her by Kiwoe and the others. A circle divided by a wavy line, an S, the surface smooth on one half, stippled on the other to give a darker effect.

"Where I come from, this is the symbol of the Voyagers," said the old man.

"And where I come from, it's the symbol of an ancient religion," said the old woman. "The earth and sky in balance, and human beings in the middle."

"It was something like that where I come from, too," murmured Catherine, trying to ignore the rising tears. Yin and Yang. She held the medallion tightly and looked up. "Thank you," she said huskily. This was one heritage she could accept.

The old man gave a little grunt. The old woman put her hand on Catherine's arm diffidently and smiled, but said nothing.

They got up together. "We're ready, Athana," said Egon.

Athana looked beseechingly at Catherine, who shook her head, unable to speak.

"Don't be afraid, Athana," said Talitha.

The girl stood awkwardly. "You really want to ... disappear completely?" she stammered.

The old woman smiled and placed a hand on Athana's head. "We'll be there, Athana, in your memory. That's enough."

"I don't know how, really.... I've never done it."

"We trust you," said Egon.

Athana stepped back and closed her eyes. The bodies of the two old people suddenly glowed through their clothing, a blue shimmering network of veins, arteries, the outlines of organs and bones, pulsing with a radiant cascading electricity. Then, like fading fireworks, the blue luminescence dissipated into even smaller particles until it faded and vanished.

Athana's eyes were still closed. She was trembling. Catherine stood up, put her arms around the girl, and made her sit down in one of the chairs.

"They've really left." Athana looked a little haggard.

"Yes."

"But where have they gone?"

Sitting on the arm of the chair, Catherine stroked her head absently. "I don't know."

Athana's trembling gradually subsided. She had taken Catherine's hand and was gripping it fiercely. "And you?" she asked at last, her voice faint but resolute. "'What are you going to do?"

"Don't you know?" said Catherine, surprised.

Athana took a great gulp of air, like a child catching its breath after a crying spell. "You are all ... each in your own head. It wouldn't be ... fair for me to be there with you."

Catherine gave an involuntary smile. "That's true."

"What are you going to do?" Athana asked once more. Then, "Do you want to leave, too?"

"Heavens, no," said Catherine. Why was it so obvious, she wondered. She tried to find the words. "I'm at home, here."

"But it's going to change."

One day, there would be no more South and North. But the human enclave created by the Voyagers and the entity would continue to exist. The country, the landscape, the cities, the people. The climate would be milder, but there would still be winters. The artificial barriers had disappeared. What would happen when contact was made with the rest of the planet? And once the North and South had transformed, what evolution would there be for this Quebec that was made up of so many disjointed elements? What relations would be established with those of its inhabitants who gradually returned to their real, indigenous form as the blue energy slowly left their bodies without being renewed, generation after generation? Only one thing was certain: it would all continue to evolve in its own way.

Catherine smiled at Athana. "I know, but I'm curious."

$$13$$

They left the next day, first by canoe to cross the lake where the island lay, then on foot to the place where they'd left the snowcar. They hadn't really planned anything, and Athana hadn't suggested any other vehicle once they'd left the canoe behind. After climbing the grassy slopes of the meadows around the lake, they entered the forest with its familiar aromas—oak, beech, walnut, aspen, mingled with the smell of alien trees and plants. At one point they heard a muffled noise in the distance. A massive shape passed through the trees on their right, fairly indistinct, but Catherine had recognized the long, serpentine neck and forked tail whipping the underbrush. She turned to Athana, who was behind her with Charles-Henri. "The green children really exist?"

Athana pushed away the hair from her forehead. "Not quite like you saw them."

"Like Kiwoe?"

"No, different again. There are many different people."

The results of arbitrary and occasional crossbreeding by the entity, over the centuries, with the indigenous life of the planet? Or imitated from the life forms remembered by the Voyagers? A multitude of theories clamored for attention in Catherine's mind, but she pushed them resolutely aside. There would always be time later for speculation, for questions and answers. She preferred to be here, now, in the forest that smelled of moss and mushrooms over all those other strange and exciting odors. It was good to walk, to feel the straps of her backpack biting into her shoulders, to experience the regular rhythm of her breathing and the sensation of her feet hitting the ground, still a little spongy between the patches of spring snow. She stopped in front of one such patch where she could see the prints of some animal crossing it diagonally. A small animal, something with a tail—that was all she could deduce, now that she had renounced her Voyager's powers.

"Are you sure?" Athana had said.

She had hesitated momentarily. The *gestalt* perception that had showed her the inconsistencies in the Voyagers' creation? She hadn't even recognized it as such—it was merely an extension of synthetic logic. Her talents as a combatant? She could get them back if she wanted, with training. Hyperceptions . . . the ability to see at will that splendor, always radiant, always quivering, of space pregnant with energy. . . . But no. Manesch had known what he was doing by renouncing everything. "I'm sure."

Athana had said, "Good. That's it, then."

"It's done?"

"Yes."

She'd felt nothing. And now, as she rose to continue walking, careful not to step on the tracks, she told herself that it was right. She had never been a Voyager. Not that kind of Voyager.

"You'll never want to use the Bridge?" Athana had asked, still a little anxious.

She had replied honestly, "I don't know. I don't think so, but I don't know. For the moment, this world is more than enough."

She had kept to herself the question that rose to her lips: "And you, Athana?" It was too soon. But she thought of it again, now, as they walked beneath the branches in the dappled morning light. Perhaps one day Athana would no longer feel linked to her creation. Perhaps she would understand that she could, that she should leave. She could explore her universe, far from the

small mother planet. And even farther—who knows? But
she wouldn't need a Bridge to cross over to other universes: the cloud must be able to reproduce the process
without needing a machine.

Amused at herself, Catherine put a stop to these reflections, It wasn't for now. It wouldn't be for perhaps
thousands of years. And who knows what will have become of Athana in thousands of years? Not me. But the
thought didn't sadden her.

Someone had caught up with her, was walking beside
her. Kiwoe. He hadn't braided his black hair again, and it
swung freely on his shoulders. Their eyes met. She smiled
at him, and he seemed relieved. Kiwoe the Alien. There
had been an alien, after all, but not the one she'd imagined. And all things considered, she was an alien too. She
wondered again what the green children really looked
like.

They were walking beside another patch of snow
with larger tracks. Another animal, or one of the children? Impossible to know. *The beasts of winter write their
name in the snow.* Where did that come from? Ah,
Manesch, of course.

Manesch. She could almost imagine him, the poet,
coming joyfully back across the snow and ice from his encounter with his Deity. Or perhaps he hadn't been joyful,
had understood too many things during this ultimate confrontation. Perhaps the joy only came later, a precarious,
passing joy, but joy all the same. Because he was liberated.
Because he then had nothing but the memory and the
words to try to express it—but they were his own words,
no longer dictated by anyone, and so what if there were
too many fine words in his poems? He had surely intended them for no one but himself.

And yet he hadn't destroyed them. Did he think
someone would publish them after his death? He had left
them, at any rate. Like a secret message, an admonition
over time, for posterity? Surely he hadn't harbored that
kind of childish hope, this man who had written, *Rupture
absence/That burnt thought/Explore/Amuse yourself/And
vanish.*

But perhaps he *had* intended them for someone, all
the same. For his creators, prisoners of their own creation

without knowing it. Who had unwittingly given him freedom by liberating him from their Voyagers' powers, a
freedom they were unable to give themselves. He was free
to imagine, to write—and this creation would never im-
prison him totally.

> At last the flash
> The primordial gleam of flint
> Everything condenses
> No heartbreak
> No convulsive humor
> Our steps define wisdom
> Children of fictional time
> We are infinite, warm and radiant.

ELISABETH VONARBURG is the author of *The Silent City* and the Philip K. Dick Special Award-winning novel, *In the Mothers' Land*, for which she was also a James Tiptree Award runner-up. She works with her translator when her novels are translated, making her work in English a true collaborative effort. She has published numerous SF stories and has worked tirelessly to encourage the genre in Canada. She has attended many SF conventions in the U.S., Canada, and Europe, and several international conventions of SF writers held in Chicoutimi. She has received various awards for her work in both France and Canada. She lives in Chicoutimi, Quebec.

JANE BRIERLEY lives in Montreal and has translated works of fiction, biography, history, and philosophy. She won the 1990 Governor General's Award for her translation, *Yellow-Wolf & Other Tales of the Saint Lawrence* by the 19th-century Canadian writer, Philippe-Joseph Aubert de Gaspé. Her translation of two Vonarburg SF novels has appeared with Bantam Books. She was until recently president of the Literary Translators' Association of Canada.